ZENOBIA

ZENOBIA

Haley Elizabeth Garwood

2005

THE WRITERS BLOCK, INC.
Franklin, Kentucky

ZENOBIA

The Writers Block, Inc. published by arrangement with the author
First Printing, March 2005

Copyright © 2005 by Haley Elizabeth Garwood

Cover concept by Mel Graham

Researched art work by Alex Horley

Cover art by Pioneer Press of W.Va, Inc.

ISBN: 0-9659721-3-5
LCCN: 2004115474

THE WRITERS BLOCK
The Writers Block books are published by The Writers Block, Inc.
P.O. Box 821, Franklin, KY 42135

Designed by Pioneer Press of W. Va., Inc., Terra Alta, WV

Printed in the United States of America
10 9 8 7 6 5 4 3 2

DEDICATED TO

Melvin K. Graham
who makes me laugh and lets me cry

Gary F. Elliot
who led me past mourning into the afternoon sun

Gene Onestinghel
who kept me from being murdered

ACKNOWLEDGMENTS

Usually the cover models who adorn the front of a book are not given credit although their talent and beauty go a long way to sell the novel. Stacy Walker is a phenomenal woman who is brainy as well as gorgeous. She did hours and hours of work for the cover from the recommendation of the Italian artist, Alex Horley, to posing and overseeing the painting. She meticulously pulled together the costume and made certain every detail was historically accurate.

I can't thank her enough.

My business partner and artist friend, Melvin Graham, is responsible for the cover concept. He took the painting of Zenobia and made it work as a book cover. He's always there when I go on a tear about something or other, and his calm demeanor helps.

All writers think they're alone, but it doesn't have to be that way. I want to thank the Music City Romance Writers—a chapter of Romance Writers of America—a wonderful and supportive group of published and unpublished authors. Their professionalism does not stop them from being a fun group of intelligent members. I found my critique partners through MCRW. Thanks to Cassondra Murray and Cheryl Martin who patiently teach me the basics of writing romance. My novels all have elements of romance, but I'm eager to try my luck with a pure medieval romance the next time out.

Thanks to my editors who correct my errors and help me to look good—not an easy task. Onie Shinn does a remarkable job with the grammar. She's been a friend, too, for years. I can count on her to keep me straight.

Gerald Swick, a non-fiction historical author, is also a good friend and a superb writer. He doesn't sugar coat anything (thank goodness) and tells me if something is historically inaccurate or just plain stupid. He's great at catching all those comma splices, too.

Cheryl Martin (yes, the critique group partner) is a copy editor with an eye for errors. She did a wonderful job with line editing, continuity, and all manner of things.

Thanks also to Lynda and Rich Hopkins, the dynamic duo of Pioneer Press, who are more than business colleagues—they've become friends as well. Their dedication to this project goes beyond the norm in this industry.

It seems magical when a mentor appears on the horizon just as she is needed. Marilyn Ross has transcended the position of guide to become a dear friend. She gave me a valuable chunk of her time to edit the manuscript with a sharp eye and a precise pen. Her ideas regarding marketing are jewels. My thanks and appreciation are not enough. To your continued success, Marilyn.

ABOUT THE AUTHOR

Haley Elizabeth Garwood has had several starts in life with interesting careers. Her time spent as a flight attendant didn't seem like work at all. The most difficult career was in education. Dr. Garwood taught special education before accepting the most challenging job of her life—that of a high school principal.

Retirement started her on another career path that made use of her degrees in creative writing/journalism and theatre. Garwood works full time as a writer.

MAIN CHARACTERS

Zenobia, Queen of Palmyra, Syria

Odainat, King of Palmyra, Syria

Hairan, son of Odainat and step-son of Zenobia

Vaballathus—son of Odainat and Zenobia

Arraum—son of Odainat and Zenobia

Tarab—sister to Odainat

Mokimu—husband to Tarab

Maeonius—son of Tarab and Mokimu

Ezechiel—general for Odainat and Zenobia

Miriam—wife to Ezechiel

Rebekeh—nurse to young Vaballathus and Arraum

Dionysus Cassius Longinus—Greek philosopher and teacher; friend of Zenobia

Timagenes—Egyptian leader and ally of Zenobia

Aurelian—Roman emperor

Marcellus—Roman lieutenant and confidant of Aurelian

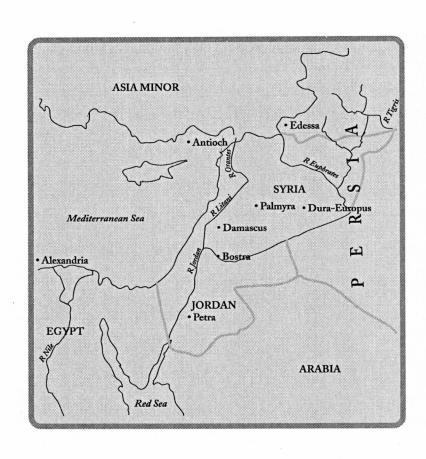

THE WARRIOR QUEEN SERIES
by Haley Elizabeth Garwood

The Forgotten Queen

First he stole her heart, then her kingdom. Empress Matilda dried her tears with rage, invaded England and, with sword in hand, fought lover turned enemy.

"*The Forgotten Queen* is the first book in what Garwood calls her 'Warrior Queen' series, in which she intends to 'dust off the forgotten women in history.' If her engaging fictionalized account of Matilda is an indication, the rest of the series should provide a most welcome addition to the genre of the historical romance."

—Leigh Ann Berry
British Heritage Magazine

"The depth of historical research is evident in Garwood's account of Empress Matilda's struggle to save England. Assuming details to create a story cleverly interwoven with fact, Garwood brings this turbulent era to life, deftly describing fickle barons, adulterous liaisons, battles for power, and misplaced loyalties that characterize medieval history. In an era when women were over-shadowed by the men in their lives, Garwood reveals Matilda's spirited and heroic struggle to overcome political intrigues and prejudice, and the significant role she played in changing the course of English history."

—Cristinia Pelayo
Renaissance Magazine

The Forgotten Queen is an imaginative, colorful look into England's past and the life of a little known, but exciting, ruler.

—Catherine Cometti
historical novelist

Swords Across the Thames

Brave, beautiful and brilliant, this warrior queen risks death to save her people from the brutal Vikings.

"Like scenes from a medieval tapestry, Haley expertly weaves history with the delicacy and expertise of a talented storyteller. She makes history come alive on the pages of *Swords Across the Thames.*"

—Constance O'Banyon
author of *Ride the Wind*

"In *Swords Across the Thames*, intriguing characters bring the pages of history to life. I could not put down this unique tale of an unsung heroine."

—Juliana Garnett
author of *The Knight*

"There are some authors who deserve high praise for their work. Haley Elizabeth Garwood is such an author. She has taken on a giant project in her 'Warrior Queen Series.' These women who took up arms in defense of their lands will fascinate you."

—Nancy Porter
Romance Communications

Ashes of Britannia

From the ashes of Britannia arose a legend. Boadicea, Celtic queen and Druid priestess, fought the massive Roman army that invaded her country. Two thousand years later this woman warrior continues to reign as a symbol in Great Britain.

"*Ashes Of Britannia* is a fabulous historical fiction tale that centers on the clash between the Druids and the ever-growing Roman Empire. The story line is filled with incredible depth that vividly brings to life Britannia and Rome through the eyes of two real people, Boadicea and Suetonius, whose war turns the island into a red sea. In her third Warrior Queen novel Haley Elizabeth Garwood writes an entertaining tale that turns history into fun reading."

—Harriet Klausner
independent reviewer
Barnes & Noble.com

"In her third novel, *Ashes Of Britannia*, Garwood interprets the clash of cultures between the ever-expanding Roman Empire and the Druids of Britain. She takes readers into the sacred groves of the priestess warrior, Boadicea and the streets of Rome with military commander, Suetonius. These two strong, independent leaders respect each other, but their conflicting goals will cover the soil of ancient Britain with blood and ashes."

—Gerald Swick
author and historian

"The beauty of Garwood's novel is that she clearly shows that in the inevitable tragedy to come, there is neither villain nor hero . . . The freshness of *Ashes* is the objective view taken, that the true cause is what must come when two distinct nations collide . . . Like the previous two novels in Dr. Garwood's series, *Ashes Of Britannia* is quick, light reading."

—Suzanne Crane
Historical Novels Review

CHAPTER

I

252 A.D. The Syrian Desert

It was a beautiful day for death. The saffron sun teased the desert with color as it changed beige sand to a rainbow of pinks, oranges, and hot red and sent the temperature soaring. Dunes laid in rows from east to west, and the sand plains in front of them were ridged like a sun-ripened date.

Zenobia tucked an errant strand of black hair under a silk scarf she wore beneath her helmet. She looked across the desert at the Persian army lined up to attack her Palmyran forces along with those of her husband.

She turned in the saddle and looked at her husband, who was always introspective before a battle. She reached over, touched his hand, and prayed to the great god, Bel, for his safety. This ritual was performed before every battle, and each time it grew more important to her. She had thought it impossible to love her husband with such depth. Her heart felt as if it would burst at times like these. She loved his powerful shoulders and arms, his decisive manner in battle, and his strength against the enemy. Most of all, she loved the man. He was a good man and a good king.

"We have been fighting the Persians for eight years now, Odainat." She inclined her head toward General Abdas to her husband's right. "Your Christian man says that we had our first battle in the 244th year after his god's death."

"It seems many lifetimes," Odainat said. He looked neither at his wife nor his general.

"It's time for me to return to my troops." She squeezed her fingers around his war-hardened hand and released it slowly as she turned her horse away from her husband. She refused to think of mortality.

"It is your turn to give the signal to advance," Odainat said.

Zenobia looked over her shoulder and laughed. "You are a stern taskmaster making me decide when to attack."

"It is good for you to practice strategy and for me to learn how you think."

"After all these years on the field of battle, you should know how I use my mind."

Odainat pulled at his beard, still black but tinged with silver. "Alas, my queen, I believe not."

"Tonight we shall play a game of Senet. Perhaps then you'll learn how I plan my attack." Zenobia smiled and saluted her husband as she rode toward her own men. This morning before dawn, she had prayed for Odainat's safety to the greatest of their gods, Bel; to the sun god, Iarhibol; and to Aglibol, the god of the moon. Odainat always prayed to his favorite, Shadrafa, the warrior god.

Zenobia reined in her horse next to her general and appraised the Persian army. Voices carried on the breeze drifted across the sand as last minute instructions were given by Shapur, the Persian king. He rode up and down the front lines, his black horse covered in blue and gold pressed wool to protect him. Shapur was not a tall man, but he was built like a granite statue.

Similar to hers, the first line of the Persian army was composed of archers standing shoulder to shoulder, bows at rest and arrows in hand. The infantry, nine rows deep, undulated through heat waves from the desert, their swords sparkling in the sun like precious water. The horse-archers were at the rear, and Zenobia could hear horses snorting and the jingle of armor as the riders tried to calm their mounts. A chain mail shirt covered each helmeted Persian rider, ending above his knees where leg coverings of protective metal bands completed the armor. An unsheathed sword and a spear five cubits long would draw plenty of Palmyran blood today.

"Their cavalry is not as deep as ours, General Ezechiel," Zenobia said.

"Nor is their <u>cataphractii</u> as well-trained. Their horses dance while ours merely swish their tails to chase away the sand flies." Ezechiel said.

"A good observation." Zenobia narrowed her dark brown eyes and glanced at the sun. It was almost time. The sun had risen behind her and shone in the face of the enemy. To her right the Taurus Mountains rose mirage-like over the horizon and hovered there. Her army, combined with Odainat's, stood between King Shapur and the Euphrates River, and cut him off from his city, Edessa. Zenobia smelled the sweat of her horse, the leather saddle beneath her, and the already burning sand. Like the Romans, whom she and her husband had vowed to help, her armor was scaled. It reminded her of fish from Lake Tiberias. She was slight in stature and slender, so she could not carry full armor. She chose to leave her arms bare to cut down on weight and to keep from overheating in the desert sun.

"We will win this battle. God has favored you," Ezechiel said.

Zenobia looked at the man next to her. The Jew wore battle scars carved out of his tough hide like badges of honor. He was loyal to her and to Odainat perhaps because she allowed his people to live in peace within the walls of Palmyra. Perchance he was loyal because she asked nothing of him except to make her army the most powerful in the world. As Rome declined, Palmyra would rise. In a bold move, Odainat and Zenobia helped Rome weaken the Persians who shared this part of their world.

"A great wrong has been done to the Romans," Ezechiel said, as if reading her thoughts.

"True. Rome's strength has been sapped over the years by the barbarians. It is in chaos without its leader. Who but we can fight the Persians and win? And maybe I can right a wrong against my father by Shapur's father, Ardishir."

Ezechiel nodded toward the Persian army. "They grow restless."

"It is part of my plan. I like for them to be nervous before we attack. It consumes their strength." Zenobia shifted in the saddle, not from lack of comfort for the saddle fit her like a well-worn shoe, but to ready herself for the attack. She didn't need to look at Odainat. She was as aware of him as if he were next to her.

Zenobia held her spear high and nudged Thabit forward. She wedged her thighs under the front pair of saddle horns that angled outward. She loosened the reins, and her Arabian stallion flew across the hard packed sand toward the Persian enemy. Zenobia's voice escaped her in a shout of ecstasy. The earth vibrated as thousands of her men followed her to glory. As she closed the space between her army and that of King Shapur, she no longer saw the details that she had from a distance. A blur of silver, bronze, blue, and flesh whirled toward her. She was used to this sensation and never tired of it.

Zenobia's army followed her lead toward the middle of the Persian ranks. It was her choice to break through the lines while Odainat's army swerved around the right flank and came in from behind. She wanted to kill King Shapur herself. Zenobia saw him surrounded by a double row of <u>clibanarii</u> on armored horses and two rows of <u>cataphractii</u>, armored men on unarmored steeds. The swine wasn't even in front leading but called his orders from four rows back.

A column of men with spears surged toward Zenobia, and she almost swerved, worried that her beloved sorrel horse would be killed. She held her spear ready, picked her victim, and bellowed out the name of the god Bel as she thundered closer to the Persian front line.

Zenobia held her head down to protect her face and stared from under her helmet as she pounded toward the infantryman. When she was close enough to see his features, but not close enough that he seemed too human, Zenobia thrust the spear through his midsection. She watched him fall to the blood-painted sand and heard the sucking sound of his body as he gave up the spear she jerked from his writhing torso. She rode past him into the middle of the Persian front lines.

A second Persian was impaled on her spear as she rode toward the retreating Shapur. She left her spear in this soldier, holding him to the sand like the desert lizards she used to hunt with pointed sticks. She drew her sword and hacked her way toward Shapur. As she got closer, she was aware of his watching her. Her quarry grinned.

"Queen Zenobia. Is your husband content to let you do his work for him?" he shouted.

She ignored the insult and concentrated on thinning out the line of protectors that surrounded him. A guard rode toward her through downed Persians, his horse slipping on the blood that hadn't had time to soak into the sand. Zenobia's sword flashed in the sun as she narrowed her concentration from several of the enemy to the one that came toward her with death in his eyes. She watched his face intently, holding her sword steady, walking her horse step by step to her destiny.

When his eyes squinted, she tightened the grip on her sword, kicked Thabit and surged toward the grim Persian before he could position himself. Her sword whistled as it sliced through the air and imbedded itself in the side of his neck, cutting through cartilage and muscle to decapitate him. He had only a second to register surprise before his head rolled across the ground in a circle guided by his pointed helmet.

The smell of hot iron from fresh blood assaulted Zenobia as she readied herself for another attack. It came from her left, her weak side, and she barely had time to pull Thabit around before running her sword straight through a spear man's face. She hated the sound of splintering bone and hoped that none of her men saw disgust on her face as she connected with the enemy. A warning shout from General Ezechiel caused her to pull back on Thabit's reins too quickly, and he reared, pawing the air. Zenobia hit the ground with a thud that rattled her spine. She scrambled up as rapidly as she could in her armor and held herself ready. Had General Ezechiel not taken care of an enemy soldier, she would have been dead. She nodded her thanks to him, slapped Thabit on the rump and sent him back to the rear of her lines. There was no way to re-mount once down, and she didn't want to use him as a shield as some cavalry did when un-seated.

"Behind you!"

Zenobia turned in time to dodge a thrown spear. It stuck in the ground next to her and quivered. She pulled it from the sand with a swift left-handed motion, swore at the man, and sailed it toward him. She tried not to show her surprise as it thunked into his chest, neatly dissecting his breastbone.

Zenobia dispatched two more soldiers. "May you live under the earth in the darkness led by your god, Ahriman," she shouted at their departing souls.

Engrossed in her task, Zenobia, nonetheless, noticed that Odainat's army had swung in behind the enemy and was effectively crushing the Persians. She advanced briskly on foot to close the gap between herself and King Shapur. "Prepare to meet your Zoroastrian god," she shouted.

"Not this time," Shapur yelled in return. He had the audacity to salute her, turn his horse and gallop down the Persian line ordering a retreat.

Predictably, the Persian army withdrew from battle. Odainat's army pursued the soldiers as they raced around the dunes and headed east toward the Euphrates River. Zenobia stabbed her sword in the sand several times to cleanse it of blood before she sheathed it. She whistled for Thabit, then grinned as the big horse raced toward her, mane flying, white blaze and stockings glowing in the heat of the midday sun. Without further commands, the horse stopped next to her. She called for two infantrymen to help her to mount, and with her legs wrapped tightly around Thabit's saddle, tore after Odainat. If he captured Shapur, she wanted to be there.

King Shapur had been too confident and had led his army into the desert to fight instead of staying on the far side of the Euphrates River close to Edessa and terrain that he controlled. Zenobia shook her head at his stupidity. After this battle, he would no longer underestimate the power of Palmyra.

Zenobia caught up with Odainat and his army at the edge of the river two hours later just in time to see the last of the retreating Persian army.

"Do we allow them to escape?" she asked Odainat.

"No. We allow them to hole up like the desert creature who thinks he is clever."

Odainat rubbed Zenobia's cheek. "You wear the blood of the enemy."

"Better than wearing my own." Zenobia loosened the reins and allowed Thabit to eat the lush grass that edged the Euphrates in a half mile strip on either side. "We could cross the river at night and surround Edessa before dawn. If we capture this city, then we control more land north of Palmyra. That puts us in a good position to take away Shapur's empire."

"You would rather pursue him than play that game of Senet you promised me?"

"You know the answer to that." Zenobia removed her helmet and unwound a blue silk scarf from her hair. Black hair cascaded down her back and rested on the rump of her horse.

Odainat laughed, his dark eyes crinkled at the corners. "Gather your army, my fierce warrior queen, and meet me on the other side. We can cross here. It is not deep, nor is it swift this time of year." He reached out, grabbed a handful of hair, and pulled her toward him, kissing her.

The passion of his kiss kindled fervent desire in Zenobia as it always did. Invariably their lovemaking was more intense after a battle. "I doubt the cool waters of the Euphrates will cool our ardor for one another."

"We will have to wait for fulfillment."

"Alas." Zenobia kissed her husband again.

"A fair reason to make short work of our Persian enemy."

"I want to deal with King Shapur myself."

"So you shall." Odainat chuckled. "You're the only woman I know who prefers swords to jewels, armor to gowns, and the acquisition of land to the rigors of the home."

"You knew my weaknesses. My father complained of them to you many times while I was growing up."

"He complained, but he was proud of your boyish ways. Was it not your father who hired the best swordsman from my army to train you? The best archer to teach the mastery of the bow? The best horseman to teach you to ride?"

"He had no choice. I worried him so." Zenobia sighed. "My poor mother. She tried to teach me to be a lady and manage a household. She should have been a queen."

"Royal Egyptian blood ran through her veins and thus yours," Odainat said. "I often think of you as my Cleopatra."

Zenobia pulled the silk scarf through her fingers, watching it swirl in the breeze from the river. "Do you? Thank you."

"What say you to taking our armies behind the dunes and waiting for nightfall to cross the river? Shapur will think we have retreated."

"We have no tent for privacy."

"No."

Zenobia shrugged. "We'll have time to plan for a siege or an attack of Edessa, however."

The cold desert air made Zenobia shiver as she rode Thabit from the water. He clambered up the bank of the Euphrates and shook himself. The camels loaded with supplies followed behind the army and would cross the river easily. She would be glad to have her bedding and a change of clothing. Fires couldn't be built to dry out man or armor, so she would have to take care of her mail as best she could to keep the rust away. She hoped the leather strips that held the scales together wouldn't shrink. She didn't relish having her breath squeezed out of her by her own armor.

When her bedding did arrive, it was damp. Zenobia lay down, her chain mail digging into her ribs even though she wore clean silk undergarments with cotton padding. She thought she would not be able to sleep, but sleep came as soon as Odainat lay beside her. They held hands in the darkness and listened to the guards pace the encampment. It was a lullaby to her.

The two armies were ready to ride to Edessa before sunrise. They rode due north until near the city, then turned eastward and skirted the city on the south side. Zenobia's army headed north to attack the city where least expected. Odainat would use the rising sun as a backdrop and enter the city from the east. It was an innovative plan developed by General Ezechiel. A twinge of jealousy flitted through Zenobia before she cast it aside. She wished she could have thought of such a furtive plan. She would have to spend more time in strategy. Lack of a good strategy could lose a battle, a war, a country. Zenobia shivered at that thought and shoved the morose idea from her mind.

Light from the east was heralding the sun as Zenobia looked over her shoulder at her men lined up behind her. Below her, Edessa was asleep. "Why are they so stupid, Ezechiel?"

"King Shapur is too confident. He doesn't expect a pursuit."

"One should always expect pursuit, for some day it may come."

"He fights as his father did. They plod along, but never learn new ways."

"To our advantage, then." Zenobia looked to the southeast where Odainat's army emerged over a dune. She saluted him, although he couldn't see her, and said her morning prayers to Bel, Iarhibol, and Aglibol for his safety. Her priests had said that Odainat would never die in battle. For that she was thankful. But still she had to pray. It made her more comfortable.

"We wait for Odainat's signal. It is his turn," Zenobia said.

General Ezechiel laughed. "You and your king play an amusing but effective game. The enemy has never guessed your stratagem because it is like a two-headed monster."

Zenobia grinned. "Your comparison to a monster is understandable, but not desirous."

"It seems appropriate. Look, Odainat prepares himself for a charge."

With one last prayer for the safety of her husband, Zenobia kicked Thabit and surged toward the gates of the walled city. As they came within fifteen feet of the walls, flaming arrows flew over her head from horse-archers behind her. The stench of palm-thatched roofs as they caught fire was followed by the wailing of the inhabitants from fear and injury. Shapur's army retaliated with a barrage of well-aimed arrows. Spears were thrown next, and Zenobia winced as one whistled past striking a soldier behind her. She barely had time to pray for his soul before pots of boiling oil were poured on her men who had thrown up ladders to scale the wall. Screams and the putrid odor of cooked flesh made her shudder.

"By all the gods, may we survive this battle." Zenobia raced up and down the front lines shouting to both the men trying to scale the walls and the archers who still sent flaming arrows across into the city. "Hold your lines. You are Palmyran soldiers, the best trained, the most god-fearing men of all times. We were chosen to help strengthen Rome because we are mighty!"

Smoke made her eyes tear, and Zenobia blinked continuously as she shouted encouragement and orders. She saw the men on the left flank falter as they scaled the vertical barriers. Three of the five ladders had been pushed away from the walls and the men had clung helplessly to the rungs as they crashed to the earth below.

"Get those ladders against the walls! More men, more men!" Zenobia didn't wait to see if her orders would be followed; she knew they would be. She raced to the right side of the huge wooden and iron bound gates where her soldiers had seven ladders still standing. Men scrambled over the top and subdued the enemy with little resistance. Zenobia barely had time to bask in their victory before General Ezechiel, clinging to his horse, came tearing across the trampled and bloodied grass toward her.

"King Shapur has escaped from the west side of the city out a narrow and not often used gate. He rides east." Ezechiel wiped sweat from his face.

"East? He thinks he'll escape to Nisibis. Send word to King Odainat that we will pursue Shapur. Ask my husband if he'll join us."

Ezechiel saluted as he rushed down the lines close to the walls of the city to look for a messenger. Zenobia watched him go, amazed that he seemingly had no fear of arrows, boiling oil, spears, or falling bodies.

The pursuit of King Shapur across the desert was tedious. Zenobia felt the heat of the noonday sun and had ordered the pace be slowed so the infantry would not faint. She also ordered the Master of Camels to increase water rations to the men. When the water was gone, the camels were to continue past Nisibis to the Tigris River and refill the goatskin bags for the march home, made doubly long by Shapur's flight. Zenobia glanced over her shoulder at Odainat and his army barely in sight on the horizon. The two armies made a grand sight, and Zenobia felt the pride she always did after a well-won battle.

Word had come to her via her husband's nephew, Maeonius, who now rode beside her, that Edessa had been captured. As soon as King Shapur had deserted them, the citizens opened the gates to the Palmyran army. A garrison had been left behind to help bury the dead of both peoples and to cleanse the streets of blood.

Zenobia forced herself to listen to the prattling of Maeonius. "What say you, Maeonius? I fear I am tired after the battles and was not attending. Forgive me."

"I can't wait to return to civilization. I abhor this incessant riding through the heat and dust."

"You should not hover at the rear of the troops. That's where most of the dust is," Zenobia said. She glanced at the man who was not yet five and twenty, but looked like a over-ripened grape.

"I . . . I didn't hover at the back. I was gathering information for Odainat."

"King Odainat to you." Zenobia watched Maeonius' lower lip protrude. She wanted to knock him off his fine Arabian stallion with the back of her hand. At least he might get a dent in his fancy brass decorated iron mail that had yet to feel a blow from the enemy.

"I am King Odainat's most valuable messenger. He has said that to me many times."

"How many messengers does your king have?"

"I . . . I don't know. As many as needed." Maeonius frowned.

"I never thought of it."

Zenobia waved her hand to dismiss the subject. She was too tempted to reveal to Maeonius that Odainat had only one messenger. His general had a score of messengers so Odainat would not be bothered.

"I see Nisibis ahead. Care you to ride back to your king and say that since it is my turn to announce the attack, I wish to do so immediately."

"Now?"

"Question you my methods? Why do you, my little dust eater, dare ask such a thing? Yes, now!" Zenobia clenched her fists to keep them from shaking. She wished that she wouldn't react thus to the little desert scorpion. "King Shapur will not expect a third battle today. It will catch him unawares. Go!"

Maeonius expertly turned his horse and headed toward Odainat's army a quarter mile to the rear.

"He is a good rider and clings to the horse as if he is one with it." Ezechiel moved into the space vacated by Maeonius.

"He is practiced in retreat."

"He impresses the ladies with his riding skills," Ezechiel said.

"If he would just be a man and have a wife and children, a home, then I would be happier. Maeonius has too much time on his hands for mischief. Enough of a disagreeable subject." Zenobia looked at the sun. "Think you that we can take Nisibis before nightfall?"

"Five hours? I think so. Shall I pass on that word to the others? From which direction do we attack?"

"Straight through the western gate." Zenobia looked at the walled town before her. Instead of being built on the Tigris River, it had grown around an oasis much as Palmyra had, but there the similarity ended. She remembered Nisibis as an irregular maze of narrow streets, airless shops, and noise. She looked back at Odainat's army. It would do well to have them as a second wave of attackers. As before, she ordered fire arrows, wall scalers, and the cavalry to cover the infantry as it attacked. If King Shapur would show his face, she could tear it apart.

The first volley of fire arrows arched over the walls with a whooshing sound. Before Zenobia could order the infantry to hoist the ladders and scale the wall, the gates were swung open. "Ezechiel! The people surrender to us, but that means King Shapur has fled."

She reined Thabit to a stop in front of the gate and waited for Odainat to catch up with her. It was common for a city without a leader and an army for protection to throw open the gates in hope that their people and town would be spared. Zenobia had no desire to kill innocent people.

"Are you disappointed, Zenobia?" Odainat asked.

"Not really. I've had enough blood and death today. Both our armies are tired, but I have no doubt that we could have taken this city, too."

"I shall arrange for the city administration to have Palmyran help with funds. That will guarantee loyalty."

"We have just doubled our lands, Odainat. Doubled." Zenobia glanced at the crumbling walls around the city. "Although I'm not certain this town will bring much revenue. Perhaps we need to strengthen its trade route."

"An army to protect traveling merchants will be the first order of business," Odainat said. "Now, my dear, do you want to stay here for the night or sleep under the stars?"

"I prefer the stars."

The buff-colored desert gave way to grasses, shrubs, and wild flowers as Zenobia and Odainat reached the huge oasis where their city, Palmyra, had been built. As they traveled from the flat desert through rolling hills, Zenobia could see dark green leaves of date palms that girdled the oasis named for them. The city of palms was like a cool drink of water to Zenobia each time she returned from a battle. She reached for Odainat's hand. "It is so beautiful."

"Always. To me it is the loveliest place on earth." Odainat kissed her hand and stopped at the crest of a hill.

"I thought we were going to chase King Shapur all over the world," Zenobia said. "Although not having killed him is a disappointment, I'm glad to be home."

"It's both good and bad to have Shapur in Ctesiphon. He is separated from us by the Euphrates and Tigris rivers and a desert, but he is closer to us."

"He can't attack Palmyra. We have weakened his forces. Our city is too lovely for the likes of him." She nudged Thabit forward.

Below them, nestled against western mountains, the city lay south of army barracks that skirted the outside area. The eastern part of the city pushed against the edge of a wadi. The natural fissure in the desert provided protection to the city from surprise attack, but prevented it from growing outward. Consequently, Palmyra grew to the north and south in a planned layout of columned streets in opulent splendor that reflected its wealth.

Zenobia smiled at her husband as they entered the north gate, the sun momentarily blocked by the twelve-foot high limestone arch. Smaller arches flanked the sides. As was custom, Zenobia and Odainat entered through the middle, their generals through the smaller arches. An honor guard of cavalry officers followed as crowds of cheering citizens welcomed home the victorious army. Retired soldiers, no longer able to fight, stood at attention with their battle-hardened bodies in never-forgotten stances.

The street was paved with limestone blocks as were all the main streets in Palmyra. Zenobia loved the sound of horses' hoofs on the stone squares as they made their way past the four columns with statues that venerated men and women from four different occupations. Her father, Zabbai, had been so honored because of his success as a merchant. A native of Palmyra, he had taught Zenobia to cherish the city. She looked at the top of a limestone column four times her height where a bronze statue of him had been placed long before her birth. She said a prayer for him to Hercules, his favorite god, and the one whom most merchants favored.

The street pushed its way almost straight south through a residential section. Zenobia waved to her childhood friends who stood in the doorways and second story windows as she passed. A few of her friends were on the rooftops of their homes, oblivious to the late afternoon sun that sparkled off their gold jewelry woven through massive piles of curls. Zenobia knew that she would be besieged with invitations to dinners and afternoon baths at the Nymphaeum so that she could tell her friends not of the battles, but what style of clothing the women wore in Edessa and Nisibis. Contrary to what Odainat believed, she enjoyed jewelry, clothing, and womanly things as well as armor and weapons. Not as much as other women, she had to admit.

Zenobia smelled the sulphurous water of the oasis for fifty cubits before they got to the Ain Efqa. As they rode past the oasis, servants and slaves stood on the steps that led to the water. They stopped dipping water into containers long enough to cheer as the army passed. She was happy to be home. Even the odor of the Ain Efqa was not unpleasant to her, as it was to some. It was Palmyra's lifeblood.

CHAPTER

II

260 A.D. Dacia

urelian pushed the leather tent flap aside and looked down the gentle sloping hill at his Roman troops who dotted the grassland like scattered coins. The sun's rays pushed through the morning clouds, peeked around the craggy mountains, and promised another life-giving spring day. Today he would allow the men another day's rest while they waited for the Dacians to attack. His strategy was to let his troops, exhausted from their march, rest while the barbarians wore themselves out clambering up the rugged terrain. He expected them from the west and had sent a cavalry officer to watch the Tisza River. He had also sent an officer to the northern pass through the Carpathian Mountains. It would not surprise him to see the shaggy haired and bearded troops tear through the pass.

Aurelian stared toward the southwest where he had been born more than four decades ago on the far side of the Danube. His homeland in the Balkans was as far away in distance as it was in time. He remembered little of his father who fought with their tribal leader against the invading Romans. His mother's face was a blur surrounded by sun-colored hair.

The Romans had captured his village when he was fifteen. He liked the army's precision, armor that sparkled, and the sound of marching troops. He'd followed the army on its southward trek running errands and learning the language that sounded like barking dogs to his ear. At twenty he joined other young men to begin his training as a Roman soldier. He became enemy to his own people, but he didn't care. Rome would prevail whereas his people were nothing but peasants who were content with hovels, rough clothing, and little food. They had no ambition.

He loved the beauty of Rome. He loved Rome's growth, the expansion of her boundaries, her civilization. He smiled. He loved the beauty of her women, too.

Aurelian let the tent flap drop and marveled at how the interior seemed sunnier than outside. He supposed it was the sun shining through the well-oiled leather. He sniffed. The oil had a rancid odor if one chose to seek it out. He was so used to the smell of oiled leather, horses, and blood that he hardly paid attention to it. He wondered what his life would've been like if he'd stayed on the little patch of ground that barely supported his small family. Boring, no doubt.

Aurelian crossed to the table that held maps, orders from the inept senators in Rome, and news of the eastern front. Odainat and Zenobia had once more turned Shapur back. The pair fought well. Too well. Some day Rome would pay for their services. Not with gold; the Palmyran pair needed no more gold. No, Rome would pay in a way more costly. Aurelian shivered. He could never trust a woman who fought like a man and, according to all reports, did it with pleasure.

He heard the commotion outside his tent and waited patiently for his aide to thrust himself through the tent flap. The snapping of leather as it was jerked back sounded like the crack of a whip.

"Commander! A missive from the east. It is edged in black and has to be bad news." Marcellus waved a scroll in front of Aurelian's face.

"Everything is bad news." Aurelian grabbed the scroll and unrolled it. He read it rapidly, then rubbed his eyes. "May Mithras preserve us!"

"The Persians?" Marcellus asked.

"The Persians, the barbarians, the world. Why is the world against us? Can't they see the wonder of Rome's civilization?"

"Most people are blind," Marcellus said.

Aurelian glowered at the scroll. "The Persians have captured Emperor Valerian. Never has Rome had an Emperor captured." Aurelian read aloud. "Our dear Emperor suffered a crushing defeat at Carrhae. He serves Shapur as a human mounting block and servant."

"Truly?"

"Rome is too weak to go after Shapur. We've had to use Odainat and Zenobia. What kind of emperor is so stupid?"

"Shhh! That is traitorous." Marcellus glanced at the tent flap. "Gallienus is emperor now."

"I don't care. He hasn't shown any sign of strength, either. Rome is weak, and she should never have allowed it. She fights battles with the barbarians that are better left unfought."

"I cannot believe this!" Marcellus whispered. "Whatever will happen to Rome?"

"I don't know." Aurelian threw the scroll on the hard packed earthen floor. "Rome was not meant to be ruled by three emperors."

"Three?" Marcellus asked. "I count Valerian as one, his son, Gallienus, as co-emperor, but who is the third?"

"Odainat. There are four if Zenobia continues to grow in strength." Aurelian kicked the scroll across the room. "Valerian will die."

"Cannot Odainat rescue him?"

"No one can rescue him. Even I would not march that far. A black curtain has fallen on Rome. Valerian is lost and so is Rome."

"But Zenobia and Odainat are able to contain Shapur."

"I don't see Gallienus fighting alone."

"Are you not afraid of spies?"

"I care not. Let my words reach the ears of Gallienus. He needs to hear them." Aurelian paced back and forth. "Don't you understand? If Rome depends on others for her defense, she grows weaker and weaker."

Aurelian pointed to the earth. "Why are my shield darts scattered about?"

Marcellus scrambled to pick up the darts. "My apologies. The slave is new and has no idea that these must fit inside the shield. I will beat him."

"Soundly, I hope."

Aurelian thumped a map with his finger. "If ever I were to rule Rome, I would withdraw all troops from Dacia. Even our gods laugh at us for fighting here. Our lines are as thin and taut as a harp string."

"What of the mines?"

"The mines are not worth the price to keep them. The Dacians are a fierce lot." Aurelian's head snapped up. "A horse pounds toward us."

"I hear nothing."

Aurelian strode outside and watched as a man leaning low on a horse thundered up the mountain trail, tore through the infantry who scrambled up from their games of knuckles and bones, and found Aurelian.

Turf scattered and dust rose around the horse's hoofs as the rider slid off before the animal had come to a stop.

"They come up the pass through the Carpathian Mountains. They will be here by tomorrow. They march by the hundreds."

Aurelian nodded, tugged on a strand of mud-colored hair, and squinted toward the north. He knew he wouldn't see the Dacians, but still he looked. "We will be ready before dawn. No fires tonight. No music, no talking. Marcellus, make certain that the shield wall will be four men deep."

"With the cavalry to the right and left to flank them?"

"No. I want all the cavalry in the center. We'll have to break through their shield wall immediately."

"Sir, no cavalry can charge a shield wall. The spears alone would down our horses." Marcellus rubbed the hooked bridge of his nose.

Aurelian grinned. His friend and second in command always rubbed his nose when he disagreed with Aurelian. Some days his nose was almost raw. "Do you think the enemy will expect us to crash through their lines with cavalry?"

"No. It never works." Marcellus grimaced.

"Put padding on the horses' chests," Aurelian said.

"We need leather. Where do we? . . ."

"Tents." Aurelian motioned for two of his slaves to come over. "Make my horse a padded leather chest protector from this." He pointed to the tent flaps. He didn't wait for them to question him, but went inside to look at the new maps he'd made yesterday.

It was an important battle needed to impress Emperor Gallienus. Aurelian had long ago formulated his personal goal. Nothing would stop him. No one would stop him. He would do anything for his own glory and to reinstate the glory of Rome.

The scout had not exaggerated. There were hundreds of them. Aurelian shaded his eyes and looked down the slope at the army who marched up the mountain with the pace of men who climbed mountains in heavy battle gear for sport. They outnumbered his men ten to one easily.

Fish-scale armor shone in the dawn light as the Dacian leaders rode toward Aurelian's shield wall. Bushy bearded and dark, these men were short, stocky, and muscular. Dark curly hair escaped from under battered helmets and seemed as disorderly as the men. Well behind the last line of archers were the women and children who tagged along. Some were known to pick up the weapons of fallen men and use them until they, too, died. Aurelian shivered. What manner of men allowed women to fight? Barbaric, of course.

Roman horses, sensing an impending battle, snorted and pawed the ground. Aurelian spoke softly to his horse and patted him on the neck. He had several names for the brute. Some were not flattering as the beast had the habit of unseating Aurelian after a battle. At those times, he called the animal Harpinna, after his mother-in-law.

"Hold your shields tightly against your neighbors'!" Aurelian shouted. "Close behind our cavalry quickly."

The enemy stopped fifty feet away to shout insults at the Romans as was custom. It didn't matter that most of Aurelian's men wouldn't understand the words; they understood the meaning. Aurelian understood all of it. He could not forget the tongue that was his for the first fifteen years of his life no matter how he tried.

Aurelian shouted for the charge toward their lines. The enemy had expected insults instead of a charge and were startled by the sudden rush. Aurelian led his men to his left where the shield wall wavered. He kicked furiously at the horse and swore at the gods who had cursed him with such a cumbersome beast.

Spears glanced off the tough leather horse armor made tougher by boiling and building layers. Aurelian used his spear to stab a shield and jerk it away from the startled foot soldier just before he was crushed beneath Harpinna's hoofs. The small gap in the shield wall widened as more of Aurelian's cavalry poured through and slaughtered the retreating Dacians.

All at once the Dacian leaders shouted a reversal. Aurelian was confused by the sound of horns to his left and in front of him. The

Dacian army curved around the Roman army like a crescent moon and Aurelian groaned. How stupid.

"Aurelian!" Marcellus shouted from his right. "Look to your left!"

"May Mithras help me to die a brave death. We are lost!" Aurelian returned the shout. Another hoard of Dacians came charging up the mountain behind his men. Half his army was split away from him. Aurelian and fewer than a hundred soldiers were surrounded on three sides with their backs to a sheer cliff wall.

"These Dacians crossed the Tisza River! Our scout must be dead." Marcellus waved his bloody sword. "We have no choice but to fight to the end."

"Fight we must." Aurelian shouted the command to form a single-line shield wall. The banging of leather-covered shields against each other sent his horse into a frenzy. Aurelian struggled with the animal, but it shot forward through a gap in the not yet formed shield wall.

"Damned animals. Always hated horses." Aurelian drew his sword.

He surprised the Dacians and took advantage of the confusion to down three men in quick succession. He felt the earth tremble as his men thundered toward the enemy. It was his turn to be surprised. They must have thought this a new tactic. He glanced over his shoulder at the running wall of shields and quickly maneuvered to his left and out of the way.

The Dacians had no time to form more than a third of their shield wall before the Romans crashed into them. The reverberation of wood-covered shields carried across the field to Aurelian. He shouted for the cavalry to follow him around the collapsed shields. They swept past the fallen enemy who were being slaughtered by Roman spearmen and rode over screaming, fleeing Dacians. Aurelian felt a surge of energy, swung his sword again and again, and left a trail of trampled and decapitated bodies.

His horse slipped on the blood soaked earth, righted itself and for once obeyed Aurelian perfectly. He and his men charged toward the other Romans who were in a tight circle and fighting to the death. There were no shields, for these were infantry who usually followed behind and killed any remaining enemy. Some of his oldest and best-trained men were in this group. Aurelian could not leave them behind.

His sword made a whistling sound as Aurelian brought it down onto a Dacian's uncovered skull. The spray of hot blood splattered Aurelian's already gory armor. He jerked his sword from the man's head, spurred his horse forward and sliced off another man's sword arm. Aurelian raised a foot, placed it against the man's chest and toppled him backward like a stone column.

A scream from his left warned Aurelian of an advancing enemy, but he could not swing his sword around in time to stop the Dacian who charged at him with an ax. Aurelian felt the bile rise in his throat. He pulled his horse around to take the assault, but the animal slipped on wet earth, and Aurelian was thrown to the ground. He rolled instinctively to his right, leaped up and faced the enemy.

Swords clashed until Aurelian thought his arm would cease to obey his commands. This old gray-haired fighter calculated every move to conserve his own energy while leading Aurelian around in a large circle. Aurelian knew the Dacian tactic was to tire him, but he was helpless to break out of the pattern.

Aurelian continued to dance around the enemy until his sword arm stung and his legs were weak. He prayed to Mithras to take him quickly.

Hammering hoofs broke through his thoughts. That brainless horse of his came charging toward him, swerved just as he got to Aurelian, and ran over the Dacian. The old soldier, cut and bleeding from a massive wound to his head, struggled to his feet and swung his sword in a half circle before the life went out of his eyes. He fell to the earth.

Aurelian shook the sweat from his eyes and, with no time to think of the lucky turn of events, charged into the closest brawl. He dispatched three unarmed spear soldiers, then turned to look for another victim. At first the large area around him startled Aurelian until he realized that the Dacian horns blared a retreat. The enemy scattered as Aurelian's cavalry galloped over dead bodies in pursuit.

Aurelian handed his sword to a slave who had come running. "Clean this well." He couldn't remember the slave's name. They'd captured him several battles ago, and the youngster seemed eager to please. He was slow-witted, however, and more trouble than not. Aurelian had started to order him executed, but the mindless, trusting eyes stared at Aurelian with awe. He was spared, but like Aurelian's horse, not worth much.

A tub of hot water had been placed inside the tent for the commander. It was a luxury, but he insisted on it. The mindless slave helped Aurelian from his fish scale armor, the leather padding, and his leg coverings. Boots were thrown away after each battle. Blood stiffened them, and Aurelian hated blisters.

Aurelian stood outside the tent while the slave dumped warm water over his head. Diluted blood, dirt, and sweat made rivers at his feet and ran down the slope. He waved the slave away after the third bucket and went into his tent. He eased himself into the water spiced with cloves and mint. At his age he needed something for muscles that ached. He slid down and rested his head against the back of the wooden tub. Even the linen lining made his skin hurt. Maybe he was too old to be a soldier. The slave tiptoed into the tent with scented oil and a set of Strigils. The rattling of the silver cleaning implements irritated him, and he sent the simpleton away. He didn't need to be oiled and scraped clean with the curved instruments that must have been invented by a Roman mother bent on torturing her offspring.

He reluctantly opened his eyes when he heard a rustling at the tent opening. The slave pushed a girl of a dozen years toward him. Aurelian frowned. He'd asked for a woman. The slave grabbed the child's thin, dirty garment and ripped it off. She shivered and stared at the floor. Thick, black hair cascaded down her back, and she leaned her head forward so that hair fell across her boy-like chest.

"Send this child away. She knows nothing of love." Aurelian waved his hand. "Marcellus! Marcellus!"

"Yes, sir!" Marcellus popped through the tent. He was clad only in under garments.

"Give this child decent clothing, some food, and send her down the mountain. Make certain that none of the men follow. She is not to be touched."

"Yes, sir."

"Are there any comely women from the village we captured? Young and untouched? I don't want any diseases." Aurelian glowered at the slave. "And send this worthless rubbish somewhere else. Have him dig new latrines."

"Of course." Marcellus chased the slave out the door. "I think there is a girl of fifteen summers or so. I'll bring her."

"Make her take a bath."

"I'll return quickly."

Aurelian stood and let the water run down his war-hardened body. He had scars, but none of his wounds had been large or deep. He stepped into a second tub of cold water and used a silver dipper to rinse. He stepped from the tub onto a linen cloth and waited for the woman.

Marcellus came into the tent pulling a slender girl behind him. "I found a beauty."

Aurelian looked at her. Hair the color of honey framed a heart shaped face. Blue eyes met his own blue eyes, then she looked at his chest, his arms, and toured his body slowly with her eyes. When she saw his well-endowed privates, she smiled and untied the strings on her tunic. She let her clothing fall to the floor, walked to the warm water tub and climbed in. Hair floated around her shoulders as she slid down into the water.

"You may leave, Marcellus," Aurelian croaked.

"Did I do well?"

"Yes. If she is good, I shall keep her close by."

"I think she's the daughter of one of the dead tribal chiefs. She did not cry or wail when we captured her," Marcellus said. "And her clothing is better than the others. See, she wears a gold torc about her neck."

"Go!"

Aurelian waited for the tent flaps to drop discreetly into place. Although he'd bedded women in front of the whole army, he didn't want to share this woman. He sometimes liked to force the captured women, but this one was different. She seemed to think she was his equal. It promised to be an interesting night. She laughed when she saw that he was more than ready for her.

He took her hand and helped her from the tub. Her hand was smooth. She did no work as was customary among the tribal women. She folded against him and nuzzled his chest before letting her tongue dart out and taste his nipples.

"I wanted a virgin with no diseases," he whispered.

"I have no diseases." She knelt before him and took him into her mouth.

With a moan, Aurelian pushed her to the pallet. Her love making was as intense as his own.

He awoke exhausted but relaxed. He reached for his new mistress, but found the bed empty and cold. He sighed and rolled over to wait for her return. He drifted off into a deep slumber. When he awakened again, the sun shone directly overhead. He glanced around the tent, but did not see his woman. Odd. Usually the ones who loved to make love came back to him for more.

He bounded off the low bed and wrapped a toga about himself, not taking the time to drape it properly. He rubbed his face. He needed a shave, but that half-witted slave nearly severed his upper lip the last time he let razor touch skin.

Aurelian looked around. Something was amiss. Nothing was quite out of place, but things had been moved. His bag of coins were hidden in a chest under his winter cloak. Aurelian opened the chest and felt for the leather bag. It was there. He held it, but the bag did not lay as it usually did. He pulled the bag open and poured out the contents. Small stones had replaced his coins.

He reached for his bag of jeweled pieces that he'd gained through plunder. That bag also felt peculiar. Instead of jewels, Aurelian found more small stones. It couldn't be that dim-witted slave. He'd never have enough sense to look for things.

"Marcellus!" Aurelian heaved himself up. "Marcellus! Where are you?"

"Here." Marcellus stuck his head inside the tent.

"Where is that whore?"

"Whore?"

"The woman I had last night."

"Ah. She went to pick berries. She speaks our tongue very well."

"Berries? You let her go?" Aurelian frowned.

"She said that you told her to find berries. I know how much you like them, so I thought she spoke true. She speaks our tongue."

"You said that. She is also a thief. What did she wear?"

"Wear?"

"I want her found. What did she wear?"

"She wore one of your togas. She didn't drape it properly and the toga kept slipping. She is well-endowed."

"She is well-endowed with my gold," Aurelian growled. "Get that damnable horse of mine."

"I cannot."

"Why not? Did she ride away on that poor excuse for an animal?"

"How did you know?"

Aurelian stared at his aide. "She took that horse?"

"She rode like the wind toward the berry patch."

"Did you see the berry patch?"

"I saw nothing but her fine upper torso," Marcellus said.

"Which direction did she go?"

"Toward the Tisza River." Marcellus rubbed the bridge of his nose. "Did I do wrong?"

"No, I did wrong. How long ago did she leave?"

"Nearly half a day. She said that she would be back before the sun was at its zenith."

"Where is the sun now?"

Marcellus frowned. "Just past the zenith. Should I go look for her?"

"No. We can't spare the men." Aurelian rubbed the stubble on his chin. "She took that horse?"

"Good riddance, Aurelian."

"I agree. Find me another. This time get a horse that is trained." Aurelian turned to check about another bag of hidden gold when he heard familiar off-gaited hoof beats. He stepped outside in time to see Marcellus pull the reins of Harpinna hard enough to cause the horse to snort.

"She's back," Marcellus said. "And here's a scroll tied to her mane."

Aurelian grabbed the scroll. The horse whinnied when Aurelian pulled out some of the hair in his haste.

"Is it from her?"

"This is ludicrous. She says that she enjoyed last night. The gold is payment for her services and will be spent to help the Dacian people gain their freedom." Aurelian looked up. "How did she learn Latin? And to write?"

"You'll never know."

"She says that she hates Romans and all things Roman except love-making with a warrior. What kind of woman is this?" Aurelian threw the scroll to the ground. As he did, he noticed writing on the other side. "She stole the scroll, too. And probably the ink and pen! If ever I see her in this lifetime, I'll choke her to death."

"I think she's interesting." Marcellus rubbed his nose. "Would you give her to me?"

"No!" Aurelian stomped back inside his tent.

The senate floor was alive with politicians who scrambled to the hastily called meeting with white togas flying. Some were stoic, but most showed the terror on their faces that they felt. At last everyone was seated and order restored. The oldest senator rose and addressed the others.

"Valerian's capture has humiliated Rome. We have never had an emperor captured and enslaved. I have just received word from one of our greatest military leaders. There is no way for Aurelian to join Gallienus' army to rescue his father. All is lost for our noble Valerian." Calix waited for the usual noisy diatribe. Instead there was an eerie silence. "We can send a strong note of protest to Shapur and ask if he will accept ransom."

A few senators nodded. One senator jumped up and yelled out, "Where do we get ransom for an emperor? Shapur would never accept it, but would keep the treasure and Valerian. I say we do nothing, for nothing can be done."

The uproar from the senators thundered across the room and echoed off the columns and walls. Calix pounded his staff on the floor until the noise died down. "We vote after we have heard from all those who want to speak for or against ransom for our emperor." Calix stared out at the senators through eyes that had misted over. He remembered the old days when Rome had power and wealth and respect. He missed the respect for his country. Rome was civilized and should not fall to the barbarians or to the eastern savages like Shapur. It would be cruel fate if the gods allowed all that Rome built to be destroyed.

"We speak by order of rank. I shall go first." Calix took a deep breath. What he had to say would take little time. "Are there any protests to going by seniority?"

"Nay, Calix, you speak. We will listen," a young senator called out.

"We still have Gallienus, Valerian's son, as co-emperor. There is no one else that could rule with Gallienus who would have his experience, his temperament, or his station. I believe that with his skills in battle, he can lead Rome to glory. I have spoken with my heart." Calix stepped away from the podium.

"My friend and colleague, Calix, is right. We need no other emperor. Rome can be glorious as she once was. One emperor was enough in the past. It shall be so in the future." Damae bowed his head to show that he was finished.

"You are both wrong. Rome is twice the size she was and needs the hand of two, nay, even three men. We had three emperors in Valerian, Gallienus, and the third generation with the late Valerian II. Rome, the Rhine, and the east need three strong rulers," Quintus said.

"Who would you choose?" Damae asked. "Who do we have to rule?"

"I would choose Aurelian who has been victorious against the Dacians," Quintus said. "He is strong. He is powerful. He could rule."

The roar of protest caught Calix off guard, and it was a few moments before he could find his staff to pound the floor. He pounded so many times that his arm tired, and he had to switch to his left hand. He continued pounding until the protests died.

"Who speaks against Aurelian?" Calix asked.

"We cannot choose Aurelian for emperor as long as Gallienus lives. One would slay the other," Damae said. "Aurelian is a good soldier, but does that make him a noble ruler? He is devious. Rome would have civil war."

Calix hid his surprise. He knew Aurelian by his reputation as a soldier, but he knew nothing more than that Aurelian could be ruthless and especially hated senators who didn't support him. He was getting too old to keep up with politics. He preferred dozing in the atrium next to the pool.

"From whence do you come by this knowledge?" Calix asked.

"From soldiers and lieutenants who serve with Aurelian. From his slaves. From his women. It is knowledge that is common," Damae said.

A murmur of agreement rolled through the senate. Calix thought quickly. If Aurelian heard of this vote, and certainly his spies would tell him, then Calix could be found murdered. Yet, the senate had to vote if only to shore up the pretense of power that they no longer held. Calix sighed. He was old. What difference did it make if he were murdered this year or died in his bed the next? Still, perhaps there was a way to prolong his life.

Calix thumped his staff on the floor. "We vote with green and white marbles. The green marbles are a negative vote for a co-emperor." Calix nodded and one page started around the hall with a lidded wicker basket full of marbles. Each senator received a green and a white marble. A second page waited until the first row had been given marbles, then he followed with two baskets that had holes just large enough for a marble to pass through. The dark basket was for the voting marbles and the light basket was for the extra marbles.

The voting took place among silent men. The only sound was the clinking of marbles as they dropped into their respective baskets. Calix waited until last to vote. He dropped both marbles into the voting basket. The page ignored his unorthodox method. Calix took no chances. If Aurelian ever asked him how he voted, he could say that he dropped the white marble in the voting basket.

Three senators plus Calix counted the marbles. There were many more green marbles than white. No one noticed that there was one vote too many in the dark basket.

"We have voted and it shall be announced that we have confidence in Gallienus. The senators believe that Gallienus is strong enough to rule Rome as a whole as was custom in the past," Calix said. He noted that the scribe wrote rapidly. His words were part of history. Whether that was good or bad, he would know only on his deathbed.

"Aurelian, you look pensive," Marcellus said. "What news have you from the senate?"

"It is news from my spies that tell me what I want to know." Aurelian quit pacing and settled in a chair.

"And what news is that?"

"That interfering Calix has maneuvered the senate into voting for one emperor to rule Rome." Aurelian tapped the scroll against his palm. "Calix is old. Death will come to him soon. It shall look natural."

"With your usual herbs?"

"My usual herbs?" Aurelian shrugged. He observed Marcellus rubbing the bridge of his nose. Someday Marcellus would no longer be useful. It mattered not that they had been friends since the day they joined the army together. The future was grander than the two of them together. How Aurelian became emperor depended on no one but Aurelian.

"What of Gallienus?" Marcellus asked.

"The gods will show me a way," Aurelian said.

"The gods have a way of forgetting man," Marcellus said.

"They will not forget me. The gods were with me against the Dacians. I am meant to be emperor. I have known this since I was a child and saw Severus Alexander ride at the head of a vast army through our lands."

"The gods have a way of turning on man. Emperors die. Severus was only one emperor to be murdered by his own soldiers." Marcellus shook his head. "To be emperor at this time in history is to ask for assassination."

"To be a soldier during this time in history is to ask for death," Aurelian said. He held up his hand. "I hear a horse racing toward the tent."

"How do you do that? You always hear horses before I do." Marcellus stuck his head out of the tent. "A messenger comes."

Aurelian waited for the messenger to be escorted into the tent. Aurelian was surprised to see two missives. He tried not to grab the scrolls from the messenger. He popped the senate seal on the top parchment. Calix's handwriting was spidery and shaky and the date a mere ten days after the voting had taken place.

Aurelian handed the messenger a gold coin and dismissed him. "Listen to this, Marcellus. 'It is with great trepidation that I have to inform you of General Cassianus Postumus' elevation by his soldiers to emperor of western Rome.'" Aurelian swore. "By the gods, this is incredible news."

"Not unexpected, however," Marcellus said. "You said that as soon as he could, Postumus would rid himself of Gallienus' young brat. He has done so. Am I not right?"

"It says that the boy is dead. After Postumus divided the spoils of war with his troops, the youngster met with an untimely end." Aurelian looked up. "Never trust your heirs to anyone but yourself."

"Who has sent you the second scroll?"

Aurelian ripped through the seal, smiling as he did so. "Did I not tell you the gods always watched out for me? It is from Gallienus."

"Gallienus? How timely."

"He wants us to join him. I am to be elevated and am to serve as his second in command in the east." Aurelian slapped the scroll against Marcellus' arm. "Don't look so dour."

"I fear your end. The wars in the east are deadly."

"Fear your own end, not mine. I am chosen to be emperor of Rome. And when I am, I shall rule alone. I shall rule without Zenobia and that husband of hers. I shall rule as men are supposed to rule. Rome needs me to lead her to glory."

CHAPTER
III

260 A.D. Danube River Valley

    The war weary Roman army still marched with precision as it followed Emperor Gallienus down the valley along a sparkling river.

Marcellus rode beside the general. "We have followed Gallienus' army for several hours now. To what purpose?"

"I'm waiting to see if the barbarians will ambush. They are a trying race. They fight with tenacity and vigorously defend their scrubby little villages. Often men from different tribes band together to fight. I've never understood their resistance to our civilized world. They are stupid."

"What is our plan for the next battle?" Marcellus asked.

"To close them in a vise between two Roman armies," Aurelian answered. He really wanted a chance to rescue the Emperor, but it was not likely to happen. He looked down the mountains at the other army.

"Don't they know we're here?"

"By now they should." Aurelian sighed. He'd have to let the gods give him another way to worm his way into Gallienus' confidence. "We move to catch them now. Give the lieutenants their orders."

Aurelian nudged his disreputable horse forward. He should get a different mount, but this one intrigued him. He'd never had an animal that didn't obey him. This one would learn, too, even if he had to beat it regularly. He wished the whore had kept the beast. Harpinna was probably not even valuable enough for the thief. If ever he saw that girl again, he would make her pay. It was not an easy trek down the Thacian mountains, but better than climbing up. Aurelian thought about walking down, but didn't want to appear before Gallienus on foot. They were near the Black Sea, but probably would not see the wide delta of the Danube as it swept into the shallow shoreline.

The emperor looked formidable as he led his army along the Danube River Valley. Generals Reolus and Domitianus rode to his left and right. Aurelian led the way down the relatively easy path and in less than half a day had caught up with Gallienus.

"Ah, you have finally found us," Gallienus said. "I wondered how much longer you would be. I thought you knew this territory intimately."

Aurelian stifled his anger and smiled. "I gave my men an easy march. We have a difficult task ahead."

"Do we need to conquer all the Balkan area? Why do we not, as General Reolus suggests, attack Postumus instead? We unseat him, then I am the only emperor."

"We could do that, but the barbarians would be striking at our backsides the entire way to Postumus. We would lose time and men. Postumus would have recruited more soldiers by the time we got there."

"Ha!" Reolus snorted.

"Do you think the barbarians would leave us alone?" Aurelian asked.

"Yes. When they see the great army led by our emperor, they will flee."

Aurelian chose not to argue in front of the emperor. He would let what he had said sink slowly into the wine soaked brain of the weakening leader. A few more years. A few more years.

"So you think we should capture this entire area?" Gallienus asked.

Aurelian was startled by the sudden interest in his plan. He thought he'd have to talk for days. "I do. It will make more recruits want to come to us rather than to Postumus. Recruits follow a winning army."

"You know the way?"

"Very well."

"It shouldn't be difficult." Gallienus smiled at him, waved, and rode behind him to confer with his two generals.

Aurelian listened to the chatter as the two generals and the emperor talked about the upcoming battles. Fools. They had no idea how to fight here. Wait until they witnessed the first hordes race up a mountain towards them.

Aurelian turned in his saddle and called back. "We need to discuss strategy for dealing with the hordes of unruly men who'll swoop down on us."

"Our general knows how to lead," Domitianus said.

Reolus chuckled. "We have led armies long before you ever thought about being a soldier. We know how to fight."

"You don't know these people. I know these people. I was one of them. You live in the past and not the future. Old men like you atrophy starting with their brains!"

The sound of a sword as it left its sheath prompted Aurelian to pull his own short sword. He stopped in mid-movement when he felt the cold tip of Reolus' sword on his throat.

"One thrust and you're dead," Reolus said. "The emperor would not care."

Aurelian had foolishly let his temper dictate his actions, and he dared not glance at the emperor's face to see his reaction. By the gods, he couldn't allow this dolt to best him.

Swiftly, he drew his own sword and knocked Reolus' sword to the ground. "I dislike being threatened." He turned Harpinna toward the front of the lines again and rode slowly away from the stupid general.

"Wait!" Gallienus called. "Come instruct us. You spoke true. You are . . . were one of them."

Aurelian rode back to the emperor. He had no choice but to obey. Should he show contempt for the emperor's favorite generals or would that make the emperor think his own intelligence had been questioned? No, that would never do.

"I would be happy to add what little knowledge I have to your vast stores," Aurelian said.

"Without a sword, I hope?" Gallienus said.

"As you command."

"Come, Reolus and Domitianus. Listen to a native tell what our battle strategy should be." Gallienus gathered the three men together like a small flock of sheep.

"They fight with no seeming method and are fierce. Breaking

through their shield wall in the middle has been most effective though dangerous. Special provisions have to be made for the horses." Aurelian paused. Reolus shook his head. His eyes revealed that he thought the plan preposterous. Domitianus was no better. He asked inane questions, then lost interest as well. Gallienus rode ahead. He, too, had nothing to contribute.

With a sigh, Aurelian gave up trying to talk with them. Domitianus was loyal to a fault. Reolus had an edge about him that Aurelian didn't trust, but he could prove useful when the time came. It would take months or even years to gain Gallienus' respect and to become indispensable to him. The wait would be worthwhile. Aurelian had time.

"We camp here close to the Danube," Gallienus said.

"The sun still has three hours before setting," Aurelian said.

"The men need to rest before climbing the mountains that I see in the distance." The emperor watched Aurelian.

Aurelian nodded. "I see. It's a good leader who thinks of his men. They'll serve better rested than tired."

"I always think of my men. They serve Rome well." Gallienus stared at the river. "Were you born near here?"

"Farther to the west," Aurelian said.

"You seem to know the territory well."

"I roamed far and wide when a child. We followed the animals. I've since led my army up and down this valley and across those mountains several times." Aurelian paused. Should he tell him about the Dacians and the others who fought so fiercely?

"Come to my tent tonight. We shall talk, eat, and drink." Gallienus pulled his horse around and galloped toward the back of the lines.

Aurelian forced himself to keep from grinning. "Marcellus!" he shouted. "Get our tents up quickly."

The meat was tough and stringy, but the cook had made an exquisite spicy sauce from local herbs. The wine had started to turn to vinegar, but it wasn't so bad when watered down. The mountain springs were clear and sweet and Domitianus flanked the emperor at dinner just as they did during the day's ride. A dark skinned woman played a lute in the corner of the vast tent laid with layers of Persian rugs after the eastern style. She stole glances at Aurelian, and he smiled at her.

More than once Gallienus caught Aurelian watching the dark eyed beauty.

"Do you fancy her?" Gallienus asked.

"Is she yours?" Aurelian asked.

"I tire of her. I have another woman. You may take her." Gallienus smiled. "She will please you, but she is demanding and likes presents."

"What woman doesn't?" Aurelian said. "They are the same no matter where they were born."

Gallienus laughed aloud as did his two generals. "Well put." He winked at the woman and she moved so that her toga slid off her shoulder and bared a breast.

Aurelian had to look away lest he lose his concentration. She was young and smooth and beautiful.

Gallienus slapped his thigh. "You have fought these people well. Tell us about them."

"They fight to the death for their freedom." Aurelian licked his lips. He had planned what to say, but now the words would not fill his brain, nor would they flow to his lips.

"What say you, Aurelian?" Reolus asked. "Have you nothing to report about these barbarians after all the years you've done battle with them?"

"My knowledge will keep you alive." Aurelian hadn't meant to answer so caustically. Reolus knew everything, learned nothing new, and belabored the point of using the old methods of warfare that had been discarded long ago by winning armies. No wonder Postumus was able to kill Gallienus' son and take over as emperor of the Rhine Valley.

"I have done well enough without you," Reolus said.

"These barbarians fight unlike anyone else." Aurelian took a drink of wine. The sour taste was no worse than listening to Reolus.

"I know how they fight." Reolus sounded like a petulant child.

"Let him speak," Domitianus said. "You always want to fight with the old methods, but we're fighting a different war now."

"You were born barbaric. Did not our Roman training erase that?" Reolus asked.

"An advantage that will help Rome win battles." Aurelian slowly set down his wine goblet and glared at his tormenter.

"Aurelian is a puppy in a large dog's collar. He thinks he can bite, but all he can do is bark pitifully and piss on short bushes." Reolus leaned back in his chair and laughed.

Aurelian leaped up, reached across the table, and jerked Reolus out of his chair by his toga. "I shall piss on you, fool!"

"Enough!" Gallienus shouted. "Save your fight for the enemy. Release my general, if you please."

Aurelian shoved Reolus back into his chair.

"Both of you will listen to Aurelian. He has won battles that no other Roman could. He knows these people, for he was once one of them. I want to hear what he says." Gallienus stabbed a piece of dove and chewed slowly.

"The Dacians fight like other peoples of this area. They have no fear of our soldiers. They clamber up these alps like those mountain goats we see. They gather together in great swarms like bees. Their sting is fierce. They study our precision marching, then come at us in globs of unruly humanity. Our shield walls are easily penetrated." Aurelian paused.

The emperor studied him intently. "How did you hold your shield wall?" Gallienus asked.

"With cavalry. We essentially had two shield walls to the right and left of the cavalry. We try to make the shield walls four deep if possible."

"Won't the Dacians realize this is a new tactic and try to change their methods?" Domitianus asked.

"Probably. They may be undisciplined, but the leaders are crafty. I have an idea, however." Aurelian glanced at Reolus whose dark face and features had the look of someone who would kill with little provocation.

"Emperor, our real problem lies not with the Balkan warriors, but with our own."

"Our own?" Gallienus set down a silver goblet before it reached his lips. Red wine splashed on the white table covering.

"Macrianus."

"You are mad, Aurelian," Reolus said. "He has been a good loyal general and fights in the east to help Odainat and Zenobia against Rome's enemies."

Aurelian glowered at Reolus. "You are either stupid or a traitor."

Reolus leaped from his chair, pulled an eating knife from a chunk of meat, and held it under Aurelian's chin. "No one calls me a traitor and lives."

"Then you are stupid." Aurelian ignored the rivulet of warm

blood that trickled down his throat. He could see Gallienus, cat-like, watching. "Macrianus would like nothing better than to place his sons on the throne as co-emperors."

"He is in the east helping Odainat and Zenobia," Domitianus said.

"Odainat and Zenobia don't need his help. They are so powerful that they protect Rome without us," Aurelian said.

"Still, Macrianus fights in the east," Domitianus said.

"Wrong. Macrianus marches west to engage us in battle."

Gallienus' left eyebrow rose. "How do you know this?"

"My man, Marcellus, has gathered details from our spies. We were informed just before dinner." Aurelian pushed the knife away from his throat. "Don't ever do that again." His voice, hard and cold, made Reolus flinch.

"Send for Marcellus," Gallienus said.

Aurelian motioned to a servant who scurried from the tent. "We need to fight two battles; one against Macrianus and one against the Illyricum, not Dacia."

"The Illyricum?"

"Take them out and we have cut the heart out of the Balkan rebellion. It effectively splits this region in half," Aurelian said.

"A march to the Adriatic Sea from here would take twenty days or more," Gallienus said.

"We could march against Macrianus first," Domitianus said.

"The longer we wait to fight the Illyricum, the stronger they become," Aurelian said. "Ah, here is Marcellus. What news?"

Marcellus bowed to the emperor and spoke to him directly. "We have learned that Macrianus has already declared his two sons as co-emperors of Rome. He marches west and is five days away. He thinks he can fight our gallant emperor and win."

Gallienus grunted.

"His troops are tired from the desert heat. Some have been left behind because they suffered from sun sickness." Marcellus looked at Aurelian.

"Go on. Tell us about the Illyricum," Aurelian said.

"They have sent messengers throughout several countries to join them near the Adriatic Sea to invade Rome. It is imperative they be stopped," Marcellus said.

"How old is this news?" Gallienus asked.

"Barely twenty-four hours. We sent our fastest messenger to our spies," Marcellus said.

Gallienus nodded. "Here's what we will do. Reolus and Domitianus will take half the army and march east for one long day. There you will rest and wait for Macrianus. As soon as you see them, attack before they have time to rest."

"We should start tomorrow," Domitianus said.

"Yes." Gallienus looked at Aurelian. "Were you not born in Illyricum and know the land well?"

"Yes."

"You will ride with me to fight the Illyricum. We leave tomorrow." Gallienus motioned toward the slave who still played the harp. "Take her. She knows love. It is my gift to a fine warrior."

"I am honored," Aurelian said.

A warm hand caressed Aurelian's back, and he rolled over to stare into dark copper colored eyes. Black hair tumbled across Sanura's slender form as she lay nude atop the linen sheets.

He grabbed her fingers and kissed each one. Her soft laughter caressed him and sent shivers into his soul. "You have no right to be so beautiful."

"You have no right to be such a good lover." Sanura nibbled his ear lobe. "I want to be yours forever. Your body is strong and smooth. Gallienus grows soft."

"I will grow soft in years to come."

"No, not you." Sanura reached for him. "One time before we march to the sea."

"One time, but that is all." He traced her jaw with his tongue. "You are sweet."

"You are hungry for honey."

"Always." He slid down and took her breast between his lips and suckled until she groaned with pleasure. "Now, Sanura."

She welcomed him with abandonment.

Aurelian sighed. He had a good lover, and life was better than he'd planned. Gallienus slowly grew to trust and need him. Aurelian would make certain he would be indispensable.

"The Illyricum are many." Gallienus motioned for Aurelian to ride forward. "Their shield wall looks strong with many spears showing through. Archers in the rear could cause problems. Let's form the wedge to break through."

"Agreed except for one thing," Aurelian said.

"Which is?"

"Let's do the wedge, but hold shields above our heads like the tortoise formation." Aurelian hoped the emperor liked innovation. Winning depended on it.

"Good. Double time march. Spear men to the right and left to come in behind the Illyricum. Give the orders." Gallienus said.

"I'll lead the spear men on the right; Marcellus will be to the left. One last thing. The wedge should not be fully formed until the enemy has begun their assault. We need surprise," Aurelian said.

"It will be dangerous, but I like it." Gallienus pulled his horse around and rode up and down the front lines while Aurelian explained the new tactics to the Roman lieutenants.

Aurelian rode with the right formation of spear men as they advanced toward the Illyricum army. He shouted at the men to keep the lines even. The Illyricum outnumbered the Romans three men to one, but they were undisciplined. Rabble danced back and forth waving spears and shouting insults. Their commander wore fish scale armor over a short tunic and trousers. Sun danced off his helmet with cheek protectors that covered much of his bushy beard. Fastened about his neck was a brown woolen cloak clasped with a silver brooch. He waved a broad sword above his head that matched the fierce look on his face.

How they ever beat the Romans was a mystery to Aurelian. He chastised himself for his disdain and prayed to Mithras.

The Illyricum army let out a roaring scream that made Aurelian shiver. They banged their spears against their shields as they ran toward the Roman first line of defense. Aurelian felt his stomach clench at the sound. He looked up and down the lines. The wedge with its tortoise shell protection moved quickly into place and advanced forward in double time.

Arrows from the back lines of the Illyricum army darkened the sky as they rained down on Aurelian and his men. He held his shield above his head and cursed. Although the arrows would do little damage, they effectively kept his spear men from fighting.

The wedge continued forward unrelentingly and broke through the three deep shield wall crushing the ill-fated enemy. Aurelian ordered his spear men around the outside of the Illyricum army during the commotion. They were in place before the enemy could recover from the wedge. The cavalry rode through the gaps along the shield wall line and, with swords drawn, cut down the enemy.

Aurelian drew his sword and leaped into the fight. He slashed vigorously with a downward swing into the bare-chested Illyricum who tried to grab his horse's reins. The man's matted, bearded face registered shock, then paled as he went down. Aurelian rode over the man and chose his next victim. The sun made its way across the sky unnoticed as the Romans created a blood bath.

Before sunset, the Illyricum, who'd been pushed to the edge of the Adriatic Sea, surged forward one last desperate time. The Romans killed the few who staggered towards them, chased down and captured the remaining men who had run.

"Take no prisoners," Aurelian shouted. He watched as the last man was dispatched to the world of the gods.

Gallienus led the army to the north toward the chief's village and stopped at the edge. Thatched roofs above round houses circled a clearing. Small plots of produce in neat rows huddled next to each hut.

"The women and children hide," Gallienus said. He turned in his saddle and motioned for a small band of soldiers to search the huts. "Find the women and children. They will bring a good price on the market. The pretty ones are to be separated. They will bring better prices."

Aurelian waited between Gallienus and Marcellus. He was anxious to see how many good slaves could be rounded up. He thought he saw movement at the edge of the forest. He stared into the woods, but saw nothing. A breeze swept aside some leaves, and he saw a shadow slip from tree to tree.

His horse, Harpinna, cooperated today and moved quietly to the woods and through the trees. The shadow ran, and Aurelian, hampered by low hanging branches, slid off his horse and pursued the young girl. She ran like a hare; first to the left, then to the right. He ran faster and, with one final leap, wrapped his arms around her.

They fell to the ground. She squirmed and almost got away, but Aurelian held her down. She managed to get one arm loose. He saw the knife too late, but she wasn't strong enough nor was the angle good enough for her to do more than scratch his arm. He bent her arm back and tore the knife from her hand. He flung it far into the woods and dragged her to her feet.

"You! You're the thief who stole my gold!"

"I stole nothing."

"And my horse."

"I returned her."

"You kept the gold." Aurelian tightened his grip on her arm.

"I earned it." She jerked her arm, but couldn't free it from Aurelian's grasp.

"I could execute you."

"Do that. Explain why to your emperor." She laughed. "I thought not. It's too embarrassing to be bested by a mere woman."

"Why did you send the horse back?"

"She is worthless. Why do you keep her?"

"She amuses me."

Aurelian turned the woman toward the field where Romans buried their dead. Other soldiers had old men, women, and children under guard.

"Their fate is in your keeping, Roman."

"Don't try to absolve yourself of sin. Their fate is your doing."

She cursed him. He recognized the words from his childhood, and he smiled. When he asked her name in her own language, she stared at him.

"How do you know my tongue? You didn't speak it before."

"It is almost the same as I used in my childhood," Aurelian said.

She pulled away from Aurelian and looked him up and down. "You are a traitor to your own people."

"I can help your people."

"To become slaves? Prostitutes? No, thank you."

"What's your name?"

"What is yours?"

"I am called Aurelian." He grinned at her frown.

"That's a Roman name."

"I have taken on the Roman ways, thus a Roman name. I have forgotten my other name."

"No, you haven't. You haven't forgotten your language, either."
She pursed her lips and studied him. "I am called Lucine."

"Moon," Aurelian said.

"I'm afraid the moon is almost dead. I'll kill myself rather than
let you touch me again," Lucine said.

Aurelian pulled her against him, held her tightly, and kissed her.
She spat at him.

"If you take me this time, I will take pleasure in killing you before I kill myself." Lucine stood perfectly still.

"If you lie with me, I will allow your people their freedom,"
Aurelian said. "If you kill me or yourself, they will all die."

A small cry like that of a trapped animal escaped Lucine.

"Your expert love-making for their lives."

"I'm not worthy of a famous general."

Aurelian laughed. "Of course you are. You are the daughter of
the tribal chieftain."

"I am not."

"The gold torc about your neck tells me so." Aurelian pushed
aside her blonde hair and touched the wide band of metal studded
with colored stones. "You have the power to save your people. They
will listen to you."

"You're not the emperor."

"He will listen to me."

"I will hate you forever. I will curse you so that your soul will
never have peace. I will get a disease from your spear men and give it
to you."

Aurelian laughed. "I will take the chance. Come, I'll talk with
Gallienus. He rides this way."

"Aurelian, you have captured one of the enemy—again! Isn't she
the one who gave you exquisite pleasure, then stole your gold and your
horse?" Gallienus laughed, reached down from his horse, took a strand
of Lucine's gold hair in his fingers and rolled it back and forth. "Like
fine gold." He opened his fingers and watched Lucine's hair settle.

"The daughter of a dead tribal chieftain." Aurelian reminded
him. "She will make love for her people's freedom."

"Agreed." Gallienus shouted to Marcellus. "Let the people go.
We have made a bargain."

Aurelian translated for Lucine. "Your women and children are
free." He wasn't prepared for the tears that filled blue eyes.

"Thank you," Lucine said. She stared at her people as they slowly walked away before picking up their children and running towards the woods. A few of the women looked back.

Aurelian could tell that they thanked Lucine with their eyes. She stood straight and watched them go.

Gallienus nodded to Aurelian. "Take her to my tent."

"Your tent?" Aurelian asked.

"Yes. A fair trade. I'm tired of my woman. You have Sanura. I'll take this one. She will interest me." Gallienus kicked his horse and rode off.

"The bastard," Aurelian whispered. He put his arm around Lucine. How could he tell her? He whistled for Harpinna and, inexplicably, the horse obeyed. He swung into the saddle, reached down for Lucine and was surprised at her grace and lightness.

"Where do we go?"

"You'll see." He clamped his teeth together. Someday when he was emperor, no one would take anything away from him.

He stopped and helped Lucine slide from the horse.

"I remember your tent. This one is too fine for you. Whose tent is this?"

"The emperor's." Aurelian dismounted.

"Why are we here? Do you share?" Lucine frowned.

"Emperor Gallienus is enchanted by your beauty." Aurelian pulled back the silk curtains and led her inside.

She looked down and wriggled her toes. "What manner of grass is this that covers the tent floor?"

"It's a carpet from Persia."

"Persia?"

"It's a land that's far from here." He poured a goblet of wine and handed it to Lucine. She took it.

"Drink."

Lucine shook her head. "You have betrayed me."

"I had no choice."

"You had a choice. You chose to betray me just as you betrayed your people many years ago." She stared at the thick wine.

Aurelian expected her to throw something, to hit him, to scream, but she did not. Lucine walked around the tent and let her hand trail across silver dishes and bowls. She touched a pear. "What manner of fruit is this?"

"It comes from far away. It's a pear."

"Is it sweet?"

"Yes."

Lucine picked it up and took a bite. "You betrayed me. Someday my death will be your soul's death."

"No."

"Yes." She wiped pear juice from her chin. "I thought you wanted me."

"And have you steal my gold? No." Aurelian turned and left the tent.

Sleep would not come to Aurelian no matter how exhausted he felt. Sanura wisely slept on the floor when he pushed her away. She wanted to comfort him, for she had seen everything, but he did not feel worthy enough for her gentle touch. He covered his head with a linen sheet, but Gallienus' tent was too close.

A thud preceded Gallienus's cursing. Lucine cried out once, then returned the Roman curses with those from her language. Something made of glass shattered. Gallienus' laughter drowned out Lucine's protests. He had to give her to the emperor, but someday, someway he would make Gallienus pay. Aurelian was ambitious and Lucine paid the price.

"If Gallienus loses the campaign in Gaul, then he will lose his status as emperor." Aurelian poured more wine for General Reolus. "You want Gallienus as emperor, not Postumus."

"How do you know what I want? You don't tell me what I can think and cannot." Reolus downed the heavy wine in one gulp. "I have plans that you know nothing about."

"You fight well for Gallienus. He must be generous with you," Aurelian said.

"He is somewhat generous."

"Somewhat?"

"He keeps most for himself." Reolus' eyes narrowed. "You know that firsthand. I saw him take your captive."

Aurelian clenched his teeth to keep from saying what he really thought. He took a deep breath through his nostrils, then poured Reolus more wine. "It was of no consequence. He is the emperor. He can do whatever he wants."

"No. Not if my plan works."

"Plan? What plan?"

Reolus blinked several times, closed his eyes, and then nodded off to sleep. His head thudded on the plank table as he passed out.

Aurelian jerked Reolus' head up by the hair and slapped his face. "Wake up and finish your thoughts, you bastard."

"I can't tell you my plans. You'll tell the emperor who will have my head on a golden platter." Reolus grinned. "I am smarter than you."

Aurelian let the drunk's head drop to the table with a loud thud. "Marcellus, call someone to take this garbage to his own tent. I don't need that stink in here."

Early morning light drifted across the valley at the base of the Alps. Aurelian looked over his shoulder at the massive mountains. It had been a difficult march to get here. He could hardly believe that he'd crossed the Alps again. This time he did it as an aide to Gallienus. He would be made a general soon.

He let his thoughts drift to memories of last night's lovemaking with Sanura. She helped him to forget Lucine who still served Gallienus. The squeak of leather, the smell of hundreds of horses, and the warm sun on his back calmed Aurelian. He basked in the quietness save for distant conversations.

Gallienus stopped and motioned Aurelian forward.

"We are ready to fight for Gaul." Gallienus pointed across the plain bordered by the Danube and the Rhine rivers. "There lies the way to Postumus' throat."

"When you capture Gaul, you'll weaken his hold on the empire. Without control of the Rhine, he can't pretend to be emperor," Aurelian said.

"You think we can recapture Gaul?"

"I know we can." Aurelian motioned across the grassy plain. "In a day's time we will overtake Postumus."

"Then we march," Gallienus said.

The next morning after breaking camp and heading north along the Danube, Marcellus came riding back. His cloak floated on the wind behind him, and his hair swept back from his face. "Postumus and his Roman army are just over the rise."

Gallienus nodded and kept the army moving forward until he crested the hill. "There lies my enemy and the enemy of Rome. A traitor trained in warfare by Rome, and now he uses that training against her."

Aurelian pointed toward the opposing Roman army. "We fight against men trained as we are. We need to do something to turn the battle to our advantage."

"You have little faith in our army," Gallienus said.

"Faith is not the same as creating an advantage." Aurelian hated to argue with the emperor. The man often did not want the truth.

"You want to create an advantage. How?" Gallienus asked.

Aurelian was startled by the question and was not ready. So often Gallienus had waved his ideas away.

"There are several ways." Aurelian stalled while frantically pulling and discarding ideas. As always, any idea was for his advantage, not Gallienus'.

"So tell me the best idea that you have," Gallienus said.

The answer came to him in a flash. He thanked Mithras. "Why not challenge Postumus to single combat for Gaul? You against him. He won't do it. He's afraid he'll lose, and it would be damaging to his troops to see him refuse. They'll have doubts about his dauntless courage."

"What if he agrees?"

"Then he is a fool."

"Can I win?" Gallienus asked.

"Of course, else I would not have suggested it."

"I am stronger."

"And quicker," Aurelian said.

"I've won more battles."

"You fight with grace, and Mithras favors you."

"True. All the gods favor me. They always have." Gallienus motioned to Reolus and Domitianus to flank him. Aurelian watched them ride down the gentle slope toward Postumus' Roman troops. It didn't matter who won, for Aurelian had plans for either. He would not let himself smile no matter how easy it had been to maneuver the emperor. Gallienus had more men and more experience. Postumus had fresher troops and more cavalry. Either could win.

The sun had not moved more than a quarter hour's worth when

Gallienus and his generals rode back up the hill. The emperor signaled to Aurelian. "He paled at the suggestion of a duel. We attack now."

Every time shield walls clashed together, Aurelian's heart thudded against his chest so violently that he thought it would pierce his armor. He wasn't frightened; he was exhilarated. He lived to lead men. He was in his usual place to the right of Reolus. Domitianus flanked the emperor's left. The push should have gone well. Aurelian rode through the Roman traitors, slashing them down one after the other, yet the troops still did not advance. He took a precious moment to look across the field at Gallienus and Domitianus, and to his horror he saw that Gallienus was surrounded. Domitianus fought his way toward the emperor.

Aurelian shouted to Reolus. "Get your men over there to help." Reolus ignored the command and continued to hold his troops back. Aurelian shook his head in disgust, turned his horse and men to his left, and raced through the center of the battle to Gallienus' side.

Blood poured down the emperor's face from under his split helmet, but he still rode straight and still swung his sword with vigor.

Aurelian maneuvered to his side and forced the traitors back. Domitianus continued his attack from the left until the enemy retreated. Postumus ordered the rebel troops to retreat, but he stopped when he realized that Gallienus, wounded and bloody, retreated with his army as well.

Aurelian sheathed his broad sword and stared at Reolus across the field and behind them. "He is a traitor."

Gallienus frowned and wiped blood from his eyes. "How do you know this?"

"He was to my left, and I know he held back his troops. He wanted Postumus to win. Why?" Aurelian shouted. He couldn't help it.

"Send for Reolus," Gallienus ordered. He watched Marcellus ride away.

Both men returned quickly with Reolus leading. He stopped and saluted Gallienus. "Sir?"

"Why did you hold your men back when a straight forward clash would have brought me certain victory?"

Reolus paled. "I tried to make Postumus think I was weak. I tried to draw them in."

"You liar!" Aurelian shouted. "You are a strong enough military man to know that with both of our armies we could have surrounded at least half of Postumus' men. Together we could have broken the shield wall!" Aurelian's hands were doubled in fists. He wanted to draw his sword and run Reolus through. It didn't matter to him which man won the battle, but he hated not having either man win. Rome was no better than she was before the fight. "You lie!"

"Enough!" Gallienus waved his hand towards both men. "We have fought our own men too many times. Enough." His voice weakened with each word. "I will err on the side of leniency rather than execute an innocent man." His eyes were expressionless as he slumped forward. Domitianus caught him.

"We need the physician," Aurelian shouted. "Take the emperor to his tent."

"The Emperor's physician has been killed on the battlefield today," Reolus said.

"How convenient," Aurelian growled. He dropped from his horse and rushed into Gallienus' tent. He stopped short at the sight of Lucine, whom he had not been near since Gallienus had claimed her.

She glared at him. "You'd like Gallienus dead, wouldn't you?" She spoke to him in their tongue.

"For what purpose?"

"I know your heart. I know who killed his physician, too." Lucine glanced from Aurelian to the emperor. "I know medicine and surgery."

"You! Don't be absurd." Aurelian ran his hands through his hair.

"I am a medicine woman."

Aurelian chuckled. "All right. Do your best. Keep him alive."

"You'd rather I kill him, then you would have a reason to kill me. For those reasons, I will keep him alive." Lucine turned away from Aurelian and knelt before a chest. Inside she had seven leather pouches, four bottles of liquid, and numerous oiled packets.

She turned back to Aurelian. "Tell someone to get water from the fire." She opened an oiled packet and sniffed the greenish brown powder.

Aurelian hurried out of the tent. Not so much to do her bidding as to rid himself of guilt. He had not forgotten he'd used Lucine as a pawn in his game.

Gallienus lay quietly on the bed while Lucine used a foul smelling mixture to wash away dried blood. She pulled the skin of Gallienus' scalp together and held it. "A piece is missing. I'll have to make a cut so that it can be sewn together. Tell him that, Aurelian. You hold him down so that he doesn't move."

Aurelian translated Lucine's words.

"Do what must be done." Gallienus closed his eyes.

The hours passed slowly while Aurelian and Marcellus paced back and forth in front of Gallienus' tent. The stench of the herbs that Lucine used drove them out to the cool night air.

"If Gallienus dies, then Postumus will take all of Rome," Marcellus said.

"Gallienus is strong. He'll live, but neither side will be able to regroup. Rome will remain with two emperors and Odainat and Zenobia as the third. It is a tragedy." Aurelian kicked a rock. "Rome cannot remain divided. Today's fiasco was Reolus' doing. Gallienus is a fool. And fools die."

"You said Gallienus is strong." Marcellus frowned.

"He won't die a natural death. His future is with the gods, not with men." Aurelian glanced toward the tent. "Lucine saves the emperor not for life, but for death."

"You speak treason."

"I speak the truth. Enough talk." Aurelian marched toward his tent. Marcellus could be a problem, but one easily solved.

CHAPTER
IV

260 A.D. Palmyra, Syria

Zenobia moved against her husband, wrapped a bare leg around his thigh, and kissed the back of his neck. "It is morning, love, and you have yet to stir. We have not had a major battle with Shapur for more than seven years. Grow you soft?"

"We still battle weekly with one or another of those roving bandits who try to rob the caravans. I am older than you and need more rest."

"Eight years is not much older." Zenobia wrapped a curl from Odainat's hair around her finger and pulled him closer. "You did not seem older last night. Aye, you kept me awake long after the moon set with your lovemaking."

"You keep me young." Odainat kissed the finger that had been wrapped in his hair. "You do many things for me that no other woman has ever done."

"Dare you talk of other women? After I have given you two sons? For shame, Husband."

"But I have loved only you. I never thought it possible to love so deeply." Odainat rolled over and gathered Zenobia in his arms. "I always thought women were only for having sons."

"A common mistake made by men who are shallow."

"What?" Odainat slapped her bare bottom.

"Do not beat me or I'll have to challenge you to a camel race."

"Not I. You know I hate those creatures. You grew up with the disgusting animals."

Zenobia grinned. "My father always said his wealth depended on the humped back of a camel. He prized them." She lay quietly, prolonging their time together. "Did you not love Adara? She gave you a son."

Odainat sighed. "I cared for her as my wife, but the love was not as deep as it is with you. I know she was your friend, but she was like the desert flower that blooms in the spring. She died before I could get used to her presence."

"Your son is handsome and looks like you."

"Hairan is fragile like his mother. I worry that he will not be able to lead after we're gone."

"He has seen only ten summers. Our boys will be a help to him when they're older."

"He should be riding with us into our skirmishes, but his trainers tell me he is not ready."

"True. I have worked with him. He does not have the rhythm for sword play nor the strength needed for archery. He is good at strategy, however. His strength is my weakness. Perhaps if he rides with us the next time, he will see the need to work harder at warfare."

"I have enough trouble with my nephew, Maeonius, who tags along like a lost calf."

"Make him stay home and take your son. All Maeonius does is eat the dust of your army."

"I have to take Maeonius. My sister demands . . ."

Zenobia untangled herself from Odainat and the cotton covering and sat up. Her feet touched the cool marble floor beneath the two person sleeping couch. "May the gods damn that sister of yours. She whines, she begs for money, she spends all day at the Nymphaeum gossiping. More times than I care to count I have heard my words repeated as doctrine spread around Palmyra no doubt by your sister."

"Tarab has been brought up as a gentlewoman."

"I was brought up as a gentlewoman, too, Odainat."

"But it did not work with you."

"Odainat! I mean that I do not have to gossip to feel important."

"That is because you already are important. Can you imagine how it must be to have you for a sister-in-law?"

Zenobia pursed her lips. "Exciting?"

Odainat laughed. "I think overwhelming is more accurate."

"I differ with you." Zenobia turned and punched Odainat in his rock-hard belly. He didn't even pretend that it hurt. "I still think that Maeonius is a hazard. Leave him behind. Sometimes when he watches you, his eyes make me shiver with fear."

"That puppy? He is but a sand flea jumping here and there; nothing more than an annoyance."

"I don't like him."

"You don't have to like him, and you don't have to worry about him." Odainat snatched up his linen clothing and bellowed for a slave. "I have to meet with my generals."

"Your obstinate view regarding your nephew will be the death of you."

"I doubt that. He is not a fighter." Odainat dropped a toga over his head and pulled on his leggings.

"A most dangerous beast." Zenobia wrapped herself in the bed covering as an angular dark-eyed, dark skinned slave crept into the room. He stood, hands folded and waited for instructions.

Odainat ordered the slave to help him dress and waited while the slave arranged the horizontal folds in the leggings that swept upwards on the sides. The slave scrambled under the low couch to retrieve Odainat's slippers.

"Not those," Zenobia said. "They don't match your clothing. Get the ones that are trimmed in gold leather that go with the brocade on your king's toga."

"The gold ones aren't as comfortable as these." Odainat pushed his toe against his favorite pair of shoes.

"No matter," Zenobia said.

Odainat sighed and held up a foot for the slave. "I shall sneak back and exchange shoes after you've gone."

"You do and they will be incinerated."

"Women." Odainat shook his head. "Four days hence is the celebration for the anniversary of Kithoth's birth. He has seen more years than I."

"I shall be lonely without you. Has he hired dancing girls yet?"

"Of course not. This is a serious celebration."

"So. He has hired dancing girls."

"Only two."

"Your sister told me twenty and four."

"She exaggerates. She is a gossip. You told me that."

"How many?"

Odainat shrugged. "Perhaps ten and eight."

"How many?"

"I know not."

"I know. He has hired twenty. They will dance without veils."

"Really?"

"Really."

"Prostitutes. How interesting." Odainat held up his left arm so that the slave could attach his sword to its belt.

"If you so much as think about bedding a prostitute I will . . ."

"I have no need." Odainat smiled.

"Good."

"I will not drink as much wine as I used to."

Zenobia loved his lop-sided grin rarely seen during these turbulent times. "And why not? Is age a problem?"

"Remember the one time I went to Kithoth's party instead of rushing out to fight the Persians?"

"How could that be forgotten? We confused them with the one day's delay and won that little border skirmish."

"That day my head was as big as a melon and was filled with a thousand braying donkeys that tramped around on my bruised brain."

"You still fought just as well."

"I was forced to live. A punishment from the gods."

Zenobia laughed, kissed Odainat's cheek and waved to him as she left his suite. She crossed the mosaic floor, the bed linen she'd wrapped herself in trailing behind her, and walked past the bathing room into her own apartment. She smiled to herself. How like Odainat to pretend not to know that Kithoth would throw his annual wild party. Men were like boys. All year they whispered plans to each other for the next year's party. Everyone in Palmyra waited for Kithoth's annual event.

Zenobia's footsteps echoed in the Funerary Temple that rose two stories high. It was cool compared to the heat that already invaded Palmyra as the sun rose toward its zenith. She walked past twenty rows of crypts stacked five high between marble pilasters. She stopped beside Adara's loculi. The flickering oil lamp that

Zenobia held made the statues of the dead seem alive. Adara, because she had been queen, had a life-sized statue carved into the closing stone to her crypt. Below her crypt rested her family. Her mother, who died in childbirth, was on the bottom. An older brother, dead through war, rested above his mother and below his father. Zenobia had known them all her life. Hairan, her stepson, was Adara's only direct descendent, and Zenobia felt compelled to protect him from danger.

"Adara, I've come to talk with you about Hairan. I fear your son does not please Odainat, and I need your advice." Zenobia lighted incense in a small dish. She sniffed the sandalwood smoke as it drifted upwards. "I have tried to teach him archery, the spear, to ride. He prefers playing the lyre to the sword." Zenobia looked at Adara's painted statue. "You played the lyre like a goddess."

"That is true, and she taught me well."

Zenobia whirled around at the sound of Hairan's voice. "Why are you here?"

He stepped from the shadows. "I come often." Hairan's voice cracked. He was at the edge of sadness.

"So you heard?"

Hairan stared at the marble floor. "I did."

"I'm sorry."

"It's all right. I've known how father felt about me for a long time. I try not to disappoint him, but I do."

Zenobia touched the boy's hair. "You're so much like your mother. I loved her like a sister."

"She didn't have to be a warrior, but I'm to be king after Father and you. I need those skills." He sighed. "I just don't seem to have the will to throw a spear, shoot an arrow, or learn swordsmanship. I try. I really try."

"I know you do. Some men don't get their coordination until later. I had an older cousin whom we thought would never learn to wield a sword."

"Who?"

"Zabbai, named for my father and grandfather."

"Zabbai! He was a fierce warrior. He had no fear."

"He served me well until a desert fever struck him down." Zenobia closed her eyes. She could see Zabbai before her, dark eyes laughing at her attempts to imitate his prowess.

"Would you work with me again? I'll try harder."

"Of course. Tomorrow. Meet me just before sunrise at the army barracks. We'll conquer archery first."

"Don't tell Father. I want to surprise him." Hairan tugged at his toga.

"Promise that you'll continue to play the lyre. We need music in times of war."

"Yes." Hairan looked at his mother's statue. "Was she as beautiful as that statue?"

"More beautiful, for her eyes were full of joy. She sang often because she was happy. I remember when you were not yet an hour old. She held you in her arms and sang a baby's ballad."

"What did my father do?"

"Odainat? His smile was so broad that I thought his cheeks would crack. You were his first born and a son."

"You were there."

"Adara was my dearest friend from childhood. I always tended her in joy and sorrow and in life and death."

"You've known me all my life."

"Yes." Zenobia put her hand on the boy's shoulder. "You have a talent for music. How I envy that!"

"Envy?"

"Yes. The gods favored you with a gift. I can fight, but that isn't a gift from the gods. I learned to fight. Your mother's music and your music come straight from the heavens. How lucky you are." Zenobia grinned at Hairan's blush. "Go and play music today. Tomorrow we take up fighting with General Abdas and General Ezechiel. When they finish with you, I shall practice with you more. You will beg me to let you rest, but I will not."

"I'll never beg you to let me rest. I will learn everything." Hairan started to leave, turned back, and hugged Zenobia. "You are a wonderful second mother. I would have no one else." Hairan turned and raced past the crypts and out the doorway.

Zenobia took a deep breath. It would take many hours to teach Hairan how to wield different weapons until he would be safe on the battlefield. Perhaps they should concentrate on the weapon he could wield the best. Maybe he didn't need to know all the weapons.

Zenobia looked at Adara's funerary statue. "He is so like you that I feel you've never left us." She touched the statue's cold hand.

Adara stood before her, lifelike in colored stone. A long white chiton with painted gold ribbons on the sleeves and bodice beneath a purple robe indicated that Adara had been of the royal house. A shawl of blue fell gracefully from her head to gold slippered feet. Adara held a spool and spindle to show that she had been a wife. To Adara, being a wife was more important than being a queen. Zenobia had chosen the clothing for her friend's burial and had overseen the carving of the statue. Now as she looked into Adara's beautiful face, she felt like crying. She touched the likeness of the gold breastpin at Adara's left shoulder. Adara had given the real one to Zenobia on her deathbed. It was a symbol of the royal house. Even though Zenobia had the right to wear the pin, she could not. It had been put in the treasury house for Hairan.

"I'm not sure I'm much of a mother to Hairan." Zenobia twisted the end of the white silk shawl that covered her hair and shoulders and flowed down her back. "I tend to be too impatient with him. I'm too much like Odainat. I have little time for listening to music and thus don't understand your son's passion for it."

Zenobia set the oil lamp on the floor and paced back and forth in front of a four columned shrine that disappeared into the shadows near the roof. A marble couple, founders of Adara's family tomb, reclined on a cold couch above Zenobia. They looked at her with empty, stone eyes from a century ago. "You must help Hairan. I fear for his future."

A banging and clattering at the door to the Funerary Temple stopped Zenobia in mid-stride. She blew out the flame from the oil lamp, stepped behind a column, and waited for the person to show himself. She checked her dagger that was hidden in the sleeve of her chiton and kicked her toga away from her feet. She never liked having bodyguards and had refused Odainat's demands that she have one.

When she heard a woman giggle and a man's voice echo through the Temple, Zenobia relaxed. An illicit love affair was in progress. She had no desire to stay in the Temple to witness lovemaking. She waited until both lovers were engrossed in each other before she slipped from her hiding place and walked toward the light of the massive front door. Zenobia gasped when she saw the lovers against the wall by the door.

"Tarab! And General Abdas! My husband's sister and his general?"

Tarab shrieked.

"What an interesting liaison. A Palmyran noblewoman, married, and a Christian man, also married. Isn't it against your commandments to commit adultery, General Abdas? By the gods, this is interesting."

"You should not swear, Zenobia," Tarab said.

"I should not swear! You should not commit adultery."

"Please do not tell Mokimu. He is a kind man and would suffer if he knew."

"Hear that, General? She protects her husband." Zenobia's words echoed off the marble and plaster walls.

"Perhaps I should go." General Abdas backed toward the door. His shadow fell across the mosaic tiles and turned the colors to black.

"You have not answered my question. Is it not against your Christian laws?"

"Yes." General Abdas stood at attention. "It will not happen again."

"It will not happen again?" Tarab screeched. "What do you mean? Am I to be thrown over like an old slipper?"

"Old is a good reason," Zenobia said.

"No, Tarab. I must end this liaison because Queen Zenobia reminded me that I have chosen to follow the laws of my wife's religion. I have done her an injustice. May she forgive me."

"Do not dare mention my name to her," Tarab said.

"No, I would not humiliate her so." General Abdas saluted Zenobia and walked quickly from the Funerary Temple.

Tarab stamped her foot. "That desert rat. It is your fault he left me. What are you doing in this place?"

"I do not have a secret lover." Zenobia frowned at the look Tarab gave her. "I was here talking with Adara."

"Oh."

"Come, let's return to the palace. We can talk."

"I have nothing to say to you."

"Interesting. I would think you had much to ask of me."

"It is not uncommon to have a lover."

Zenobia grabbed her arm and jerked Tarab around to face her. "It is if you are a member of the royal family. We are supposed to be above reproach. I have enough trouble keeping Maeonius from being the center of gossip. Like mother, like son."

"Let go of me." Tarab pulled away from Zenobia. "You do not like my son because he is a better soldier than Hairan."

"I shall not discuss that subject with you. We shall have a pleasant conversation on the walk to the palace. You will be polite all the way to your own apartments. I shall have a guard placed on the door so that you may not stray." Zenobia walked down the steps of the Funerary Temple to Odainat Way, named not for her husband but for his grandfather, a Roman senator. Every four cubits a column rose that held a roof the entire length of the street. Halfway up each column a statue rested on a platform. Zenobia loved the statues that celebrated Palmyra's citizens from two centuries past to the present.

"You cannot put a guard on my door. What will you tell Odainat and Mokimu?"

"I will tell Odainat the truth, but I will tell your husband that I fear for your life. That you've been threatened."

"I have not been threatened."

Zenobia glared at her sister-in-law. "You have now. If you so much as flutter your eyelashes at a man other than Mokimu, I will make certain that you meet with an accident."

Tarab's eyes widened. "You cannot."

"I am the queen. Of course I can. You could be a political enemy."

"But, but . . ."

"Political enemies have a public beheading. Perhaps in the Oval Piazza. It is my favorite part of Palmyra."

Tarab's brown eyes were dark with fear. "You would not do that."

"Enough. You have never given me any peace. I could not even talk to Adara without your indiscretion interrupting me. The two of you were panting like dogs in heat."

"You are disgusting. You talk like the soldiers."

"I am a soldier." Zenobia strolled up the busy street, barely aware that her subjects parted so that she could walk unrestrained. She moved quickly, her usual pace learned many years ago when she started walking with her infantry to keep her strength for battle. She noticed that Tarab breathed with difficulty.

"It is too far. Let's go behind the theatre. My shoes are thin and the paving blocks hurt. I am so hot." Tarab's voice had its customary whine.

"I should march you across the desert a few times. You are soft."

Tarab stopped. "I will not go another step further. I am going behind the theatre."

"I do not have time to argue. Your preference rules." Zenobia turned between the columns and cut across the hard packed earth that encircled the building. They were behind the amphitheatre looking down the rows of stone seats when Zenobia felt the nerves in her spine come alive.

She whirled around in time to see three men dart behind a storage building that held scenery. "Did you see those men?" Zenobia pulled off a silk shawl that would hinder her actions. She threw it to Tarab.

"I see no men. What men did you see?" Tarab caught the shawl.

"I saw three." Zenobia pulled her dagger from its sheath in the sleeve of her chiton and tugged at her toga that had wrapped itself about her ankles as she walked. Thank the gods that when she rode into battle she could wear leg coverings instead.

"What are we to do?"

"I will kill them. You stay out of my way."

"Perhaps I should summon help."

"I fear that one will overtake you and slit your throat."

Tarab's hand flew to her slender neck. "Oh."

"We walk toward the palace. I hope it was my imagination." Zenobia pushed Tarab in front of her. "Go quickly, but do not run." She listened for sounds behind her, filtering out the normal din of everyday life in Palmyra.

They had not walked far when Zenobia heard the men running behind her. She shoved Tarab into a doorway of a second storage building and swung around. She caught the first man unawares and sliced through his neck. Blood spurted, hot and sticky, down the front of Zenobia's clothing. She heard Tarab gasp as the man dropped with a thud at their feet.

Zenobia stepped from the doorway into the advance of the other two men. Smiling, she crouched and circled crab style away from Tarab who was defenseless and thus, useless. Zenobia waved her knife, with its perfect balance, back and forth. As the men tried to separate and rush her from both sides, she backed up.

"Which of you dies first? Who will die at the hand of Zenobia this fine day?"

"You die today, unworthy queen."

"Perhaps, but I think not." Zenobia moved toward a stand of trees and used them to shield her back. "Come, come. Who is brave and throws the first knife? You don't look like fighters to me. Hired killers who do not get paid well. Your clothing is dirty and ragged. You speak with an accent. From whence come you? Persia? Asia Minor? No matter. I have many enemies, but none live long."

The man to her left lunged at her. She stepped away from him and let him crash to the ground at the base of a tree. She kicked him between the legs and turned in time to study the advance and technique of the other man coming toward her. He was used to dirty fighting, but was not trained. She stepped into his lunge and stabbed him in the stomach. The surprise in his eyes mirrored the eyes of soldiers in battle who met their death at her hands.

As he fell, Zenobia pulled the blade from his belly and turned toward the man on the ground who still groaned. She kicked him in the head. "Who hired you?"

"I don't know. I was along for the money. I did not know it was you. I never would have attacked the Queen of Palmyra." The man heaved himself to his feet. "Forgive me. Let me go. I have children who need me. A sick wife."

Zenobia kicked him in the face and sent him sprawling. "You lie. Who hired you? Tell me or I'll cut you apart in little pieces."

"I don't know."

"First the little finger. It is a small chop, but so effective. Then I do the other little finger. Do you know how much pain is caused by the loss of a finger? When the fingers are gone, I cut off a hand, then another." Zenobia flashed the blade of her knife in the sunlight. Blood already dried in the heat and flaked off, drifting down on the man at her feet. "Who?"

"I don't know a name. We were supposed to kill you so that the king would be in anguish and vulnerable. Someone else is to kill the king. We were paid by a Persian. He said the orders came from the city of Ctesiphon."

"Shapur."

The man rolled toward Zenobia, grabbed her around the legs, and threw her to the ground. The knife flew from her hand and, as she reached for it, the man grabbed it. Zenobia doubled up her fist and hit him in the jaw. He fell back. Zenobia jerked the knife from his hand, and they rolled across the dirt. He wrapped his hands around her throat. Zenobia sliced him from his intestines to his heart.

She pushed the dead man away, got up and looked at her clothing. "I am a mess." She looked for Tarab. "Are you all right?" The woman's face was pale.

"I may faint."

"We do not have time. We have to sneak back. If Odainat sees me thus, he will make certain that I am under guard at all times." Zenobia brushed dirt from her gown. "He lied."

"Who lied?"

"That man. Shapur is not an assassin. He fights on the field of battle, but he has too much honor to murder."

"Here. Cover yourself before someone sees you." Tarab thrust Zenobia's shawl toward her.

"I have killed three men and you're worried about social conventions? Do you think I care that my hair is uncovered?"

"You're a married woman."

Zenobia pulled her shawl from Tarab's fingers and draped it across her dirty hair and filthy clothing. "I have other things to worry about than whether or not my hair is covered. Someone wants Odainat and me dead. I will find out who. May the gods help anyone who tries to kill my husband." Zenobia marched toward the palace, not waiting for Tarab to whine about the pace.

"You could have been killed!" Odainat shook his fist at Zenobia.

"I was capable of defending not only myself, but Tarab. I had no need for a bodyguard. Three men are dead because of my skill with the blade." Zenobia had never seen Odainat's face as flushed as it was now.

"They were not well-trained. General Abdas checked the area behind the theatre himself."

"General Abdas? Why was he at the theatre?"

"He was there at my request when I was told three bodies had been found."

"How convenient for him." Zenobia turned away from Odainat and stared out her apartment window. The wadi dropped off below the walls of the palace, separated them from the desert, and made it difficult for the enemy to approach from the east. If she leaned out, she could see the bottom of the wadi.

"You will be guarded from this moment forth."

Zenobia whirled around. "I will not be treated as some child. I am a warrior as are you."

"I am stronger."

"Not much." Zenobia turned back to the window.

"I could not bear it if anything happened to you. I would understand if you were killed on the field of battle, but to think that you could be assassinated is unacceptable."

"I will not allow a guard to follow me around."

"General Abdas would not be intrusive. I think you like him."

Zenobia turned, leaned against the marble window frame and crossed her arms. "If I must have a guard, then so shall you. Why, I would be only half a person without you. I would be as the night sky without the moon."

"No one has tried to kill me. I don't need a guard."

"No one has tried to kill you? How do you know?" Zenobia smiled at her husband's shrug. It had always signaled the beginning of a winning argument for her. "I choose my General Ezechiel to guard you."

"He is unavailable. He is teaching Hairan to use the sword."

"I have asked General Abdas to work with Hairan's archery skills. If one general is too busy, then so is the other."

"Wife, you are cunning." Odainat pulled her into his arms. "I behaved badly because of fear. I would not like to live the rest of my days without my best soldier."

"Nor would I. If the gods answer my prayers, we'll die together— gray haired and wrinkled."

"You pray for that?"

Zenobia stared at the floor. "Enough talk. I grow restless. We need a hunt."

Odainat laughed. "You always want to hunt when there is no battle to fight. All right. Tomorrow we hunt."

"We'll take our two youngest boys. And Hairan. He needs to learn more of hunting."

"Zenobia, he doesn't like killing animals."

"He has to learn."

"All right, but I will have to take Maeonius."

"Maeonius! Just one day I would like to be away from that whining, conniving nephew of yours."

"Don't remind me of Tarab's offspring. I wish I had listened to you years ago and sent him to Rome or Greece or somewhere. Especially after he got roaring drunk and rode through the Temple of Bel."

"You couldn't send him away. Tarab wouldn't allow it. You did the only thing you could do. You punished his blasphemy through his vanity by taking his horse away. He could not impress the ladies with his riding skills for six months."

"I was too easy on him. I should have banished him from Palmyra whether my sister liked it or not."

"No. It is better that we know what he's doing." Zenobia laid her head against Odainat's chest and wrapped her arms around his waist. "Fear for my safety made you angry. I often fear for the lives of our sons."

"A sorry pair of warriors we are." Odainat said.

"I like my warrior." Zenobia kissed Odainat and said nothing about her own fear for his life that adhered to a corner of her heart like a thorn.

"Tomorrow we ride into the mountains to hunt."

"Good. I would like wolf fur to line my cape," Zenobia said.

"Bear would suit you better," Odainat said.

"Husband, you tread on dangerous territory." Zenobia smiled at his booming laughter.

CHAPTER
V

264 A.D. Western Mountains in Syria

"*P*ull the string back, Hairan! Further! You must be strong." Odainat rode up to his son who sat astride a large horse. "The hare is a difficult target."

Sweat poured down Hairan's face. He had disappointed his father again. "He's tied down. By your orders."

"Still he thrashes."

Hairan closed his eyes and let fly the arrow. It thudded into the hard earth next to the hare. "I cannot kill, Father. It isn't in me."

"It had better be. Who is going to rule this empire? You are. Try again."

Both horses danced in circles, and Hairan grabbed the pommel to keep himself on the horse. He lifted the bow and pulled back again. He had the hare centered in his line of sight, but he could not let the arrow go. He heard his father sigh. His father didn't know that his exasperation showed, always showed. Hairan would rather that his father scream or beat him like other boys' fathers did. It would be easier. It had been four years since Zenobia pestered his father to let him hunt. Four difficult and horrible long years. Hairan hated to kill.

"The hare will break his neck before you put it out of its misery. Shoot!" Odainat bellowed.

Hairan let go and the arrow hit its target. He felt his stomach churn as the hare twitched and blood flowed. "No more!" He flung the bow to the ground and rode away from his father and the rest of the hunting party. He saw the dismay on his father's face, the concern on Zenobia's face, and the laughter from his cousin, Maeonius. He didn't know whose face pained him the most.

He stopped at a grove of scrub trees that clung tenaciously to the rocky mountain and stared across the ripples of rugged terrain. He had been here before, but instead of killing, he had given birth to a song. Songs! What good was music? He was called girl-boy by Maeonius when no one was around. Once Maeonius and his friends had caught him, held him down, dressed him in woman's garb, and put make-up on his face. He was afraid of what else they were going to do to him, but a young Jewess, Rebekeh, had come upon them in the alley behind her home. He had been further humiliated when she threw rocks at them. They ran, their laughter echoing off the walls of the houses that lined the alley. He felt his face get red. It always did when he remembered Rebekeh. He hoped he'd never see her again. Sometimes he dreamed of kissing her.

"Well, here is our great hunter," Maeonius shouted. He rode so close to Hairan that the flanks of their horses touched. "Here is your bow. It is such a fine bow, the best. The queen only gives you the best of everything except courage. How is our girl-boy today?"

"Get away from me."

"I have your bow. Don't you want it for practice at sunrise? I've seen you out there with the queen and General Abdas."

Hairan jerked the bow from Maeonius' hand. He hoped that it hurt him. "Go away."

"I rather enjoy the view from here. Have you written a song about it?"

"Why do you pester me? I don't do anything to you." Hairan clutched the bow so tightly his knuckles were white.

"I taunt you because you're the next king, and you don't deserve to be. I should be king but for an accident of birth. You are that accident. You weren't supposed to be born. My mother told me so."

"What does Tarab know of anything?" Hairan refused to look at Maeonius.

"She gave your mother a potion every morning to keep her from conceiving. Before you, I was next in line for the throne."

Hairan's head snapped around and his mouth dropped open. "Your mother is crazy."

"Don't you call her that! She is not!" Maeonius grabbed Hairan's arm.

"Let go of me, you bastard!" Hairan raised the bow and brought it down on Maeonius' head. He liked the cracking sound that it made. He didn't like the silence as Maeonius glared at him.

"You will be sorry. There is more than one way to gain a kingdom." Maeonius ignored the trickle of blood that ran down his forehead. He jerked his horse around and rode off.

Hairan's stomach was full of moths. Maeonius scared him.

Zenobia almost intervened when she saw Hairan's bow come down on Maeonius' head. She pulled Thabit up short and watched as Maeonius galloped away, whipping his horse unmercifully. She pushed the anger at his cruelty to an animal to the back of her mind. She would deal with him later. Curiosity surfaced to the top of her thoughts, and she rode slowly toward Hairan.

"Hail." She noticed the startled look on Hairan's face and wished that she hadn't let him know she was there.

"Zenobia." Hairan sheathed his bow. "How much did you see?"

"I saw your bow come down on that hard headed cousin of yours. I am glad."

Hairan grinned. "So am I."

"Maybe the bow is your best weapon."

"Did Father say anything about the rabbit?"

"Not really."

"I embarrassed him."

"Your father is king. He is too much of a man to be embarrassed. You did nothing wrong."

"It is easier to hit a non-living target. I won't make a good king for Palmyra. I wish I were dead."

"Hush, lest the gods hear you!" Zenobia said three prayers in rapid succession to Bel, Iarhibol, and Aglibol.

"I'm going home."

"It is close to midday. The mountains are deceptively cool. You'll have to cross the desert to get to Palmyra."

"I don't care."

Zenobia rubbed the back of her neck. "The horses would be put at risk."

"I can't do that. Perhaps I can follow the hunting party and not get in the way."

"Escort me back to your father. It would be the proper thing to do."

Hairan looked at her like a trapped hare. "Yes."

Odainat waved to them as they rode toward him and their two youngest boys. Vaballathus held a hare by its ears.

"See what I brought down on the run? With one arrow, too."

"Good." Zenobia tempered her enthusiasm for Hairan's sake.

"I am proud of him, Zenobia. He has a fine eye and will be a great warrior," Odainat said.

Zenobia could almost feel Hairan wince. She glanced sideways at him. He rode to Vaballathus and clapped him on the back.

"Good job. You have mastered what I cannot."

Vaballathus' grin was wide. "Will you sing a song about my first kill? Write one just for me?"

"For you? Do you think I have nothing better to do than sit around writing songs about dead hares? Who would listen to such a tale as that?" Hairan smiled to soften his words.

"I would."

"Me, too," Arraum said. "I like your songs. Especially the funny ones."

"All right. Tomorrow evening before bedtime, I will sing a song for you about this poor creature."

"Does Hairan write many songs for you?" Odainat asked.

"Many. Some we don't like because they speak of girls and kissing, but we like his funny songs," Arraum said.

"Interesting." Odainat looked at Hairan until the boy blushed.

"Odainat, we waste daylight hours when we could be hunting the wolves." Zenobia gave Thabit his rein and headed up the mountain behind four guards. She knew Odainat would follow her.

"I've had no luck in finding wolf tracks." Zenobia leaned over and scanned the ground. "Do you see any?"

"None. Perhaps the heat has driven them farther up the mountain." Odainat looked at the sky. "No rain for awhile either."

"I'm afraid our hunt is merely an exercise," Zenobia said.

Odainat grinned. "Alas, the wolves are safe from my lovely huntress today."

"I'm no huntress. There is nothing to hunt."

"Look up here," Hairan shouted. "I've found bear tracks!"

"Bear tracks? I'd rather hunt a bear when I'm better prepared."

Zenobia rode to Hairan and looked where he pointed. She followed the tracks slowly. Hairan dropped back as Odainat cantered to her.

"Let's track him." Odainat and Zenobia followed the bear tracks from a crystal stream to the edge of the forest farther up the mountain.

"It isn't a large bear," Odainat said.

"Any bear is large enough for me." Zenobia pointed to a thick undergrowth of arbutus and boxwood. "He's in there. I can't ride Thabit in there. It's too dangerous. The bear is close. See how Thabit tosses his head. I can hardly hold him."

"We'll leave the horses. The brush is too dense for them."

"The brush may be too dense for us and the bear," Zenobia said.

"Remember the cave?"

"In the clearing. Yes, and that's where we'll catch our bear."

Odainat led the hunting party as Zenobia brought up the rear. Soldiers, turned hunters for the day, had bows ready as well as long swords. She watched the men in front of her tread as quietly as possible on the leaf covered path. A twig snapped occasionally, and there was labored breathing as they climbed the steep mountain in thin air. Hairan hung back with Vaballathus and Arraum who pestered him about writing a song all the way through the brush and into the clearing despite Hairan's frequent motions to quiet them.

"Zenobia, they'll be safer behind you," Hairan said.

Zenobia nodded. "Take them back to the stream. They'll be content to play in the water. Take two guards."

"I can watch them."

Zenobia pursed her lips. "It isn't you I worry about. It is Maeonius who concerns me."

"Ahhh. My dear cousin. I'll take two guards." Hairan turned and motioned the boys to follow him.

A snort and thrashing caused Zenobia's heart to lurch. She caught up with Odainat and focused on the clearing. The bear, a young male reared up and stood taller than Zenobia. She sniffed the air; a musky odor wafted across the clearing.

"Do you want him?" Odainat whispered.

"No. You take him down. It is customary for the king to get the first kill."

"You are equal to me. You take the shot."

"I don't want to." Zenobia patted Odainat's shoulder. "I'm not confident, yet. Wolves are more to my taste."

Odainat raised his bow.

An arrow whistled past Zenobia's ear and thudded into the bear's leg. The bear bellowed and stumbled into the brush leaving a trail of bright blood behind. She whirled around. "Who did that! Who has dared to break tradition and shoot before the king?"

Odainat turned, his face a mixture of surprise and anger. "Who let loose with an arrow from behind me?"

"My king, it was your nephew Maeonius," General Abdas said.

Odainat's face turned purple as he stalked toward Maeonius and stopped in front of him. "You have caused me nothing but trouble since your mother birthed you! How can you be so stupid as to let fly an arrow from behind a crowd of people? Did you wish me dead? Are you treasonous?"

Maeonius' face lost its color as the blood drained from it. "Uncle, forgive me. I was so excited that I didn't think."

"Don't call me uncle. I am your king at this moment. You didn't think? When ever do you think when on a hunt or in battle? Your punishment will be severe."

"But Uncle, it was a mistake. Excitement caused my hand to shake and my arrow to fly. I am good with the bow and so no one was hit."

"I might have been, but worse, you might have killed your queen." Odainat's voice dropped to a deeper range to wrap itself around his fury. "Stand back from your queen and me. Because of you, we have a difficult task ahead—to track an angry and injured bear so that he can be killed properly. You have made a genuine mess of this hunt and have ruined my day—again!" Odainat stomped off.

The next hour bored Zenobia. She always had problems with tracking after the first fifteen minutes. She liked hunting, but this was tedious. They had to find the injured bear to put him out of his misery. If he couldn't hunt because of his leg, then he would prey on domestic animals and put their people in danger. Maeonius caused too much trouble. Perhaps she could convince Odainat to send him to Rome to fight the barbarians.

The guards gathered around Maeonius in such a tight knot that he couldn't have raised his bow without hitting someone. Maeonius' face was filled with thunder, and he kicked pebbles repeatedly; some bouncing off the guards' ankles.

A paralyzing roar followed by the sounds of the bear crashing through the brush stopped everyone in mid-stride. Zenobia's breath caught in her throat as she realized the bear was not running from them, but toward them! She drew an arrow from its quiver and placed it in her bow. Sweat ran down her face and dripped onto her clothing. "I'd rather fight the Persians than an injured bear."

She stood ready next to Odainat more to protect him than to be protected by him. It was ignoble of her to think that her warrior husband would need her arrow, but she would rather take the claws of an angry bear than to see Odainat injured. The sounds of breaking twigs and small branches seemed to come from everywhere as the bear took an erratic flight through the forest. The small group of hunters stood in a cluster at the edge of a pond. Tall trees and scrub brush seemed to close in on them. The odor of pine trees pressed into Zenobia's nostrils and made her ill.

The bear burst out of the undergrowth in front of Odainat and Zenobia. He stopped out of range and bellowed, his teeth white against a bright pink mouth. Zenobia thought that the bear had grown, but she knew that was impossible. Her imagination did odd things.

"Hurry, Odainat."

"Too soon. I need a perfect shot through an eye." He stood ready with hunters and guards who flanked the royal couple.

The bear dropped to all fours and retreated into the forest only to explode out of the trees a second time.

"He wants water," Zenobia said. "He's lost much blood."

"Indeed." Odainat's arms never wavered as he held his aim.

The bear roared and lunged in circles, getting closer with each pass.

"Almost," Odainat said.

The thunk of an arrow as it hit the bear's flank, and its subsequent roar, confused Zenobia because Odainat had not yet shot. His arrow was still in place. The bear charged toward them, his bellowing filling Zenobia's ears.

"Shoot!" Odainat yelled. "Shoot before he attacks!"

Zenobia let her arrow fly and was pleased when it hit the bear in the chest along with a half dozen more arrows. The bear kept coming, and she re-armed herself, letting fly another arrow aimed at the bear's eye. The arrow bounced off its head and fell to the ground as the bear reared up on its hind legs in spite of its injuries. "Odainat, he still comes!"

It seemed an eternity before Odainat's arrow whistled through the air. The sound of the arrow hitting soft tissue was a relief. Zenobia expected the bear to fall immediately, but it stumbled forward, blood running from its eye, down its fur. At last, the bear thudded to the ground and remained motionless. Zenobia breath was ragged from tension, and her knees shook.

Instead of looking at his kill, Odainat turned and stared at Maeonius who stood ten cubits behind him. "Why did you shoot this time?"

"To protect you, Uncle. The bear was attacking."

"You cannot obey a simple command. Again, you put your queen in danger with your too soon arrow. You wounded the bear a second time. Your shooting has no purpose other than to irritate me. We will talk about this tonight."

Odainat turned to the guards. "I do not hold you responsible because all of you were intent on killing the bear. However, the hunt is over. Seize Maeonius' bow and arrows and march him back to the palace double time. We'll bring his horse."

Maeonius glared at Odainat until he saw Zenobia watching him. He looked at the ground, said something that caused one guard to push him toward Palmyra harder than he should have. Maeonius spit on the ground.

Zenobia held back the urge to box the insolent cur's ears. He was old enough to be dangerous. She would have to warn Odainat about his sister's son. Odainat had been too busy giving instructions on field dressing the kill to have seen Maeonius' behavior.

Odainat glowered at Maeonius as the guards ushered him to the dias that Odainat shared with Zenobia. The cub knelt before his king and queen, but Odainat sensed the boy's impertinence. Zenobia's posture straightened, a sure sign of anger. It was time to listen to Zenobia. She had an uncanny ability to understand people's motives especially if detrimental to Palmyra.

"You have made a grievous error against your king. Twice you let an arrow fly from behind your queen and king. Twice you broke custom and twice you put our lives at risk. On purpose, no doubt. Do you forget that Zenobia rules if I die? She has as much power as I." Odainat rubbed one of the claws on his new necklace.

Odainat couldn't see any changes in his nephew. It was like talking to a statue in the Funerary Temple. "What have you to say in your behalf?"

"My sorrow is great, Uncle." Maeonius raised his head and stared at the king.

Odainat was startled to see the eyes of a desert snake peering back at him. How could Maeonius hate so strongly? He had never been denied anything. Odainat glanced sideways at Zenobia. She watched Maeonius with contempt.

"What say you, Wife?" Odainat whispered.

"I say send him to Rome to become a real soldier." Her whisper was loud and echoed off the walls of the throne room.

"A fine idea." Odainat enjoyed watching Maeonius squirm.

"May I speak, Uncle?"

"You may speak to your king, not your uncle."

"King Odainat, I would prefer to stay in Palmyra and learn our army's ways. We are even more powerful than Rome who loses the power and glory that was once hers. Gallienus has to rely on Aurelian to beat the barbarians."

"What do you know of Gallienus and Aurelian?" Odainat asked. "I thought you had no interest in politics."

Maeonius blushed, then shrugged. "Sometimes I try to study military strategy. I want to be a better soldier for you, Uncle. That is why I need to stay here."

"Nonsense. Rome's army will toughen you and teach you to follow orders. If you disobey a Roman commander, your mother will not be able to stop that punishment. I wager that you would be executed before we even heard about it."

"No! No! No!" Tarab screamed as she ran across the marble floor and threw herself at Odainat's feet. "Brother, spare my only child, my son."

"Why are you here?" Zenobia asked. "You were not supposed to be here. No one was to be here."

"You played with Maeonius when he was but a child. You held him on you knee, you gave him his first horse, you clothed him like a prince. . . ."

"Enough! Get to your feet, Tarab, and quit your babbling." Odainat sighed. This woman caused him more problems than the Persians.

"Yes, my king."

"Do not talk with that quiver in your voice." He watched as she dried her eyes with the back of her hand, a habit she'd had since babyhood. His little sister had always followed him around as a child, had spied on him when she was almost marrying age, and had begged him to introduce her to Mokimu.

"Yes, my king."

"Tarab, my tolerance is low." He wished that Mokimu had kept her shut in their apartment. Odainat should have listened to his father who said that Mokimu was too weak to deal with Tarab, but his father hadn't withstood Tarab's tears either.

"I have the mother's fear for her only son. He is not bad. He made a little mistake." She sniffled.

"Stop that!"

"I can't," she whispered. "Are you going to send my son to Rome? They'll send him far away to fight the barbarians. No more will he have a fine bed, fine clothes, or the warmth of the desert. It is a death sentence for one brought up gently as Maeonius has been."

"If you brought him up too gently, that was your fault." Odainat tugged at his beard.

"I reared him to serve Palmyra."

Zenobia choked and clutched the arms of her throne. "You reared him to take from Palmyra."

Odainat wanted to rest his hand on her arm to temper her anger, but it would do no good. Zenobia was right. He had to send Maeonius to Rome. He looked at Tarab's tear-streaked face. Her hair was uncombed and her clothing wrinkled. She'd not slept at all. Without sleep, she would become ill.

"Maeonius, you have been a thorn in my foot since the day you were born."

"I know, Uncle. I mean my king."

The answer was true, but the remorse was false.

"I beg you, Brother. . . ."

Odainat could no longer stand the trembling voice of his sister that caused Zenobia to glare at her and Maeonius. "Guards! Take Princess Tarab to her chambers!" He winced as she stumbled between the guards who gently, but persistently escorted Tarab from the room. The last thing he heard was her plaintive cry like that of a she-wolf who'd lost her cubs. It haunted his heart.

Odainat glowered at his nephew and rushed the words out before he could change his mind. "Maeonius, your punishment is to be assigned to the infantry in Palmyra. You will no longer have rank, but will be a lowly soldier to march without armor, without horse, and without privileges given to the royal house. You will live in the barracks." Odainat could feel his queen stare at him. He couldn't help it. He could not torture his sister because of her only child's transgressions.

"Odainat, you know not what future you've shaped with your tender ways," Zenobia said.

"There is nothing that the two of us cannot handle. Maeonius will be tempered." Odainat wished that his nephew would protest, whine, or beg as was his usual manner, but the young man was silent as he waited to be dismissed.

"You may go." Odainat watched Maeonius retreat, still silent, still expressionless, still a puzzle.

Tarab ran across the chamber and threw herself at Odainat's feet. "My king, thank you. You have saved a mother from months, nay, years of grief."

Odainat stared at the guards who ran back to the throne room. He waved them away. They were not at fault that his sister had escaped them. She had escaped him often when they were children.

"Get up, Sister. Do not grovel. You are a princess."

"I am prostrate before my kindly brother, not my king. You have not taken my son from me, and I will be in your debt."

"Get up!"

Tarab rose and stood before Odainat. "May I take my leave now?"

Odainat sighed. "By all means."

"Thank you, Brother." Tarab grinned as she left the throne room.

"Did you see the look she gave me," Zenobia asked.

"Yes. She smiled. She is content."

"She is shrewd and has you twisted about her finger."

"You misconstrue her delicate nature, Zenobia." Odainat could not understand his wife's explosive laughter.

His mother was a fool, but she had served him well with her tears. Women were only good to serve men. Maeonius leaned against a limestone column and waited. Several times a week, one of the palace girls, he couldn't remember her name, would return this way from the Jewish sector. She was a pretty thing. He'd noticed her dashing about the kitchen one day. She had argued with the cook about something or other and hadn't even flinched when he had waved a meat ax at her. She intrigued Maeonius enough that he had forgotten the kitchen wench he hustled into a doorway until she pinched him. He grabbed her breast and twisted until she screeched, then Maeonius shoved her away. She jerked down her clothing and scurried off to another part of the palace. Maeonius uttered an obscenity. Later he would take care of the wench for having drawn attention to him.

The gods were with him! The Jewess appeared like a dream on the far side of the street carrying a basket of folded linen. A horse and chariot raced past Maeonius and raised a cloud of dust. He squinted through the brown haze to keep her in sight. He didn't want to lose her in the crowd of shoppers. The sun shone on her long, dark hair highlighted with auburn. He wanted to lace his fingers through the waves that rippled across her shoulders.

Maeonius walked quickly to keep up with her. She stopped to talk with another young girl, and Maeonius crossed the street dodging pedestrians, horses, and push carts. They left the residential section of Palmyra and were in one of the smaller market places.

"Out of my way!" Maeonius pushed a man out of his path and caught up with his quarry.

It took the girl a moment to notice that he matched her stride step for step. He grinned at her enjoying her confused look, but said nothing.

"Leave me alone."

"You have beautiful eyes. They're as blue as the sky."

"Your pretty words do not interest me." Rebekeh slipped into a crowd of women.

"Your pretty mouth interests me," Maeonius shouted.

Rebekeh gasped. "You're rude."

"Allow me to carry your basket." He trotted up beside her and tried to take it from her.

"Absolutely not!" Rebekeh jerked the basket from his hands.

It hurt, but he kept his anger hidden. She would pay for that. "I am a lowly soldier in need of soft company."

"You're no lowly soldier, but Prince Maeonius."

"I am pleased that a lovely girl knows me. What may I call you?"

"Call me irritated."

"I'd call you ungrateful." Maeonius grabbed her arm, but she jerked it away.

"I don't care if you are a prince. I shall have to tell the queen of your advances. She would not be pleased."

"You think you're safe from me? I could have you killed for treating me thus."

"Your idea of your own worth is inflated. I don't fear my king or queen. They are just."

"I always get what I want. You're Rebekeh. I've seen you in the gardens talking with that idiot Hairan. I could have you killed for treating me thus."

"He is a gentle man; something you'll never be." Rebekeh scowled at the prince and marched away from him. He hated her arrogance. He was a prince. A ruler of men. And women. There were plenty of girls who would do anything he asked. He glared at the retreating figure. He would have her, and it would pleasure him to give her pain.

He had to walk fast to keep up with Rebekeh. Once she looked back and scowled at him, but never slowed. Sweat ran down his face. By the time they reached the palace, his toga was soaked and his hair was plastered against his head. She looked cool and that irked him. He followed her into the kitchen. He didn't think she worked here. She sailed through the normal kitchen chaos and continued up the back staircase.

Halfway up, Rebekeh confronted him. She held the basket between them like a shield. "I don't care to have you follow me any further. I have no desire to be anywhere near you. I will tell the queen about you."

"You slut!" Maeonius lunged at Rebekeh, jerked the basket from her hands, and threw it down the stairs. He pushed her down on the stone steps, ignoring her yelp of pain and surprise. "I'll take whatever I want from you whenever I want."

"Get off me! You're disgusting." Rebekeh grabbed a fistful of hair and pulled.

He slapped her so hard that her teeth clacked together. He grabbed her toga at the shoulder and jerked it until he heard the cloth tear. He liked the sound. It made him feel powerful. He kissed Rebekeh, but snapped back and howled with pain when she bit him. Blood dribbled down his chin from his bottom lip. He inadvertently loosened his hold on her, and she brought her knee up hard between his legs. He rolled off, doubled over, and tumbled down the stairs ending in a heap beside the spilled laundry basket.

He had managed to get to his hands and knees, ignoring the startled cooks and helpers, when Rebekeh had the nerve to kick him once more in the crotch from behind. He could see her beside him as she picked up the linen, folded it neatly, and placed it in the basket. It angered him further that she hadn't run and even had the presence to fold linens.

"Don't do that to me again, or I will kill you." Rebekeh picked up the laundry basket. She kicked him as she walked past and up the stairway. Part way she looked down at him. "Don't ever threaten me again or come near me or touch me. I find you pitiful."

The last he saw of the slut was when she climbed the stairs to the second floor of the palace. He vowed to get even.

At the top of the stairs, Rebekeh leaned against the wall and let the tears flow. She shook so hard that the basket threatened to fall from her hands. She slid down the hallway, keeping her back to the cool walls until she was across from the apartment she shared with the boys. She couldn't tell the queen about Maeonius. It would be too hard to explain what Maeonius had done.

She slipped into the apartment and put the linen sheets in the chest. When she passed a mirror, she started. Her cheek was red and would be bruised by morning. She traced the four-fingered pattern that branded her, ran her hand down her exposed shoulder and pulled her stola together where it had been torn. Through her tears she could see that her hair was disheveled. She needed to bathe and change clothes before the boys or Miriam saw her.

"What happened to you?"

Rebekeh whirled around and stared at Hairan who stood in the doorway. "What are you doing here?"

"I'm looking for my brothers. I promised to sing and play my newest song for them." Hairan walked across the room and stood before Rebekeh. "You look terrible. Who hit you?"

"No one."

"Did you slap yourself?"

"Don't be ridiculous." Rebekeh turned away from his probing stare.

"Someone hit you. My father and Zenobia don't allow servants to be mistreated. Was it the cook?"

"No."

"You argue with him all the time."

"Because he doesn't feed the boys enough, that's all. It's a game with us."

"So who slapped you and tore your clothes?"

"I did and I'll do it again to the little slut." Maeonius lurched across the room, his face pale and his eyes full of fury.

"Don't you come near me." Rebekeh hid behind Hairan.

"You're crazy, Maeonius. Get out of here before I call the guards and have you hauled off like a criminal," Hairan said.

"The guards have been sent on an errand. There's no one around." Maeonius staggered toward the two of them. "Get out of my way, you weakling." He pushed at Hairan.

"You'd better go," Hairan said.

"Don't tell me what to do you pitiful writer of songs. You're not fit to be king. You can't even fight." Maeonius swung at Hairan.

Hairan side-stepped the blow, grabbed his cousin from behind, and wrapped his arms around Maeonius. Both fell to the floor and rolled. Rebekeh sidled away from them. She grimaced when she heard the squish of flesh beneath a fist. Hairan would have a terrible black eye.

It must have made Hairan angry, for he rolled until Maeonius was beneath him. Hairan grabbed Maeonius' ears and pounded his head against the marble floor until he went limp. Hairan sat on his cousin's chest while he caught his breath, then looked at Rebekeh.

"I hope by all the gods in heaven that I haven't killed him."

"I hope by my one true god that you have," Rebekeh said. She bent down and looked at Maeonius closely. "Damn, he breathes."

"Who breathes?" Miriam asked from the doorway. "I heard peculiar noises, so I came right away. You interrupted a most pleasant game of Senet, Rebekeh."

"I am sorry."

"Maeonius looks as if he's been run over by a chariot." Miriam pursed her lips.

"Yes," Rebekeh said. "I think that's what happened."

"Odd for a chariot to be inside the palace."

Hairan scrambled up and straightened his toga. "We had a disagreement."

"I see." Miriam grinned as she looked from the downed Maeonius to Hairan to Rebekeh. "That explains everything." She chuckled and retreated.

"Now what?" Hairan asked. "If she tells her husband . . ."

"What do I care if she tells General Ezechiel? We have done nothing wrong. Let's drag Maeonius out of here." Rebekeh picked up one leg and pulled. Hairan grabbed the other leg and together they hauled Maeonius out of the room, down the hall, and into an empty apartment.

"He'll have an aching head tomorrow," Hairan said.

"And a swollen lip." Rebekeh giggled as they walked back to her apartment.

"If he bothers you again, send for me." Hairan touched her cheek. "He did this to you, didn't he?"

"Yes."

"He'll not touch you again. I'll see to it."

"Thank you." Rebekeh looked at Hairan who was so kind and gentle and wrote songs. He was special. It was comforting to have an oasis of calm in the middle of all the fighting with the Persians. Her heart pounded against her chest so loudly that she knew Hairan could hear it. Rebekeh stood on tiptoe and kissed Hairan's soft lips, then ran into the apartment out of sight.

CHAPTER
VI

267 A. D. Palmyra, Syria

Odainat leaned against a shadowed column in the atrium. The cool limestone felt good against his bare arm after having been on patrol the entire day along the trade routes. He smiled at the giggles of his two youngest sons who sat at Hairan's feet. Their sweet voices drifted across the pool to him.

"Sing the song about the soldier who kissed his camel by mistake," Arraum pleaded.

"Are you not tired of that song? I sang it twice yesterday," Hairan said.

"I never tire of that one," Vaballathus said.

"You are certain I won't bore you?" Hairan strummed his lyre, tightened a string, and began singing, the notes floating above him and out the open roof in the center of the atrium. Candle light flickered in rhythm to his music.

The sureness of his voice surprised Odainat. He had never listened to his oldest son sing. A bittersweet memory of Adara tugged at his heart, and he frowned. What had he told Adara about her music? She played effortlessly and her lyrical voice shamed the birds. When she sang, even the servants stopped to listen heedless of their tasks. Often, she was asked to sing by her friends. Her friends, for he never told his friends of her talent. It didn't seem to fit with his fighting, his politics, his lusty appetite for life. He had never told her that he liked her playing. He had pretended not to hear her songs. If the truth had been known, it was that her songs had wrapped themselves about his heart too tightly, and it had frightened him.

Hairan had the same talent. Odainat, older and wiser was not frightened of his talent, but he had been too busy to pay attention to his gifted son. He was here because Zenobia asked that he learn to appreciate the boy.

The laughter of his two boys sliced through his thoughts, and he listened to Hairan who grinned as he sang.

"Her lips were softer than ever before, and her breath was honey sweet. I sought her lovely cheek in the dark to feel her silky skin."

Odainat slapped his hand across his mouth to keep from laughing. The rest of the verse caused him to guffaw. He didn't want his sons to discover him lurking in the shadows.

"Your lashes that caress my neck are long and ebony and curled so sweetly about eyes that are as dark as the desert night," Hairan sang.

First Vaballathus flopped to the floor, helpless from giggling, then Arraum rolled in merriment.

As the song continued, Odainat found that he could no longer conceal his laughter. He stepped into the light and noticed Hairan's surprise. The boy did not falter and finished the song. His two younger sons wiped tears from their eyes as the last notes died away. Odainat had to use the hem of his toga to stem the flow of laughter-caused tears.

"Where did you learn that song?" Odainat asked.

"I wrote it."

"You write words?"

"The music, too." Hairan stared at his father. "Did it please you?"

"Very much." Odainat said. "May I?"

Hairan scooted over, leaving more than half the bench free for his warrior father. "I'd be honored." His face turned red.

"Do you have other songs like that one?"

Hairan laughed. "Yes. I sing them to the soldiers often. They ask, you see."

"I understand why. Would you be so kind as to attend Kithoth's birthday party with me?"

"I . . . I would be flattered, but for what purpose? I can hardly speak to such venerable men."

"Can I go?" Vaballathus scrambled up from the floor and tugged on his father's toga. "I would like to see you drink yourself stupid like Mother says. I have never seen you stupid before."

"I'd like to go, too," Arraum said. "I want to see you bray like a donkey in pain. That's what Mother says you do when you're drunk. She says you think you're singing."

"Does she?"

"Can we go?"

"No."

"Hairan gets to go."

"Hairan is almost an adult. He will entertain us." Odainat studied his oldest son. "Do you sing songs of love and songs of sadness, too?"

"I remember many that my mother sang when I was but a baby."

Odainat looked away from Hairan. Could he listen to Adara's words and music? "Perhaps the party will be too rowdy for you. You are but sixteen summers."

Hairan wiped the lyre with his sleeve. "I would like to go," he whispered.

"I see." Odainat pulled at his beard. Zenobia would be angry if he left Hairan at home. He didn't want her angry; she was worse than a wounded bear when she was angry. "Could you sing without embarrassment?"

"I have strength when I play and sing."

"Good." Odainat patted Hairan's knees. "At Kithoth's party, start with a ballad, then switch to the camel song. That should surprise them."

"I have other silly songs." Hairan looked at his younger brothers and grinned. "I have songs that I sing just for the soldiers."

"Hairan! That's not fair," Arraum said.

"Is life fair?" Hairan laughed.

"No! Why did you get to be the oldest?" Arraum asked.

"Silly, he was born first," Verballathus said.

"I am not silly."

"Excuse me," Odainat said.

"Yes, Father," the boys said in unison.

Odainat stood. "Be ready at dusk seven days hence."

"Thank you, Father," Hairan said.

Odainat stopped at the doorway. "One more thing. We never

reveal all that goes on else the wives would stop us." He left quickly before Hairan could ask questions.

"Sing some more, Hairan," the boys begged in unison.

"I think not. Rebekeh gestures from across the room. It is bedtime for you." He glanced away from Rebekeh and fiddled with the strings on his lyre. Her eyes were so beautiful. He could not let her see how much she made his heart pound. She was sought after by many, but she spurned them all. She would do the same to him, and it would be more painful than anything.

"No, no, no!" Arraum said. "I want to listen to more songs."

"Yes, yes, yes." Rebekeh strode across the room, stopped in front of the boys, and crossed her arms. "You will lose the privilege of listening to Hairan another evening if you cannot behave."

"Come on," Vaballathus said. "She never gives in to us."

"Never," Arraum sighed.

Hairan smiled. "I'll come with you. If you ready yourself for bed quickly, there may be time for one more small song."

"The camel song," Arraum shouted.

"Not in front of Rebekeh!" Vaballathus said.

The boys scurried off to their apartment with Rebekeh and Hairan in tow.

The last notes of Hairan's song drifted across the drowsy boys. He winked at Rebekeh, and the two of them left the bed chamber.

"Please sit with me for awhile." Rebekeh put her hand on his arm. "You are very good with your brothers."

"You are better with them than I. I would have sung for them as long as they had begged for more." Hairan felt his face flush. He thanked the gods that he hadn't stammered.

"You sing beautifully. Zenobia says that you sing as well as your mother did." She patted the couch next to her.

Hairan shrugged. He felt his face get hotter. He hated it when someone complimented him. "You're kind." He sat on the small couch next to a shallow pool.

Stars could be seen overhead through the open roof. The heat of the day was brushed away by a cool breeze that barely rippled the water. Reflections of wall sconces made the sun seem as if it had been broken in the pool.

"I like you, Hairan." It was Rebekeh's turn to blush.

"Really?"

Rebekeh smiled. "Yes, really."

"Thank you."

"You're much more suited to rule Palmyra than anyone."

"Maeonius doesn't think so."

"Your cousin is a self-centered, egotistical, spoiled prince." Rebekeh leaned over and peered into Hairan's eyes. "You must be careful around him. He has the look of a desert snake. He doesn't walk, he slithers. His eyes are narrow and glassy." Rebekeh shivered. "I wish he'd broken his neck when I pushed him down the stairwell."

"So do I. If he ever bothers you again, tell me. I will kill him." Hairan started at the harshness of his voice.

"I know you would." Rebekeh took Hairan's hand. "You should have your future read. I know a woman who is excellent."

"I know my future. I am to rule Palmyra."

"That isn't the only thing in your future. You will have a queen, sons, and maybe a daughter or two. Your children will sing as beautifully as you."

"You speak of all that's expected of me. There is no way to know the future."

"Do you not believe your gods have set a pattern for your life?"

"I don't know. Even if they did, I wouldn't want to know it." Hairan squeezed her hand. "You are so beautiful. You're beautiful enough to be a queen."

Rebekeh gasped, but did not pull her hand away. "I could never be a queen. I have no royal blood."

"No one needs royal blood to marry into our royal line. Zenobia's father was a merchant."

"But she's descended from Cleopatra." Rebekeh glanced around the atrium. "See the Egyptian influence? She admires Cleopatra."

"Egyptian influence? What do you mean?"

Rebekeh sighed. "Never mind. It's just a way of decorating."

Hairan leaned over and kissed Rebekeh's cheek, then pulled back astonished at his boldness. She smiled at him.

"That is not a kiss. This is a kiss."

Rebekeh pulled Hairan to her and kissed him gently on the lips. Hairan could not explain the feelings that surged through him. He'd never felt this way before even when he sang love songs.

There was only one thing he could do. He kissed her in return, then wrapped his arms around her, held her close to his heart, and kissed her again.

"Oh, Hairan." Rebekeh pulled back.

"Don't I please you?" Hairan asked.

"Too much so."

"I don't understand that."

Rebekeh blushed. "I want what I can't have."

"I told you that you don't have to be royalty."

She shook her head. "I know better. Surely the King and Queen have someone suitable chosen for you; someone from a neighboring kingdom."

"They've never said." Hairan pulled Rebekeh back into his arms and kissed her forehead. "I'll explain to them that I want you for my queen."

"Hairan! You move too quickly. We may not really love each other."

"I have loved you since we were children." Hairan stroked her hair. He had always loved the way the sun made it shine like obsidian with ruby highlights.

"Children? Whenever did you see me?"

"Whenever you came to the palace with your mother. She brought linen that she had woven."

Rebekeh smiled. "Every week. I begged her to allow me to come with her. She still weaves a fine piece of cloth."

"And why did you want to visit the palace?"

"To see the handsome boy prince that was named Hairan." Rebekeh touched Hairan's cheek.

"Didn't you see me often?"

"Yes."

"That's because I always knew when you were coming."

"That means nothing. We were children."

"It means that our love is meant to be. It means I've always loved you and will never love another." Hairan kissed her again. Her lips were as soft as silk, and energy flowed through him.

He was aware of a presence in the atrium before he heard his name being whispered. He pulled away from Rebekeh and felt his face get hot. He jumped up and bowed.

"My queen. How . . . how good of you to . . . to . . ."

Rebekeh leaped to her feet. "My queen. The boys are fine. They sleep soundly."

"Please sit." Zenobia's mouth twitched, and she finally smiled. "I'm sorry to have interrupted you."

Hairan was speechless. He should have known Zenobia would check on her sons.

"I must go." Rebekeh glanced at Hairan and almost ran from the atrium.

Zenobia watched her leave. "She's lovely."

"I . . . I . . . we . . . were . . ."

"Don't explain, Hairan. You can't explain love. I understand. I've come to see the boys. Are they asleep?"

"I sang them to sleep."

Zenobia smiled again. "Good." She crossed the atrium, her stola flowing behind her.

Hairan grinned. He loved the pretty Jewish girl, and she loved him!

The cella was bright with extra candles and wall sconces. Cream colored silk drapes had been pulled aside to let in cool desert air. Insects flirted with candle flames and died a sizzling death. Odainat could smell their toasted remains mixed with the aroma of sandalwood incense from India and the whisper of Jasmine perfume that Zenobia wore. She loved the perfumes and silks from Carthage.

She looked particularly beautiful tonight with eyes that sparkled like black diamonds. Her ebony hair was loose and flowed about her shoulders. He ached with desire and wanted to be near her, but she was surrounded by their guests except for General Abdas who stared at her from across the room. The court physician, Iason, tried to sit close to her, the silly old fool; and even steady, reliable General Ezechiel was enamored with his queen. Odainat had no reason to be jealous.

"Timagenes, you are not paying attention to the game," Zenobia said. "See, I have taken a game piece."

"Alas, you are too good at Senet these days," Timagenes said.

"An Egyptian, especially a warrior, should play this ancient game better." Zenobia patted his hand. "One more move and I have won."

"You are more Egyptian than I, Zenobia."

"Nay, my lineage through my mother is Greek as are all the Ptolemy's. You are Egyptian in birth and temperament. Perhaps you have not had time to play games. You've had to keep Egypt wealthy so that the Romans can strip her of her resources."

"We should not talk politics. It is not wise." Timagenes glanced toward General Abdas.

"Do not be alarmed. We have had to rescue the Romans so many times that I fear them no more than I do that moth. See, the moth behaves as do the Romans. They fly toward light, but destroy themselves at the same time." Zenobia slid a white chip across a black flowered square and took Timagenes' marker.

"We do not perceive Rome as weak as do you." Timagenes sighed. "I hate to play this game with you."

"We must do something to entertain ourselves until the Persians arrive." Zenobia glanced at General Ezechiel. "Do they still cower in their tents and refuse our escorts?"

"Yes, even when you said they could come armed."

"How are we to have a peace meeting if they are afraid to come to our palace?" General Abdas grumbled.

Odainat heard his queen's velvety laughter, and he knew she had a diabolical plan for the hapless Persians. She grinned at him as she pushed her chair back.

"Come, Odainat, shall we search out our guests? Perhaps they'll feel more comfortable if we met them in their own quarters."

"Do you not fear a trap?" Timagenes asked.

"The Persians are brainless but not stupid." Zenobia reached for her silk cape and draped it about her shoulders. "Come, Husband. It is a pleasant walk through Palmyra to the West Gate where they've raised their tents."

Laughing, Odainat motioned to the others in the room. "We shall escort ourselves since they would be afraid to send guards."

"Leave your weapons behind," Zenobia said.

"Do you think that wise?" General Ezechiel asked.

"I fear them not." Zenobia sailed across the room and out the door, her silken robes fluttering in the wake.

King Shapur's Persian ambassador trembled as Zenobia and Odainat were escorted into his tent. He rose from a plump, silk cushion and bowed.

"You honor me with your presence," Balthasar said.

"Thank you." Odainat looked around the leather tent. It didn't look as if anything had been unpacked. A few patterned rugs were scattered about the floor, but not as many as customary. Tables were not covered with cloths nor were there plates for the food that had been sent to them from the palace.

Zenobia walked to the table and pulled a fig from a basket. "Do you not like our figs?" She bit into one. "These are the sweetest in all our lands."

"I had no time to eat them." Balthasar retrieved a fig and took a tiny bite. "It is sweet."

"The roasted bear meat is exceptional." Zenobia picked a piece off a palm leaf and swallowed it. "I'm sorry you haven't had time to eat. Perhaps you have time now?"

"Of course." Balthasar signaled to his servants.

Cushions were hurriedly unpacked and placed at the table for Odainat, Zenobia, and their entourage. Her eyes sparkled as she settled herself slowly.

"Come, General Abdas, General Ezechiel. Sit." She patted the cushions on either side of her. "Timagenes, you old Egyptian, sit across from me so that I may admire your handsome face."

Odainat maintained his serious countenance with difficulty. How smoothly his wife took over the Persian's tent. He sat at the end of the table and watched Balthasar struggle to try and guess how he lost control so easily.

"Iason, my fine physician, do sit next to Balthasar. He looks ill."

Odainat had to cough to cover the chuckle that slipped out.

"Who are the gentlemen who have accompanied you?" Zenobia took another fig. "These are not poison, you know."

Odainat winked at General Abdas who must have noticed, as he had, the startled look on the faces of the three Persians. So, he thought. Zenobia has guessed their fears. The fools sent by King Shapur to discuss a treaty were terrified.

"We would never think that. . . ."

Zenobia dropped the half eaten fig back into the basket. "You did, but I am not offended. I would have thought the same of you had we agreed to go to Persia. Now you know why we stayed here."

"I hope you do not think that we are cowards," Balthasar said.

"Of course I think that. Who are your friends?" Zenobia lifted a woven lid from another basket. "Dates. These are very good. Would you care for some?"

"No thank you." Balthasar said. "The gentleman to my right is

Kansbar. He is master of our treasury. At the end of the table opposite your husband is Saeed. He is master . . ."

"I am master of nothing." Saeed leaned across the table, took Zenobia's hand, and kissed it. "Ah, the lingering taste of honey-coated dates. A wonderful appetizer."

"Honey attracts insects far better than vinegar," Zenobia said.

Saeed chuckled. "I have heard of your barbed wit. I adore that in a woman." Saeed squeezed her hand.

"You are master of women, I see." Zenobia withdrew her hand slowly. She took a date and popped it into Saeed's mouth.

Odainat laughed at General Abdas' shocked look. Ezechiel hid a grin behind a handful of dates.

"My dear Queen Zenobia, perhaps you would honor us by having a drink. We have brought some exceptional wine." Saeed snapped his fingers and two servants appeared. "The best wine for our guests."

"By all means," Balthasar said. "Do not frown so much Kansbar. It will not hurt our treasury to share our wine."

Odainat laughed aloud. "Your treasure master is the same as ours. One would think we were destitute the way he cries when we spend gold or use the silk from the treasure house."

"To our new friends. May peace come with understanding." Balthasar lifted his chalice in a toast.

"Blessed be our new found friends," Zenobia said. "May your gods protect you." She downed the wine in one long swallow. "That is quite good."

Saeed snapped his fingers and instantly Zenobia's silver chalice was refilled. He sipped his wine as Zenobia smiled sweetly at him.

"My queen loves good wines," Odainat said. He noticed that the Persians drank from smaller chalices than what the Palmyrans had been given. A common trick when dealing with a treaty, and one that he had used on occasion.

"Your wine is good." Zenobia grinned at Balthasar. "Drink up. I am one ahead of you already."

Nodding, Balthasar motioned to the servant. He downed his wine almost as quickly as Zenobia, then signaled for more.

"Good," Zenobia said. "Saeed, you're slow."

"I savor everything exquisite as if time does not matter," Saeed said.

Odainat nudged Zenobia's foot with his. She nudged in return. He glanced at the candles in tripods that had been placed about the tent. They had barely burnt. Dawn was many hours away. Behind Balthasar sat a trunk of camel leather painted with intricate geometric designs. The treaty was probably in there ready to be signed. It would not be written to Palmyra's advantage.

The candles had burned low; some had sputtered and died, but the singing continued. Zenobia's voice joined with Generals Abdas and Ezechiel. The physician, Iason, and Timagenes had passed out long ago and were draped across the table. Iason, his silver hair as limp as he was, snored quietly. Timagenes' eyes were half closed, glazed, and stared at the draped ceiling of the tent.

Odainat couldn't help grinning as Zenobia held out her chalice for more wine. She patted his arm, leaned over and whispered, "You grin like the Bacchus. Is there debauchery in your heart?"

"I think so. You look lovely." Odainat hiccupped.

"You'll have a head twice the size of a camel tomorrow."

"I don't want to hear that now." Odainat reached for the double chalice that floated before him.

"I think not." Zenobia pulled the chalice from him.

"You are depriving me...."

"An answer to my prayers." Zenobia chuckled.

"Did we sign any treaties, yet?"

"No." Zenobia thumped her hand down on a stack of parchments in front of her. "These are ridiculous."

"My head is inside a cavern, for every word you say has an echo. Will you make certain the treaty is all right? I fear the Persians planned to get us all drunk." Odainat grunted. "They did not know about your capacity for wine."

"An odd talent, but convenient."

Zenobia pushed the treaty across the table toward Balthasar. The scratching of parchment on the marble top sounded far away to Odainat. He tried to clear the roaring from his mind.

"This is no treaty. It's an insult." Zenobia's voice was clear and forceful. She glared at Balthasar.

"It is a fair treaty," Balthasar said.

"Fair!" Zenobia banged her chalice down on the table. Wine

sloshed over the top and splattered angry maroon patches that pointed toward Balthasar.

"This treaty asks for two thousand denarii in gold, fifty camels, seventy donkeys, and one hundred containers. . . ." She leaned over the document and scanned it. "One hundred man-sized containers of grain. All this for payment of our prisoners?"

"A fair price, I assure you," Kansbar said. "I wanted to demand . . . ask for more grain for our people, but King Shapur would not allow . . ."

"King Shapur is a jackal." Zenobia drained the chalice and wiped her mouth with the back of her hand.

"We want compensation for the prisoners for the sake of their families," Saeed said. "The wives and children need food and shelter."

"Ha! They would see none of this."

Balthasar rose to his feet and swayed like a palm tree in a gale. "Our king wants compensation."

Zenobia stood and with each word, poked Balthasar in the chest. "We have no Persian prisoners. They are in Rome."

Balthasar's eyes closed slowly and, just as slowly, he folded downward into his chair.

"Well done, Zenobia. What now?" Odainat said. He wasn't sure that she heard him above the pounding of a thousand hammers against stone.

"A new treaty."

"Wasn't theirs to our liking?"

"No. I have already asked General Abdas to write a new one for us."

"Is he sober? The Persian wine is strong." Odainat squinted to try and make out one of the twin generals.

"It doesn't matter that he is drunk. He writes well under the most adverse conditions. He writes what I tell him."

Odainat raised his eyebrows and blinked. He focused on General Abdas who leaned across the papyrus and scratched away, the bronze pen bobbing and twisting in a dance that made Odainat's head thump. "How fare our Persians?" he whispered.

"Kansbar has fallen over the treasure chest. See, his arms are outstretched as if he's trying to protect all the silver and gold they brought with them."

"Is that Saeed who watches General Abdas so intently?" Odainat rubbed his eyes.

"He is not yet drunk enough to sign the treaty," Zenobia whispered. "Balthasar will sign when I promise him medicines to clear his head."

"Are you sober?"

"No." Zenobia giggled.

"No matter. You've never been too drunk not to do what was necessary for Palmyra." Odainat sat straight and tugged at his belt. "Where is my dagger? I should kill the Persians for trying to get us drunk. The wine is strong."

"Hush, Husband. I will have the army marching through my head tomorrow, but it won't be a problem." Zenobia tuned to General Abdas. "How fares the good general?"

"My hand is steady, which belies my brain." His red-rimmed eyes stared at Zenobia. "I am finished, my queen."

"Good." She turned to Balthasar. "Wake up, Persian. Your snoring is like the rasping of a sick donkey."

"I am awake."

Zenobia motioned to General Abdas who pushed the treaty toward Balthasar. "As the king's representative, you may sign this."

"Have you signed the treaty?"

"I have."

"And the copy?"

"Of course."

"It satisfies you?"

Zenobia shrugged.

Balthasar struggled to maintain his balance. He ran his hands down the front of his chest to smooth his clothing, ran his fingers through his beard, then tried to get his hair in place. "I, as representative of the king, will sign the treaty that we so gallantly prepared for our friends to the south."

Zenobia handed him the bronze pen and watched as he wrote with a flourish. Odainat chuckled, then winced as Zenobia's foot connected with his shin. He coughed to cover his faux pas.

"Thank you, good Balthasar. I think that this will do nicely." Zenobia rose, signaled to Balthasar's guards, and strode with dignity toward the tent flap. "Would you guards be so good as to transport my drunken comrades to our palace? I would not want them to clutter up this Persian tent. It would be a shame to ruin the lovely carpets. Come, General Ezechiel and General Abdas. I think your king would appreciate your assistance."

Odainat nodded to General Ezechiel. "My wife is quite a woman. Even drunk, she thinks as she does when sober. The Persians should not have tried to trick us."

"Zenobia! I am dying." Odainat felt a cold cloth on the back of his neck.

"You bellow like the jackass who has no reason to." Zenobia touched a cup to his cheek. "Drink this."

"It smells foul." Odainat pushed it away.

"It doesn't smell as foul as you do."

"I have camel dung for breath."

"That you do. Drink."

The cup was warm. The liquid was bitter and hot. "You don't have to burn the foul Persian wine from my gut."

"The Persian wine was not foul. It was strong." Zenobia tipped the cup.

Odainat was forced to swallow. The medicine dribbled down his beard. "I am ugly."

"You are never ugly, my handsome warrior." Zenobia kissed his forehead.

"Why do you never get drunk or ill?"

"Blessed by the goddess Allat who protects women." Zenobia laid another cool cloth across Odainat's head. "I have a pounding in my temples, but I choose to ignore it."

"Have the Persians gone?"

"Soon. The Generals and I will escort them to their border . . . their new border. They gave us more land in trade for peace."

"Good land?"

"No, desert, but it gives us more space between their army and Palmyra. I shall assign more border guards for awhile."

"You are a clever woman."

"I learned from you, Odainat."

"You should have seen her, Miriam. She was in complete control."

Ezechiel laid his head on the kitchen table. He liked the roughness of the planks against his cheek. He was probably alive, although his body felt like a three day dead jackel and his head was a pulsating stone.

Ezechiel sat up and rubbed his eyes with thumb and forefinger. "I was able to direct the Persian guards to the palace, nay, even to Odainat's chambers. They deposited him gently on the sleeping couch as one might a sleepy child." Ezechiel drank. "What is this disgusting tonic?"

"Queen Zenobia sent it by messenger just before the sun rose." Miriam pushed the cup toward him. "A mere hour, Husband, after you stumbled in. Drink."

"It is bitter."

Miriam crossed her arms. "Drink."

"They gave us powerful wine." Ezechiel blinked. His head still throbbed. He drained the liquid.

"And you had to partake."

"They tried to trick our king and queen."

"Did they try to trick you, too?"

"I drank a little to be pleasant. It was a trying time."

"Ha!" Miriam said. "A noble sacrifice for the sake of peace."

"I had to."

The silence that settled around Miriam like a shroud was more horrible than the worst noise of battle. "Our queen did well."

"Really?"

"Not once did she refuse their wine. Not once did she waver; not once did her hand shake; not once did she lose her thoughts in her cups; not once did she . . ."

"Enough!"

Ezechiel belched. "Excuse me."

"I don't think so."

"My love, are you jealous of Zenobia?"

"Don't be like the donkey."

"You are! You're jealous of our queen." Ezechiel hiccuped.

"I am not jealous, you idiot. Just leery of your attentions to her."

"There is no one more beautiful than you, Miriam."

"Except our queen."

"Her love is for no man save Odainat."

"I know."

"You are foolish to fear that I would do anything. . . ."

Miriam laid her hand on Ezechiel's arm. "Forgive me. I trust you, for you're an honorable man."

"One who loves you more than the stars. . . ."

"Easy to say."

"More than Ain Efqa with its precious water."

"Ain Efqa smells like eggs that have rotted in the desert sun." Miriam sighed. "I am silly. I admire our queen as much as you do."

"Perhaps I talk too much."

"No, Ezechiel. My thoughts were with you the entire night. I was frightened for you and could not sleep. When you're in battle, I know what to expect."

"But last night?"

"You went unarmed to the Persian delegation. I don't trust them."

"Neither did we." Ezechiel reached across the table, wrapped his war-toughened fingers around the back of Miriam's slender neck, and pulled her toward him. "I see your face when I'm alone." He kissed her, savoring the sweetness of her mouth, her quick intake of breath, the softness of her.

Miriam pulled away. "I pray to God every night for your safety."

"I pray to God that we'll have a long life together." Ezechiel kissed her again.

"I feel trouble coming, Ezechiel, and it scares me."

"You were always the one who worried even when we were children."

"I had to help your mother worry. You were always somewhere that you weren't supposed to be."

"In the mountains."

"Daydreaming."

"Hunting."

"You roamed the desert."

"Hunting."

"Daydreaming."

"Don't worry about me, Wife. I will always survive just to come home to you." Ezechiel pulled her toward him again. "I pray to God that I will live through every battle just so I can come home to you. I love the way your hair smells of desert flowers, the smoothness of your skin, the way you gasp when I enter you. . . ."

Miriam placed her fingers on his lips. "No more talk, Ezechiel. I need you."

"You always speak your mind."

She traced a scar that ran down his chest. "I always felt compelled to make the most of our time together. Don't waste it."

Ezechiel swooped Miriam into his arms and carried her toward the outside entrance.

"Where are you taking me?"

"Under the stars."

Miriam giggled. "The neighbors will see us."

"The neighbors are asleep."

"Dawn comes soon."

"Let it." Ezechiel pushed aside the leather curtain.

"I love you." Miriam snuggled closer and draped her arms around her husband.

"And I love you. More than life." Ezechiel placed her on a pile of clean straw near the stable, and eased down next to her. It took only a moment to remove her stola and loosen her hair from its pins.

It took her less time to grasp his tunic and pull it over his head. He grinned as her fingers explored his war-hardened chest. He would tease her many times before allowing himself to love her.

"This cannot be our border." Balthasar jerked the reins; his horse skipped sideways, pushing Zenobia's mount aside. "Our border is half a day behind us."

"The treaty indicates that this is the border." Zenobia arranged her veil to keep the sun from her eyes.

"Treaty! I signed no treaty that gave you a third of Persia."

"General Abdas, would you bring the treaty chest forward?" Zenobia enjoyed the fleeting look of alarm that danced across Balthasar's face.

"Kansbar! Get our copy of the treaty!" Balthasar bellowed. His voice rolled across the dunes like thunder.

"Yes, sir." Kansbar motioned to two of his guards who came running from the back, the decorative camel hide trunk banging against their legs.

Balthasar jerked the scroll from Kansbar's hand, read rapidly, then glared at Zenobia. "This is no treaty."

"It is signed by you, witnessed by Kansbar and Saeed. Your seal is affixed alongside Odainat's and mine."

"I have been tricked!"

"Tricked? The crafty Balthasar tricked? The ever alert Balthasar signed a document in error?" Zenobia watched in alarm as his face turned sunset red. If his heart exploded now, the treaty would be worthless.

"You got me drunk."

"With your wine? I matched you chalice for chalice—you saw to that."

Balthasar sputtered. "You . . . you . . . you did this."

"King Shapur wanted peace. It cost him nothing in gold, nothing in denarii, nothing in gems. He gave us worthless desert in exchange."

"This is not what he expected us to bring back."

Zenobia glanced at General Abdas. He nodded. His troops were ready to fight. General Ezechiel was to her right, his hand clenched around the hilt of his sword. He, too, was ready.

"No, Balthasar. Shapur wanted that which he did not deserve. Shapur forgets who the power is in this part of the world. It has not been Rome for a long time."

"Bitch!" Balthasar shouted.

Zenobia held up her hand to stay General Ezechiel who had drawn his sword. "You return to Shapur and tell him that he is lucky we didn't take all of Persia. I wish we had—it would save much trouble." She turned Thabit and rode slowly toward Palmyra.

"I will see you on the field of battle!" Balthasar shouted after her.

Zenobia whirled Thabit around. "I do not think so. Your head will not be long attached to your body." Even from this distance, she saw her adversary wince.

Balthasar's horse leaped forward as he drew his sword.

Zenobia heard the familiar swish as she pulled her own sword from its sheath. General Abdas drove toward her from the left while General Ezechiel and his men rode around Balthasar's right flank and closed in on his army. Her mistake had been in pointing out the inevitable to Balthasar. He had nothing to lose and much to gain. If he won this skirmish, killed or captured her, then he would keep his head.

She watched as he bore down on her, his sword held out in front. He meant to skewer her like a piece of meat. Zenobia sucked in her breath and raced toward her fate.

Balthasar had cleverly moved so that the late afternoon sun was behind him, but Zenobia had the advantage because she could see his sword as the sun set it afire. As Thabit pounded toward the enemy, Zenobia dropped the reins over one of the double saddle horns. She waited until Balthasar was close enough that she could see the gray hair in his black beard, then she grabbed her sword with both hands. As Zenobia swept past the Persian, she broadsided his sword with the flat side of her blade and knocked the weapon to the ground.

Balthasar roared, indignation entwined in his voice. He pulled his horse up short and dropped to the ground, scrambling for his sword.

Pulling Thabit around in a tight circle, Zenobia stopped next to Balthasar. She leaped from her horse and kicked the sword from Balthasar's reach. Sand splattered in his face, and he cursed her.

"Such language." Zenobia placed the point of the sword between Balthasar's shoulder blades. "Turn over slowly so I can see your eyes."

He rolled over and stared up at Zenobia as she held her sword to his throat. "Go on and cut. I prefer dying on Persian soil."

"This is no longer Persian soil. Remember the treaty?"

"It will always be ours no matter the words. Finish what you started. Kill me."

"That would be too good an end for you. No, you'll be better off explaining the treaty to King Shapur."

"He will have my head."

"In the town square, I imagine."

"Do you enjoy thinking of my death?"

"No, Balthasar. I regret that it has come to this." Zenobia inclined her head toward Kansbar and Saeed who were held by General Ezechiel. "I regret their deaths as well."

"Have you no mercy? Kill us in honor on the field of battle."

"I need you to take the treaty to your king."

"You are cruel."

Zenobia clamped her teeth together to keep from answering, but it did no good. "Do not accuse me of that which you are. I did not try to get you drunk. I did not try to take what was not mine to take. I protect Palmyra. It is my duty."

"Cruelty guides you, Zenobia."

"Don't keep hammering away at that chorus!" Zenobia glanced around. "General Abdas! Escort this baggage and his comrades to King Shapur. Take a goodly number of men with you, for I trust neither these men nor their ruler."

"My death will be on the list that the gods check after death."

"You won't be the first or the last." Zenobia sheathed her sword, whistled for Thabit, and waited for a young foot soldier to assist her in mounting. Once on her horse, she turned with a small division of cavalry and infantry falling in behind her and headed toward Palmyra.

General Abdas settled into a gold brocaded chair and watched the Persian king order food and drink. The king had a plan, and Abdas wasn't sure he liked it. A messenger had ordered him to appear before the king without guards or entourage. He could have refused and been mistaken for a coward. He had too much pride for that.

"Tell me, how do your king and queen fare?" Shapur poured wine for Abdas, then for himself.

"Their strength and cunning grows daily." Abdas noted the wine was poured from the same jug. However, the chalice could be poisoned. There would be no gain for Shapur to poison a lowly general. Not after he had humiliated the Roman emperor, Valerian.

"Too bad." Shapur held out a golden plate of fruit. "You must be hungry after the long trek from Palmyra."

"We had provisions." Abdas frowned. "You did not ask me here because you were concerned about my having food."

"No." Shapur's eyes narrowed. "I want to defeat your king and queen at any cost. They have been nipping at my heels for years, and I'm tired of it."

"What do you want with me? Am I to take them that message?"

"No." Shapur nodded toward a small chest that rested on a table. "That chest holds gold, gems, and silver. It is yours."

Abdas glared at Shapur to hide his astonishment. "You are not in the habit of giving gifts to your enemies."

"Are you really an enemy? You appear to like fine things. Your clothing is fit for a king, your horse is the finest that can be bred, your home, I'm told, is almost a palace. You are a man who thinks like a general for someone else so they can rule you, be wealthier than you, have an adoring public."

"You think that I might betray those who've trusted me and made me wealthy?"

Shapur leaned forward and stabbed a piece of lamb with his knife. "I think you're greedy."

Abdas glanced at the chest. He could do much with what lay in the chest. He could disappear to another part of the world and live like a king. Beautiful women would throw themselves into his bed. . . .

"What do you want?" Abdas asked.

"I want Odainat and Zenobia dead."

Abdas blinked. "I am to be an instrument of death for you?"

"It appears to be so." Shapur leaned back from the table and watched Abdas.

Abdas wanted to look at the chest again, but he forced himself to stare at Shapur instead. He couldn't stop thinking about what the chest held. There would be more gems than he had ever seen in one place; more gold than one man could spend in a lifetime; silver enough for his heirs. What did he owe Zenobia and Odainat? Just because they were all born in Palmyra didn't mean he couldn't be loyal to someone else outside of that oasis.

He could pay someone to attack them; he could misdirect a battle. . . .

"This is only half of what I would give you. An identical chest will be delivered to wherever you want after the . . . ah . . . deed is done." Shapur cleaned his fingernails with his eating knife.

Abdas shook his head. "No."

"No?"

"I do not wish to betray my king and queen." Abdas stood, bowed, and walked toward the door. He walked slowly and expected to feel the quick impact of a knife between his shoulder blades.

He continued to walk deliberately through the palace until he was outside. He nodded to the master of horses, climbed on his beautiful Arabian stallion, and led his men away from temptation.

CHAPTER
VII

267 A. D. Palmyra, Syria

aeonius stared at the hob-nailed sandals in his hand. They were disgusting. He never had to wear these when riding in the cavalry. He had always worn fine leather boots. Maeonius threw the shoes to the ground. The irritating sounds of marching, the noise of men shouting back and forth to each other, and the smell of camels assaulted him. He stayed outside most of the time because he hated the barracks where he fell into a fitful sleep every night exhausted and bored by the daily routine.

He was not a commoner. He should be heir to the throne instead of that girl-boy Hairan. Maeonius spat on the ground. He should be the one to wear the purple silk cape and lead the army like Odainat did. A shadow fell across him, and he looked up.

"How fares the cast-out prince?"

"Go away, Nishan, you Roman dog. You are not amusing."

"Are you not going to join the others and listen to your cousin sing? He will entertain us with his wit and wonderful voice," Nishan said.

"He is witless and cannot sing."

"He always has a large crowd."

"Those who think he will be king fawn after him."

"Think you that Hairan will be king?" Nishan shrugged. "There are many who think he is sickly and will die young."

"He looks sickly, but is not." Maeonius stared across the compound where Hairan had settled himself under the shade of the

overhanging roof. He plucked and adjusted the strings. The result-
ant twangs and pings irritated Maeonius further.

"There are poisons. . . ." Nishan said.

Maeonius' mouth dropped open. "Are you in need of having
your head separated from your shoulders?"

"I have said nothing that you have not thought about." Nishan
nodded toward Hairan. "Your cousin sings well."

"If you like the sound of a belching camel," Maeonius growled.

"He has the soldiers laughing."

"They flatter him." Maeonius tried to force the straps on his
knapsack to close.

"You haven't packed it properly," Nishan said.

"I don't need to know how to pack this! I'm a prince! I have
servants." Maeonius threw the knapsack to the ground and slid his
feet into the disgusting hob-nailed sandals.

Nishan moved the knapsack with his toe. "Not anymore. You
must hate watching Hairan rise in favor while your own favor di-
minishes. I have heard the queen hates you."

Maeonius leaped to his feet and swung a fist at the offensive
soldier's jaw. Nishan stopped his fist in mid-flight.

"Fool! Do not draw attention to us! You'll ruin everything."
Nishan said.

"Let go of my hand."

"Calm yourself and think of what I've said." Nishan waited, then
let go of Maeonius' fist.

"You have said nothing that I want to hear. You have a peculiar
way of committing suicide."

Nishan chuckled. "I thought you were brave. I thought you would
make a good king. Perhaps I was wrong." He walked away. "I hear
that you no longer hunt with the royal party," Nishan called back
over his shoulder.

Maeonius sprang up and tore across the hard-packed earth. "You
cloven-hoofed beast." Maeonius grabbed the soldier's brown hair and
jerked him backward.

Nishan growled, tumbled into Maeonius' arms, and the two of
them rolled on the ground, kicking up a cloud of dust. Maeonius
yelled obscenities in his adversary's ear. He was aware that a crowd
had gathered. He could hear voices calling for him to hit Nishan
harder. Nishan's friends also called for blood.

Maeonius wanted to kill. He tried several times to reach his dagger, but Nishan, bigger and stronger, held his hand away easily as if Maeonius were a child.

"I will kill you, Nishan. I will kill you."

Nishan panted. "You kill the wrong one. You hate another. Can you not single out the cub and the lion?"

"Stop the fighting! I order it!"

Maeonius was so taken aback by Hairan's command that he stopped and looked up at his cousin. "What did you say?"

"I order this to stop. There is no reason to fight. If you want to fight, get transferred to the border."

"You can't stop me." Maeonius sat up.

"Are you fighting?"

"No." Maeonius spat on the ground.

"Then I stopped you," Hairan said.

The smug look of triumph on Hairan's face incensed Maeonius. He wanted to blot out the girlish face before him, but he could not. Voices faded, faces faded until only Hairan's eyes locked onto Maeonius'. Maeonius gritted his teeth until his jaws ached.

Beneath him, Nishan shifted his weight and whispered, "Take care or your chance will be lost."

"Get up," Hairan said.

Nishan scrambled to his feet and bowed. "Forgive us. We fight over the same girl."

Hairan's mouth twitched in a half-smile. "There are plenty of women. Why fight?"

Maeonius got to his feet slowly. He refused to bow. "You are right. There are many women for me. I should allow Nishan to have one."

Nishan's chuckle raised Maeonius' spirits. At least it was amusing to have him around.

"Good. I see no need to report this scuffle," Hairan said.

"Report! Who are you to? . . ." Maeonius asked.

"Thank you for your kindness and understanding, Prince Hairan." Nishan bowed. As he did, his elbow banged into Maeonius' ribs.

Maeonius watched Hairan stride away like a peacock. Maeonius stomped away from the sound of the lyre and the insipid singing.

"Wait!" Nishan caught up with Maeonius. "You are our guiding light. Our only way to victory."

"Victory?"

"There are those who feel the time has come for new leadership. Youth with intelligence and a desire to fight."

Maeonius stared at Nishan. There was no sign of jest on his face. Indeed, he looked serious. "You're talking of killing Odainat."

"And Hairan. Come, we must plan with the others."

"Plan? There is nothing to plan."

"There is a plan—from Rome."

Maeonius gasped and stopped so suddenly that minute clouds of dust rose, then settled on his sandals. He stared at Nishan. "Zenobia and her army protect him always, and he protects her."

"Not always. What one night do the men in this town leave their wives for dancing girls? What night do they drink themselves silly?"

"Kithoth's birthday party in Emesa." Maeonius grinned. "But Emesa is a two day ride from here across the desert. We cannot follow without being seen."

"We may go before and wait for Odainat. It would be easy. Come talk to your followers."

"I didn't know I had any." Maeonius thought of the purple cape. He would look good riding in front of the army with the cape billowing like a sail on the sea. He would have many women come to his bed. Maybe he would make Rebekeh his mistress, whether she liked it or not. Hairan wrote songs about her, the fool. He hated Rebekeh because Hairan loved her. He grinned as he thought of all the ways he could hurt her.

"Zenobia! Zenobia!" Odainat shouted. He scrambled off his sleeping couch and pushed aside the messenger who stood between two servants. Odainat wrapped a multicolored striped cotton cover about his naked body and raced across the cella that the two apartments shared.

"What is it?" Zenobia sat up and rubbed her eyes. "Are we being attacked?"

"Not yet. That Persian beast, Shapur, has sent an army towards Palmyra. We must ride. We will push him back as far as China to rid ourselves of this pest. I have sent word to our generals to get the armies ready."

"He didn't like our treaty." Zenobia leaped from her sleeping couch and signaled to her servants. The women scurried off to get her riding clothes.

"Odainat, this would be a good time for Hairan to ride with you."

"I want you by my side."

"I will be to your left, but your oldest son should be on your right."

"No one rides to my right but you."

"It is time for Hairan to ride into battle. What better way to show you his improvement with the bow, the sword, and his riding?"

"He will ride behind me with our other lieutenants. I . . . I don't want him at the front of the line."

"I understand." Zenobia grabbed her riding pants from a servant and tugged them on. "What of Maeonius?"

"He marches at the end of the army."

"Perfect. Now go, Husband, for I am anxious to ride against Shapur. Our treaty will be more solid when we win this battle."

"He is but four days away."

"Already he treads on our land. The fool. We'll double march and meet him in two." Zenobia grinned. "Send for Hairan. Tell him he rides as a prince today into his first real battle."

"My son rides today with me. It is the first time." Odainat laughed. "How I remember my first ride into battle with my father. It was the most invigorating feeling in the world. It is time that Hairan enjoyed his first battle. Yes, I will go tell the prince he rides with us."

Dust whirled about Maeonius, refusing to settle. His eyes felt gritty, sand imbedded itself in his clothing, and he had no saliva with which to spit out dirt. He had blisters on his feet from the stupid sandals. He should be on a horse. He had an urge to prod Nishan in his rear end with the heavy spear that he was forced to carry. It was Nishan's idea to make certain they marched with the army. What better way to get to Kithoth's birthday party? Rumor had it that Odainat planned to march double time back to Palmyra so that he wouldn't miss the yearly affair in Emesa.

Their plan to assassinate Odainat and Hairan was simple. Maeonius scowled. Was it too simple? Did he have enough followers?

How many of the Romans who marched with the Palmyrans would really come over to his side?

A simple plan. Let the fools get drunk, then attack. Zenobia would not be there with her army. What soldiers were there with Odainat would be drunk, too. Kithoth's birthday party was legendary.

Maeonius grimaced. Emesa was a two day march past Palmyra. The desert cloud settled briefly. Ahead was Hairan. Riding. The fool. Maybe he would be killed. Maeonius checked his dagger. He'd honed the edge to perfection. If there were an opportunity . . .

"Is that Shapur's army?" Nishan shouted over his shoulder.

"How should I know? I can't see anything from the ground." Maeonius glared ahead at his cousin who rode ahead of the dust cloud. "May the gods frown on you today, Hairan."

Hairan stared past his father and Zenobia at the approaching army. Sun glinted off shields, swords, and the silver adorned bridles of Shapur's horse. Hairan's throat constricted. There were so many of them. He was glad that his father had made him ride three rows back. He ran his fingers over the new bow that Zenobia had given him not more than three nights ago. It hung off the saddle in a special leather carrying case. A quiver of the finest arrows hung off the other side.

He didn't know if he could hit a living target. As much as he had learned to hate Shapur, he did not think he could hit a living target. The picture of the hare thrashing about on the ground made him grimace.

The armies moved closer. Hairan could see King Shapur's face. The black bearded man wasn't as tall as his own father, but he looked formidable with thick, muscular arms. He traveled in front of his army with his son by his side. Hairan grimaced. Shapur's son was younger than he by two years. King Shapur's youngest son had ridden with him for the last three years. Odainat had told him that one day in a fit of anger.

Odainat raised his arm and gave the signal to rush the front lines. Hairan kicked his horse, but got a late start. He was three paces behind the others in his line. He struggled to remember what he was to do. His bow and arrow was useless while tearing across the desert at this speed. His horse stumbled and Hairan jammed his thighs against the double saddle horns that angled outwards. They kept him from tumbling to the ground.

When the horse righted himself and the dust settled, Hairan could see that the fight had already begun. The two men assigned to him, probably as bodyguards, had surged ahead. They were already in the middle of the fight, swinging their short swords furiously.

Hairan drew his own short sword, but pulled his horse to a stop. He glanced over his shoulder and saw the infantry marching double time straight into the brawl. He heard Zenobia's scream of warning over the clashing of swords, the whinnying of injured and dying horses, and the shouting of men. Hairan saw her forcing her way toward Odainat who was surrounded by four of Shapur's men. She would never get to him in time.

"Not my father! No!" Hairan kicked his horse so hard that he leaped forward and sped toward Odainat.

Hairan took out the closest man with a quick thrust to the ribs as his sword was raised. The second man swung around, but Hairan remembered a trick taught to him by his stepmother and swung his sword with both hands. The enemy's head flopped to the side as Hairan's sword detached it from its neck. The stench of blood forced acrid bile from Hairan's stomach into his throat. He forced it back.

Odainat bellowed and took out the other two men with two clean swipes to the left and to the right with his sword. He nodded at Hairan and rode into another group of men. Zenobia flew past Hairan and galloped after his father. Hairan smiled. She was a goddess protecting her own.

The notes of a trumpet drifted across the desert as King Shapur sounded a retreat. Hairan watched the Persian army spin as one and race across the desert toward their walled city. He groaned. Zenobia shouted orders for the cavalry to pursue the Persians. Hairan kicked his horse and galloped after her. Ctesiphon was two days away. He would be glad when the fighting was over, and he could go to Kithoth's birthday party with his father. At least at the party they could forget about war and fighting. At the party would be the sweet smell of incense instead of the bitter smell of death.

"Odainat," Zenobia called from her bathing room. "Did you see how Hairan rushed in to save you?" She waited for her husband to answer.

"Every day you have told me that story." Odainat leaned against the door opening. "I have heard it a least ten days in a row."

"Five days. No more. You have not said anything to Hairan. He mopes around and steals glances at you. He needs your praise."

"Why should I praise him for a job he is supposed to do?"

"Wouldn't you have said something to General Abdas or General Ezechiel had they not done the same?" Zenobia stood and took a drying cloth from her servants. She waved a hand at her favorite pair of eunuchs. They bowed before leaving the bathing room.

"I probably would praise them, but Hairan needs to grow up. Praise would spoil what progress he's made." Odainat took the ends of the drying towel and pulled Zenobia to him.

"He needs your words to give him pride. Our old generals know they're good. They need your kindness less than does Hairan."

"You're right. I will thank him." Odainat frowned.

"A frown, my love? Why?" Zenobia kissed the tip of his nose.

"We need to think of a suitable queen for him. I have no idea who would have the strength to shore up his weaknesses."

"His weaknesses are temporary. Why, they're hardly weaknesses now. He was wonderful on the field of battle."

"A young Roman aristocrat might do."

"Roman! Oh no. A Roman woman would not survive here. It's too hot. And she would be spoiled."

"We need to find him a woman worthy to be his queen."

"I agree, but one who is Palmyran." Zenobia grinned. "One who is right under our noses. One whom Hairan has already chosen."

"Who?"

"The daughter of our Jewish weaver. She's been helping care for the boys for the last few months. Her name is Rebekeh. The boys like her." Zenobia put her arms around Odainat. "I wonder if we should have her trained in warfare?"

"It would be a good idea." Odainat wrapped his arms around Zenobia. "Let's talk of this later. I need you more than anyone. I need you now."

"Don't you have a birthday party to attend?"

"Kithoth will have women there, but none as exciting as you." Odainat kissed her.

"I'm to stay home and celebrate our victory over Shapur alone?"

"True." Odainat kissed each eyelid. "Come. Let's celebrate before I have to leave."

"My love for you is stronger each day. If we were to conceive a child today, he would be strong and powerful."

"She may be strong and powerful—like her mother."

Zenobia laughed. "I do love you more than all the lands we conquered, more than my gems, more than . . ."

"No more talk." Odainat scooped Zenobia into his arms and carried her to his sleeping couch.

"My warrior husband is strong in war, but gentle in love." Zenobia sighed.

Rebekeh paced back and forth in the garden. She had slipped out of the palace long after the boys had been put to bed. She often walked in the garden, but not at night. She wasn't frightened. Palmyra was strongly defended and powerful. She no longer feared Shapur and the Persians. Palmyra's strength even outshone that of Rome.

Hairan had asked her here, but she wasn't certain he meant it. It was one thing to steal kisses when they were in the palace, but another to meet him in the privacy of the garden. What was she doing here? She sighed. Hairan was different from the other boys she knew. She loved him.

She sat on a marble bench and watched the moon rise. Pale color bathed the garden in creamy light and forced the heat of the desert to be a memory. She should leave. She knew why she was here, and her mother would not approve.

Hairan slipped up behind her and wrapped his arms around her. He leaned down and kissed the top of her head. "How pleased I am to see you."

"Are you?" Rebekeh leaned back and looked up. Hairan was so handsome. "Are you still going to Kithoth's party with the king?"

"Yes."

"Will you drink a gallon of wine as the other men do?" Rebekeh asked.

"No, I'll be too busy singing."

"Will Kithoth have a woman for you?" Rebekeh blushed.

110

"I'll be too busy singing." Hairan moved in front of Rebekeh and pulled her into his arms.

"My mother says that none of the men who go are too busy for wine and women. She won't let my father go."

"They don't sing. I sing. I won't have time for wine and women." Hairan smiled. "I think you're jealous."

"No, just concerned about you."

"Rebekeh, I cannot look at another woman. None is as beautiful as you." Hairan kissed her. "Come, promise that you'll miss me."

"That's an easy promise. Promise me that you'll not look at another woman."

"An easy task." Hairan kissed her again. "I love you."

"You don't know what love is." Rebekeh shivered. His kisses did something to her that made her want to get so close to him that nothing would part them.

"I love you." Hairan took her hand and pulled her to a hillock covered with moss. "Come, lie here with me for a little while."

"I can't do that!"

"Just for a while." Hairan drew her down next to him, wrapped his arms around her and kissed her eyes, her ears, her cheek.

"Hairan, you're making me weak."

"That's love." He kissed her as he untied the girdle that held her stola in place. When it fell open, he kissed first one breast then the other. His toga fell away.

Rebekeh felt the heat of his body mix with hers as his leg parted hers. "We must not."

"Why not?" He moved until he lay on top.

Rebekeh gasped, but did not push him away. She felt the hardness of him, and she wrapped her arms about him. So many sensations coursed through her body. Each made her feel so wonderful that she could not stop Hairan. And she didn't want to. She wanted him to make love to her. She cared nothing for the consequences.

"Please love me. I need you," Rebekeh whispered.

The sun had not set when Odainat kissed his wife goodbye and left for Emesa. Zenobia hung over the balcony wall and watched father and son ride toward the north gate along with soldiers and other silly men who made the yearly trek to Kithoth's birthday party.

Vaballathus and Arraum bounced up and down on either side of her, pointing and talking about all the things they'd heard about last year's party. Rebekeh stood apart from them, quiet and introspective today. Zenobia wondered, but did not ask whether all was well. Rebekeh was a pretty girl who would grow into a beautiful woman. Zenobia liked her for her intelligence as much as anything. It was obvious from the way Rebekeh tentatively waved at Hairan and smiled, that she loved him. Zenobia had love with Odainat, and she wanted the same for their sons.

She giggled as she heard Odainat singing with Hairan. Although she couldn't hear the words, she recognized the music. It was Hairan's song about loving a camel. He had taught it to his father. Already the two of them were making fools of themselves. Odainat had told her that they would ride in the cool night by the moonlight. He planned to get to Emesa in less than the normal two days.

"Mother, they sing the funny song," Arraum said.

"Why is Hairan going when I can't go?" Vaballathus asked.

"You will get to go one day. Perhaps after you've ridden into battle with your father." Zenobia ran her fingers through her son's hair. She loved the silky feel of it.

She waited until her men were out of sight and there was not even a cloud of dust to show where the road lay before she turned to her two boys and Rebekeh.

"I have a surprise for you, but it will have to wait until tomorrow night."

"A surprise!"

"Tell! Tell me first," Arraum said.

"Tomorrow night. Now off to bed." Zenobia's heart filled with joy at the sight of her two sons. She was blessed.

A cool breeze from the desert washed across Zenobia as she sat in a chair on the flat roof and watched the sun disappear behind the buildings. A hard day of working with the troops had invigorated her. She always worked hard when Odainat was gone so she could sleep at night.

The sun had barely set when Vaballathus and Arraum bounded into her sleeping quarters. Zenobia rose from the chair and stepped into her chamber.

"I couldn't hold them back any longer, my queen," Rebekeh said.

"I want you to tell me about the surprise first! I'm the oldest," Vaballathus said.

"I will tell both of you at the same time, but first I have to ask that Rebekeh tell you good night. It's her Sabbath."

Rebekeh kissed the two boys, then smiled at Zenobia. "Thank you, but I have begged the rabbi to excuse me tonight. I don't want to miss the surprise."

"He is a gentle and understanding rabbi." Zenobia turned to the boys. " I have a panther under my sleeping couch."

"No, you don't," Vaballathus said. "Your sleeping couch is too low."

"I will show you." Zenobia stretched belly down on her double couch with her head and arms hanging off the side. "You see, you must fool the animal into coming out." She looked at the two dark haired sons who sat on the floor before her. Rebekeh smiled and settled into a chair next to them.

"I do not believe you have a panther under there." Vaballathus leaned down and peered under the couch.

"You are doubtful of my words?" Zenobia grinned at her oldest son who had been born a hardy and spirited child nine summers ago. "Rebekeh found the panther for you."

"General Abdas has told us stories of a man who doubted the prophet, Jesus. Maybe Vaballathus is like him. Thomas always doubted everything." Arraum looked at his mother with great dark eyes surrounded by long lashes.

"You are the serious child and the gatherer of stories," Zenobia said, mostly to herself. How she loved these sons of Odainat's. She loved them as much as she did Hairan who had been placed in her care when he was but four summers old.

"Look, I shall show you, my doubting Vaballathus. You'll see a panther." She dragged a feather across the mosaic floor, tracing the pattern. "Come out, my little panther and kill this fierce beast." She laughed at the gasps of surprise from her sons when a small furry foot swept out from under the sleeping couch and snagged the feather.

"Again, my pretty kitty. Kill, kill." Zenobia grabbed the kitten as she leaped out and pounced on the toy. "You are the loveliest kitten I've ever seen."

"He is beautiful. Let me hold him, let me." Vaballathus reached for the kitten.

"You may both play with him if you will not argue. He does not like fighting."

"We will be good," Arraum said. "I will let Vaballathus hold him first."

"That is noble of you." Zenobia was nuzzling the black ball of fur when a servant entered the room.

"What is it?" Zenobia asked.

"General Ezechiel is here to see you."

"Show him to my cella." Zenobia waited until the servant had gone, then kissed the kitten and put him on the floor between the boys. She handed Rebekeh the feather and smoothing her stola, left the boys.

She sighed. A peaceful moment broken by a crisis. It always happened. She hoped she wouldn't have to disturb Odainat. He was probably still singing as he rode toward Kithoth's. It didn't hurt him to imbibe in too much wine once a year. He would probably be going to Kithoth's yearly party when both men were in their eighth decade.

"General Ezechiel. How nice to see you." Zenobia waved her hand. "Don't bow. It's unnecessary in private. What may I do for you?"

"I have distressing news, my queen."

"Shapur has attacked?"

"No, worse than that. We caught two men who were climbing out of the wadi just below your windows. They are either stupid or bold for sneaking in before the moon set. We have them in the scroll room where there are no windows. Four of my best men guard them. We think there are others."

Zenobia didn't wait for her general to say more, but called for Rebekeh. As soon as she appeared, Zenobia studied the young girl. Rebekeh had always been reliable. "Know you this woman?" she asked Ezechiel.

"Yes. She is the cousin of my good friend."

"Trusted?"

"Yes."

Zenobia nodded. She remembered the look of adoration for Hairan by Rebekeh. "Rebekeh, take the boys and the kitten to a safe place until I contact you personally. Sneak out of the palace in disguise. Take no guards to identify them."

"Yes, my queen."

Ezechiel scowled. "Do you think it wise to take them from the sanctity of this palace with its high walls and guards?"

"I have reason to believe that the traitor is within these walls. Go, Rebekeh. May your god and mine be with you."

"Shall I send for Odainat?" Ezechiel asked. "He is not far away."

"No. I will discover the problem first, then we will see. The gods help anyone who plots against Palmyra."

The man screamed as Zenobia gave the order to cut off a third finger. She didn't wait for the blood to gush forth before she asked the same question for the fourth time.

"What were you doing climbing up the wadi? Who sent you?"

"No more, no more," the man whimpered. He slumped forward.

Zenobia grabbed him by the hair and pulled his head back until his glazed eyes met hers. "Who sent you and for what purpose?"

When the man didn't answer, she slapped him once on each cheek. "Who?" Frustration had built up in her until she wanted to run her knife through his heart. The first man had fainted and was no good to her. This man was her only chance. "Another finger?"

"No, no."

"Who?"

"Your husband's nephew, Maeonius, sent us to kill you and your sons."

Zenobia let go of the man's greasy hair. "Coward! He could not face me himself. This is too big of a conspiracy for that sniveling pig. Too much planning, too much money has gone into this assassination attempt. Now who is really to blame?"

"Maeonius is to kill the king tonight, and then part of Maeonius' army will storm the palace. We were to let them inside after you had been assassinated."

"Another finger. Then another. Perhaps your toes will have to come off, but by the gods, you will tell me the truth!" Zenobia nodded. A soldier raised the curved knife.

"No! No! Please. It was the Romans. The coins we were paid with are Roman."

"Fool. Anyone can have Roman coins."

"I saw the coins. Newly minted and from Rome."

"Not enough. Why would Rome?. . ."

"I saw the order. It had Emperor Gallienus' seal."

Zenobia felt as if the world had stopped. She took a deep breath as she stared at the assassin before her. "The simpleton. He wants to kill his strength? He is too weak to fight our army man to man, so he resorts to deceit." Zenobia paced back and forth.

"Maeonius is but a pawn, but he is too stupid to know this." Zenobia's shock at confirmation of her distrust for Maeonius turned to hatred. In blind fury, she pulled her dagger from the sleeve of her chiton and ran it through the would-be murderer's heart. Warm blood flowed across her fingers. She pulled the knife from the man, wiped it on her stola, and sheathed it.

"Ezechiel, gather your most trusted soldiers and come with me. We have to catch Odainat before he reaches Kithoth's. I pray that we are not too late." Zenobia closed her eyes and whispered, "Bel, you are our most powerful god. Please keep Odainat for me. He is my future, my life."

Aurelian watched Gallienus read a missive from Palmyra.

"Interesting," Gallienus said. "You're right about Palmyra's strength. Their army grows in number and riches. Palmyra is the only country that challenges Rome for power."

"They grow stronger daily," Aurelian said.

"Soldiers captured our men, but our spy is still safe."

"Good," Aurelian said.

"You know how to tempt him." Gallienus' eyebrow raised.

"An easy task. All men have a price. Gold sways many."

"And Maeonius?" Gallienus asked. "What was his price? He has much gold."

"Power, the aphrodisiac." Aurelian lifted his goblet. "Here's to Maeonius' leadership. May he always be weak."

The rhythm of hoofs against limestone paving blocks as Thabit raced down Odainat Way sounded like hideous music to Zenobia. She leaned forward as if that would help her get to Kithoth's sooner. Thabit's mane whipped her face with knife-edged fury, but she didn't care.

She could hear General Ezechiel's horse and General Abdas' mount six cubits back followed by the cavalry that guarded the palace minus the six soldiers who had accompanied Odainat and Hairan.

Because of her, Hairan had gone with his father. Adara's only son was in danger because Zenobia wanted father and son to be together. If he died, it would be her fault. She hoped Adara's soul would haunt her for the rest of her life. It would not be punishment enough for the mistake she had made.

Zenobia's bellowed curse at Maeonius echoed off the walls of the buildings as she raced through the streets thankful that most citizens were in their homes. Her speed through the dark would not have given her time to avoid a collision with anyone who walked the boulevards that were normally devoid of horses.

After she had passed the lighted Sanctuary of Bel and the oddly cheerful Diocletian Baths, she would have been in darkness save for lights from doorways of shops and small apartments that laid across the streets like a Senet game board. Zenobia led her horse from one rectangle to another. It was the only light that she had to guide her toward the north gate and the road to Odainat.

"Please, Bel, guard Odainat and Hairan." She said the prayer automatically over and over in time with the pounding of Thabit's hoofs.

At the first cross street, Zenobia turned north. Out from under the pillared and roofed boulevard, Zenobia could see better in the light of the half-moon, which served her well. She knew Palmyra's streets since she had traveled them daily as a child. There were not many side streets that led straight north to the gate, but Zenobia unerringly worked her way toward the road to Emesa. Odainat would have to camp somewhere tonight. If only she could fly like the birds.

The moonlight on the desert road made it look like a silver ribbon. Thabit's hoofs pounded relentlessly against the hard packed earth. The distance to Emesa seemed to grow longer. Hot wind blew through Zenobia's stola and the desert sand stung her skin as whirlpools of dust attacked her. She had taken no time to armor herself. It didn't matter. Without Odainat, she wouldn't want to live. She prayed to Allat, the goddess who protected women. She would understand the fear in Zenobia's heart.

Zenobia wished she had ridden with Odainat to Emesa, but she wanted this to be a time for father and son. Besides, no wives had been invited. She thought of her friend, Hairan's mother. "Adara, I have failed you."

She raced on, the rhythm of Thabit's hoofs dulling her senses. Ezechiel's voice penetrated the stone wall she'd built around her feelings. She ignored him. All her energy was directed toward reaching Odainat.

"My queen! My queen! You must stop before your horse drops from under you."

The words that he shouted pierced through the wall. Thabit! How could she have been so dull-witted? She pulled back on the reins, slowing Thabit until they stopped. Dust swirled around his legs. Zenobia gasped and scraped the froth off his neck. She rubbed her fingers together. The odor of Thabit's sweat assaulted her senses.

"I almost killed him."

"Almost," Ezechiel said.

"How stupid of me." Zenobia patted Thabit whose head hung low. "We stop here for the night. I pray that Odainat stopped, too, somewhere ahead."

"A few hours rest, then we ride again. Thabit recovers quickly. He is a war horse." Ezechiel slid off his horse. "Let me groom Thabit for you."

"No, I want to undo the damage myself." Zenobia slid off Thabit and wrapped her arms around him. Thabit's nostrils flared, and his breath came in short, hot bursts. "I'm sorry my friend."

"I'll set up a watch command. We'll arise in three hours and continue," Ezechiel said.

The noise from Kithoth's party could be heard echoing off the stone walls of the homes that lined the streets. There was no need to be quiet. Maeonius looked at Nishan who rode next to him on a stolen cavalry horse. All Nishan wanted was to be second in command.

Maeonius glanced over his shoulder at the small army of twenty, but soon he would command thousands. And he would be wealthy beyond his imagination.

Flowers in full bloom perfumed the evening of death. The full moon reflected off limestone buildings that lined Emesa's streets making it a perfect night for a change of command. King Maeonius sounded good. He scowled. The first thing he would do as king would be to banish that yapping, whining thing that claimed to be his mother. His father could go with her. He didn't yap and whine, but Mokimu had no backbone.

"We are close," Nishan said.

"Yes." Maeonius shook his head. "I don't understand how my uncle could ride so far so fast."

"He slept like a dead man from sunset to sunrise. I am surprised he is here at all." Nishan grinned. "I guess the promise of wine and women is not as strong in him as it used to be."

"He took far too long to get here. I am eager to end his reign," Maeonius said.

"We should walk rather than ride."

"Why? The party's noise will cover our sounds," Maeonius growled.

Nishan stared at him. "As you wish."

"We'll dismount up there," Maeonius said.

"A good place."

Maeonius felt no fear, had no quaking or sweating hands, had no rapid heartbeat as he had expected. It was as if the gods favored him. He could smell the strong wine, hear the music. . . .

"Hairan!" he whispered.

"It does sound like your cousin," Nishan said. "How fortunate for you that they stopped to rest."

"The gods must favor me," Maeonius said.

"Of course."

"Where are the guards?" Maeonius asked.

"There were only two by the front door. My men. . . ."

"Your men!" He glared at Nishan. "Your men?"

"Friends of mine who chose to follow your lead. Admirers of your . . . abilities."

"These friends of yours . . . what did they do with the guards?"

"A simple ambush and a quiet throat slashing. Now two of my . . . your followers stand in their place." Nishan slapped Maeonius on the shoulder. "All is well."

Maeonius frowned. "All had better go as planned."

"Your plans are excellent," Nishan said.

"They had better be perfect." Maeonius dismounted, motioned to his men. He stopped, hand upright and stared at it. With this hand he commanded men. Odd. Nishan waited for him, and Maeonius shook himself from his reverie.

"Spread out and climb the garden walls. Advance when you see my signal," Maeonius said. "We wait for a while longer. I want to savor this moment."

CHAPTER
VIII

267 A. D. Emesa, Syria and Palmyra, Syria

$\mathcal{M}$usic and light cascaded between the columns and spilled into the garden. Maeonius and Nishan crept forward followed by twenty soldiers. Maeonius stopped behind a limestone column, one of many, that rose above him to hold up the open air roof of the atrium. Light from the full moon danced across the pool and wrapped itself around two dozen nude dancing girls.

"Look at the whore on the left, Maeonius. I want that one," Nishan said. "Then I'll kill her."

"As you wish," Maeonius said. How easy it was to grant favors. He slapped Nishan on the back. "Anything you want is yours."

Two of Kithoth's friends threw aside their togas and leaped into the pool after the laughing, screaming women.

"We go," Maeonius said.

Nishan put his hand on Maeonius' arm and gently pushed it down. "Watch a little longer. See, the slaves pour more wine."

Maeonius jerked his arm away. "So?"

"They'll soon be too drunk to lift a sword. Or too dead. If all has gone as planned, the wine has been poisoned."

"Poisoned? Who gave such an order? I doubt the poison. See, they suffer only drunkenness."

"It is a slow acting poison."

"I don't believe you," Maeonius grumbled. Who was this idiot who thought he knew everything?

Odainat's laughter bubbled across the atrium. He gently pushed a dancing girl away. "No, no, my dear. My queen would kill me."

"Only if she knew," Kithoth said. His words were slurred.

"I can keep no secrets from Zenobia." Odainat winked at Hairan. "Visit my son. He is young and virile. He needs you."

"Father!" Hairan blushed and his fingers slipped on the strings. A sour note mixed with the sweet ones.

"When I was your age . . ." He winked at Hairan.

"When you were his age, you were too busy hunting and fighting to be with a woman," Kithoth said.

"How do you know?" Odainat drained the last of his wine.

"I was riding next to you. We always complained that we had no women."

Maeonius stepped deeper into the shadows and away from the atrium. "Hairan is a fool like his father."

"More reason for you to rule," Nishan said.

"The time to strike is now."

"Think they are drunk enough yet?" Nishan asked.

"Maybe."

"Odainat's hand is steady."

"His hand is always steady." Maeonius shivered. He blinked the sweat from his eyes and cursed under his breath. Why should fear grip him now? He looked inside at the dancing girls, the fifty stupid men drinking, and that cousin of his, grinning and singing. "Let's go!"

"Not yet!" Nishan whispered. "Not yet or all is lost!"

"You are not the commander, I am." Maeonius thought briefly about killing Nishan. He was like a pesky insect that buzzed in one's ear.

"I know you are, but I am here to help you. Patience will assure us a victory. Besides, two of my . . . your men are on a secret mission to the palace."

Maeonius had to clamp his mouth shut, it had dropped open so far. "What kind of mission? Why was I not informed?"

"There was no time. The opportunity arose." Nishan pointed to Odainat. "See, he is still steady."

Laughter assaulted Maeonius' ears. They were stupid men who led Palmyra. But not for long. "We go."

"A little more time. They're not drunk enough." Nishan laid his hand on Maeonius' sword arm. "Patience will give us victory."

"I'm sick of your advice." Maeonius jerked his arm away. "We go now."

"It is too soon."

"Your mouth flaps like the old hag who sells fortunes in the market square. We go." Maeonius raised his arm and signaled the assault.

He saw Hairan across the atrium as the small army burst from the garden and into the columned atrium. Odainat was to Maeonius' right, but it was the sight of Hairan—puny, girlish singer of songs—that infuriated him.

"You die, my cowardly cousin!" Maeonius shoved a naked dancing girl into a pillar. As he passed her crumpled form, he saw a streak of brains and blood that followed the limestone column to the floor.

Men scrambled for swords and daggers and naked girls ran in all directions or crouched behind furniture. Blood already flowed in the shallow pool where a man lay face down, his hand frozen around the arm of a screaming woman.

"Fool," Maeonius whispered. He stared at Hairan who stood with his mouth open. One of the men charged toward his cousin. Hairan crashed the lyre into the man's face. The strings acted like a garotte and wrapped around his throat. Hairan pulled the loose strings tightly about the man's neck. Hairan let out a satisfied grunt as the soldier dropped to the marble floor, his head lolling to one side and a gusher of blood flowing down his body.

"A fine job, Son," Odainat yelled. He staggered once under the weight of two men who leaped on him. He threw off the one man easily, but the other clung to him with a hand clutching Odainat's face.

"I'm coming, Father!" Hairan, still holding the broken lyre, ran across the room. He swooped down, seized a sword, and ran it through the man's ribs.

Odainat shrugged and the man slid off his back. "Well done, Hairan." He slapped his son on the shoulder, then stumbled.

"Father! Are you hurt?"

"Only by the wicked grape. Look to your left." Odainat grabbed a short sword from the hand of a dead friend and charged the soldier who threatened his son.

"Thank you," Hairan said.

"I saved one who saved me." Odainat grinned.

Maeonius could not let them stand together, for the father would protect the son. He ran across the room, sword in one hand and dagger in the other, stopping short of Odainat.

"Maeonius?" Odainat said. "Have you come to help?"

"I have come to help myself." Maeonius swung at Hairan, but Odainat was too quick and pushed the boy from harm. A Roman infantryman charged Odainat, and both went down.

Odainat wrapped his powerful arms around the soldier's chest and squeezed until the man went limp. He snatched a dagger off the floor and sliced the traitor's throat.

Swords clanged as Maeonius stepped into a fight with his cousin. It was difficult to see Hairan through sweat and hate, but he was predictable with his moves. It was a surprise when his cousin let out, not a bellow as other soldiers do, but a whimper before he knelt on the floor clutching his stomach.

Maeonius had no time to finish Hairan off, but time would do it for him. He turned to face Odainat. Nishan and two others advanced toward the king.

"Back away! He is mine!" Maeonius shouted.

Nishan grunted, but kept advancing.

"You are a traitor, Nephew, and will die a traitor's death," Odainat lunged toward Maeonius, ignoring Nishan and his soldiers. He saw too late another soldier hidden behind a column, and turned to fight him. They performed macabre ritualistic movements across the atrium, the enemy soldier pulling Odainat away from Hairan.

Zenobia strained to hear sounds of music and laughter from Kithoth's, but the paving stones acted as drums to Thabit's feet and clattered out a rhythmical tune of their own that became a backdrop to Zenobia's prayers.

As soon as Zenobia saw lights from Kithoth's peristyle house, she felt as if time were caught in honey. She plowed through the thickened interval intent on saving Odainat. She almost called out for her husband, but let her soldier training block the wifely fear. Zenobia stopped the horse twenty cubits from Kithoth's and slid from the saddle. Gripping her sword, she raced toward the gaily lit house.

The sounds were not of laughing, dancing, and music. Zenobia fought her honeyed pace and ran up the dozen marble steps to the atrium that housed pandemonium. Kithoth was sprawled between two columns, his sword arm severed and lying beside him still clutching a dagger. They had been set upon by cowards.

Zenobia's war trained eyes sought the enemy through the chaos of fighting. She slipped on blood-slicked marble, but righted herself without losing sight of the tragedy that played before her. A pack of Maeonius' friends swung swords at Kithoth's guests who fought back, their alcohol stupor slowing actions. Most had to fight with table daggers or the broken legs off couches and chairs. One man smashed a pot over an assassin's head and brought the man down.

She saw him. Hatred turned from blistering hot to cold calculation. Maeonius was across the room with two dozen of his own between them. Zenobia skirted the atrium pushing her way past dancing girls who hid behind columns and under brocaded couches. She ignored their squeals of terror and concentrated on locating her quarry.

"Maeonius!" Zenobia screamed. He paid her no heed but continued slashing through the air above Hairan's head and waited for Odainat's son to rise.

Hairan was down on one knee, blood gushing from his abdomen. With his left hand holding his stomach, he swung his sword in an ineffectual arch in front of him.

Zenobia fought her way through the confusion, slashing the men she knew were fighting her husband's friends, and grimly advanced toward Hairan. She knew he would not survive, but neither would his murderer. Adara's only son had wanted to play the lyre instead of the sword; Zenobia should have let him.

Hairan plunged forward and jabbed his sword at Maeonius, nicking his sword arm. Maeonius laughed and brought his sandaled foot to his cousin's face with more force than was needed to topple the half-dead youth. Hairan laid across the tawny mosaic tiled picture of a lioness, and his blood turned her to crimson.

A bellow from Odainat startled Zenobia, and she watched in horror as her husband staggered across the atrium with no weapon other than his fierce temper and his bare hands. Maeonius wasn't much of a swordsman, but Odainat was already injured; the muscles of his upper left arm laid bare.

"Odainat! Catch!" Zenobia heaved her sword through the air. It whistled above the heads of the attackers, and Odainat caught it neatly with his good arm.

Zenobia drew a dagger from the sleeve of her chiton and sent one of the enemy to the underworld with a swift thrust between the ribs and into his heart. She was almost to Odainat's side. If he died, she wanted to die with him.

Maeonius stepped across the body of Hairan and faced the boy's father. "Uncle, your time of death has come. Not on the field of battle, but at a party. An ignoble end, but one that I shall cherish."

"Close your mouth. It flaps like the vultures who cannot hunt, but feed off the dead."

"A few more insults to add to the long list. I care not. Palmyra soon will be mine. I shall have the glory, not you."

"A puppy cannot take down a stag." Odainat held his sword steady and advanced across the slippery floor slowly, measuring each step.

"A wounded stag half drunk? The wine has been poisoned. You die by the sword or by the fire. It matters not to me."

Zenobia screamed. "You will die by my hand, Maeonius, a coward's death." The hot fury in her turned to cold metal as she shoved a dancing girl out of her way and was finally at Odainat's side.

"I have not long," he whispered.

"Cling to life, my love. I know anecdotes to poisons." Zenobia grimaced at Odainat's torn and bleeding left arm. She had seen worse wounds on the battlefield, but not on one she loved.

"Step back, Zenobia. I want to kill my nephew alone."

"You cannot."

"You are not safe. Flee to the desert. I fight this battle alone."

"I have always fought by your side. I will not leave. He comes." Zenobia stepped aside so that Odainat could swing. She saw too late that Odainat's sword arm quivered and his eyes were glazed as he lunged toward Maeonius.

Maeonius neatly sidestepped the thrust and brought his sword down across Odainat's back. Odainat fell to the floor, the sword clattered as it dropped beside him. Zenobia grabbed the sword and in one smooth motion, knocked Maeonius' sword from his hand.

"I will kill you a piece at a time like the cat who toys with a rat." Zenobia stepped toward Maeonius. She cared not whether anyone guarded her back. She had but one target, and she believed that even in death she could kill Maeonius.

"No!" Maeonius drew his dagger, parried with impotent movements then yelled, "Retreat! Retreat!" as he and his men ran from the atrium. Their footsteps clattered against the limestone paving blocks, a peculiar epitaph for a dying king.

Zenobia fell to her knees beside Odainat; her hand hovered over his body. She could not touch him while he still breathed for fear she would make his injuries worse. "Send for the physician!"

"Too late," Odainat said.

"No."

"The cloak of purple silk that you made for me . . ."

"It matters not. I will fashion you a new one."

"Find it."

"I will sew you another."

"I will not live past this night. I want you to promise that you'll wear the cloak."

Zenobia laid on the floor in a scarlet pool of Odainat's blood in order to see her husband's eyes. She touched his cheek. "The cloak was for the ruler of Palmyra. The Romans say that purple is the color of royalty."

"You must protect Palmyra from Maeonius, from any enemy. You must rule."

"Rule? We have sons."

"Too young."

"I will be regent."

"No. Wear the purple."

"I have no need. You will live." Zenobia kissed Odainat's cheek. "I have loved you more than I can say. Our love has protected us always."

"And I, you. Be strong for our people." Odainat sucked in his breath, let out a rattling sound and was still.

"Odainat, awaken. The physician comes." Zenobia felt strong hands pull her to her feet, and she jerked away. "Who dares take me from my husband's side?"

"I do, my queen." General Ezechiel bowed.

"Do not interfere! The king needs me."

"No more, my queen. He has gone to the land of your gods. Come, we must go. You're in danger."

"I will not leave. Don't you come near me. All of you, listen to me." Zenobia looked around the atrium at the dead, the dying, and the wounded. "I stay by King Odainat's side until he awakens. Where is the physician? I demand that he appear at once."

"I am here, my queen, tending to the wounded. The dead have no need of my services." The gray-haired physician wiped bloodied hands on his robes.

Zenobia grabbed her sword from the floor and leaped across bodies until she had the weapon under the man's chin. "You will tend to my husband. He will rise in the morn."

"Yes, my queen." Iason gathered his medicines and stood slowly. The sword followed him upward and rested against his long beard. His dark eyes were rimmed with the milk-white of old age and nestled in a woven wicker of wrinkles, but his muscles still held strength.

"Make haste, old man. His life's blood pools on the floor." Zenobia allowed the physician to push aside the sword.

Iason walked past her deftly skirting the carnage until he was at the side of Odainat. He knelt beside the king. "General Ezechiel, he is dead."

"Speak to me. I am queen."

"The king is dead."

"He is resting. Give him a potion."

"Iason is right," General Ezechiel said.

"No." Zenobia glanced around the atrium. Her soldiers and Odainat's had dropped to their knees and bowed their heads in tribute to a fallen leader. "There is no need to mourn. Odainat will rise." The dancing girls huddled together in twos and threes. Zenobia knew their tears were from fear. They had no other reason to cry.

"My queen, you must be strong. Palmyra can't exist without a leader. You have to be our leader lest Maeonius take the city." General Ezechiel put his arms around Zenobia. "Come, it is time to go."

"I will not leave my king."

"Others must tend to him. You have your sons."

"No, I cannot fight without my husband." Zenobia's sword clattered to the floor, and she knelt beside it, hunched over, and rocked back and forth, her arms wrapped about herself.

General Ezechiel threw up his hands. "General Abdas, tend to your queen."

General Abdas looked at the carnage that lay around him and backed away. "I can't."

Zenobia shook her head. "I need no one." She pushed away the hand that touched her shoulder.

Ezechiel stood before her. "You are a warrior."

"I have failed my king, my husband. What manner of warrior am I?"

"A good warrior who thinks not of a battle lost, but of a war to be won."

"I have lost more than a battle. This war is over."

"A weak thought for a strong woman."

"My strength has been cleaved in half. The right arm of my soul lies dead before me."

"What of Rome's treachery? Dare you let them wrest Palmyra from you to give to Maeonius? Will you let that fool make a mockery of King Odainat?"

"I have no heart to fight."

"Perhaps your heart is wrenched, but it still beats strong with a warrior's craving for justice." Ezechiel knelt before Zenobia. "I fall to my knees to pay homage to the ruler of Palmyra."

"Stand. I deserve no homage."

Ezechiel reached toward Zenobia, but did not touch her. His hand wavered above her shoulder. He gently grasped a strand of hair that had fallen and tucked it behind Zenobia's ear. "Do not sit on the floor like this," he whispered. "Palmyra has lost one leader tonight; let her not lose two."

"I stay."

"Your subjects must not see you like this. Word will get to Maeonius, and it will fuel his dark heart." Ezechiel allowed his hand to rest lightly on Zenobia's shoulder. She did not push it away.

"I sit close to my husband and hold his hand. What care I about subjects or Maeonius?"

"Care you for your sons?"

"My sons?"

"We must find your sons. Maeonius has vowed to kill them," Ezechiel said.

"Odainat's sons."

"In them lives the father."

"I have not the strength, Ezechiel. Help me."

"I have enough strength for both of us. Come. I know a safe place for you, and we'll look for Rebekeh and the sons of a king."

Zenobia allowed her general to pull her to a standing position. With a glance at her prone husband, she said a prayer for his safe passage to the other world. No matter her denial of his death, she could see that his soul had flown. She felt numb.

"Your sword, my queen."

"No. I cannot touch it." She walked away.

"How fares Zenobia?" Ezechiel dropped into a chair by the eating table and stretched out his legs.

His wife was a good-natured woman seemingly unaware of her beauty. Her hair wasn't ebony as was the hair of most of the women in Palmyra, but a deep brown with flashes of red when the sunlight shone on it. She never questioned him about what he did or why, although she seemed a little startled to see the queen placed on their sleeping couch two nights ago.

"Is she lucid yet?"

"Husband, I fear for her life on two counts. She sleeps as if drugged." Miriam knelt in front of her husband and removed his sandals. "I flinch every time I hear footsteps. I am certain that Maeonius has found us."

"My men have our home surrounded."

"I still fear for her." Miriam wrung a cloth out in warm water and spices. She washed the dust from her husband's feet. "What have you discovered tonight? Have you found Rebekeh and Odainat's sons?"

"Not yet."

"Do you think?. . ."

"I fear the worst. Rebekeh is but a girl. She is not used to intrigues."

"She is clever, Ezechiel." Miriam rose and placed the bowl of dirty water outside the door for the servants to tend to.

"I pray you're right."

"I have prayed to God often these last few hours."

"For what do you pray?"

"I ask that Zenobia be given the strength to fight Maeonius. I ask that you come home to me safely. I ask that justice be served." Miriam laid her hand on Ezechiel's shoulder. "I would be lost without you. Seeing our queen grieve for her husband reminds me how tenuous life is."

"Do you think God will find it in his heart to help a woman who prays not to him, but to many others?"

"I do."

Ezechiel chuckled. "How can you be so certain when our own rabbis argue against other gods?"

"I believe that God is just and loves all good people." Miriam shrugged. "I care not for learned arguments. They are too lofty and fail to see real life."

Ezechiel laughed aloud. He had always loved this intelligent woman for her wild thoughts, and he pulled her down onto his lap. "If our rabbis learn of your beliefs, they'll descend on our home like carrion."

"They would find me a poor student." Miriam kissed him. "Where can we go? I have need of you. Our queen sleeps in our couch and our daughters in theirs."

"Blow out the lamps. The floor will not seem hard."

"Ezechiel! What will the servants think?"

"That we love each other."

"You are wicked." Miriam leaned over and blew out the kitchen lamp.

Zenobia awakened and stared about the room. Sun filtered through a goatskin window covering that kept out the desert night chill. Shafts of sunlight draped themselves across the striped couch on which she lay amongst tangled linen bedclothes. The room wasn't large, but it was clean with freshly painted walls. A mural directly across from her showed a sunset on sand dunes done in shades of reds and pinks that drifted toward dusty purples. The familiarity of the scene saddened her. She didn't know where she was, but she knew that she was heartsick.

Ordinary household noise—the banging of pots in the kitchen on the other side of the hide curtain that hung across the door and the shouts of servants as they went about their duties—was familiar, but different. Zenobia as not in her own dwelling. In her own dwelling she would not hear those noises from her sleeping room.

She sat up. Next to her on a plain wooden table was a pitcher of water and a drinking mug. It smelled of sulphur, so it was from Ain Efqa Spring. She was in Palmyra. Frowning, she shook her head to rid it of confused thoughts. She listened to the sounds of the household again. She heard children singing and the soft voice of a woman telling them to be quiet. Outside, Zenobia heard a steady march of hob-nailed sandals on limestone walkways. If she were a captive, it was an unusual situation.

Zenobia untangled herself from the bedclothes and crossed the small room to the window. She peered through the edge of the covering. The guards were her own. By the gods, it had better not be a mutiny! The sunlight flashed on their armor as they marched in perfect unison.

She gasped as the horror of Odainat's death pushed through her hazy thoughts and planted itself full-bloomed into her consciousness. Zenobia screamed as she fell to her knees, her fingernails scraping down the plastered walls.

The sounds of feet hurrying into the room did not arouse her curiosity. Zenobia huddled on the floor and tried to shut all thoughts from her mind.

"My queen, allow me to help you back to bed," Miriam whispered.

"Leave me." Zenobia tried to push away the woman's soft hands that gripped her upper arms.

"I cannot in good conscience leave you prostrate on the floor. It is unseemly."

"I care not."

"Come. I care." Miriam gripped Zenobia's arms hard enough to lift her to her knees. "Come."

Zenobia knew a commander's voice when she heard one. It would be useless to argue with Miriam. She knew, now, in whose dwelling she had been sequestered. She allowed herself to be guided back to the sleeping couch. "Where is Ezechiel?"

Miriam poured a mug of water from the pitcher and held it to Zenobia's lips. "Drink."

"No."

"It will replace the tears you have shed in your sleep."

"Need I more tears? Are my sons found? Dead?"

"They are still in hiding. A good thing, for Maeonius has stormed the palace in search of them. I fear that he will come here next although Ezechiel says that the coward and his men are too fearful to attack such a well-guarded place as this." Miriam held the mug closer to Zenobia.

"Maeonius lingers here? Why has he not turned tail and run to hide in the desert?" Zenobia drank all the water before handing the mug back to Miriam.

"Have you need of sustenance? You should eat to keep your strength." Miriam snapped her fingers at a servant who hovered near the door. "Bring bread and honey and goat's milk for your queen."

"You avoid my question."

"I am not a political person. I cannot guess the motives of an usurper." Miriam clapped a hand across her mouth. "I am sorry. Maeonius has not the brains to be an usurper."

"Does he have the palace and commands some of the soldiers?"

"Yes."

"You have spoken in truth. How many follow him?"

"I know not. Ezechiel is trying to discern this. He rages at your nephew."

"Not my nephew. I have disowned him many times in anger, but this time I will do so formally in front of the senate." Zenobia plucked at the covers. "How fare the people in the palace? My servants, my palace guards?"

"Your loyal servants were cut down by disloyal soldiers. Some of the palace guards put themselves to the sword rather than take the oath that Maeonius tried to force on them. Others died protecting the palace."

"Poor guards. I left but a few. The rest went with me to save Odainat." Zenobia blinked to hold back tears. "I thought I had no tears left."

Miriam sat on the bed next to her and gathered Zenobia in her arms. "Cry for the king, for yourself, and for Palmyra. It is a bleak day in our history."

"I have no time for tears. How long has it been since . . . since Odainat died?"

"This is the fourth day since Kithoth's party. It is early in the morning."

"How do the citizens view Maeonius?"

"I was at the Ain Efqa with the laundress seeing to the bedding. The women did not speak at first. I took it that they were afraid that Ezechiel had turned traitor." Miriam sniffed. "I started things by talking loudly of the cowardly Maeonius. Soon others were showing their anger at his disruption of their peaceful lives. From that, I believe that most of Palmyra would like the vulture removed. Most women reflect the views of their husbands."

"I have much to do. I must secure the throne, find my sons, and . . ." The rest of the sentence would not pass Zenobia's lips.

"See to the king's burial." Miriam dabbed at her eyes with the sleeve of her chiton.

"Where lies my husband?"

"In the Temple of Bel. Ezechiel said that in your religion, he is the supreme god. General Abdas said that Bel is in armor, and that it is fitting for a warrior to lie in his temple."

"That's true. I would have chosen the same." Zenobia stared at the mural of the sun setting over the desert. "I have asked Bel to protect Odainat in battle, but I never thought to ask him to protect him in everyday affairs until it was too late."

"At times it seems the gods—God—has plans that we cannot change no matter how many prayers." Miriam sighed. "I question the wisdom of my God almost daily. I shall probably be punished for my blasphemy."

"I think not, Miriam, for you have a good soul."

"Do I? With blasphemy in my heart?"

"You judge yourself too harshly."

"Do you hear that? I think Ezechiel has returned."

Zenobia heard marching, then footsteps in the kitchen. "Allow me a few minutes to make myself presentable, then I should like to see my general. I have sore need of advice."

Ezechiel stood before Zenobia, helmet tucked under his left arm. A thin white line wound its way around the upper part of his arm, and Zenobia remembered when he had received that wound as a young infantryman. When his lieutenant had fallen, Ezechiel led the men toward the Persian army with no fear. Even when slashed badly, Ezechiel continued to command the charge. That had been more than ten years ago.

"You have seen the situation in Palmyra. Which do we do first? Seize the palace or bury my husband? Or find my sons?"

"The Temple of Bel is guarded; the senate, and other government buildings; this dwelling is guarded; the Ain Efqa Spring is protected by General Abdas' troops, although not well; and we have surrounded the palace."

"How many of our troops have crossed to Maeonius?"

"Not more than one in ten. Some Roman soldiers from the Palmyran units joined Maeonius also. They who have joined him are of no consequence."

"I yearn to bury Odainat. The gods wait for him." Zenobia watched her general's face for a clue to his thoughts. There was none.

"As you wish."

"I love my sons and miss them sorely."

"Understandable."

"However, our troops are stretched thin trying to protect the city in pieces instead of as a whole. Have many citizens have been killed?"

"Not as many as I feared. Several have whispered to me that they wish you to fight Maeonius."

"I will fight him. The question is how." Zenobia smoothed the cover beneath her hand. "I can wait to bury Odainat. I presume he has been preserved?"

"Yes."

"If I find my sons unharmed, then a spy may tell Maeonius where they are. I have to assume that Rebekeh is so naïve that no one can fathom her thoughts, including us. If . . . when I find my sons, then we will have no kingdom to rule."

"We have plans to make," Ezechiel said.

"It will be an easy battle, for Maeonius never listened to battle strategy. I thank the gods for his ignorance." Zenobia glanced about the room. "I do not see my sword."

"You rejected it."

"I was but a wife in pain who wanted no part of the instrument of death. Now I am a vindictive warrior and have need of my sword."

"I rejoice that the warrior queen returns to her people." Ezechiel bowed. "I have your sword in our cella."

"One never looks to the weak as killers. How wrong that is. The weak have moments of power." Zenobia stared across the colored dunes of the mural behind Ezechiel. "I am ready to face Maeonius. It is best to kill the scorpion before he stings again."

CHAPTER
IX

267 A. D. Palmyra, Syria

Zenobia counted the number of men as they marched past the small room at the army barracks where she had taken up residence. There were more than enough soldiers to accomplish her mission. She had moved here as soon as she had come to her senses. She needed to be close to the men so that they would be used to her presence. They had to understand that she was in control of most of the men even though she no longer controlled the palace or the southeastern section of Palmyra.

She had had to leave Ezechiel's home. In a minute she would have to solve the problem of which general to use and couldn't deal with it as long as she was in the middle of Ezechiel's family. She had to be certain that her choice was made with reason, not thankfulness.

Odainat's general, Abdas, was capable, but he was used to her husband's ways, not hers. She was more comfortable with Ezechiel although he had less experience. She could not command two armies. They had to be merged.

The dreaded knock on the frame of the open door caused Zenobia to sigh. She signaled for General Abdas to enter. He stood at attention before the table where she sat with drawings of the palace spread before her.

"Relax, General Abdas." Zenobia pointed to the only other piece of furniture in the small command room. "Please sit."

"As you wish." General Abdas placed the chair carefully so that he was at an angle and could view the door.

Zenobia wondered whether this was habit. "I have a difficult task ahead of me."

"Maeonius will not be difficult to capture."

"It is not that battle of which I speak, but the one that rages in my mind." Zenobia forced herself to keep her hands folded motionlessly in her lap. She had Abdas' attention. She looked steadily into his dark eyes.

"You were my husband's confidant, his first in command, his best officer. He rewarded you with the rank of general. He is no longer here, and I can't command two armies. I plan to merge King Odainat's army with mine, hence there will be one general." With a start, Zenobia saw pride in Abdas' features. He even sat straighter, if that were possible.

Zenobia broke eye contact and stared at the drawings in front of her. She had chosen her general, but at what cost? Forcing herself to look at Abdas, she continued. "I have always admired your methods, but General Abdas, I can't work with you as well as I can with General Ezechiel."

"General Ezechiel? What do you mean?" Before General Abdas' face turned impervious, anger had flashed across it. "He can't command. He is too young, too inexperienced. It was not long ago that he was a foot soldier."

"I know that you have more experience, but I fear that our methods are too different for us to work together effectively." Zenobia refused to glance away from his brown-eyed stare that bore into her own dark eyes.

"I would not be afraid to disagree with you."

"I know that, and it's a valuable trait, but . . ."

"I know how Odainat thinks . . . thought." General Abdas blinked.

"As much as I value how well you fought with the king, my strategies are different."

"I can help you change."

"You don't understand. I don't want to change. I want someone who will work with me, not someone who expects me to follow them. I have never followed any man except Odainat. Even so, I fought the way that was best for me."

"All you want is someone who will not tell you your absurdities in battle."

"Don't be ridiculous. I need someone who will be a guide, an advisor. I need someone who can point out my weaknesses. However, I must have a second in command who understands my thinking in battle, but does not feel a need to change me."

"I see." General Abdas said. "Is it because your sister-in-law and I were? . . ."

"No, I had forgotten the incident in the funerary temple." Zenobia clutched the maps in front of her to steady her hands. She felt remorse for not having wondered at the fate of her sister and brother-in-law. Had Tarab known of her son's plans to assassinate Odainat and Hairan? "General, what happened to Tarab?"

"She and Mokimu fled to Damascus."

"They don't support Maeonius?"

"Mokimu disowned his son."

"They were afraid of him?"

"They were afraid of you."

"Me?"

"Tarab knows you don't like her. She was afraid that you would use Maeonius' assassination of her brother as an excuse to execute her," General Abdas said.

"That's preposterous."

"Is it? I saw anger in your eyes that quickly turned to hatred."

"Toward Maeonius and other traitors."

"I provided Mokimu and Tarab with a military escort."

"Really? Without my consent?"

"You were . . . unable to be found at the time I had to act."

"Very well." Zenobia dismissed the conversation. It was another unpleasant reminder of the last few days that she could do without.

General Abdas rose. "May I leave, my queen?"

"Yes. You are still a general in the army. I will have your orders later. I would like for you to be in charge of training new officers. You have invaluable experience and can serve Palmyra skillfully in that capacity."

"Very well." General Abdas saluted and marched from the room, his hob-nailed sandals rang against the stone floor.

Zenobia leaned against the brocaded cloth of her chair. She had expected anger, but not the quiet acceptance after a meager argument. Perhaps he felt as uncomfortable serving her as she was in having him second-in-command.

General Ezechiel strode through the door. "You look pensive. Is there a problem?"

"Only that I can't have two generals whose methods are so different." Zenobia motioned to the chair that had been vacated by Abdas.

Ezechiel sat. "I understand. General Abdas has many more years experience than do I. I would be content to serve in whatever capacity you think worthy of me."

"You give in too easily." Zenobia wondered why she hadn't talked to Ezechiel earlier. She might have been tempted to let Ezechiel step down.

"I am realistic."

"So am I. We work too well together for me to retrain an old general to my ways. I want you with me as my second hand."

"Not General Abdas?"

"No."

"He is not likely to take this well."

"He was all right."

"Be careful of him. His pride rules his emotions," Ezechiel said.

"He is a military man and used to following orders."

"For years he received his only orders from his king."

"He wouldn't have been happy following my orders. He would've expected me to change," Zenobia said.

Ezechiel laughed. "He doesn't understand you—or any woman."

"Be careful, General, lest you insult your queen."

"I think you should be careful." Ezechiel glanced toward the door, then leaned forward. "I don't trust General Abdas," he whispered.

"Why not?"

"I don't know. There have been no improprieties that I've ever observed."

"Perhaps we're overreacting to everyone because of Maeonius." Zenobia choked on the name.

"I pray you're right."

Zenobia grinned as she noted the confused look on Ezechiel's face. "You have some questions?"

"I am not certain what to do now."

"Prepare for a sunrise battle. We send troops through the main gate as well as the back. Have men cover the wadi if we have enough."

Zenobia tapped the drawing. "It would be easier to invade the palace if Odainat's ancestors hadn't planned so well."

"No secret entrances?"

"None."

"I'll report to you at dusk as usual. I'll do my duties well. Thank you for believing in me." General Ezechiel saluted as he turned and left the room.

The only light in the small bedroom next to the command room was an oil lamp beneath a statue of Bel. The Babylonian god was flanked by the two gods of Palmyra, Iarhibol and Aglibol. Offerings of dates lay at their feet. Before she had gone to her sleeping couch, Zenobia had stared south toward the palace she couldn't see and promised her sons that she would hold them in her arms again.

A knock on the door frame awakened Zenobia. She sat up quickly and slid her dagger from its hiding place in the sleeve of her chiton, then realized that an assassin wouldn't knock. She had no need of guards since Ezechiel was close. She was surrounded by sleeping soldiers inside the compound. "Who is there?"

"General Ezechiel."

"Enter." Zenobia pulled the linen covers about her shoulders.

The general pulled aside the leather curtain.

"Why do you come in the middle of the night?" she asked.

"It is nearly dawn."

"A fleeting night too short for rest, but I care not." Zenobia rose from the sleeping couch and tossed her long, thick hair behind her shoulders. "Is there any woman to attend me?"

"My wife has asked for the honor."

Zenobia's mouth opened, then closed as she tried to hide her shock. "She is not of the servant class."

"In troubled times Miriam says that rules must be broken. She says to trust no one, not even the servants. We know not who has joined Maeonius."

"A clever woman, your wife. I have no armor, so she won't have any trouble helping me. Please send Miriam to me with my gratitude." Zenobia motioned toward the statues of her gods. "Will these discomfort her?"

"No. She is liberal in her ways of thinking." Ezechiel chuckled.

"She would set our rabbis into spasms if they knew her thoughts. She reminds me of you. Neither of you care what others think, and you like to ponder ideas yourselves."

"Life is a maze." Zenobia looked out the small window at the sky. "It's still dark. I fear the sun will not shine for us. We should all pray this day."

"Don't speak of such things. Think of the glorious battles you have always won," Ezechiel said.

"I won them side by side with the man I loved."

"He will ride with you today."

"I can only hope."

The sun rose behind Zenobia as she rode Thabit toward General Ezechiel. A breeze ruffled through her chiton and riding pants. She felt unclothed without her armor. As reassurance, she touched the hilt of her sword. It felt good to have it at her side once more. Thabit's hoofs on the packed earth as she rode toward the mall between the barracks sounded lonely without Odainat's horse to echo the cadence. Zenobia had no more tears to shed. She had cried herself to sleep again last night for Odainat, for her missing sons, and for her stepson, Hairan. Poor Hairan, who never liked to fight, had died fighting.

"Ezechiel, where are the troops? Why are they not ready?" Zenobia looked around the mall and quickly counted. Only her men and a few of Odainat's soldiers were suited up and ready to march on the palace.

"They are nowhere to be found."

"Check with General Abdas or his aide. Perhaps they had to chase after Maeonius." Zenobia shrugged. "Unlikely, however."

"We have half as many men to attack Maeonius. The palace is too large to surround in a siege. Need we postpone the battle?" Ezechiel asked.

"We can't. The longer we wait, the weaker we appear. Some people always cross over to what they perceive as the stronger side. We cannot afford to lose support. We attack as planned. A thin battle line is better than none."

Zenobia looked at the small number of soldiers beneath her command. The others who had disappeared would be dealt with later.

Now she had to decide how best to proceed. Maeonius would know that she was coming. He would not expect an army to march through Palmyra, but go around and come in from the south. Zenobia would use no cover, but march her men the quickest way to the palace. She gave the orders and turned Thabit out of the compound onto the paved streets. She hoped Maeonius would quiver with fright at the sound of her army.

As they marched through Palmyra, word flew in front of them; and soon, the people lined the streets from the Honorific Column to the Monumental Arch. As Zenobia, flanked by General Ezechiel, and the army flowed through the Arch, they turned southeast and followed Odainat Way past the Temple of Bel. Zenobia returned the salutes from the sentinels at the Temple who guarded Odainat. She prayed for her sons and the souls of Odainat and Hairan, then pushed away thoughts of what might have been and concentrated on what had to be.

The palace rose before her, two stories high, with a plain facade behind columns that hid the opulent beauty inside. It was deceptively quiet. Ezechiel pointed to the soldiers on the flat roof at the front armed with spears. Zenobia nodded. Archers would be in place behind them.

"Ezechiel, there seem to be more men than I had thought."

"It could be for show. The back of the palace might be unguarded. We didn't come in secret. I'll attack from the rear." Ezechiel smiled. "May your gods and mine give us victory today."

"If they don't, we'll pray some more and fight again." Zenobia waited until the army had disappeared behind the palace before she gave the order to attack. Under cover of a hail of arrows, she rode Thabit up the stone steps to the palace and watched the soldiers heave the battering ram against the thick, wooden doors. The rhythmic thud, thud, thud, made her shiver as she realized that the fight had really begun.

The doors were sturdy, and it wasn't until she had lost count that Zenobia heard the first splintering of wood. A few more thrusts with the giant tree trunk, and they were able to push the doors inward. She withdrew her eight inch hunting dagger from its sheath; her sword would be useless in the tight space of the atrium.

She hadn't expected Maeonius to lead his men in the fight, and he was not in sight. As she pushed through the flimsy line of soldiers, she wielded her dagger with such ferocity that she sliced between scaled sections of armor with ease. The curved blade hid its silver color beneath ruby red blood that matched the jewels on its handle. Zenobia refused to think of these men as former infantry-men in Odainat's army or hers. They had chosen to follow the trai-tor and thus became traitorous.

She faltered once when her blade caught a young soldier in his midsection. He gasped, said he was sorry, and collapsed at her feet. It was the remorse in his youthful eyes that made her hate Maeonius even more.

Ezechiel was on the far side of the atrium, having fought his way through from the back of the palace quickly. That surely meant that Maeonius had to be in the upper levels. Zenobia pushed one soldier into the atrium's pool in her haste to get to the steps. She didn't have time to kill him. She raced up two at a time and burst into the wide hall that led to the many apartments. The noise of fighting was muted. No one guarded the curtained archway into Odainat's chambers. Maeonius would be there. He coveted every-thing that had been the king's.

Zenobia crept toward the drapes that billowed gently in the breeze and drifted back and forth across the marble floor. She stopped. The last time she had been in Odainat's chambers, he had been alive. She didn't want to view it empty, or worse, with Maeonius inside, but she had to. She forced herself to pull the drapes back with the blade of her dagger, smearing the blue silk with crimson. She looked inside the large cella that served as a gathering place for friends and family. No one was there. Zenobia stepped through the doorway and slid along the marble wall past the alabaster pillars that disappeared in the silk draped ceil-ing.

When Maeonius burst into the cella from Odainat's sleeping room, Zenobia was not surprised, but her heart constricted just the same. Hatred for her husband's assassin crowded everything from her vision except his nephew's ugly face.

"So the scorpion has retreated to Odainat's rooms." Zenobia's thumb rubbed against a ruby in the handle of her dagger.

"I expected you." Maeonius held his sword in readiness.

"I see you finally learned how to hold a sword."

"General Abdas taught me." He nodded to his right.

General Abdas stepped into the center of the room from behind a marble pillar and stood behind Maeonius.

"Seize him, Abdas."

"I can't," General Abdas said.

"Seize him!" She shouted. Maeonius laughed, a high pitched squeal that made Zenobia clench her teeth. "Why do you laugh? You sound like the hyenas in Africa."

"He laughs because I am second in command in Maeonius' Royal Army," General Abdas said.

Zenobia felt her mouth drop open. She closed it with a snap that cut off her surprise and turned it to anger. "You traitor! How could you do this to me? To Odainat?"

"You had no need of me."

"You are worse than a traitor, Abdas. You are witless to think that you could beat my army."

"Part of your army is with me. Actually, more than half have followed me to Maeonius."

Zenobia stared at Odainat's former general. She catalogued his weaknesses, what few there were. Her husband had chosen his general well. "A fair fight dictates that I be allowed to draw my sword."

Maeonius leaped toward her in a motion much faster than Zenobia thought possible. He ignored a shout from General Abdas and had her backed into the wall, his sword inches from her midsection. She let loose with an ancient Egyptian curse. She had failed to consider that the untrained often act irrationally. She had misjudged him a second time.

With nothing more than her dagger between her and being maimed by Maeonius, Zenobia hunched low to avoid the two-handed swing of her nephew and lunged forward. She slashed Maeonius' left thigh as his sword whistled above her just before she drove her head into his gut. His sword flew from his hands and clanged against the wall. If he had been experienced, he would have killed her with the first swing of the sword. She rolled over.

They collapsed on the floor and rolled together across the cool marble. Maeonius bent her hand back until she could no longer grasp her dagger. It clattered across the floor, and slid out of reach.

"I will kill you, Maeonius, with my bare hands." Zenobia clawed his face and left deep scratches across his left cheek.

"One thing I want before you die," Maeonius panted as he

wrapped his legs around hers and pushed her under him. He pulled at her gold shoulder brooch and tore it away from her stola.

Zenobia tried to cover her breasts, but Maeonius jerked her arms down and wedged them between their bodies. No man but Odainat had ever touched her. "You are not man enough." She wriggled around and brought her knee up, but Maeonius blocked her.

"I have waited years for this." Maeonius bit her nipple.

Zenobia ignored the pain and pushed back the gasp. "Stupid, insipid little boy. You'll never be the man Odainat was. You'll never get it up."

Zenobia heard the sharp slap before ringing in her ears told her that she'd been hit. Her anger dulled the pain, and she felt nothing but the weight of her assailant. "You can't do a man's job when you have to fight the woman for love." Zenobia taunted Maeonius with her laughter. She remembered his deficiencies all too well.

He slapped her again, and she seized the moment to jerk her knee up. This time she hit Maeonius in the vulnerable spot between his legs. Zenobia felt the satisfying squish of contact. He let out a bellow and slid away from her.

The marble floor was cold against her breasts as she squirmed away from Maeonius. She brushed hair from her face as she stood. Zenobia drew her sword. "On your feet. You can't even rape a woman." She kicked Maeonius' sword toward him. "Fight like a man."

"Abdas, kill her!" Maeonius shouted.

"It is not my fight," General Abdas said. "You must battle the queen alone for the keys to the kingdom."

"I can't," Maeonius wailed.

Zenobia glanced at General Abdas. The muscles in his jaw were bunched tightly, and his face was red. A vein stood out on his forehead. She had only seen him this angry once before. "Raise your sword, Maeonius, for I care not if you fight. I will run you through. General Abdas will not help you."

"No! Don't kill me. Send me into exile. Forgive me. Forgive me for my mother's sake." Maeonius dropped to his knees in front of Zenobia.

She backed away from the quivering bundle on the floor in front of her. Aghast, she stared at Maeonius, then looked to her right where

General Abdas stood. He seemed as confused as she.

General Abdas shouted and slammed into Zenobia, pushing her to the floor where they fell in a heap. She felt stupid to have let her eyes stray from the snake that had moments before been begging for his life. She was astonished to see that General Abdas had blocked the dagger thrown by Maeonius. The jeweled handle quivered as it protruded from his back.

Zenobia pulled the dagger from General Abdas with a smooth movement and sent it sailing across the room as Maeonius came toward her with his sword.

The cur dove to the floor and rolled out of harm's way. Cursing, Maeonius scrambled to his feet and ran from the cella. "I live to kill you, Zenobia," he shouted as he escaped.

"I fear not you, Maeonius, but my own demons." She looked at Odainat's fallen general. "I will get Iason, the physician, for you Abdas."

"No. I don't want to live." Abdas coughed.

"Because of your betrayal of me? It was my fault. I have never handled people as well as Odainat. Forgive me."

"Death is better than living with my treachery."

"A mistake, not treachery."

"Don't be easy with your enemies. It will haunt you. Hang my body outside the walls for the vultures to pick apart. It is what a traitor deserves." Abdas sucked in air and the wound in his back frothed with bright pink bubbles.

"You saved my life," Zenobia said.

General Abdas' eyes were as glassy as the Ain Efqa when there was no breeze to ripple the water.

"Abdas?" Zenobia knew he couldn't answer. His last wish was for a traitor's hanging, but she could not do that to Odainat's general. He had betrayed her, but for years Abdas had been loyal to Odainat. He would have a hero's funeral. He had saved her life, thus could not be what the Christians called a Judas. He would have an honorable Christian funeral.

Clattering in the outside hall warned Zenobia that soldiers were coming. She pulled her sword from under General Abdas' body and scrambled to her feet. She waited to see whose soldiers would burst through the silk draperies.

General Ezechiel burst through the door and skidded to a stop.

He stared at Zenobia's breasts, blushed, and looked at the floor. "The palace is yours," he stammered.

"Thank you."

Ezechiel disappeared into Odainat's sleeping chamber. When he returned, he threw a cloak to Zenobia.

She caught the purple silk easily and held it in her hands.

"It is to cover yourself."

"I know."

"Please."

"It's the royal cloak I made for Odainat. It is soft and still smells of Odainat." Zenobia held it to her face and rubbed her cheek against it. "He wore it into battle. Look, here and here. It is stained with blood. His or the enemies? No matter."

"Cover yourself. It pains me to see the queen standing so."

Zenobia threw the cloak around her shoulders and let it settle gently against her bare skin. "Am I fit to rule Palmyra now?" Zenobia couldn't hide the bitterness in her voice.

Ezechiel did not answer.

"I'm sorry, Ezechiel."

"No matter. We have the palace. I will make certain that all the treasonous soldiers are executed in the desert and left for the vultures."

"No!"

Ezechiel stared at her.

Zenobia looked down at Abdas. He had been right. She could not be weak. "Let the executions be in the theatre so the public can attend. Let no one think that Zenobia is an impotent queen."

"It shall be so," Ezechiel said.

"Leave me." Zenobia glanced around Odainat's apartment. "I need to tend to some things."

"May I send in men for General Abdas?"

"Tell them to hurry." Ezechiel nodded and left. Zenobia heard him give orders to the soldiers who had waited in the hall.

Zenobia pulled the purple cloak tighter about her shoulders and walked from the cella without looking at the dead man who lay there. She stepped into Odainat's sleeping room. Why was it emptier now than before? There had been times when she had tended to his clothing while he was not in the room, but now it echoed her pain.

Zenobia drifted about the spacious room and touched the sleeping couch, Odainat's favorite chair that held Hairan's second favorite lyre, the table at which so many decisions had been made. She saw a string ball in the corner. Odainat always played ball with the boys during the heat of the day while Hairan played lilting tunes that were drowned out by youthful voices of the younger sons. Remnants of her family haunted this room to remind her that she was alone.

The silk draperies at the window billowed and danced, mocking her with their cheerful movements. She hugged Odainat's cloak closer to merge his essence with hers. He hadn't worn it to Kithoth's party as she had thought. Zenobia would wear this vestige of her husband as he had; on the field of battle and on the throne.

When Zenobia entered the amphitheatre the following morning just as the sun rose, she heard the gasps that rippled through the audience. She knew it wasn't the palace guards in their polished armor that had caused the stir, nor was it her presence as their ruler, or the one hundred and fifty men waiting to be executed. They had expected her to take over the kingdom.

It was the visibility of Odainat's purple cloak that gave her subjects tangible evidence of her intent to continue to rule as a nation independent of Rome. She looked neither right nor left as she was escorted to the dias that was halfway down the steps. Zenobia settled herself on the cushioned throne, nodded to Ezechiel who stood on the stage below her with the condemned traitors, and listened as the crowd settled to an eerie quiet.

Zenobia forced herself to look at the men lined up in five rows, thirty to a row on the stage where usually Roman and Greek tragedies and comedies played. She was shocked at the youthfulness of some of the men, and she wondered if they had families. She noted that the scarred, grizzled soldiers showed little emotion. It was a sorrowful day for Palmyra. After today, there would be many widows.

Five of her most powerful soldiers stood next to granite blocks, their swords shining in the sun. Ezechiel had chosen the executioners, for she did not have the gall. It had been easy to try to kill Maeonius. It had been easy to do whatever necessary to save Odainat. But here there was no battle, no hatred flowing from an enemy's eyes, no fight to survive. She had to have the executions, but it would be one of the most painful moments of her life. Zenobia wondered if layers of painful duties would callous her heart.

The first five men were made to kneel and place their chins over the edge of a block of stone, their necks exposed and hands tied behind their backs. All the men had been stripped of their uniforms and stood before the crowd naked.

The executioner's swords were raised in unison at Ezechiel's command. Zenobia clenched her teeth together so tightly that she felt the muscles in her jaws bulge while at the same time she feigned relaxation by making her hands lay in her lap. There must be no show of weakness.

When the swords came down swiftly and cut through life, Zenobia had to force herself not to flinch as they rang against the stones. She blinked when the traitors' heads thudded down to the stage floor like goat-skin jugs that had been filled to bursting.

The crowd cheered as each successive group of five men was beheaded. The executioners were covered with blood, some of it already drying in the heat. It flaked off like poorly applied paint on a mural. Blood flowed across the stage, dripped down the front, and soaked into the cracks between the stones.

One executioner slipped in the blood as he was brought down his sword and accidentally cut an old, but muscular soldier across the back. The man's scream of agony brought a gasp from the crowd followed by hissing. Zenobia lost composure, and a tiny scream escaped. It was smothered by the noise of the crowd. She didn't have to tell Ezechiel to order the stage washed. Soldiers with buckets of precious water from the Ain Efqa tossed the water across the stage until it was clean. The lifeblood of Palmyra washed away the lifeblood of the traitors. Three more times the executions were halted while the blood was washed away. Each time, Zenobia settled into a deeper depression. So many had betrayed Odainat and her that she wondered whether she could save Palmyra.

The last of the men had been executed before noon. Zenobia followed her palace guards out of the amphitheatre. She tried not to look at the people as she passed them. They were so quiet that she could hear her slippers scrape against the steps.

This was the easiest of her tasks, as repugnant as it was. Odainat's funeral would try her strength. Seeing Hairan in the temple would rip out her heart. And finding her sons would take what remained of

149

her fortitude. She vowed, as she left the theatre, that she would never have a moment of weakness again. If she had to march across the world to prove Palmyra's power, then she would do so. Odainat's name would live in history.

CHAPTER

X

267 A. D. Palmyra, Syria

    It was not yet light when Ezechiel made his way through the palace to the queen's apartment. His footsteps echoed against the marble walls and floors too loudly even though he wore soft-soled shoes rather than his hob-nailed sandals.

He sent the lady-in-waiting to tell Zenobia that he must see her. He paced back and forth in the cella and tried to ignore his sweaty palms. Why did he feel like a young stallion every time he was near his queen? He had a beautiful wife and two charming daughters. He believed in being true to his wife.

The task at hand was difficult, but who else could convince the queen? He heard a rustling behind him and turned. Zenobia paused in the doorway as if to assess the situation. She looked beautiful. Her almond shaped eyes were half-closed from sleepiness. Dark hair flowed down her back, unbound and uncovered, and wisps of hair floated about her face.

"Ezechiel, is anything wrong?"

"No."

"You're acting odd." She bent her head and stared at him with pursed lips. "It isn't my sons, is it?"

"No."

"Please don't stand there like a young boy with a dreadful secret. Tell me why you've dragged me from my sleeping couch."

Zenobia's frown was like honey to him. Ezechiel cleared his throat. "My queen, the ceremony is ready at the Temple of Bel for our king. It is time to lay King Odainat's body to rest."

"I will not allow King Odainat or Hairan to be buried without my sons present. Vaballathus and Arraum should see their father and brother one more time." Zenobia turned away from Ezechiel and stared out the window at the rising sun.

Ezechiel went to the window and stood as close to Zenobia as he dared. He looked out to see what Zenobia saw. The sun hung low and shadowed the wadi below.

She rubbed her eyes with the fingertips of both hands. Zenobia pushed back her uncombed hair and held it off her neck. She had no idea what it did to his composure. He felt flecks of perspiration on his upper lip.

"You're right, Ezechiel. We can wait no longer. King Odainat needs to join his ancestors. The family funerary temple is waiting for him, and Adara waits for her son. Our son."

Ezechiel nodded. "Yes, he was as much your son as hers." He cleared his throat. "It's time to send them to your gods."

"Not yet."

"Tomorrow, then." Ezechiel held his breath. He was not used to giving the queen a direct order. He expected her eyes to flash with anger; he expected her to whirl around and dress him down as she had done a young soldier only yesterday.

"All right. It shall be tomorrow." She looked at him with a thousand years of sadness in her eyes.

He wanted to hold her, to take the hurt away. Ezechiel waited until the moment passed. "We will have the parting ceremony without your sons if necessary."

"Do you think they're dead?"

"I don't know."

"I can't bear the thought of losing all my family at once," Zenobia whispered. She looked at Ezechiel, blinked rapidly, then asked, "What of the statues for the funerary temple?"

"I have the best stone carver working on them. He will do a magnificent rendering of the king." Ezechiel wiped his hands on his toga. "He has shown me sketches of Hairan's statue. The lyre will be a part of it as you requested."

"I would like to see the sketches."

"That shall be done."

"Let's hope we will not have to do statues for my other children."

Zenobia shivered. "I wish that I could have tortured Maeonius."

Already the temperature was soaring. Zenobia would have time for a quick bath, nothing more. But she did not want to leave the cool scented water of her tub. She slid down in the water until it was up to her neck and stretched out her arms. She could not touch the sides of the marble and copper pool. Even her feet could not touch the end. Two of her handmaidens hovered nearby with cotton cloths to dry her. They had survived the palace bloodbath of Maeonius' followers by hiding behind huge urns of grain in the storehouse. More than half of her servants and slaves had not been so resourceful.

One of the handmaidens was Christian, like General Abdas, and had answered her questions about his funeral and placement in the vault with a hesitant tremor. Zenobia found the ceremony much like the Jewish ones. Both the Jews and the Christians believed that one god could oversee everything. She had pondered that idea, but had finally dismissed it as too much work for one god. One god. One ruler. She hoped that she could run her kingdom without Odainat.

Zenobia rose from her bath and waited until her handmaidens had dried her with the soft cloths. She glanced down the hall to her sleeping chambers and to Odainat's that lay further away. She had stayed in his room last night and had fallen asleep to the fading odors of his spicy bath oil that lingered on the bed coverings. It had not been in her plans to tell Odainat goodbye so soon. She had always imagined them growing old together, perhaps dying of old age together. It was unnatural to bury a son with the father. Sons were the threads to the tapestry of the future. Today she had to tell Odainat goodbye. And Hairan.

Mixed in with the crowd that lined the streets were many mothers and wives who wore the saffron ribbons of mourners in their hair to show they'd lost a loved one. The wealthy women had replaced their jewelry with simple scarves of mourning. As Zenobia rode in a litter carried by four of her palace guards, she couldn't help but wonder which women mourned the soldiers who had been executed and thrown to the vultures in the desert. General Ezechiel had told her that the people were there to show support for her.

The thin gauze curtains that kept out the dust and some sun allowed Zenobia to be viewed by the people. She could not wave and smile at them today. It took all her energy to maintain composure.

The shadow of The Temple of Bel engulfed the swaying litter as Zenobia was carried up the shallow-stepped ramp on the west side. She didn't want to look inside the temple where Odainat lay with his first born son, so she stared at the fluted pillars that rose above her eight times the height of a man. Above the Corinthian columns on the entablature, a carved design of olive leaves, lotus flowers, and vines surrounded the building just under the eaves of the stone roof.

Too soon Zenobia was inside. The litter stopped and she alighted with help from General Ezechiel. She looked toward the adyton, a small secret room that housed statues of the three gods, Bel, Iarhibol, and Aglibol. In front of the steps to the adyton, lay Odainat on a golden bier. Purple silk covered the king and matched his cloak that she wore. Gold tassels hung to the floor from each corner of the bier. Hairan lay to the left separated from his father by a throne—a single throne. Pain wrenched Zenobia's heart. Odainat was handsome, but it was Hairan's youth that twisted her resolve not to cry.

Zenobia clung to Ezechiel's arm as he led her toward the single throne that had been placed at Odainat's head. She stumbled at the sight of the throne, for it appeared lonely and severed. For the first time, Zenobia truly understood that Odainat would no longer sit beside her.

She forced herself to walk to the forlorn throne. She would be compelled to watch the mourners who, undoubtedly, would watch her. Zenobia commanded herself, as one would a slave, to look at Odainat. He was handsome with a beard as black as obsidian. His eyes, dark as the deepest well, were closed and shut out his laughter. Odainat's hands were folded across his chest like the pharaohs of old. Sandalwood incense, her favorite, burned at the head and foot of both biers. A strong odor of spices, salts, and other preservatives assaulted her in spite of the incense. These were the smells of death, not of life.

Odainat wore his crown, but she would not allow it to be enclosed in the family burial vault. It must be saved for Vaballathus, the oldest surviving son. If she allowed it to be buried with him, the gods may view it as a belief in the demise of her children.

On his middle finger of his right hand, Odainat wore the wide gold band that symbolized their marriage. That was to be buried with him, for she wanted the gods to know that she never would marry again.

"My queen, are you ready for the others?" Ezechiel asked.

Zenobia nodded, not certain she could speak without a quiver in her voice. She laid her hand on Odainat's shoulder one last time before seating herself on the throne. She closed her eyes and listened to the rustling of togas as people filed into the main cella of the temple. She heard a woman sniffling, and she looked up.

Horrified, she saw that Tarab and Mokimu stood before Odainat's bier. How dare that woman show herself. "Get them out of here!" Zenobia bellowed. Her words echoed off the marble walls of the temple. A shocked hush fell over the already quiet crowd. She could see Ezechiel, inanimate, as he stared at her.

Zenobia leaped from the throne and pointed her finger at Tarab. "She is the mother of the king's murderer. Seize her!"

Tarab cowered and stumbled backwards. Her husband, Mokimu, steadied her. He shouted, "No! Leave her alone. She has two reasons to grieve. Her brother was murdered by our son, and our son will live in history as a traitor denied an honorable burial and will not cross over."

"Seize her!" Zenobia watched as the guards rushed over and dragged Tarab towards the door.

"Do not do this to me! Let me see my brother a last time. I have come out of exile. You may have me banished or beheaded, I care not, but allow me to see to my brother's passing over." Tarab would've fallen to the floor had not the guards held her up.

Ezechiel leaned toward Zenobia and whispered, "Your people have always trusted you to be true to the facts."

"Dare you speak to me of trust? Look at the mother of the most untrustworthy person in Palmyra. Dare you speak to me of forgiveness? Is that the next word that will flow from your lips like honey?"

"A leader is consistent for her people. Look at the ones who have come here. See their faces?"

Zenobia glanced from Tarab to the mourners who stood packed tightly together. The look on their faces was the same—fright mixed with bewilderment. When she looked at Mokimu, she was surprised to see tears flowing down his cheeks. Why, he loved Tarab, even though his wife had not honored their marriage vows. Zenobia had discovered that Mokimu knew of Tarab's affair with the late General Abdas.

"Do not make a mistake because of emotion," Ezechiel whispered.

"Tarab, you consent to being beheaded in public if I allow you to stay for King Odainat's crossing over?"

Tears dripped onto Tarab's toga and soaked through to her chiton. She stared at the floor, then looked up at Zenobia. In a powerful voice, Tarab said, "I agree. Behead me. I don't wish to carry the shame of Maeonius any longer."

The gasp from the audience echoed from the high ceilings and settled about Zenobia's heart like an iron band. She could not carry out her vindictive wishes. It darkened her soul.

"Who among us can predict what our children will do?" Zenobia asked. She looked at Tarab's swollen face and puffy eyes. It looked as if the woman had been crying for days, and she had aged badly in the last week. It was a ghastly burden that she bore.

"Release her. Come, Tarab, to the place where you were. There will be no beheading. We have had enough blood flow through Palmyra to last for centuries. Come, I will not harm you." Zenobia waited for her sister-in-law to come to the front of the crowd. "Come, come. I do not bite. I have promised you safety, and you shall be safe." The woman had the timidity of a hare and the brain of a camel. "If you do not walk over here at once, I shall have to come and get you." Zenobia almost laughed as Tarab scurried across the cella and grabbed hold of Mokimu's arm to steady herself.

Zenobia waited for the people to fall back into a respectful silence before she nodded to the high priest. The ceremony of crossing over started with the priest and forty-five priestesses, one for each of Odainat's years on earth, filing through the western portal and circling the crowd. The priest held a gold staff above his head that held a large golden globe of burning incense. Each of the priestesses chanted as they carried similar but smaller globes of incense. Sandalwood smoke drifted and danced across people like snakes of the desert. No longer would the scent of sandalwood remind her of nights with Odainat, but of his funeral. Zenobia blinked back tears.

Next followed fifteen priestesses who circled the crowd for Hairan's short time on earth. Tinkling bells reminded the crowd that

Hairan was a youth without issue. That sound haunted Zenobia to remind her that Adara's blood would not flow through Hairan to grandchildren. Maeonius had dealt a double death blow to Hairan.

The intonation began as a low murmur and rose to a crescendo as the procession reached the adyton. The crowd, unnaturally silent, waited for the priest to open the curtains and reveal the statues of their gods. Even though expected, when the multicolored curtains were pulled aside, the people gasped.

The statue of the god Bel stood on a pedestal in the center of the adyton dressed in armor and holding thunderbolts in his right hand. Zenobia stared at the thunderbolts, a symbol of Bel's control over man's destiny. He had certainly sent her a thunderbolt—straight to her heart. The other gods, lesser in power, flanked Bel, and were not on pedestals. Aglibol's toga was pinned at the shoulder with a crescent moon. He controlled the night sky. Iarhibol clasped the sun to his breast. All three gods were dressed in the Roman style with laurel wreaths in their hair.

Zenobia pushed back her anger at the gods who had served her so well until now and, horrified at her blasphemy, chanted three times over the prayer for exculpation. She forced herself to look at Bel's eyes painted a deep brown under brows of black. He stared back at her, and Zenobia prayed again for her soul. She appealed to the other two gods to intervene on her behalf. Never had she felt so alone. It was like being in the middle of an endless desert.

The crowd had settled into such an eerie quiet in the presence of their gods that Zenobia almost forgot they were there. She listened to the chanting of the priests, but kept her eyes on the beloved face of Odainat. She had no tears for herself. They had fled long ago. It was Odainat's fortune to cross over to reign with the gods, so she would not cry for him or for Hairan any longer. The gods must have need of Hairan's songs.

The chants of the priest, with their sing-song rhythm, almost put Zenobia to sleep. She blinked, forced herself to breathe even though the incense was thick and pungent, and focused on the prayers for Odainat and his son. The last hours with her husband would be long and short at the same time. She wondered how she would get through the temple feast and the grave feast.

The temple feast had been a mosaic of color, noise and blurred conversation. Zenobia lay on an eating couch covered with red silk. She drank wine and partook of the holy fish, served only at the funeral feasts, but could not taste it. Rice dishes and fruit were spooned onto golden plates by servants, even the one that was placed in front of the empty eating couch draped with blue and purple silk. The food would stay on Odainat's plate guarded by priests until it was consumed by Odainat to show that he had crossed over.

Zenobia almost cried when the servants put Odainat's favorite palm dates on his plate. She almost cried when she saw the lyre on Hairan's eating couch, and guilt rushed through her like fire. Would she ever forgive herself for trying too hard to make Hairan something he was not?

Zenobia laid on a pallet on the roof of the palace and stared at the stars. She stared at three stars in a row that the ancient Egyptians called The God of the Dead. The light from those stars shone down the shaft of the great pyramid and helped the god-kings rise to the heavens. She wondered if those same stars had helped Odainat to his place in the sky.

"My queen, would you like some wine?" Miriam asked.

Miriam's voice startled Zenobia even though she knew that Ezechiel's wife had asked permission to stay with her this night. "Please."

"It is the best that I could find. Maeonius and his men . . . ."

"Do not speak of him."

"I beg your forgiveness."

"It is no fault of yours that my heart seeks vengeance where there can be none. Have the priests come yet to say that the food is gone from Odainat's plate and Hairan's?"

Miriam nodded and poured cool water into the thick wine before she gave the silver goblet to Zenobia. "Just a moment ago. Both plates were empty."

"I want to get even with Maeonius, but I don't know how."

"Sometimes an eye for an eye comes in unexpected ways," Miriam said.

"How much wine have I had?"

"Not enough."

"Two or three goblets?"

"This is your fifth."

"I will have the ache of head that feels as if a Roman army is marching through it in hob-nailed sandals." Zenobia drank the wine quickly, hoping the numbing effect would block her pain. "What of Tarab and Mokimu?"

"They were escorted back to Damascus where they will reside in exile."

"Self-imposed," Zenobia said. She swirled wine around in the goblet. "Although I cannot say I am unhappy with the arrangement."

"It is best."

"Are the families of the deserters afraid of me?"

Miriam set down the jug of wine too hard and the metallic ring sounded loud in the still night air. "Most are mortified that their sons or husbands went against you. They are saddened two ways; by the death of their men and their traitorous ways. Some families blame you and would have preferred Maeonius as their ruler." Miriam snorted. "Fools."

"Which families?"

"Most are gone. Ezechiel's men have been escorting them out the north gate."

"To the desert."

"They deserve it."

"Your holy book says an eye for an eye," Zenobia said.

"Yes. 'It shall be life for life, eye for eye, tooth for tooth, hand for hand, foot for foot.'"

"I like that. I will remember every word." Zenobia's eyes were heavy, and she closed them. The only sound she heard was that of Miriam as she moved away from the pallet. She felt a light cover settle across her as she sank into oblivion with a prayer on her lips for the safety of her two sons.

Voices, whispered and angry, awakened Zenobia. She searched the night sky for a clue as to the time. The stars had shifted three hours worth, so it was still two hours before dawn. She listened, picking out Miriam's words.

"My queen is too exhausted to be disturbed no matter how important you say it is. What is the nature of this message?"

"I can't tell anyone but the queen."

Zenobia didn't recognize the voice of the woman who spoke to

Miriam. She rolled over and looked into the cella. Miriam had positioned herself between the woman and the sleeping porch. Two guards hovered just beyond the oil lamps, weapons ready for a signal from Miriam.

Zenobia stopped breathing so that she could better hear the whispered exchange.

"If you cannot tell anyone other than the queen, you'll have to return tomorrow morning." Miriam's arm was raised to block the stranger from stepping forward.

The woman wore the robes of the poor who lived along the caravan route just inside the gates. Zenobia noted that her hair was tangled and limp beneath a head covering that indicated the woman was married. Her age could not be determined; it could be anywhere from twenty to fifty.

"I must see the queen."

"No."

"I will not leave until I see Queen Zenobia." The woman folded her arms and glared at Miriam.

Zenobia leaned over to see around Miriam. This woman didn't act like a lower class servant or slave. Perhaps she was in disguise; a spy.

"Guards! Seize her." Miriam stepped aside as the men grabbed the woman and pulled her toward the door. "Take her to the south entrance and send her back from whence she came."

"I must see the queen! It's a matter of life and death for her sons!"

"Her sons? Wait!" Miriam called to the guards. "What know you of the princes?"

"I know they are to be sold into slavery to the next caravan that goes to Carthage."

Zenobia flew from the bed, heedless of her unbound hair, her rumpled clothing, and her shoeless feet. "What makes you say that?" she called as she rushed into the cella.

"My queen, forgive me," Miriam said. "I had no idea. . . ."

Zenobia's mind raced. "Speak clearly and quickly about my sons."

"Some young woman has them. She said that they were her brothers. She works at the brothel."

"As a prostitute? Poor Rebekeh. My sons are in a brothel?"

Miriam gasped. "Not the princes."

"Where will we find them?"

The woman shrugged. "Rebekeh learned of the plot and sent me, but she has slipped back to the brothel."

"Rebekeh? Rebekeh can't be a prostitute," Miriam said.

Zenobia glanced at the guards. "Release this woman. Send for General Ezechiel. We will search every brothel in Palmyra. Miriam, stay with this woman and keep her under guard. She is not to talk to anyone and let no one near her save you." Zenobia saw fear in the woman's eyes for the first time. She noted how scrawny the woman's arms were. "Have food prepared for her. Send a soldier to help me with my armor." Zenobia whirled around and marched to her bed room where her armor was kept. She had not donned it since the last battle with Odainat. No time to think about the past. The future depended on finding her sons.

Zenobia grabbed a silk scarf and bound her hair. She turned as she heard footsteps behind her and servants running back and forth. "You have come to help me with the armor? Good." She pointed to the corner of the room where it hung neatly on a headless manne-quin and waited for the young foot soldier to bring it to her.

"Hurry." Zenobia stood quietly as the soldier and two servants slipped the scaled armor over her head and adjusted the straps. Her short sword, buckled about her waist, hung comfortably against her hip. Zenobia refused leg coverings slipping into boots instead. "Let's go with haste."

"I was supposed to work in the kitchen!" Rebekeh jerked her arm away from the mistress of the house.

"You're too pretty to hide in the kitchen. I have a man who'll pay good money. . . ."

"I'm a kitchen helper, not a whore."

"You're what I say you are. Haven't I fed you and those two brats for five days running?"

"We're earning our keep!"

"Ha!" The woman's thin, henna-colored hair drooped across her shoulders. "They aren't worth a half a denarii between them. The caravan from Carthage arrives soon."

Rebekeh had heard the threat every day since she'd come. And every day her fear for the boys increased. She hoped the old woman had gotten through to the queen. She stamped her foot. "You can't sell them! They are . . . they are too valuable to me."

"I will get a lot of denarii for them. They are valuable that way to me."

"They're young."

"And lazy!" The woman grabbed Rebekeh's arm and dragged her from the kitchen.

The woman, Fadilah, was bony and her sharp fingers dug into Rebekeh's flesh. She could've jerked away, kicked her way to freedom, but what then? There was no place else to hide. She had heard that Maeonius lived and had taken over the palace. She had also heard the queen had tried to kill him, but failed. When she'd asked the prostitutes quietly one by one, she got only shrugs.

Rebekeh blinked back tears for King Odainat, for the boys, for her queen, and for herself. She would get out of this some way. Hairan had died. She couldn't think of him without his music drifting through her mind. This was no time for music. She'd always remember losing her virginity to Hairan, and she was glad they'd made love in the garden. She would never let another man touch her. Never.

"She's lovely, Fadilah, just as you promised." The man barely came up to Fadilah's shoulder. Bald and toothless, he looked like an ugly baby. Skinny, twitching arms and legs protruded from a grain-jar shaped trunk.

Rebekeh felt her stomach churn. Maybe she could vomit all over his befouled toga.

Fadilah pushed her toward him. "She will cost you twenty-four denarii."

"Too much."

"She's untouched."

"I am not!"

"Shut up, fool!" Fadilah slapped Rebekeh hard across the mouth.

The man stared at Rebekeh. "No one here is untouched." He pinched Fadilah's breast.

She slapped his hand and giggled. "This one's different. Twenty-four denarii, Hagop."

Rebekeh held her breath. The man stank of cheap wine, sweat, and animal grease.

"Ten denarii."

"She has strong teeth and sweet breath," Fadilah said.

"So does my donkey."

"Then go make love to your donkey, Hagop." Fadilah pulled Rebekeh up a narrow stone staircase. "Hagop will pay."

Rebekeh took short breaths until they were almost to the top, then she inhaled. The air was stale, but better.

"Get in here." Fadilah held aside a ragged mud-colored curtain and shoved Rebekeh through the doorway into a tiny room.

"No!" Rebekeh jammed her elbow into Fadilah's stomach.

A whoosh of air and a groan followed Rebekeh's escape down the stairway.

She was halfway down the steps when she saw Hagop grinning up at her. He took a step toward her; she stepped backwards up the stone staircase.

"You want to play? Good." He inched closer.

"Get away from me." Rebekeh backed up another step.

"You may be worth twenty-four denarii." One step closer.

"I will kill you."

"With your bare hands?"

"If I have to." Rebekeh waited. The man took one step, two steps closer. She stopped breathing.

"Young and pretty."

"Get away." Rebekeh put her hands against the walls and braced herself.

Hagop came up two more steps. Rebekeh shuddered with disgust. Another step. She kicked out with her right foot, her sandal making a smacking sound as it caught him under the chin. The squat little man tumbled backwards down the stairs.

"What have you done?" Fadilah screeched. She grabbed Rebekeh by the hair and dragged her up the stairs. "You will pay for that!"

"You let go of me now." Rebekeh was surprised at the coldness of her own voice. She was even more surprised when Fadilah let go. Rebekeh pulled her toga into place. "I will work in the kitchen in exchange for a place to sleep in the kitchen with the boys. You will not bother me again."

"I will give you half of the denariis that you earn." Fadilah nodded toward the room. "It would be a better life than that of a kitchen maid."

"Not for me."

"You would have enough money to support the three of you."

"No." Rebekeh turned away from Fadilah and found herself staring at the top of Hagop's head. She backed away, banged into Fadilah, and shoved the woman into the wall. "Don't come near me."

Hagop pulled a knife from his toga. "I will have you. Piece by piece."

The look in his eyes frightened Rebekeh more than before. It was the look of madness that men get when out in the sun too long. She turned and ran down the hall. Hagop, even with his short legs, was right behind her. Rebekeh could hear Fadilah's cursing.

Rebekeh darted through the dirty curtain into the last room at the end of the passageway. A window looked out into an alley, and Rebekeh checked the height. It didn't matter that it was too high. She had to escape.

She had one leg out the window when Hagop caught up with her. The knife gleamed in the moonlight, and Rebekeh's breath jerked to a stop. Her heart beat so loudly that she was afraid it would burst. She stared at the blade that Hagop held in front of her.

"A little excitement is good for the blood." Hagop placed the tip of the knife under Rebekeh's chin.

She reached up slowly and gently pushed the knife away. "Don't."

Hagop grabbed her toga and tore it from her shoulder. "Come here."

"Stop him, Fadilah!" She shoved at the little man, but he wrapped his arms around her and clung like a burr.

He smelled. Rebekeh pushed him away so quickly that his head hit the stone window frame with a clunk.

He bellowed in pain and glared at her. "I was going to be good to you, but now I'll make sure you hurt for days."

"No." Rebekeh pushed against Hagop, but he grabbed her wrist and twisted. She refused to acknowledge the pain.

"I know you."

Startled, Rebekeh stared at Hagop. "I don't know you."

"Are you not Rebekeh?"

"No!"

Hagop laughed. "Too quick to deny. I have watched you change from a scrawny child to a lovely woman. Yes, you are Rebekeh who works at the palace. . . ."

Suddenly both were aware of what he had said. "You are mistaken. Perhaps your drunken stupor has addled your eyesight."

"I drink, but I don't get drunk." Hagop ran the knife blade across her throat. "Fadilah! Come see the prize that's worth more than twenty-four denarii. Maeonius has a price on your head."

"No reason to. You mistake me."

"You have the two princes in hiding."

"Not in hiding any longer," Fadilah said. "I know where they are."

Hagop's eyes glowed. "Where?"

"Think that I'll tell you? I'll collect the money from Maeonius, then give you some for your information."

"A woman should not go to Maeonius. I hear he is crazed with power and kills at will. You wouldn't be safe. I'll go."

"You know nothing," Rebekeh said. "I am not Rebekeh." All she'd worked for was lost. If only she'd tried harder to get back to General Ezechiel's home. Soldiers surrounded his dwelling, and she had not known if they were the enemy or loyalists. She should have tried to slip past them.

Rebekeh thought of the boys. Since their escape from the palace, she had grown to love them more. They hardly complained, tried to protect her, and were so sweet. She couldn't let anything happen to them. She looked at the ground from her perch on the window sill, then back at the lowly prostitute.

"Fadilah, send word to Queen Zenobia. She'll tell you that she has her sons and that my brothers are not whom you seek."

"Queen? She is no longer queen. Maeonius reigns. She'll never have the strength to fight him. Every day I hear that more and more of the army join our new king."

"King! He is not fit to be king!" Rebekeh lashed out at Fadilah, pushed her backwards with one hand so hard that the woman tumbled to the floor. "I hear that Queen Zenobia has the palace and Maeonius is dead!"

"So! You are Rebekeh. The queen has the palace, but Maeonius escaped, and he wants the three of you." Hagop chuckled as he poked her with the knife. "Money, money, money. All mine."

"Mine!" Fadilah shouted. "I know where the boys are! The money is mine!"

"You won't get them—either of you!" Rebekeh tightened her knees around both sides of the window and grabbed Hagop's throat. She choked him as hard as she could.

"Kill him!" Fadilah yelled. She scrambled up from the floor, ran over to Hagop and pushed against his arm.

As Hagop tumbled out the window, the knife he had held against Rebekeh's throat slipped down and dragged diagonally from her shoulder, across her chest, and down under her right breast. The cut burned, but she had no time to acknowledge the pain.

Rebekeh watched Hagop fall. He hit the hard packed dirt alley below with a thud that sounded like a melon breaking into pieces. She turned away from the sight, more gruesome in her imagination than what she could see in the moonlight and the light from the kitchen doorway.

Fadilah grabbed her. "We go to Maeonius now."

"He is dead."

"A rumor. I saw him yesterday on the Queen's balcony."

"He will kill me."

Fadilah shrugged. "Life is difficult."

Warm blood oozed down Rebekeh's front. She patted the flow with her dirty toga and wished that she had some of Queen Zenobia's medicines. Corruption would surely settle in. It looked as if she would die for nothing. She needed time to think.

"Would you allow me some water to wash my wound?"

"Of course. I am not heartless."

"Thank you." Rebekeh climbed from the window and was half-way across the room, Fadilah in tow, when she heard marching.

"Which army?" Fadilah asked.

Rebekeh ran to the window and peered down the alley. "I don't know. It sounds small, so my guess would be just a patrol."

"Or Maeonius' army."

"I thought you said . . ."

"A lie. He has hardly any followers, but I'm told he kills at will. He looks for the princes. Come, let's go meet the soldiers."

"You are a fool. Queen Zenobia would pay you in gold and precious jewels for the safety of her sons." Rebekeh led the way down the steps. She walked quickly hoping to get distance between her and Fadilah. The woman was right behind her.

They had just entered the kitchen when they heard the front door splinter amid screams from the prostitutes. There was an ear-splitting screech, thuds, and men shouting for their swords. Fadilah rushed through the curtained doorway into the front part of the house.

Rebekeh spied the two boys huddled in a corner. "Come, we have to run." She grabbed Arraum's hand and pulled him toward the back door.

"No, Rebekeh! My kitty! My kitty!"

"We don't have time," Vaballathus said. He pulled Arraum toward the door.

"My kitty! My Panther!"

"Oh, Arraum!" Rebekeh dropped to her knees and looked under the table. Panther, oblivious to the noise, chewed on a piece of fat. "I'll get your kitty. Vaballathus, take your brother and run."

"I can't. There are soldiers coming down the alley."

"God, help us!" She looked around the kitchen. "Where to hide? Where to hide?" She grabbed three dirty rags from the table and pointed. "In there. Quickly."

CHAPTER
XI

267 A. D. Palmyra, Syria

The night was clear and the full moon shone off marble streets and columns and made it easy to ride through the dark. With a twinge of memory, Zenobia remembered a similar ride with a futile ending. She could not fail this time.

They rode north toward the barracks where her soldiers were housed, the clattering of hoofs bringing citizens to their front balconies and windows.

The largest of the brothels was there. Miriam had told her that Rebekeh was loyal and crafty. She might have thought the brothel safer near the army. Zenobia looked at the moon. They wouldn't have light much longer.

This part of Palmyra reflected opulent splendor of long ago. The stone buildings were no longer well-kept and seemed frayed about the edges like a well-worn rug. At one time, these buildings had been private homes for the wealthy, but now most had been turned into two-or three-family dwellings. Except the brothel. It sat at the end of the street close to the north wall.

Zenobia chose to rush through the back door of the brothel with a contingent of four men while Ezechiel and his men rushed the front door. Other soldiers surrounded the ramshackle building to capture any residents that might leap from windows.

Zenobia drew her sword as she charged through the sagging wooden door into the kitchen. Servants screeched as she glanced quickly around the darkened room where pots of nondescript gruel sat congealed in fireless fire pits.

No one could hide in this small room, so Zenobia pushed through the cowering servants into the peristyle. Women of every age and description, clad and unclad, leaped from the laps of red-faced, panting men. She ignored their screams, glanced around for Rebekeh, hoping she'd be able to see what the girl looked like in the dim light. She saw no one young enough and dashed out the front door shouting for the soldiers to follow.

Another brothel was two streets over, and Zenobia chose to run through the alleyways instead of riding. Again, she rushed the back door and entered the kitchen. This time, there was no one in the back. Startled, Zenobia halted in the middle of the room and looked around. Shadows hugged the corners, and she had to wait for her eyes to adjust. Her soldiers stopped beside her and listened. They crept down the hall toward the peristyle. It was empty, too.

"Most unusual for a business that depends on the night," Zenobia whispered to no one in particular.

A thumping sound from behind a curtained area alerted Zenobia, and she held her sword ready. She nodded to Ezechiel, who had come in the front way as planned, and she moved swiftly across the cracked marble floor. She took her sword and with one swift downward slash of her arm, shredded the drapes and pulled them down. The rod and material landed in a heap on the floor. No one was there.

"They have to be here. We don't have time to ride to the southwestern part of Palmyra to the other brothel." Zenobia chewed on her bottom lip. "Where is everyone?"

Several doors around the peristyle had curtains that hung lifeless in the night. It struck Zenobia that there was a familiar odor of iron that she had always associated with the battlefield and Odainat's assassination. "No!" she screamed as she rushed toward the closest doorway.

Ripping open the curtain with her sword, she expected death, but was still shocked to see the bodies of a prostitute and her customer each slit from ear to ear. It was the same behind each curtained room.

Zenobia ran from the brothel and toward the southwestern section of the city, whistling for Thabit. He came flying toward her, mane and tail billowing out behind him, sparkling in the moonlight.

A soldier appeared from the shadows, cupped his hands for her foot, and she swung into the saddle. As Zenobia raced through the streets between the buildings, she could tell when she left the less affluent part of Palmyra and was amongst the wealthy class. This section was only a few blocks square and soon she was in a second poor section of town.

The clattering of horses' hoofs reminded her she was not alone. General Ezechiel and his men rode behind her. Zenobia wanted to ride Thabit as fast as she did in the desert, but she could not for fear he would slip on the granite blocks that paved the streets.

The screams from the brothel cut through the night. Zenobia shivered because it was not like the sound of men dying in battle, but higher pitched like something from the other world. She kicked Thabit, and he bolted forward. He kept his footing, and only slipped once as they rode up the broken steps to the brothel and through the curtains that had replaced the door.

Lantern light took the place of moonlight as Zenobia glanced around the smoke filled room. Once it had been the home of a wealthy merchant, but now it was neglected and festered like the women who worked here.

Two women lay at the edge of the room, their throats cut like the prostitutes in the other brothel. Screams and scuffling could be heard from the back, and Zenobia rode Thabit across the peristyle and into a second large room. Some of the women were alive and writhed on the floor, but Zenobia knew they were beyond help. The absence of customers was puzzling until Zenobia slid off Thabit and dashed into the kitchen with sword drawn.

The back door that led to the alley was open. Customers, in varying stages of undress, ran in all directions. They were pursued by men in dark robes. General Ezechiel and his soldiers came around the corner of the brothel. Zenobia pointed toward the figures, and the general chased them down the alley.

She turned and surveyed the kitchen. A lantern had overturned and a wide flame flickered in a pool of spilled oil. A table held a few worn and cracked dishes with scraps of food. A dark kitten jerked its head up from a dish and hissed at her as it jumped off the table and ran to a curtained area to the left. Zenobia stared at the curtain that rippled in the breeze from the open door. She walked softly across the cracked marble floor and used her sword to hold the curtain aside. The light from the lantern made the four-foot high storage jars appear alive. They danced before Zenobia, and once more any hope of finding her sons was lost.

"So close my sons, so close. But like stars reflected in water, you disappear when I think I can touch you." Zenobia let the curtain drop and turned to go.

A sneeze startled her. She whirled around, grabbed the curtain and ripped it down. Now she noticed precious grain lay in heaps across the floor. She slid the tip of her sword under the lid of the closest grain jar and flipped it off. The noise of the clattering of the clay lid against the floor sounded like the entire Persian army had invaded. She flicked a lid off a second jar and watched as it hit the floor and spun like a toy until it lost momentum and sank to the floor ringing in protest.

"Come out or I will run this sword through the grain until it is red with your blood," Zenobia whispered.

Although she expected it, it still startled Zenobia to see a figure rise from the grain in the nearest jar. Coughing and sputtering, the apparition pulled a rag away from its face and gasped for air.

"Please, my queen. Put your sword away. Do you not recognize Rebekeh?"

"Rebekeh?" Zenobia blinked, but the frail young girl standing chest high in grain did not look like the Rebekeh she knew. This Rebekeh had dusty, stringy hair, broken fingernails, and a nasty wound that oozed as it dragged itself across her collar bone, down her chest, and disappeared under a ragged and colorless stola.

"You . . . are you all right? Where are Vaballathus and Arraum? Are they? . . ."

"They are here. It's safe to come out," Rebekeh called. "It is my queen, your mother, who stands before us."

Zenobia watched, fascinated, as grain shifted from two jars that stood behind Rebekeh's jar. Vaballathus popped up first, flinging aside a dirty rag. He drew deep breaths of air and grinned.

"Good morning. I would bow, but alas, I can't."

"As always, my oldest son is polite." Zenobia touched his cheek. He was warm and living.

Arraum rose next from the depths of the grain jar and shook seeds from his once dark hair that was now powdered. He spoke through a rag, making his voice sound as if it were from the underworld. "We were brave."

"You must have been wonderfully brave." Zenobia reached over and pulled her youngest son from the grain jar and gave him a quick hug as she placed him next to her. "Stand near. The enemy is lurking close by. I feel it. Come, we must get safely to the palace."

"Not without Panther." Arraum dropped to his hands and knees and called for the kitten.

Slowly, the tiny black kitten crawled out from behind a grain jar. Crouching and looking furtively from side to side, he made his way to Arraum. The boy scooped the kitten up in his arms and handed him to Vaballathus. "You take him. He scratches when he's scared."

Vaballathus nodded and tucked the kitten into his toga and tightened his girdle. "He tickles."

Both Zenobia and Rebekeh chuckled. It seemed that Rebekeh had saved the kitten as well. Zenobia whistled for Thabit who made his way through the kitchen debris carefully, his eyes rolling at the unfamiliar. "Come, Thabit." She led him outside.

Zenobia breathed in the night air as she glanced at the shadows. Perhaps they were alone. She heard Ezechiel and his men as they searched the rooms in the brothel. She grasped Arraum under his arms and perched him behind Vaballathus who had already mounted Thabit.

"Hang on tightly, my son. Vaballathus, be prepared for anything. If you must, ride Thabit to the palace, but make certain it is safe before entering. Rebekeh, stay behind me."

"Give me a sword, Mother, and I will fight beside you."

"Your brother needs your protection more than I. Do as I say." Zenobia grasped the reins and led the horse down the middle of the street toward the palace. Eight of her men positioned themselves around the quartet. Ezechiel and his men were fifty cubits behind.

Rebekeh pointed to a moving shadow, and Zenobia drew her short sword. The clang of weapon against weapon as many shadows swept toward them was all that Zenobia heard. She dispatched one of the traitors quickly and had time to count more than twenty of the enemy.

"Vaballathus!" Zenobia slashed her way toward Thabit who was held by an assassin, but she could not get to him. The horse reared, but was brought down hard by the shadow-man. "Vaballathus, ride!"

Frantic, Zenobia sliced through the jugular of a man who had stepped in front of her. Two more took his place, and as she fought them, she could hear Thabit's hoofs hit the paving stones over and over as he struggled to free himself.

Arraum yelled as a man tried to pull him off the horse. Vaballathus kicked the man in the face and sent him sprawling, but another man held the horse. She could not lose her sons now! She fought harder than ever she had in battle, but could not get closer.

A screech cut though the fighting. Zenobia looked up in time to see Rebekeh push her way toward Thabit, heedless of swords whistling around her. Rebekeh leaped on the back of the man who held the reins. The surprise attack dropped both of them to the street. Rebekeh scrambled to her feet and slapped Thabit hard on the rump sending him tearing up Agora Street toward the palace. Arraum had his head buried in his older brother's back, and his arms were wrapped tightly about Vaballathus' waist.

When the boys were safely past the sword-wielding enemy, Zenobia turned and sliced off the arm of the man who had tried to cut Rebekeh's throat. "Here," Zenobia shouted. She tossed Rebekeh the dagger she always kept up her sleeve.

Rebekeh caught the dagger easily, backed up to the façade of a stone house, and dared anyone to come near her. When one man did, he realized too late that the young girl meant to kill. He dropped to his knees, the surprise showing on his face that he, a soldier, had been stabbed by a slender wisp of a girl. When he fell and sprawled in front of Rebekeh, she wrinkled her nose and stepped over the traitor. Zenobia watched as the girl walked up Agora Street without looking back, the dagger held loosely at her side.

"You killed Nishan. No matter. He was bothersome." Maeonius stepped from the shadows.

Zenobia grinned. "At last. I thought you had fled."

"I found your sons."

"They are safe. Your words put no fear into my soul."

"I will torture you to death, but not before you watch me kill your sons piece by piece." Maeonius lifted his sword.

"You are a braggart and a fool." Zenobia swung her sword swiftly. It whistled past the startled Maeonius who had jumped aside just in time.

"You gave me no warning!" Maeonius' mouth hung open.

Zenobia laughed. "You, the breaker of rules, expect rules?" She anticipated his lunge and stepped aside as Maeonius' hatred blinded him.

"I want to kill you," he whined.

"And I, you."

The clash of swords echoed off the buildings as Maeonius parried stroke for stroke with Zenobia.

"You have learned, but not well enough." Zenobia let his first mistake pass. As much as she wanted him dead, she needed to draw out his end for her own revenge.

Her fighting took on a languid rhythm in contrast to Maeonius' staccato punches with his sword.

"You are old, Zenobia, so you will tire." Maeonius barely got the words out through his labored breathing.

"Too bad you didn't practice more." Zenobia chuckled, then started when she realized the crafty desert snake had drawn her into an alley. She hoped her arrogance wouldn't cause her death.

Maeonius' eyes flicked for an instant to a place behind her left shoulder. Zenobia whirled around and sliced through the man's neck who'd sneaked up on her.

She heard Maeonius come at her back, and she dropped to her knees, rolled and leaped to her feet. "Poor fool."

"I'll live, but you'll die." Maeonius charged, his sword held straight out in front of him.

"You'll not skewer me." Zenobia brought her sword up swiftly underneath Maeonius' sword. The sound of metal against metal was music to Zenobia, and she felt renewed vigor.

She was also impatient to get this diversion finished. Maeonius was ill-trained for a one-on-one sustained skirmish.

"I am sorry for you, Maeonius, though hatred tempers my feelings."

"I hate you and feel nothing else." Maeonius' words came out in gasps.

"Enough prattle," Zenobia said. She swung her sword with all her power and caught Maeonius. He wavered, lunged, and Zenobia sliced open his midsection. The look on Maeonius' face was not one of pain, but that of a spoiled child who didn't get his way. Maeonius folded downward like a dying camel and sprawled across the paving blocks.

The sounds of the skirmish escalated, then died as Ezechiel and his men surrounded the enemy. The quiet of the night seemed eerie to Zenobia as the last man lay dying on the street, blood running between the cracks of the paving stones in miniature rivers that shone dark in the moonlight.

The palace lights beckoned Zenobia like the beacon from a lighthouse she'd seen on one of her journeys with her father. She wished that she felt as safe in the palace as she used to. Now it was not secure, and she worried about her sons. Had they made it back? If Rebekeh had caught up with her sons, she would protect them. Rebekeh would be rewarded well for her bravery and ingenuity.

The gates to the inner yard opened and Zenobia rode through. She couldn't wait to see Vaballathus and Arraum. She was no longer alone.

The laughter of Vaballathus and Arraum as they splashed around in her sunken tub brought tears to Zenobia's eyes instead of the smile that she thought she would have. She watched Arraum swim from one end to the other; the tub at least four of his lengths. Vaballathus floated toward his younger brother, seemingly uninterested in him, then pulled the boy under. Both of them came up sputtering and howling with abandonment.

The old physician, Iason, bowed as he was led into the room by a servant. Zenobia looked at his face, but could tell nothing of what he thought. She blinked, hoping he had not seen her misting eyes. She could not show signs of weakness.

"What of Rebekeh? Is she comfortable?"

"For now, my queen, but it is the condition of her soul that worries me more than her body's condition."

"Don't speak in riddles." Zenobia rubbed her temples that continued to throb even though Iason had given her white powder in wine.

"She needs a rabbi."

"Why?"

"Rebekeh tells me she doesn't want to live because she has lied, cheated, stolen, and killed. She has refused all food and medicine. We had to force medicine down her, and we'll have to force her to eat by tomorrow. I thought you could talk with her. You have killed often." The physician clapped his hand across his mouth.

Zenobia laughed at his discomfort. "You have spoken true, Iason, so there's no need to feel shame at your words." She rose from her chair. "I'll go see Rebekeh." Zenobia glanced at the youngsters cavorting in the pool. "Without her, we wouldn't have them."

The sun shone through the west window and spilled across the mosaic tile floor in the room Zenobia had given to Rebekeh. It was between the boys' apartments and from her sleeping couch, Rebekeh would be able to see each of them as they slept. The kitten was curled up next to Rebekeh as she lay quietly.

Rebekeh, her face to the wall, did not stir as Zenobia sat in a chair next to her. Zenobia placed her hand on Rebekeh's shoulder.

"This is no way to repay those whom you've helped," Zenobia said. She waited for a response, but there was none. "My sons owe their lives to you, and that is worth more than all the kingdoms in the world. It distresses me to know that you want to die for having come to my aid. Your courage was dauntless, and yet it fails you now. Look at me, Rebekeh. I command it."

When Rebekeh turned over, her eyes were red and swollen, which contrasted with and exaggerated her sunken cheeks. For the first time, Zenobia believed the girl would die. She looked at the stark whiteness of the bandage that began at her throat and disappeared under her tunic. Peeking out from beneath the bandage, the long, thin red scar looked like bright blood running down Rebekeh's chest. Zenobia recognized it as a knife cut. She wondered at its history, but now wasn't the time to ask.

"Rebekeh, you were within a thread of having your throat sliced open. Does not your god protect the good? Does it not seem that you were protected? Have you asked for what purpose you have been spared?"

Rebekeh shook her head and sweaty curls stayed in place against her skull, giving her the ludicrous look of a death statue. Her color was that of pale, translucent marble.

"Do you not believe in destiny? That the lives you saved were so the boys could do noble things?"

"I killed two men and helped with the death of another."

"You killed my enemy. Your enemy. Do I not kill many enemies? If you feel you have sinned, then what of my soul?"

"You have many gods. If you anger one or two, you have more to protect you. I have one god and many rules. I have broken one of our rules and have angered my only god."

"How do you know he is angry? You may have taken one life. . . ."

"I have taken three." Rebekeh's voice was flat.

"Three? How so?"

"The first night I ran with the boys, Arraum couldn't run as fast, and he was caught. I picked up a loose paving stone and bashed in the head of the man who held him."

"Good! The betrayer was in the wrong, not you." Zenobia watched as Rebekeh's eyelids flickered. "The second time you killed?"

"It was for myself."

"Not a poor reason, I assure you."

"I had taken the boys to the brothel to do kitchen work. I couldn't think of any other place where they would be safe without endangering family or friends. I was promised that I would work in the kitchen, but one night . . ."

Zenobia placed her fingers on Rebekeh's lips. "Speak no more. It is best left unsaid. Pretend it didn't happen."

"He did not touch me. After he slashed me with his knife, I helped push him out the second story window." Rebekeh squeezed her eyes shut and the corners of her mouth turned down. Her fingers traced the bandage. "He sounded like a ripe fruit when he hit the pavement below. I cannot forget that sound or that night."

"Again, he was the one who broke the rules, not you."

"I cannot live with those men's souls on my conscience."

"Those men had no souls," Zenobia said.

"I want to die."

"If you die, will you go to a good place or a bad?"

"I will go to the bad."

"Then I would fight for life for many years to avoid the forthcoming pain."

Rebekeh's eyes opened. "My queen! You are . . ."

"Practical. Above all else, I am practical." Zenobia kissed Rebekeh's forehead. "Get some rest. I will send one of your rabbis to talk with you."

"I am not clean enough to talk to a rabbi."

Zenobia pointed toward the boys' bathing room. "You have been told you could bathe in there."

"In my heart, my queen. In my heart."

"Ahhh." Zenobia turned and left the room. She would ask Ezechiel which of the holy men would talk sense to Rebekeh.

Ezechiel arrived in Zenobia's cella in less than an hour by the water clock. Zenobia greeted him and asked that he sit. She poured wine for him herself, having sent all the servants and slaves out of the room. "I have another favor to ask of you, Ezechiel."

"As always, I am honored."

"I need a rabbi for Rebekeh. I don't know enough of your religion to argue with her. She wants to die because she killed three men while saving the lives of my sons as well as herself."

"Rebekeh? The girl who has the look of a lamb? She fought like a lioness?"

"She did. I may want to make her a soldier."

Ezechiel chuckled. "A fine one she would be." He shook his head. "But she has not been brought up as a soldier and feels she has sinned. I know a superb rabbi who will talk with her. He is old and bent, wizened and white-haired, but Rabbi Uriah is gentle and persuasive."

"It will not be easy. The same stubbornness that kept her alive may cause her death."

"I will tell the rabbi to be successful else you will cause his head to be separated from his shoulders."

"Ezechiel! Do you think that I'm an ogre? No, tell him that Rebekeh's life is precious to me, and I would appreciate his wise counsel for her."

"And you, my queen. How do you fare?"

Zenobia traced a gold leaf pattern on the arm of her chair. The question had startled her, for she hadn't thought about herself or what was to come. "My husband and companion, in love and war, is gone and with his death went my future."

"You must plan a new future."

"I do not want to think about the days, the weeks, the years without Odainat." Zenobia lifted the wine goblet to her lips. Her dark hair contrasted with the bright white of her chiton and reflected in the polished gold cup.

"Palmyra must have a future or she dies with Odainat. It would be a pity to lose the city he loved, that his father and grandfather before him helped to build." Ezechiel drained the wine from his goblet and wiped his mouth with a linen cloth.

"Palmyra," Zenobia whispered. "I know no other city that is as beautiful. Even Rome is not as grand as Palmyra."

"Emperor Gallienus would disagree with you." Ezechiel placed his goblet on the copper and silver inlaid table next to him.

"Emperor Gallienus is weak. He could not avenge the death of his father, Valerian, so Odainat and I had to do it for him seven summers ago."

"His army is not well led."

"His government is addled because he is addled. He continues to persecute the Christians; although, he says it is because they side with the barbarians," Zenobia growled.

"He outlawed oppression of the Christians."

"He has the laws written, but they are not followed. Ask the Christians who have come here to live. They flee from the tyranny of Rome. He should recognize that to harass them is to undermine the already weakened government in Rome."

"Is that why you allow Jews and Christians to live in Palmyra unmolested—to serve your government?"

Zenobia shrugged. "To some extent. Don't look so pained, Ezechiel. I am not altruistic. I am a political creature by habit. It has helped me survive."

"I would rather think that you are charitable." Ezechiel picked at the brocaded border on his toga. "You treat all people the same."

"I do not care what gods people follow. If they are good for Palmyra, then so be it. Really, Ezechiel, you look as if I had spoken blasphemy to all the gods in all the heavens. To ease your heart, I'll tell you what my mother taught me. Enemies do not exist because of different religions, but because some men are naturally evil and want what is yours. She always told me to fight the man, not the beliefs." Zenobia grinned. "I see that you are relieved."

"I am."

"So. Now I need action. I'm taking my sons to market today. They have begged me."

"Do you think it is safe?"

"I mean to find out. If assassins lurk still, then may they come forth. I want to show my people that I am not afraid of them nor are my sons fearful."

CHAPTER
XII

267 A. D. Palmyra, Syria

The rainbow of clothing reflected the rainbow of languages spoken in the market place. The contrast of color against the limestone columns of the Oval Piazza made Zenobia almost lighthearted. She chuckled at the look of awe on the faces of Vaballathus and Arraum as they stared at a snake charmer who sat near the west entrance of Damascus Gate. A basket of odd looking snakes with wide necks rested on paving blocks in front of a dark-skinned man from the east. He played a bone flute and the snakes shimmered before him as they rose toward the turquoise sky. A dirty brown blanket served as his seat and probably covered him at night.

"May we get closer?" Arraum danced up and down in front of Zenobia.

"The snakes may be poisonous." Zenobia wanted to grab Arraum's hand and jerk him away from danger.

"Arraum, those snakes have been milked of their poison, so there's no joy in getting closer," Vaballathus said.

"What do you know?" Arraum scuffed his foot across the paving stone closest to the snakes.

"I learned it from that man who stands by the gate."

Zenobia looked toward the large arched entrance that was flanked by two smaller ones. In the shade of the wide arches stood a man dressed after the Greek fashion. His bow was almost as imperceptible as his smile.

"Vaballathus, when did you talk with that man?"

"While you were sniffing the oils in the alabaster jars. Ezechiel went with me. That man is a philos . . . phil . . . something. He thinks big thoughts."

"Philosopher. Greece is full of men who do not work, do not fight, but have to eat so they call themselves philosophers."

"He knows about snakes and stars and many things." Vaballathus waved at the man whose bald head glistened in the sun.

"You must have dragged much information from him in a short while," Zenobia said.

"He said my Greek was good, but he could teach me to read the ancients myself, and he could teach me rhetoric as well as philosophy."

"Indeed."

"Could he teach me?"

"Vaballathus, we do not know this stranger. He could be a spy from Persia or sent to worm his way into the palace by the Romans."

"He doesn't look like a worm, Mother," Arraum said.

"Enough, both of you." Zenobia turned away from the Greek and walked across the colonnaded street to the stalls that held silks from the east. She picked up a corner of red silk and let it sift through her fingers. She felt the philosopher's eyes follow her, but she was used to men watching her. She turned too suddenly, and her gold bracelets and massive gold necklaces jingled, making a lilting music. Embarrassed at causing more attention than usual, Zenobia pulled her white silk head covering forward to hide her face.

The boys danced beside her chattering and pointing to camels that had folded their legs under them and settled along Caravan Street on the other side of Damascus Gate. Camel drivers and merchants unloaded incense from India, silk from China, wool from Gaul, and wine from Rome along with countless other treasures that most people did not see in a lifetime.

"Take us outside the gates, Mother. Pleeeaaase!" Arraum skipped around his mother and brother, took a whirl around two guards and ended up next to Ezechiel. "Take us to see the donkeys, Ezechiel."

"If my queen agrees." Ezechiel grinned.

"You, my fine general, are as eager as the boys to see what this caravan brings," Zenobia said.

"I'd like to see the slaves, Mother," Vaballathus said.

"I'm glad I'm not a slave. I rather like being a prince," Arraum said.

Zenobia laughed along with Ezechiel. She noted that the quartet of guards had to work hard to control their smiles. "How can I refuse such an enthusiastic request? We'll look at the caravans."

"If there's dried fish, could you send someone to purchase it for us?" Vaballathus asked.

"Only if it is from Lake Tiberias in Palestine," Zenobia said. "No other fish is as good."

"I thought the goddess who has the tail of a fish and the body of a woman didn't want us to eat fish," Arraum said.

"Her name is Hierapolis-Membij," Vaballathus said. "She protects fish. They are sacred."

"So why do we eat them at grave banquets and at funeral feasts, Ezechiel?" Arraum asked.

"Jews and Christians eat fish, but I can't answer your question about the feasts. You'd better ask your mother."

"Many have asked the same questions and have found no answers," Zenobia said.

"You eat fish, Mother, when other people don't."

"I was brought up with the Egyptian beliefs; Hierapolis-Membij is a Syrian goddess. When we have fish, the Syrian servants don't have to prepare it. They don't have to be in the kitchens and are allowed to do something else."

"Don't people get mad at you?" Arraum asked.

"I don't eat fish often. The servants never mention it. However, the fish from Lake Tiberias are too good not to eat. Look! I see the caravans."

Zenobia made her way toward Damascus Gate and through the crowd that parted for her as grass before a wind.

Caravans were a daily occurrence in Palmyra, but this caravan was especially huge and had come in from the east. The camels, goats, sheep, cattle, and even the drivers were covered with dust of many miles and many countries.

Zenobia stopped next to a merchant who had spread his glasswares on a blanket before him. He smiled a toothless smile and held up a beautiful green glazed vase. The sun shimmered through the vase and transformed it into a translucent emerald. "How much?"

"Two hundred denarii." The merchant flicked his fingernail against the fluted edge of the vase. It sang with the clarity of fine glass.

Before Zenobia had a chance to protest the price, the Greek philosopher called out, "Too much denarii even for a queen."

Zenobia looked at the man who stood on the other side of her guards. "Sir, how do you know the worth of such a piece?"

"I have traveled many places. This type of glass is made in Antioch. Although beautiful, it can be purchased for fifty denarii."

"I'll give you forty denarii; no more," Zenobia said.

The merchant shook his fist at the Greek. "I will starve. My camels will starve. My wife will starve."

"I see no wife," Zenobia said. "I am generous, however. Fifty denarii."

"Sixty. So my children will not starve."

"No." Zenobia walked toward the next merchant.

"All right. Fifty denarii." He held out his hand, palm up, and waited for the money.

Ezechiel counted out fifty denarii and dropped the coins into the dirty hand. "Be certain to pay your taxes to Palmyra. I will remember you if you don't."

Zenobia turned to the Greek. "Sir, I would like to thank you. Your name?"

"I am Dionysus Cassius Longinus of Homs, late of Athens." He bowed.

"You are Syrian, not Greek." Zenobia looked at his toga and sandals.

"I have not had the privilege of changing back to my preferred mode of dress." Longinus said. He tugged at a wisp of white hair above his ear.

"Have you lodging for the night?" Zenobia asked. His blue eyes were penetrating, but kind.

"I have just arrived."

"Ezechiel, see that Longinus has a room at the palace. I think that he would make a fine tutor for my sons. I believe they like you. Vaballathus would like to study the ancients and rhetoric." Zenobia smiled. "I have heard of you through my brother-in-law, Mokimu, who liked to read philosophy and study rhetoric."

"Yes, Mokimu and his wife are the unfortunate parents of . . ."

"We will not talk of sad things," Zenobia said. "Ezechiel?" The frown on Ezechiel's face was a foreshadow of the lecture Zenobia would get tonight. She sighed. It was time to put away fears of assassination and get on with life. She could not be immobile with trepidation much longer. "Would you like a position as teacher to my sons and to me? I would like to learn the neoplatonic philosophy you teach. Perhaps your philosophy could help Rebekeh."

"I had heard that you were well educated, my queen," Longinus said.

"So you will accept my invitation?"

"To refuse would be disrespectful." Longinus motioned to a dark-skinned boy about ten years old who stood apart from the crowd guarding two pieces of baggage. "My slave, Aswad. He is intelligent and learns easily, but alas has no fingers on one hand with which to write."

"He will be cared for. You can go with two of my soldiers to the palace. A room will be found for you and your slave." Zenobia turned away from Longinus, motioned her sons to follow her, and sauntered past the merchants and their goods that were spread across colorful blankets until she came to the jewelry merchants. Sunlight bounced off rubies, emeralds, sapphires, and diamonds set in gold and silver.

"Are the rubies from India?" Zenobia asked.

"From the best mines," the merchant said. "Tell no one, but the rajahs would kill if they knew that we had taken these from their country. The rubies are the finest."

"I will pay you one thousand denarii for the ruby ring."

"My queen, that is too little. I have a wife and children. It was dangerous for me to get this ring out of the country. I need two thousand denarii, and that is too little." The merchant picked up the ring and wiped it with the hem of his robe.

"One thousand, five hundred. No more."

"Done." The merchant grinned and handed the ring to Zenobia. "My family thanks you."

"Of course." Zenobia waited for Ezechiel to count out the gold coins, then turned to her sons. "We return to the palace. I think that our guest from Athens would like a little company at dinner. I would also like a stimulating conversation. Ezechiel, would you and Miriam join us to welcome our newest guest?"

"Yes." The frown had not gone away.

The wine was from the finest vineyards in Rome, and Zenobia swirled it around in her goblet before she took another sip. It had just come in yesterday with a caravan from the west, and she cherished every swallow. She set the goblet down on the ivory and gold inlaid table in front of her and looked at the blue-eyed, bald philosopher who sat across from her.

"Will you start the instruction of my sons tomorrow?" she asked.

"I started their instruction this afternoon, although they were not aware of it," Longinus said.

"Do they please you?"

"Very much. It seems they have the intelligence of their mother."

"You flatter me. Do not presume that it will soften me."

Zenobia started at the growl she heard from Ezechiel who sat next to her with Miriam to his right. She and Miriam glowered at him in tandem.

"Ah, here comes Rebekeh with my sons." Zenobia smiled at the girl. "Come and let me hug my brave boys."

The boys scampered across the cella and fell into their mother's arms. They had had many moments like this, for Zenobia couldn't get close enough to her sons. It was a miracle they had survived. She knew she would do anything to guarantee their existence.

"Rebekeh, honor me by sitting here." Zenobia patted the silk cushion next to her. She hugged Rebekeh who was more slender and pale than ever. She had fought men and won, but could not fight herself.

Rebekeh almost fell as she dropped down. Zenobia glanced at Longinus. His face was passive. She would talk with him later.

"We have some exquisite honey loaves, Rebekeh. Here, have one."

"I can't." Rebekeh's eyes filled with tears.

Of all the battles that Zenobia had fought, this one seemed the most difficult and frustrating. She chewed on her bottom lip—a habit that hadn't surfaced since she was a girl. "I fear for your health, child."

"I am sorry." Rebekeh stared at the table. "May I go?"

Zenobia wanted to order her to stay, to eat, to smile, to laugh. There were some commands that wouldn't be followed. "Yes. Have a good night's sleep. Take the boys." She kissed her sons and squeezed Rebekeh's hand.

She waited until the three had gone, then turned to Longinus. "What do you think of Rebekeh?"

"It's obvious that her heart stings with barbs of her own mind."

"Do you know how to remove those barbs?" Zenobia asked.

"I would have to discover the nature of the barbs first," Longinus said. "I will try."

"Thank you."

Ezechiel tapped his fingers against the table. "We have rabbis who will see to her."

"They may do what they can, but if something isn't done for Rebekeh, she'll die before the next full moon," Zenobia said. "Someone comes."

Ezechiel stood and laid his hand on his sword.

Zenobia nodded at a soldier who appeared in the doorway to the cella. He came across the room, glancing about as if he had never been inside anything other than a barracks. He was dusty and road weary; his eyes appeared to be moonlight white against a dirty face.

"What brings you into the queen's private chambers," Ezechiel snapped.

"I have important news that your lieutenants said I needed to bring to the queen personally." The soldier bowed.

"Why did not the lieutenant come as is customary?" Zenobia asked.

"They are busy getting the army ready for an invasion."

"What!" Zenobia leaped from her chair. Her hand went to her side where she kept her sword, but the weapon hung on the wall in her bed chamber. She had been idle too many days.

"Who comes this way?" Ezechiel asked.

"An army sent by Emperor Gallienus that is led by General Heraclianus."

"It seems that Gallienus thinks a woman cannot lead an army. Does he believe that I will open up the gates of Palmyra and invite him in?" Zenobia paced back and forth across the mosaic tiles, her sandals slapping the floor echoing her agitation. "Why must I fight to prove my worth? Does not my reputation stay the same with or without Odainat?"

"Unfortunately, my queen, the Romans are not aware that women have intelligence and the means to use it," Longinus said.

Zenobia stopped pacing and whirled around. "If it takes a battle to prove Gallienus wrong, then so be it. If it takes two battles, then so be it. If it takes many battles and the Palmyran army marching across the world, so be it. I will no longer allow Gallienus to think Palmyra is a jewel to be snatched at will. Henceforth, my army marches. We will take what Rome has taken from others and from us." Zenobia almost choked when she saw Odainat's face with his crooked grin flash through her memory.

"We will fight, and we will conquer the world. Rome cannot stand against us."

"My queen, at sunrise you'll see the Roman army who waits for us," Ezechiel said.

"Led by General Heraclianus. How fares his reputation in battle? Has he improved?"

"He is known to flee rather than stand and fight. His army is undisciplined and deserts easily," Ezechiel said.

"He doesn't have the qualities of Julius Caesar. Too bad he didn't study Caesar's works."

"As you did?"

"Yes. The strategies are solid even after three centuries." Zenobia looked toward the east. "The sun rises. Take your men and ride to their right flank."

Zenobia breathed in the fresh desert air cooled by the moonlight, touched her sword, and patted Thabit's neck. It was a ritual she'd performed before every battle. This time her prayers were for Ezechiel rather than Odainat, and the thought pained her heart. She prayed that Odainat would ride with her in battle safe in her memory and as a shield against her Roman enemy.

The army, five thousand strong, appeared against the horizon on top of the dismal hills to the northwest of Palmyra. Good. Her army easily matched the Roman's in size. Zenobia pulled her short sword from its sheath; the sound of metal being freed was a tonic to her. A surge of energy coursed its way through her as she shouted to the soldiers behind her. They charged en masse.

The sun glinted off Roman armor as Zenobia tore across the hard packed earth. She saw Heraclianus riding up and down the front lines, and she rode toward him slashing at his infantry with abandonment. It felt good to be in command of an army again and on the battlefield. She had almost forgotten the joy of controlling one's destiny.

Heraclianus saw her coming and turned to face her, his horse dancing sideways and snorting. He charged sooner than Zenobia expected, and she was momentarily caught off balance by his premature race toward her.

"Fool!" Zenobia dug her heels into Thabit's side, clung to him with her legs held tightly around his midsection, and rushed toward Heraclianus, her sword held above her head. It was an insult to him. She had no fear of his prowess as a fighter.

He advanced toward her with his sword ready, but Zenobia noticed he held it too high for a good thrust. Emperor Gallienus must think Palmyra had been weakened by the death of Odainat to send such a poor general. Time to show Rome what the Palmyran army could do.

The first clash of their swords as Heraclianus raced past Zenobia was ineffective for both of them. Zenobia had had to counter his too high thrust with her own high jab. The swords clunked as they glanced off each other. Zenobia pulled Thabit around and dashed back toward Heraclianus, sitting as tall in the saddle as she could to make up for her slight stature. This time, just as Heraclianus thought she would pass him on his left, she pulled Thabit hard to the right. Thabit responded quickly and as Zenobia flew past Heraclianus, she raised her shield and knocked him from the saddle. He crashed to the ground and rolled, his armor clattering.

Zenobia chuckled at the sight of Heraclianus covering his head with his shield. She couldn't even bring herself to run him through. "Get up, you coward. I will let you live to fight another day and a day after that. May there be many days of battle ahead of us." Zenobia reined Thabit around and tore off to a real contest.

The sun's rays in purples, grays, and blues settled across the battlefield and turned dried blood into inky blackness. Zenobia wiped her bloody sword on her trouser leg and sheathed it. The Roman army had been trumpeted to retreat, and she watched them go, unready and unwilling to stop fighting.

"We have beaten General Heraclianus, my queen." Ezechiel wiped sweat from his brow.

"He will try to ambush us. No, I cannot let him escape. A snake is a dangerous enemy."

"He flees."

"Then we follow him."

"How far?"

"To the end of the earth. I will not allow Rome to swallow up Palmyra and enslave my people." Zenobia spurred her horse forward and raced up and down the lines, giving her lieutenants orders to camp for the night and prepare to follow the retreating Romans at first light.

The blue water of Tatta Lake was inviting, but Zenobia had been told by the local soldiers the water was salty. She looked back across the rolling hills at the dust raised by her growing army. Men had been recruited each day of the last three weeks from the populace of Asia Minor. Eager to throw off the yoke of Roman rule, many had joined her army.

"My queen, General Heraclianus still rides; although, the sun is close to setting."

"Let him. We'll catch his army tomorrow." Zenobia watched the cloud of dust float across the arid land. Each day the dust cloud had gotten smaller as Heraclianus' army had shrunk. She would chase him through Gaul to the edge of the giant sea if she had to. From the size of his army, pitiful and dragging, it looked as if there wouldn't be enough men to get that far.

The sun would be up in a short time. Zenobia relished the coolness of the early morning air as she prepared herself for today's battle. It wouldn't be much of a fight. She held up her arms while her servant stood on a stool in front of her and draped chain mail armor down her body. She tugged at the sleeves of her chiton that she wore under the sleeveless mail to keep the links from pinching her. Maybe she should go back to the fish-scale armor she used to wear. It didn't pinch.

The servant strapped her short sword about her waist. It hung too far down and Zenobia instructed the youth to tighten the belt one more notch. It was always thus when she rode and fought. She lost weight. Food was not as interesting as a good battle, and she only ate to keep up her stamina.

The flap of her tent flipped back with a slap, and Zenobia turned to see who had entered in such a hurry.

"My queen, Heraclianus has reinforcements. Come see the dust cloud that rises with the sun," Ezechiel said.

"How many?" Zenobia grabbed a silk scarf and bound her hair.

"Several thousand come from the northwest."

"This should put fire into our soldiers. I fear they were becoming as bored as I." Zenobia took her helmet from the stand and carried it outside. She looked toward the northwest and could easily see the cloud of brown dust that blocked the blue sky.

"Send two of our legions to attack Heraclianus. You and I will take the remainder of our men and attack the reinforcements. They should be tired from their march, double time, no doubt."

"As you wish."

"Our men should be in good form since we haven't had more than a skirmish here and there with Heraclianus." Zenobia motioned for the groom to bring Thabit. "Tell the two legions to spread out so it looks like more men are going after Heraclianus."

"To frighten him?"

"To fool the general who commands the reinforcements." Zenobia grinned. "It's an old trick of Julius Caesar's." Zenobia stood on a mounting stone, grabbed Thabit's mane, and propelled herself into the saddle. She saluted Ezechiel as she rode toward the front lines.

Zenobia blinked sweat from her eyes as she drove against the new army in hand-to-hand combat. She killed more soldiers than she could remember. Blood caked on her sword and made it so unbalanced that she had to wipe it against her pants legs. Her wet pants clung to her legs, then dried stiff in the hot air. Chunks of blood flaked off and dropped to the ground making a macabre mosaic around her. From the carnage around her, Zenobia knew death had released many spirits to the other world.

"My queen! Behind you!"

She stepped sideways at her soldier's shout, but not in time to avoid a crushing blow that fell on her shoulder and sent her sprawling. Zenobia rolled away from the Roman swordsman as her man ran him through. She closed her eyes to keep the Roman's warm blood from burning them as she scrambled to her feet. Zenobia moved instinctively when she heard a noise behind her. As a Roman infantryman ran at her, looming above like an angry god, she waited for the right moment to dispatch him while she still knelt on the ground. The new troops were not any more adept at fighting than Heraclianus', but their greater numbers made the task dangerous.

Just as the hot sun hovered half-way between its zenith and setting, Ezechiel and his men appeared behind the second Roman army that had joined Heraclianus. Caught in a vise of Ezechiel and Zenobia, the Romans turned and fled across the arid land toward the Paphlagonia Mountains to the north.

"I will follow you across Asia Minor to Chalcedon and Byzantium and beyond!" Zenobia shouted. She whistled for Thabit, who came galloping toward her, mane and tail flying. A soldier helped hoist Zenobia into the saddle, and she flew after the defeated Roman army.

"Ezechiel, what is the meaning of this report?" Zenobia tapped a papyrus scroll against the palm of her left hand rapidly in time with the beat of her heart. She sensed that she was on the verge of a daring decision that would change her life and history.

"Our compatriots in Bostra have asked that we come to their aid and rescue them from Roman rule," Ezechiel said.

"I know what the words say. I want to know what the Arabian governor really means. I do not trust him. Baghel bends like grass before the wind."

"My queen, you have taken all of Asia Minor from the Romans by defeating Heraclianus. Perhaps you should consider strengthening your position against them." Ezechiel poured wine from a silver pitcher into silver goblets for them both. He leaned back in the brocaded chair and looked out beneath the rolled up sides of the tent. The sun shone brightly, outlining the small outcropping of mountains to the northwest. He pointed to the mountains. "There huddles the remnants of the Heraclianian army routed by a strong and formidable foe, Queen Zenobia. Have not your gods and my god favored our armies?"

Zenobia raised her goblet and touched it to Ezechiel's. "A toast to the future."

"What is that future?"

Zenobia shrugged. "I know not."

"You will make your own future." Ezechiel grinned. "I remember your vow that only a strong Palmyran army would protect you, your sons, and your people."

Zenobia stroked the purple silk cloak that she always wore before and after a battle. "We should strike while the Romans are weak. Thirty years of anarchy has taken its toll on the Romans."

"We are far from Palmyra."

"True. We have chased Heraclianus from Asia across the Straight of Byzantium into Europe. We passed Byzantium three days ago. Look at the town below us. What is it called?"

"Plotinopolis," Ezechiel said.

"We are thirty days from Palmyra and another three days to Bostra. Our men will be tired."

"They are the finest army the world has seen since the days of Caesar. Odainat would have been proud of you."

"Odainat," Zenobia whispered. The cape rustled as she crossed to the east side of the tent and stared at the town that lay below her. Land spread out as far as she could see, and most of it was hers. She lifted her goblet to the sky and smiled. Yes, Odainat would be proud of her.

Turning, Zenobia said, "Ready the men. After three days rest, we strike out for Bostra. The world's finest army should have the world."

The blue eyes never failed to startle Zenobia. She looked across the banquet table at the Greek philosopher who was still laughing at her latest story. He looked younger than his six decades of living. During the last month, she had enjoyed watching him tutor her sons. Rebekeh stayed close by during the tutoring sessions. The poor child was still too thin, but with Longinus' gentle questions and his soft voice, Rebekeh had responded. No one else, not Rabbi Uriah, not even Zenobia, had been able to convince the child that she had not sinned by killing the enemies around her.

Zenobia watched as Longinus motioned to his young slave and handed him a gold plate filled with delicacies. When he caught Zenobia looking at him, he flushed.

"It's for the girl. She likes figs."

"Good. I see more than figs on that plate."

"She likes the dried fish from Lake Tiberias. Rabbi Uriah told me so."

"It is healthy for her." Zenobia motioned to the pitcher of goat's milk. "Perhaps you should send that to Rebekeh."

Longinus nodded and placed the silver pitcher on the tray with the food. He waved Aswad, the slave, away. "I will check on Rebekeh later to see that she has eaten."

"Thank you. You've done wonders for the child."

"She is highly intelligent. I did not know that she learned my lessons until I heard her helping the boys with their rhetoric."

"She's learning along with them?"

"Quickly. Alas, I don't know what good learning will do her. There's no future for learned women unless they're royalty."

"Sometimes learning is good for the soul," Zenobia said. She looked at the fifty people who graced the banquet table. Tonight she didn't want to talk with anyone, and the noise of clattering dishes and murmuring voices threatened to give her a headache.

"Shall we play a game of Senet? The Egyptian game seems to elude most of my opponents except you and my late husband."

"It is a game of strategy that takes patience. I am honored that you think me worthy as an adversary."

"I learned the game from my mother. She should have been a soldier. She was cunning, but of course she was Egyptian and descended from Cleopatra."

"Therefore of the Greek Ptolemy line."

"Mostly." Zenobia rose and crossed to the atrium where the board was set up next to the pool. She settled herself on a stool and leaned forward to study the black and white board. Longinus had almost trapped her last night, but today she had thought of a way out.

"Do you feel vindicated yet, my queen?" Longinus moved a Senet marker and took two of Zenobia's pieces.

"Vindicated?"

"Has your anger at the Romans abated now that you've taken some of their land?"

"You tread on dangerous ground, my friend."

Longinus smiled. "I fear no one as rational as you. I fear not any person who likes to be challenged to think, even if it is as irritating as the hair shirts the Christians wear."

He sat opposite her and studied the board. "I see one way out for you."

Zenobia rubbed the round playing pieces together as she thought about the game. In that moment, playing a game she loved with someone who challenged her, she was almost happy. It had been a long time since she had played Senet with Odainat. It had been a long time since she had fought a battle with Odainat or loved him or laughed with him.

As soon as the army had returned to Palmyra after their victory in Bostra, a quick and easy conquest, she had given her offering of perfume and incense to Odainat's favorite god, Shadrafa, and then had gone to talk with Odainat in the funerary temple. She tried not to brag about Palmyra's control of Asia Minor and Arabia, as well as all of Syria, but she could not keep the pride from her voice. Our army, she had said, yours and mine, is the strongest in the world. The soldiers had marched thirty days to Palmyra, rested for three, and marched south to Bostra.

Startled, Zenobia glanced up from her reverie to find Longinus watching her. She blushed.

"My queen, you had such a wondrous look on your face."

"Odainat," she said.

"A fortunate man even in death."

"I can never love another."

"Do you think not? You are young, intelligent, brave, and beautiful."

"Qualities that frighten most men." Zenobia stared at the flowered square on the Senet board. Eight black petals against a field of white wavered before her. She forced her thoughts to leave those of Odainat and concentrated on her game. She shook the dice and moved her white disk from the geometric square to the flowered one that the Greek controlled. "Your move, Longinus."

He laughed aloud. "My queen, you have beaten me soundly."

"Shall we start another?"

"Of course."

The sound of dice being shaken in an ivory cup was a lonely one for Zenobia.

CHAPTER

XIII

268 A. D. Northern Italy and Rome, Italy

        *A*urelian walked swiftly toward the emperor's tent in answer to the bellow that had issued forth. A nervous messenger hurried past the guards at the tent's entrance. He glanced at Aurelian with frightened eyes and shook his head, his ringlets dripping sweat.

"The news is not good?" Aurelian asked, but didn't wait for an answer. He grinned. The emperor's troubles cascaded down on him. He noted that Gallienus' left eyebrow rode higher on his forehead than his other one. Lucine had done a remarkable job of stitching Gallienus' head wound, but too much skin had to be pulled upwards to cover the missing piece of scalp. His dark hair had grown back thick and had covered the battle scar.

"There you are!" Gallienus waved a scroll at Aurelian. Tattered edge pieces fluttered to the floor.

"Read this!" Gallienus shouted.

"Certainly." Aurelian held out his hand and the missive slammed into his palm. He ignored his stinging hand and read quickly.

"So. We march to northern Italy," Aurelian said.

"We have to. We can't let that traitor live. How dare Aureolus think I am so weak." Gallienus stomped across the dirt floor to the far side of the tent, then back to Aurelian. His hob nail sandals churned up clods of dry, packed earth. "By land or sea?"

"Land. It is spring and the seas are stormy." Aurelian reread quickly. "He can't gain control of the north or all is lost for you." He couldn't resist a little twist of the blade of truth. Did Gallienus wince or had he imagined it?

"You and your army come with me. I'll leave Marcianus here to hold the Danube frontier."

Aurelian's mind worked quickly. How best to use this good piece of fortune to get one step closer to the throne? "We can leave a third of the combined armies to hold the frontier. We need to make a strong showing."

"For Aureolus?"

"For all who think they can conquer the powerful."

Gallienus nodded. "I am invincible."

"Yes. The most invincible emperor in history. I'll prepare to leave immediately. Pray to the gods for good weather so that we will be in northern Italy by early summer."

"Send Marcianus to me."

Aurelian nodded and let the tent flap fall behind him the familiar sound of leather snapping against itself underscoring his contained anger. Gallienus must think him an idiot to use him like a common messenger. Time would solve that problem. Aurelian frowned. If Gallienus didn't die by Aureolus' hand, the emperor would die by his.

"Coins from Milan, Emperor. Newly minted two months ago when we started the campaign to hold northern Italy." Aurelian let the gold coins trickle through his fingers into Gallienus' outstretched hand.

"Aureolus minted coins in the likeness of Postumus?" Gallienus held one up and twisted it so it would sparkle in the lamp light. "Not a good likeness either. Why did Aureolus bother?"

"He seeks to ingratiate himself with Postumus."

"Aureolus is afraid of me and seeks the protection of Postumus." Gallienus laughed. "Postumus thinks he is the emperor of the west, but we know better. Minted coins won't make Postumus emperor. Power comes from an army that is strong and formidable and from generals who are loyal. As you are."

Aurelian glanced toward the walled city of Milan. "All the coins in the world can't help Aureolus now. We have had him under siege for a month. Poor fool didn't have enough army to defeat us."

"Nor will Postumus risk coming to meet us. We have won the battle even though the siege will not end for a long time."

"Send for my other generals so that we may relax tonight. Send for those most loyal to me." Gallienus smiled. "We will have the best wine tonight, the best food, and the best women."

"Your most loyal generals, Emperor? That would be Cecropius, Heraclianus, and me." Aurelian bowed, then left the tent. Again, indignation crept over him as he was, as always, a messenger for an emperor who should not be.

The two generals waited for Aurelian in his tent. "All is well." Aurelian accepted the goblet of wine and flopped onto a stool.

"Aureolus should never have listened to you, Aurelian." Cecropius poured wine for himself.

"A brilliant strategy," Heraclianus said.

Aurelian swirled his wine around in the goblet. "Thank you. It gave you a much needed victory after the debacle with Zenobia." Aurelian could hardly keep from laughing aloud at Heraclianus' red face. The man would not be difficult to push toward suicide.

"My troops were ill prepared for desert fighting."

"A good general can overcome all obstacles. We are taught that the Roman army is superior to any force in the world." Aurelian looked at Cecropius. "Don't you think so?"

Cecropius blinked. "We are taught that, yes." He glanced at Heraclianus. "We may not be taught desert warfare effectively even though some of our troops have been trained by Zenobia."

"She is formidable," Heraclianus said.

"A worthy enemy, do you think?" Aurelian asked.

"I have seen her troops firsthand. Do not underestimate her," Heraclianus said.

"I have studied her tactics. She fights like a Roman. I have word that she's studied our great generals, then has adjusted her method of attack to make desert fighting her strength." Aurelian took a long drink of wine. "In that strength has to be a weakness. I will find it."

"Do you plan to attack Zenobia?" Cecropius asked.

"The time is not right, but it will be done." Aurelian held the goblet toward Heraclianus and waited for it to be filled. He knew it galled the general to be treated as a servant. No slaves were present at this meeting. Not even Marcellus, his most trusted lieutenant, was privy to this meeting. There could be no spies.

"She will be content with the land she has now," Heraclianus said.

Aurelian laughed until tears came to his eyes. "You don't understand Zenobia at all."

"She is but a woman."

"No, she is a leader of men. She is a soldier. She has left behind her womanhood to behave like a man except . . ." Aurelian glanced from one man to the other. "Except that she still thinks like a woman sometimes."

"An advantage, then," Cecropius said.

"An advantage? Do you understand it when your wife is angry with you? What makes your daughters cry? Do you know? Why does a woman laugh? Tell me." Aurelian grinned. "I thought not. What man understands the female mind? No, we have a disadvantage when we decide to fight Zenobia."

Aurelian slugged down the thick wine. He fought the impulse to wipe his mouth with the back of his hand like a common man. "On to more important things. I believe that to save the empire, we must have new leadership. You know there is only one way to unite Rome."

"Kill Gallienus," Cecropius whispered.

"And Postumus," Heraclianus said. "That should reunite the divided empire."

"Not completely. Remember I have always said the empire is split three ways, not two," Aurelian said. "After Gallienus and Postumus are eliminated, then we must dispose of Zenobia."

"A daunting task," Heraclianus said.

Aurelian frowned at him. "For some of us."

Cecropius leaned over and whispered again. "Why not send Gallienus in to deal with Zenobia? Perhaps she can kill him for us."

"No, that would take months. The time to rid ourselves of this ineffective ruler is now." Aurelian glanced from one general to the other. "Who wants the honor?"

"You should have the honor." Heraclianus broke eye contact with Aurelian and stared at the dirt floor.

"I am to be emperor. I can't have blood on my hands." Aurelian snorted in disgust. "Do you not see the wisdom of our plan? We are to trap Gallienus. Then find a way to eliminate Postumus. We knock them down one by one to make Rome whole again. We do this for the glory of Rome. We have been chosen by the oracles to lead Rome."

"I will do the deed," Cecropius said. "How to do it is the problem."

Aurelian leaned forward and grabbed a fig. "I have a plan. Gallienus knows that if Aureolus escapes from Milan, his position of emperor is precarious."

"We can't help Aureolus! It would put us in jeopardy." Heraclianus leaped up and paced back and forth. "He has followers and Postumus might decide to throw in with him. We can't defeat both of them."

"Did I say to help Aureolus escape? You're a fool. No wonder Zenobia bested you." Aurelian chewed the fig. He liked the flavor, but hated the seeds that stuck between his teeth. He watched Heraclianus squirm. The truth couldn't be denied. Another truth was that Heraclianus was afraid of him. Good. He believed fear controlled men better than gold.

"What plan do you have?" Cecropius asked.

"A simple one. You, since you volunteered, go to Gallienus and tell him that Aureolus and a large contingent of soldiers plan to ride out of Milan."

"When do we tell this fabrication?" Cecropius asked.

Aurelian grinned. "Now. Gallienus should be dining at this moment. Urge him to rush out to see for himself."

"His bodyguards will be there."

"Gallienus is careless with his bodyguards. He doesn't always want them with him, and they won't follow unless ordered."

Cecropius nodded. "May the gods be with us."

"Heraclianus and I will wait in the dark. Agreed?"

"A simple plan. Perhaps the best plans are simple." Cecropius laughed. "I like it."

"Then go." Aurelian waved his hand at Cecropius to dismiss him as he did his slaves. The silly man acted like an eager boy. "Remember that we give Gallienus a more noble death than his father, Valerian, had at the hands of the Persians."

"Well said." Cecropius slapped Aurelian on the back, then let his hand drop when he realized that his gesture wasn't appreciated.

"Aren't you coming?" Heraclianus asked.

"I follow the two of you." Aurelian stood, spit seeds on the ground, and sauntered out of the tent. He slowed as the two generals became engrossed in the task ahead of them. He hadn't told them what to do. If they failed, so much the better. He looked up at the September sky. The stars did not foretell Gallienus' future, for he had none.

Cecropius burst forth, running and shouting for the emperor. "Stand aside. I have need to see our emperor." He pushed past the guards at the door.

A few minutes later Gallienus dashed from the tent and ran toward Heraclianus. "Where is the traitor? I'll ride him down myself."

"Now! Go now!" Aurelian whispered to Heraclianus.

Moonlight glinted off the blade of Heraclianus' knife as he ran toward the emperor. Another blade shone in the light, then disappeared into the flesh of Gallienus. Soft sucking sounds rhythmically spoke of doom for the emperor.

"Do you betray me?" Gallienus' quiet voice, full of surprise, did not alert his guards. He staggered toward Aurelian in a macabre dance. "Help me. I have been . . ."

He fell to his knees and in the light of the moon, Aurelian saw the emperor's eyes reveal the truth of his death and who had betrayed him.

Aurelian had no knife. He stood back from the carnage as blades flashed over and over in staccato tempo until a river of black soaked the emperor's toga and saturated the ground, the smell of iron a prelude to death. Only when the emperor could no longer speak, did Aurelian shout for help as he ran toward the guards.

"Heraclianus and Cecropius have betrayed our emperor and Rome! Seize them! Seize them!" Aurelian ran to the fallen emperor and pulled the knife from his belly. He switched the blade to his left hand and slashed his right arm, and his midsection from left to right, then held the knife, handle first toward Heraclianus. Warm blood snaked toward the earth and soaked in along side Gallienus'.

"The emperor is not the only one betrayed tonight." Heraclianus sighed and took the knife. "I was twice defeated; once by Zenobia and now by you. May the gods haunt you forever." Heraclianus pushed the knife into his abdomen and twisted. His screams brought the guards to a halt.

Cecropius dropped his knife. "I won't make it easy for you."

"I am in command now. It won't be difficult to arrange your execution. You are treasonous to Rome. A crime punishable by death." Aurelian nodded to the guards. "Send for a physician. I have been wounded by these traitors as I fought to save our glorious emperor."

"I go to my fate willingly. I no longer care to live in a world of your making." Cecropius walked in front of the guards toward his tent.

"Take care that he doesn't escape or none of you will see another sunrise." Aurelian stood over the bodies. Steam rose from them like smoke and drifted upwards toward the stars.

Aurelian sat easily in the chair outside the new Emperor's chambers. At least he tried to appear that he had nothing to fear. Claudius, named for another emperor two centuries earlier, was difficult to decipher. He led his army well, fought like a tiger, and pursued every last enemy until they were dead. He had swiftly ordered Cecropius' execution, but the wily general had escaped only to be captured at the home of Gallienus' widow, Salonina. Claudius would not be a man to have as an enemy.

Aurelian, stunned that the senate hadn't even considered him, decided to bide his time. He didn't want to be emperor yet. He wanted total control before he sought Zenobia's downfall, but Rome needed to be shored up first. He wanted to start his regime from strength.

He scratched the linen wrapping that covered his right arm. His midsection felt warm to the touch and was red, but did not itch. He had not clipped any of those stitches as he had done his arm.

He clawed the bandages some more until blood soaked through. It wouldn't hurt to remind Claudius of his intended intervention in Gallienus' death. It needn't be known it was for show.

Aurelian nodded to a guard posted at the door. Immediately the guard knocked and just as quickly the heavy door to Claudius' rooms opened. Lucine motioned Aurelian inside.

His eyebrow raised in surprise. "Apparently you have become part of the bedroom furniture," he said.

"I am a survivor. I would've preferred survival in my own land, but fate has twisted my life." Lucine swept past Aurelian, slamming the door behind her.

Aurelian heard a fountain tinkling in the atrium just beyond the main chamber. It sounded too cheerful for what could transpire. He knew he was too valuable to execute, but did Claudius?

No one else seemed to be present. Oddly, the door seemed larger than it had when he had visited here with Gallienus. It was the same door. A chunk was missing where young Marinianus, the emperor's son, had thrown a sharp rock a few years back. The wood was darker around the handle where countless hands had opened and shut the door to their destinies. And what was his to be? The gods knew. Aurelian's lips tightened. The gods did not control his destiny—he controlled his own. He could stay alive. He had the power to appease Claudius.

"Do you find the door an opportunity or a barrier?" Claudius moved silently across the room from the direction of the atrium.

"It is a door. Nothing more." Aurelian turned and faced the emperor.

"Is there no poetry in your soul?"

"I am a soldier. I deal with reality. Poetry has no room in my life."

"The language of love. A pity." Claudius adjusted his toga and arranged the purple stripe in a perfect diagonal. "Sit." He gestured toward two couches that flanked a gold table. Two goblets and a jug of wine waited.

"After you." Aurelian said.

Claudius chuckled. "I keep forgetting. You were senior to me as a general."

"Only because I knew the Balkans. Not by the gift that you have for leadership."

Claudius sat and again motioned toward the other chair. "We have much to discuss regarding Gallienus' assassination."

"A terrible tragedy, but the gods plan our destinies."

"So they do. I had not thought to be emperor. I believed that the young Marinianus would follow in his father's footsteps." Claudius sniffed the wine. "Sour. You'd think sweet wine could be found."

"Gallienus' line is stamped out by his enemies. Even Salonina met death. Why did his widow have to die?" Aurelian sipped the wine. It was sour.

"The excuse given by Cecropius before we captured him was that no seed of Gallienus should survive. With the death of his brother

Licinius Valerianus, Gallienus' family is no more. There are no cousins, no nephews, no one. How sad. No lineage into the future." Claudius put the goblet down and stared at Aurelian.

Aurelian wanted to squirm under the glare of the blue eyes, but did not allow himself to.

"You bleed. Does your recent wound bother you?"

"Only in that I could not save Gallienus. He was a fine warrior and a good emperor."

"A good general might have seen the treachery afoot."

"I will carry that failure to my grave. Once I mentioned my suspicions to Gallienus, but he convinced me that I feared for nothing. It is difficult to believe that his best and most trusted generals would turn on him." Aurelian sighed. "Is nothing sacred in Rome these days? It is difficult to have to fight the enemy without."

"Without having to fight the enemy within," Claudius said.

"I tried to watch Gallienus' back, but expected the enemy to come from Postumus' camp or Aureolus."

"What do you think of Aureolus? He has made overtures to me. He asks that I forgive him for trying to step in and become emperor." Claudius grinned. "Forgive the viper? I think not."

"You need to order his execution immediately," Aurelian said. "Choose a new general to lead the troops that Cecropius and Heraclianus left behind."

"What of the troops still under siege at Milan?"

"Aureolus' men? They, too, need to be under a new general. It is better to have fewer generals than to have too many ambitious ones."

"Hmmm. An interesting thought. We have problems with loyalty and problems with the barbarians. How do we solve these problems?" Claudius' eyes narrowed.

"You are a wise emperor who knows there are too many knives behind your back. Rid yourself of Aureolus and put his army with the other two legions. Do it quickly." Aurelian pretended to absently rub his arm.

"What of Postumus?"

"Postumus will irritate his men to the point that they'll dispose of him for us. A few coins and some bad rumors spread through his troops will do the deed."

"A good plan. Consider it done. I have arranged for Aureolus' execution immediately." Claudius laughed. "How easy to order deaths. I command and I get."

"It is a solemn responsibility."

"There is another problem. Where do you think the barbarians will strike next?"

"Aureolus is no longer in Milan, and therefore the northern frontier is open. The barbarians will pour down the Alps to invade. They can do it. You know firsthand how formidable they are."

"That I do know. The whole republic is fatigued and exhausted. We are in want of darts, of spears, and of shields. The strength of the empire, Gaul, and Spain, is usurped by our former ally. We blush to acknowledge that the archers of the east serve under the Banners of Zenobia."

"Rome will be powerful again, then our enemies and Zenobia will crumble."

"Shall we fight them together?" Claudius' keen eyes were fixed on Aurelian.

Aurelian froze. One simple sentence had declared his future. His life spared. He breathed in slowly to calm himself. "We will be good together. The glory of Rome is in your hands." Aurelian held up the goblet. "A toast to a glorious leader."

Claudius touched his goblet to Aurelian's. "To strength through friendship and trust. And need. Your men respect you and your views. I want you to make certain there are no further uprisings against me."

"You command and I follow. It is the will of the gods."

Both men drank.

"Prepare your army and the Dalmatian cavalry to ride to Lake Garda."

"The Dalmatian cavalry?"

"Yes. Cecropius has no need of them. He is dead."

Aurelian nodded. "To Lake Garda for the enemy without."

"On your way out, send in the guards with Aureolus." Claudius' grin was lopsided.

"He is here?"

"I said I'd arranged for his execution immediately."

"True." Aurelian bowed and left the chamber. He motioned to the guards who flanked a defiant Aureolus. "The emperor wishes your presence, General."

"I am certain you helped my cause." Aureolus' face betrayed his hatred.

"I helped Rome's cause." Aurelian's words were clipped. He had no use for this stupid pig.

"You helped your own cause. Emperors come, but emperors go. You will rule but a short while, Aurelian."

"I am a simple soldier. I have no need of a throne. I rule my troops from the honorable seat upon a horse. That is all I need and want."

"You lie." Aureolus spat, then entered Claudius' chambers.

"Pig," Aurelian whispered. "Always rooting in the dirt, never once to look at the sky."

Aurelian leaned against a pillar outside Claudius' chambers and waited.

Claudius' voice overpowered the thick door and Aurelian heard him shout, "Traitor!" A thud of a falling body told him that the deed had been done. One less obstacle between him and the throne.

He watched the floor in front of the door until he saw a dark pool slide under it. Blood, still steaming, made its way across the corridor toward Aurelian. He smiled and walked through the blood on his way out. His footprints, dark against white marble, littered the hallway.

Aurelian leaned back in a camp chair and looked out over the Balkan mountains. It was a rare moment of peace for him. Eight months had passed, and each day brought forth another march or another battle. He and Claudius had defeated the barbarians at Lake Garda, but not without problems. Always problems with the barbarians. Would they never give up?

He refused to think about more war. He closed his eyes and let the chilly mountain air be pushed away by the warmth of the spring sun. The fragrance of flowers washed over him and reminded him of his boyhood in these very mountains. His mother always had wild flowers in their hut. He never understood why. It did nothing to diminish their poverty. She said it made her world better. He fought hard to make his world better, and it wasn't with wild flowers.

He couldn't help but think of war. War ruled his world. He and his Dalmatian troops had recently saved Claudius' hide. The emperor had not believed Aurelian when he said the barbarians were strong enough to break through the lines. If Aurelian hadn't sent in the Dalmatian cavalry, Claudius might've been captured. Aurelian was shocked the emperor had misjudged the barbarians. Now the emperor owed him. That alone would make his world better and his future as secure as could be expected.

Aurelian shifted in his chair and the sound of fabric ripping made him stop squirming. There was no way to get comfortable anyway. Odd how a single thread would not hold his muscular body nor would a thousand single threads hold him up, but when twisted together to make fabric, it was strong.

He thought about the barbarians. The different tribes had banded together; and, like a rope, became stronger as they twisted together. It would be too easy to defeat Rome. The rope needed to be unraveled. Aurelian liked the idea of a frayed enemy.

Without opening his eyes or moving, he bellowed. "Marcellus! Come forth you lazy soldier! We have wars to fight."

"I am stretched out in the sun next to your chair. Don't shout. Your voice sounds like the braying of an ass."

"How long have you been there?" Aurelian asked. "I thought I was alone."

"You were snoring, so I decided to take advantage and rest, too." Marcellus opened one eye and peered at Aurelian. "What is so important that you had to awaken me?"

"I know how to fight the barbarians and win. Come, we have plans to make." Aurelian leaped from the camp chair. "The maps. I need all the maps of the barbarian's movements."

"They know we've come," Marcellus said.

"No matter. They have won enough battles that they think they can bring down mighty Rome. 'Tis not so." Aurelian sniffed the air. The pungent smoke odor, mixed with recently cooked game, drifted across the grassy slope from the barbarians' camp. "They eat well."

"So do we." Marcellus looked at the Roman troops scattered across the hillsides. "Our men wait for your command. They're prepared."

"As soon as we mount up, I want you to go around the right flank and try to break through. I'll do the same on the left. When you see me pull back as if in retreat, you do the same."

"Retreat! Why fight if we plan a retreat from the start?"

"It's not a true retreat. We pull back in the middle and let the barbarians come after us. It's like a vortex. We suck them in."

"Ah! We reverse the retreat and our lines wrap around theirs. They'll be trapped in the middle."

"Yes. You do the same and we'll have their armies split in two. Two halves are easier to beat than a whole. Divide and conquer. It's an old saying, but appropriate here." Aurelian sniffed the air again. "Eat well, for tomorrow will bring you death."

Aurelian glanced at the sky as he gave the order to take no prisoners. He slipped off the battle weary horse and handed the reins to a groom. He smiled and felt invigorated. It was a scant three hours later by the sun when Aurelian declared victory in Emperor Claudius' name.

"I congratulate you, Aurelian!" Marcellus pounded him on the back. "A job well-done; a ruse that worked."

"I learned that trick from two great warriors." Aurelian smiled. If only Marcellus knew that Odainat and Zenobia had baited the Persians with just this trick many years ago. He had studied their tactics for years. It served his purpose to know their fighting style. Now he had spies in the Palmyran army who reported to him weekly about Zenobia's tactics as well as her general, Ezechiel. He wanted to know his enemy intimately no matter whether that enemy be Roman or Palmyran or barbarian.

CHAPTER
XIV

270 A. D. Palmyra, Syria and Alexandria, Egypt

     *E*zechiel gave the messenger a denarii and sent him to the barracks kitchen. He tucked the papyrus scroll into his tunic and walked between the buildings to find Zenobia. The sun had barely risen, but she would already have had her breakfast, visited with her sons, and be ready to work with the soldiers. The news he had was distressing, and he did not want to share it with her.

He found Zenobia outside the walls marching in full armor at the head of a troop of young soldiers. "Ah, Zenobia, always showing the men you can lead them." He watched with pride as she ordered double time and filed the troops past him. Through the dust cloud that she raised, Ezechiel could see that Zenobia had stamina that her young charges had not yet developed.

"You are weak! How can we beat the Romans if we are as weak as they are! Double time! Double time! I've seen your grandmothers do better!"

It amazed Ezechiel how her shouts could bolster the most mediocre of infantry. He had seen it over and over—Zenobia could whip a group of men into shape in two weeks of hard work. Maybe it was because they didn't want to admit that she could out march them, out ride them, and even out drink them.

Just before the men were about to expire from the heat, Zenobia halted the marching and dismissed them. Most staggered toward the well where buckets of cold water waited. She, still marching double time, was next to Ezechiel in a flash.

"So, I saw you smiling. Good news?"

"No. I smiled because I remember the many times that unscrupulous men have tried to gain secrets from you by trying to get you drunk. There was the time long ago when King Shapur of Persia thought he could out drink you. Then the Roman general, the Greek mathematician, a diplomat from Byzantium . . ."

Zenobia grimaced. "Please. It was necessary. It's a trait I possess, but there is no pride in it."

"Convenient, however, to be able to turn the tables and get secrets from them." Ezechiel laughed at her scowl.

"You didn't come here to talk to me of my drinking habits." Zenobia bent over and let her helm slide off. She caught it neatly with the ease of someone who had spent years in armor, took a linen cloth from a young soldier and wiped her face and neck.

"We need to talk. Privately." Ezechiel took the helmet and tucked it under his arm.

"Come." Zenobia led the way across the compound to her command center. She shooed out the soldiers who were copying her orders for the day and sat behind the table where maps and scrolls were neatly placed.

Ezechiel should have been surprised that she didn't remove her armor, but he wasn't. Even on the hottest of days, Zenobia wore it all day. She had told him it would make her stronger.

"What have you? Are the Romans invading?" Zenobia unbound the silk scarf that held her hair in place to keep the helmet from snagging it. She draped the scarf across her shoulders. Her long, ebony hair floated down her back.

Ezechiel held back a sigh.

"Ezechiel!"

"Sorry, my queen." He pulled the scroll from his toga and held it up. "Bad news from Timagenes of Egypt."

"Bad news?"

Ezechiel handed the scroll to Zenobia and watched while her eyes scanned the Greek letters rapidly. She pursed her lips and frowned.

"I see no bad news. Timagenes wants our help in expelling the Romans from Egypt. What is bad about that?"

"The Romans have been there three hundred years."

"Since Cleopatra and Marc Anthony's unfortunate failure."

"It was more than a failure."

Zenobia waved her hand to dismiss the subject. "Timagenes has been a friend for many years." She read the scroll slower the second time. "He says that the Romans are starving his people. They send taxes in the form of grain and cotton, but always the Romans want more. His people grow food, but watch as it sails away to be consumed by the ungrateful. I know he speaks the truth, Ezechiel."

"Maybe he speaks the truth, but we have no right to go to Egypt."

"We had the right to take Asia Minor and Arabia and Syria." Zenobia scowled at him.

"We were attacked. We won the battles and therefore the land."

"It is no different. Ten and seven years ago we helped Rome avenge the death of Emperor Valerian. Was that wrong?"

"Rome was our friend." Ezechiel plucked at his linen toga.

"Rome is not your friend if you care for your people. Claudius continues the tradition of persecuting the Jews even though it is supposedly outlawed."

"And the Christian sect," Ezechiel said.

"Yes, especially the Christians. Timagenes is our friend. Listen to me. Egypt is in my blood. I can feel the same desires to conquer that Cleopatra felt. Look at our army. It is the finest in the world. Look at Palmyra. It is the most beautiful place in the world. And it's the strongest. We grow wealthy because the caravans know that they are protected by our army. Our men wear the uniform of Palmyra far to the east, to the north, and to the west. Why not wear the uniform far to the south?"

"If we spread ourselves thin, then like a stretched piece of rawhide, we will break." Ezechiel shook his head. "Remember what happened to Cleopatra."

"I shall not make the same mistake. She tried to fight a sea battle without knowledge of the sea."

"I would rather that we try to talk Rome into cutting the Egyptian taxes."

"Claudius is a fool. He will not listen any more than Gallienus did."

"You must try." Ezechiel sat still and waited a long time for Zenobia to answer.

"I know Claudius. He has no pity for the people who serve him. He has no fondness for Jews, Christians, or anyone. Sometimes I

wish that Gallienus had not died from battle wounds. I could understand him, but Claudius . . ." Zenobia shook her head to dismiss the
erratic emperor. She tugged at her sword belt, pulled it loose, and
laid the belt and weapon on the table. The metallic clank underscored her sigh. "All right. I will send a messenger to plead for Egypt's
cause."

"A wise plan."

Zenobia laughed. "It is your plan. Do not think you can fool me
into thinking otherwise." She leaned forward, her chain mail clinking against the table. "If I decide to help Timagenes, will you still be
at my side?"

"Always."

Bold red granite columns inlaid with geometric designs of white
marble stretched toward the sky. The roof had rotted long ago leaving not one splinter of cypress to attest to its ever having existed.
Zenobia walked farther into Cleopatra's palace; the shadows of the
columns lay suppliant across the marble floor having been cast there
daily by the sun for three centuries.

Deeper in the interior, solid columns of limestone rose startlingly
white against the blue sky. Tiny flakes of gold paint clung tenaciously
to pillars whose glory had died with Cleopatra.

"I had to come here first, Timagenes. It is as beautiful as I remember it." Zenobia heard a rodent scurry across the marble floor
and disappear behind a wall, and she frowned at the intrusion.

"To confer with Cleopatra?" Timagenes asked.

"How did you know?"

As Zenobia left the vast atrium, she passed a pool filled with the
dust of centuries. She hesitated, imagining the Egyptian Queen resting on a couch by the water surrounded by slaves who fanned her.
Chills danced down Zenobia's spine, and she hesitated at the top of
wide marble steps before walking down to the street. She traversed
the same steps that Cleopatra had. Did Cleopatra smell the sweet
flowers of summer as she did? Did Cleopatra see the double row of
sand colored sphinxes with silent stone eyes that stared at each other
across the boulevard?

"You have not been here for a long time," Timagenes said.

"When a child, I once came with my mother to meet her family.

She told me the story of Cleopatra and Caesar and Antony. I have been back here many times in my heart." Zenobia strolled past the pock marked sphinxes and stared at the Lighthouse of Alexandria perched at the end of the island.

"A fire burned each night in the top to warn ships of the harbor made double by Heptastadion Dike down the center," Zenobia said. Her voice felt detached from her body as she slipped into the past.

"That is so. Wood was taken to the top with a pulley system that ran through the hollow core of the lighthouse." Timagenes took Zenobia's elbow to guide her around a broken piece of granite paving stone.

"Is it true that the lighthouse mirror was used to reflect the sun's rays and burn enemy ships that sailed into the harbor?" Zenobia asked.

"Very true." Timagenes said.

"How wonderful."

Timagenes laughed. "You should see the light in your eyes."

"I do not thirst for blood. I just admire creative wars." Zenobia stopped next to the lighthouse and read the Greek inscription at its base. "The lighthouse is dedicated to the men who sail the sea." She looked up the shaft of limestone and marble. "Poseidon is still on top, guarding the sea and protecting the ships."

"For all eternity," Timagenes said.

Zenobia inhaled fresh sea air that smelled of fish and salt. On the horizon, ships skimmed through turquoise water as they glided between spots of sun reflected on the waves. Sails slapping in the wind reminded her of the last time she had been near the sea with Odainat. She grinned and hoped that Timagenes would not see her blush. Her oldest son had been conceived on a beach. An odd beginning for a child of the desert.

Insects and bees buzzed as they criss-crossed in front of Zenobia and brought her back to the present. In the distance, she heard both land and sea birds calling to each other. The intrusive clank of her honor guard's armor reminded her of the promise she'd made to Timagenes and his people. "We must go. It won't be long before the Romans discover that I've brought seventy thousand Palmyran, Syrian, and Arab troops with me."

"The Romans have fifty thousand men in Egypt, mostly in Alexandria and Cairo."

212

"Good. Two small battles are easier won."

Ezechiel grinned as he rode toward his queen. Both battles had been hard fought and the winning tasted as sweet as wine. Zenobia, beautiful though covered with the blood of battle, took off her helmet and shook her hair loose from under a silk scarf. Ezechiel held his breath. The sight of her always stopped his breathing.

A breeze whipped strands of curly dark hair across her face, but she paid no heed. Ezechiel reined in his horse. After battles, especially ones as fierce as these had been, Zenobia needed time alone. He had never asked, but he imagined that she prayed to her gods before she talked with Odainat. Once, when he had been too close, he had heard Zenobia talking to the king as if he were beside her. Her eyes had been full of love as her soft voice drifted across the desert toward him. He hadn't wanted to overhear her tender words, but he had been afraid to move. Her devotion struck him as beautiful and sad. A gorgeous woman should not spend her life alone. Ezechiel blinked in surprise when Zenobia smiled at him and motioned him to her side.

"General, a job well done. Together the three of us have beaten the Roman Legions."

"Three of us?"

She pointed. "Timagenes has proven himself a fine warrior."

"Ah." Ezechiel felt foolish. He thought she had meant that Odainat was with them.

"We leave at sunrise tomorrow for Palmyra. I can't wait to sleep in my own bed." Zenobia laughed. "I have grown soft in my old age."

"You will never be old, my queen. You have not aged one year in almost three decades that we've fought together."

"Oh, General Ezechiel, you talk in decades and make me feel as ancient as the pyramids in Cairo."

"My queen, I meant no disrespect. I still think of you as beautiful and desirable." Ezechiel felt his face redden. His traitorous tongue had given vent to thoughts that he had worked hard to keep hidden. Zenobia's lips pursed, and she rode away from him toward Timagenes.

Minutes later, she motioned for him to join them. Ezechiel had no choice but to force pride down his throat and go to his queen.

"Timagenes thinks that Claudius will retaliate and send a second wave of Roman Legions to try and wrench Egypt from us."

"Possible, my queen." Ezechiel hoped that his voice sounded normal.

"We will leave five thousand troops here permanently, Timagenes. Is that enough?"

"Your troops are well-trained and will work to train my Egyptian legions, but I can't understand Claudius and therefore, can't judge what he will do."

"What say you, General Ezechiel? Should we stay?"

Ezechiel looked into Zenobia's tired eyes. Thabit's head hung low, and Zenobia's posture matched it. The two battles had taken their toll. Maybe she needed to be home in her beloved Palmyra. "We have beaten the Romans soundly in many battles the last two years. We have taken much from them including their pride. I think Claudius will pull back and lick his wounds like the crippled lion."

Zenobia nodded. "Most of our troops are ahead of us. We go tomorrow as planned to take four hundred men home. Timagenes, you have shown that you can fight a good war. I leave you in charge. With your men and mine, we should not fear the Roman Legions. If ever you need Palmyran soldiers, we are but a few weeks away."

"I understand. I will serve you loyally and well, my queen." Timagenes held out his arms and laughed. His horse danced sideways at the noise. "You have given Egypt back to the Egyptians. Trade between our two countries will make us both prosperous." He bowed his head. "Thank you."

Zenobia liked the feel of the hard earth beneath her feet as she marched along with the infantry. Perspiration ran down her face, but she ignored it. Every step brought her closer to Palmyra. She dreamed of the cool temple where she would give thanks, the quiet of the funerary temple where she would talk with Odainat, and the perfumed water of her bath. She hadn't had a real bath for three days, but she was a soldier, and she liked it.

Zenobia looked at the sun that had dropped lower in the western sky and now touched the horizon. Ahead, her camp would be waiting. A simple tent was all she required and the same food that the soldiers ate suited her as well.

Thabit walked beside her, frisky for a middle-aged horse, and Zenobia recognized his joy at going home. He nuzzled her shoulder, and she chuckled.

"I shouldn't think you'd care where you were, but you're getting old and lazy, my friend. You want the soft life of a stud. Not for many years, Thabit. I have another horse in training, one of your sons, but he is still foolish."

It was not yet dark when Zenobia flopped down on her sleeping pallet devoid of armor, but not her sword or dagger. She controlled this land, but there were always enemies. She grinned. Rome as an enemy made life intriguing and tenuous. As she slept, she dreamed that she whittled a giant down to a dwarf with nothing more than her dagger.

When Zenobia awoke, she gripped her dagger tightly and peered into the darkness. "Who is in my tent? Speak before I cut out your tongue." She was irritated that her guards had not warned her of the intrusion. Were her guards dead? She reached out for her sword and slid it silently from its sheath. "Who slips into my tent like a thief?"

"It is I, Ezechiel, my queen. I had no wish to startle you."

"Ezechiel? Is anything wrong? Have the Romans attacked?"

"No."

"Then what? Light the lamp."

"I can't."

"Are you ill? You sound strange. Wounded?" Zenobia laid the sword aside and replaced the dagger in its customary arm sheath. "Come sit beside me." She patted the pallet.

"I should not have come."

"Nonsense. Sit." She felt Ezechiel's weight as he settled beside her. As her eyes adjusted to the darkness, she could see his broad outline.

He took her face in his hands and kissed her. Zenobia's heart fluttered. She felt the stirring of passion that she had not allowed to invade her soul since Odainat's death. Zenobia put her hands on Ezechiel's broad chest to push him away, but instead she kissed him in return. When the kiss was over, she nestled against his chest. It felt so good, so right to have a man's arms about her again.

Zenobia frowned and pushed Ezechiel away. "Miriam."

"I know." Ezechiel's voice broke.

"We left Miriam in Palmyra to watch over Rebekeh and my sons."

"My wife trusts us. She wished me well and asked that I bring you home safely."

"Oh." Miriam's kind thoughts of her safety were worse than a dagger through her heart. Zenobia rose from the pallet and leaned against the tent pole. "It is no good, Ezechiel. I would not love you as Miriam does because . . ."

"Because Odainat's presence would crowd me from your heart. I know. I have seen the love for him that lingers in your eyes."

"It would not be fair to Miriam. She has borne your daughters, has waited for you to return from battle, has kept your hearth and home . . ."

"I know all that. It still does not stop me from loving you. You're beautiful, vibrant, intelligent. I can't help myself."

"You will have to help yourself. I will not destroy Miriam's love for you or her trust in me. Don't your gods forbid adultery?"

"One god. We have one god who demands much of mortals. The rabbis teach us to have one spouse until death. We are to remain true to each other." Ezechiel scrambled off the pallet and moved to Zenobia. He put his arms around her and laid his head on hers. "It is too difficult to follow those rules when you're so close."

"You're a soldier and, as a soldier, are used to discipline. I suggest you discipline yourself. I can't believe my general is so weak. Perhaps you are too old to command my army." Zenobia stepped away from Ezechiel.

"No, do not send me away. I have angered you by my need to be near you. No soldier can protect you as well as I," Ezechiel dropped to his knees. "I beg you to keep me as your commander."

"Ezechiel, rise." Zenobia moved away from him. "I will keep you as my commander on one condition, and that is to forget any notions of love you have for me. I can't love a married man, especially one who is married to my good friend. She is one of the few people I can trust. I would like for her to think the same of me. Go. Forget this night, and never presume to enter my tent again unless invited."

"Yes, my queen." Ezechiel rose. "You are wiser and more loyal to Miriam than I. It is a humbling experience to come face to face with one's weakness. I'll strive to be strong."

"As shall I." Zenobia stood as still as a statue and listened to

Ezechiel's departure. "Forgive me, Odainat. It would have been easy to welcome Ezechiel into my arms. He is handsome and desirable. Would that he were not married, for I could love him."

Shouting and hoof beats brought Zenobia from her tent at the sun rise. She had spent a restless night, but the encounter with Ezechiel seemed like a hazy dream. A rider on a sweaty horse came bounding toward her tent. She recognized the dress of an Egyptian soldier. Zenobia frowned. What now?

"Queen Zenobia, a message from Timagenes." The man dropped from his horse and handed her a papyrus scroll. She broke Timagenes' seal and read the Greek quickly. "That conniving Claudius." She turned to the guards posted by her tent. "Find General Ezechiel. I must see him at once."

Ezechiel came to her in less time than it took for Zenobia to put on armor and strap her sword into place. She noted that he looked like a man who had not slept for days. No matter. She couldn't worry about that now. She had other problems.

"Ezechiel, we have to return to Egypt to help Timagenes. Claudius has sent one of his generals, Probus, I believe, to attack. Get our troops ready."

"Yes, my queen." Ezechiel turned to go.

Zenobia put her hand on his arm. "Ezechiel, we are still comrades in battle and so must be friends when not in battle. Forgive my harsh manner last night. It was armor for my heart." Ezechiel nodded as he walked away, not looking at Zenobia. She shook her head. She had wounded him deeply, and it was no one's fault. Were her gods playing games with her? Well, they could just stop it. She was in no mood for their diversions.

Zenobia kicked Thabit with her heels and clung to him as he leaped forward. Gravel spewed out from Thabit's hoofs accenting each torturous step he took. Flecks of sweat sprayed Zenobia's face as she leaned against the horse's neck to help him up the steep incline. Twice he slid backwards and sat on his haunches. Zenobia couldn't dismount as the path was dangerously close to the edge of the mountain.

Thabit scrambled up both times and, gulping great mouthfuls of thin mountain air, lunged toward the fighting.

Zenobia saw the dust of battle ahead and heard the shouts of combat. The Roman legions had cut halfway through the five thousand troops she'd left to guard Egypt. She would find out later what had happened. With a roar of outrage, Zenobia pulled her short sword and drove Thabit through the lines to the front. Slashing left and right, she cut down three startled Roman infantrymen before they realized they were attacked by fresh Palmyrans.

"Egypt is mine!" Zenobia hurled herself into enemy cavalry as Thabit expertly made his way through the chaos. A quick thrust, a strong slash, and a wicked backhanded swing took down the cavalry officer she had chosen for death. She fought for the land of her mother's ancestors, but mostly she fought for the right to keep what she had taken. How dare the Romans think they could snatch Egypt back. How dare Claudius think that she was no match for his legions.

Ezechiel shouted at her and his strong voice carried across the fetid air. "We can't win. Probus' men are killing us. We must retreat."

"Retreat! That word is not in my language. I can never retreat!" Zenobia underscored her point with quick death for the Roman who rode toward her.

"Your men will die! Back off and regroup," Ezechiel shouted.

"I will not!"

"This is no time to let pride rule your intelligence. Look around you. Save the men you can and attack at a later time." Ezechiel grabbed Thabit's bridle and pulled Zenobia around so she could see behind her.

The carnage horrified her. Battles had casualties, but this was more than she had ever seen. Her men, some had no beards yet, dead by the hundreds. She looked at Ezechiel, then squeezed her eyes shut.

"Order the . . . the retreat." The last word was whispered.

Trumpets sounded. Zenobia's army turned and ran from the battlefield. Zenobia followed as soon as she dispatched another infantryman who'd slashed at Thabit's tendons. The proud Palmyran army poured down the mountain side. The Roman army stayed behind content with victory. As soon as she could, Zenobia ordered her army to halt. They would sleep on the ground tonight in full armor under heavy guard.

It was her training that allowed her to sleep without dreaming, without waking until the next morning. She rolled off the blanket that she had thrown to the ground, wandered to the bushes to take care of necessities, then toward the mess area. The cook handed her two strips of dried lamb and a chunk of bread. She washed it down with stale water. Never had anything tasted so good.

"My queen, I fear we can't take on General Probus with the men we have left." Ezechiel spoke from behind her.

Zenobia looked around the camp. "Did the messenger ride out yesterday to bring back our troops?"

"He did. Our army is a full two days ahead of us."

Zenobia looked toward the southwest. "How many died on that mountain yesterday?"

"Of our four hundred, little more than two hundred remain. Of the five thousand that we left in Egypt, more than three thousand remain with us." He waved his arm to encompass the camp that stretched across the desert. "The Romans had seven thousand. We don't know how many we killed."

"We have to attack. Get the men ready. Unfortunately there is only one way up the mountain."

"So we fight on the desert."

"Our strength." Zenobia smiled. "Of course. I will take a thousand troops and ride into the mountains after General Probus. You follow behind by an hour. When I retreat, be ready to close in on both sides."

"Too risky. I will ride up the mountain . . ."

"No. General Probus will chase me. He, like all the other Romans, thinks women are weak."

"Timagenes told me the Romans call you the 'Iron Lady.' "

"Do they? Then I will show them that I do not bend." Zenobia looked toward the mountain. "We ride within the hour."

The sun glinted off the Roman armor as Zenobia and her men struggled up the mountain made barren by men and horses who'd negotiated its terrain yesterday. Bushes, grasses, and flowers had been trampled into the dirt, and now a dust cloud arose behind the Palmyran army as it worked its way toward fate.

General Probus waited for her near the peak. He wasn't short and stocky like most Romans, but tall and lean. He looked imposing in full armor. Zenobia swallowed. If she died, her beloved Palmyra would be under Roman rule. She could not let that happen. As clearly as if he were beside her, Odainat's voice whispered encouragement. She was so used to her memory of him, or his spirit, or whatever it was that she would've felt alone had he not spoken to her. Deep conversations with Longinus had given her more questions about Odainat's voice than had been answered. She no longer cared why she heard Odainat clearly. She needed him.

Zenobia drew her sword and loosened the reins on Thabit. She didn't have to look back to know that her men followed her. The earth shook like thunder as the cavalry and the infantry charged, and more dust swirled skyward blotting out the sun.

They fought for more than half the hour. Zenobia had tried to catch Probus and slay him, but he evaded her. Heeding the time, Zenobia ordered a retreat, and she and her men fought their way back down the mountain. She could see surprise on the faces of her lieutenants at her retreat because they were holding the lines against General Probus' Roman Legions.

Down, down the mountain and into the trap. It had to work. Zenobia shouted the orders for the trumpets to blow another retreat all the way down the mountain. She wanted Ezechiel to know they were coming.

Surprisingly, the Roman army turned suddenly and marched back up the mountain. Zenobia ordered a halt and watched, fascinated, as General Probus, now at the back of the lines, pushed his army away from her.

"It can't be a retreat. He wasn't losing," Zenobia said to no one in particular.

One of her lieutenants answered. "I don't understand it. We were not winning."

"We weren't losing, lieutenant." Zenobia's words were clipped. It was all she could do to keep from lashing out at him.

"Sorry, my queen. I only meant that . . ."

She waved her hand to shut him up. "Let me think. The only reason an army would turn is if they were in retreat or being attacked from behind." Zenobia looked past the mountain peak.

"See the dust cloud?"

"Yes."

"An army comes to join General Probus. Not more Romans," Zenobia whispered. "Not more Romans with a second victory so close."

The second army came into view, and Zenobia was momentarily stunned. "What army is that?"

Her lieutenant shook his head. "I would say that it is an Egyptian army, but how did they arrive so quickly? And who leads them?"

"Timagenes! Timagenes leads them! He is a genius." Zenobia let out a whoop of joy. "Send a messenger to General Ezechiel immediately. Tell him plans have changed. He is to bring his men up the mountain to lock General Probus into a vise. Here, take my ring so that he knows it is not a trap." Zenobia pulled off the gold band set with emeralds that Odainat had given her on their wedding day. She kissed it and gave it to her lieutenant. "We fight." She kicked Thabit and charged toward the rear of the Roman army.

"I love to swim. I never really learned how, Ezechiel, but I love the water." Zenobia squinted at the sun above her. "What's this river called?"

"Jordan."

"I should remember it since all this land belongs to Palmyra now." She splashed water on her arms and face. Her gold and emerald wedding band sparkled in the sun. A wave of sadness swept over her. "I need to go home."

Ezechiel laughed as he waded from the river. "You are home. You have so much land that almost anywhere you go is home."

"An odd thought. And since Timagenes surprised General Probus and defeated him, I still have Egypt."

"We helped."

"Without Timagenes, I'm not certain we would've won." Zenobia climbed up the bank and took a large cotton cloth from her servant. "Home is Palmyra and will always be no matter how much land we have. If ever I have to leave Palmyra, it would be worse than a death sentence." Zenobia looked to the northeast. "Odainat is there."

CHAPTER
XV

270 A. D. Palmyra, Syria

"My sister-in-law has returned from Damascus? For three years she has stayed away. Why does she come now?" Zenobia threw the papyrus scroll across the cella. Thoughts of revenge raced through her mind. "How dare she."

Longinus' blue eyes never wavered as he stared at the queen from his position in a gold brocaded chair. "Perhaps she has had her fill of grief."

"Her grief could never match mine." Zenobia jumped from her chair and paced back and forth across the mosaic tile floor.

"Your husband died an honorable death. Her son is a traitor and an assassin. History records both facts." Longinus stood, as was customary, but reclined again when Zenobia motioned for him to sit down.

"Tarab's son was spoiled by her."

"Does not a mother ask over and over where she misled the child? She suffers much."

"I suffer much."

"You have two sons; she has none."

"She has one husband; I have none."

Longinus leaned back in the chair, held his hands together, and rested his chin on the tips of his fingers. He waited.

"What do you want me to say? That I forgive her? No, I can't."

"Won't."

"My heart does not allow me to forgive her. Can't." Zenobia

stared out the window. "Her son killed my best friend's son. Adara died before her time as did Hairan. His only crime was to have been with his father at the wrong time."

"Your friend was married to Odainat?"

"Yes. I loved her son as if he were my own."

"I see."

"No, you don't. Because of Odainat's death, I hate the mother of the assassin. For Hairan's death that ended Adara's lineage, I can hate Tarab doubly."

"You must keep that hidden from your people."

"Why? My people understand my hatred of Tarab." Zenobia put her hands on her hips and glared at Longinus.

"It gives your enemies someone else to use."

"Ah." Zenobia grinned. "You are more than a philosopher, my friend; you're a politician."

"I survive. I have always been a survivor. We are very much alike, you and I."

"So, I will pretend to like Tarab." Zenobia sat in the broad marble window sill and looked at the darkening sky above the wadi. "The sun sets every day on the far side of the palace and leaves my rooms cool. I could invite Tarab and her husband, Mokimu, to live here. I will give them a western apartment. It will be hot."

Longinus laughed. "Why?"

"She sweats in the summer. Enough to fill the pool in the atrium." Zenobia chuckled. "It would please me to see her suffer."

"That is a facet of you that I've never seen."

"What facet?"

"Vindictiveness."

Zenobia plucked at the ribbons on her chiton. "I don't want to be vindictive." She walked to the Senet board and stared at the pieces. She moved the white disc and covered Longinus' flowered square.

Longinus reached across the table and held her hand. "You are too fine a person to be rancorous. Do not let hate eat you from the inside out."

"I won't. Your move."

"I can't. You have trapped me."

Zenobia smiled. "Good."

"You need to be kinder to me else your insides will rot."

Laughing, Zenobia scooped the playing pieces into the drawer of the table. "My insides feel wonderful. I hardly ever beat you."

"Not true." Longinus looked at Zenobia, his bright blue eyes shining. "When will you grant Tarab and Mokimu an audience?"

"Tomorrow. But I can't make it easy for them. I'd like to make her beg, even at the cost of my insides."

Tarab stood before the throne in a dirty, smelly chiton and stola. Her hair was grayer than Zenobia remembered, or maybe she could no longer afford the dye. Mokimu knelt before Zenobia, but Tarab had made no effort to kneel. Zenobia forced herself to relax. She had clamped her teeth together so hard that her jaw ached. It would be difficult to follow Longinus' advice. She glanced across the atrium where he sat with Vaballathus and Arraum. The boys were writing furiously, but Longinus watched her instead of his students. Rebekeh also watched her, but looked down at her lap when Zenobia made eye contact.

She should have seen Mokimu and Tarab in the throne room, but she preferred to treat the matter as a family problem, not a political one. Zenobia didn't want to give significance to this meeting.

"You have no wish to live in Damascus anymore. Why?" Zenobia's voice was harsh.

Mokimu cleared his throat. "I have no way to support us."

"That is not true," Tarab said. "We don't like the city. It is ugly."

"Wife, do not lie for me." Mokimu shook his head. "Her pride makes her lie."

"You could not get a position as a merchant? Mokimu, you are one of the best silk buyers I have ever encountered," Zenobia said.

Mokimu shrugged. "I . . . we were shunned even by the traders from India and China."

"Interesting," Zenobia said. "Why?"

"I am certain that your fame as a warrior has spread world wide. You are called 'Iron Lady' by them."

Zenobia grinned. "And by the Romans. It has a nice ring."

"By the gods, how absurd," Tarab said.

"Tarab, you are in no position to flaunt your dislike for me. You've come here to seek food and shelter because you have no money. It is not the fault of Mokimu that he could not work. You are the one who . . ." Zenobia stopped speaking at the warning look from

Longinus. It would be more difficult to be charitable than she had thought.

Mokimu reached up and grabbed Tarab's hand. He jerked her to her knees. The cracking sound as her bony knees hit the marble floor made Zenobia wince. She noted that Tarab did not react. The woman had mettle.

"Forgive my wife. She knows not what she does."

"Yes, I do." Tarab yanked her hand from her husband's.

"Enough of your babbling," Zenobia said. "You will stay here, protected by me. As the daughter of a king and the sister to Odainat, you will have clothing that is fit for a princess. You may choose which apartment in the palace that you want."

"Maeonius' apartment?" Tarab's voice choked.

"Yes." Zenobia felt compassion for her sister-in-law, and it surprised her.

"I want that one."

"Tarab, do you think . . ." Mokimu put his hand on her shoulder.

"I want that one!"

"Then you shall have it. I will assign servants to you to ready it. Nothing has been changed since . . . since Maeonius' death."

"By your hand," Tarab said.

"Tarab!" Mokimu slapped his wife's face. The sound echoed off the mosaic floor.

Tarab glared at her husband.

"Forgive her, Zenobia, for she has grieved too much for a son who assassinated a king. And forgive me for losing control."

"There is nothing to forgive you for, Mokimu," Zenobia said.

"There are many things. . . ."

Zenobia shook her head. "Hush."

"Thank you," Mokimu said.

"I understand a mother's loss, for I, too, have lost a stepson who was like my own. Let us try to live together peacefully. Now go. I have much to do."

"What? Conquer another part of the world? Don't you have enough?" Tarab hissed.

"Oh, Tarab. Your hatred consumes you," Zenobia said. "And both of you, please rise. It is not necessary to be on your knees when we are as family."

"She will learn to keep a civil tongue." Mokimu put his hands

on Tarab's shoulder and hoisted himself to a standing position before helping his wife rise.

Zenobia, surprised at Mokimu's weakness, stared at him as the
couple left the atrium. The man was gaunt almost to starvation. He
nearly waited too long to return home. It was probably Tarab's pride
that had kept them away.

The chatter of her sons made Zenobia smile. She loved to hear
the solemn voices of the boys as they helped each other with their
work. She noted, too, that Rebekeh leaned close to Arraum and peered
over his shoulder. Her lips moved as she read silently. Rebekeh needed
to be elevated to a higher station in life. It would be a pity for her to
have no use for her learning. She looked beautiful and healthy.
Longinus and his friend, Rabbi Uriah, had done wonders for her.
Zenobia had to chuckle. Longinus and the rabbi argued philosophy
and religion for hours and with such fervor that one would think
they were enemies.

It was the unmistakable sound of hob-nailed sandals against the
marble floors that brought Zenobia to her feet. Her hand rested on
the dagger hidden in its usual place. "Rebekeh, hide my sons." She
didn't have to look at Rebekeh to know that she and Longinus were
spiriting them from the atrium. She ignored the sounds of papyrus
falling and chair legs scraping against the floor as she waited for a
soldier to appear at the opening to the atrium. Her heart raced when
she saw that it was Ezechiel. He always came himself when the news
was grave.

"Has someone attacked us?"

"No, my queen. It's a caravan from India. They have just arrived
—what is left of them."

"What's wrong?"

"They were attacked by a band of marauding desert tribesmen.
Most of the caravan's people are dead except those who pretended
death."

"Where were our troops? Do we not provide safe passage?"
Zenobia frowned. The matter was serious. If the caravans could not
travel safely through her lands, then Palmyra would cease to have
the trade that kept her prosperous.

"The caravans were attacked in Persia. The Indians caught some
of their camels and rode here because they were afraid of King Shapur
and the Sassanians."

226

"You have seen to their wounds and have provided them with food and a physician?"

"I have. Two of the men wait outside. Do you want to question them?"

Zenobia nodded. Ezechiel motioned to a guard at the entrance and two blood covered and disheveled men were brought before her.

"If you need food, this meeting can wait," she said.

"We have no time to lose. There is a second caravan led by my brother who follows by a week. He will be attacked if you do not help us. I fear it is too late."

"What matter of men attacked the caravan?" Ezechiel asked.

"Well-armed, but not led by anyone we could identify. We think they were desert pirates who were paid by King Shapur," the second man said.

"Why?" Zenobia asked.

"We pretended to be dead, even when they took money from our money belts." The man shuddered.

"Any soldier does that," Ezechiel said.

"These men bragged about how well Shapur would pay them for destroying the caravan," the first man said.

"How odd. King Shapur has always allowed the caravans through. If caravan traffic ceases, he will suffer more than Palmyra." Zenobia chewed on her bottom lip as she thought about the peculiar actions of her long-time enemy. "Does he want to destroy Palmyra?"

"I think so."

"If he cuts off our supplies, then we would be in a weakened state. Palmyra has resources, but not enough to support her army and the civilian population." Zenobia paced back and forth, the colors of her chiton reflecting in the atrium's pool. "Ezechiel, get the army ready. We ride at once. Shapur has chosen to be foolish."

"We ride into his country?" Ezechiel asked.

"At the invitation of the Indians. I care not for treaties. He has broken the treaty by preying on the caravans, which is a direct affront to Palmyra. Quickly, Ezechiel." Zenobia whirled around and ran up the wide steps to her apartment. She needed to get into her armor.

Hot wind blew sand into Zenobia's eyes through her silk veil, but she dared not stop. The remains of the doomed caravan were behind them by a day, and they hoped to intercept and save the next caravan. She looked at the sky that had turned camel colored from the blowing sand. The roar of the wind made conversation impossible, but she was glad of that. She hadn't felt like talking since she'd seen the bodies of men, women, and children scattered in the desert. Those were the lucky ones. The prettiest women and girls would be sold into slavery along with some of the strong young men. Some were destined to be slaves anyway, but their lives would be miserable under the Sassanians. Better to be dead.

The rocking motion of the camel she rode nearly put her to sleep. She would have preferred to walk, but the sand was soft here. She squeezed her eyes shut, but the grit stayed in them. It was so hot her eyes were as dry as the desert. How different from the mountains they had crossed.

Shouts made her instantly alert, and she could see a scout riding toward her at a fierce rate. He leaned around the pointed saddle horn and whipped his camel on the flank. "My queen, my queen! The caravan is ahead, but it is being attacked. There is much fighting."

"We attack!" Zenobia pulled her bow off the saddle horn and reached down beside her for an arrow from the quiver.

The camel thudded across the desert. Its splayed feet helped it move faster than a horse, but the rocking made it difficult to shoot with accuracy. Zenobia was first to ride into the carnage with Ezechiel and the master of camels right behind her.

Nocking an arrow and sighting a pillaging thief was more difficult on a camel than her trusted horse. Zenobia hit her target, but only in the arm. The master of camels finished off the enemy neatly. She had to smile at Krikor's face with its fierce deliberation as he let fly the arrow. She would have to practice more with Krikor as a teacher, for he had his second kill, and she had none.

Aiming carefully, Zenobia chose a bigger man, thus a bigger target. She couldn't slow the camel, for they were obstinate creatures. She waited for the precise moment, then let her arrow sail across the space between her and the man who held a knife to a child's throat. The arrow cut cleanly through his chest and stuck out the back. He fell to the side and dropped to the desert like a boulder. The child scrambled up and ran.

It wasn't obvious who led this rag-tag band of larcenists. Zenobia wasted no more than a few seconds looking for the leader. She raced her camel down to the end of the caravan where the fighting was the worst. Ezechiel rode next to her, and dust rose behind them in a great tan cloud.

Arrows whizzed past Zenobia, but she didn't care. It angered her that innocent people were being killed to try to destroy Palmyra. Once more she let an arrow find its mark, but she was not content. Her speed at putting an arrow to the bow was too slow for effective fighting. If her army hadn't outnumbered the bandits . . . Zenobia refused to finish the thought. It would call to the wrong gods, and the battle would be lost.

She pulled back on the reins and surveyed the slaughter around her. It would be over soon. Even now some of the enemy had re-treated. Zenobia turned in time to see a rider tearing across the desert on a camel. Sun glinted off his sword, and he rode straight toward her. "You fool! You come at me with my weapon of choice!" Zenobia shouted even though the man couldn't hear her. She hooked her bow across the spiked saddle horn, drew her long sword, and yanked the shield off its hook on the saddle.

As the man rode closer, she recognized him as one of Shapur's lieutenants. "So, the Indians were right after all." Zenobia had no more time to think. Her left arm held a leather and wooden shield by double straps. She hugged it closer to her body.

At the last minute, the swordsman swerved and forced his camel past her camel's nose. Zenobia had no time to be confused before her mount bellowed in pain. Hot blood squirted in an arch as the camel swung its head back and forth, then dropped to the ground spilling Zenobia from the saddle. Her sword flew from her hand as she rolled across the hot desert. The sound of chain-mail scraping across the sand sounded like a desert storm.

She heard the peculiar muted thud of camel hoofs running to-ward her, and she jumped up. Her antagonist sprinted toward her at an alarming rate. Zenobia whirled around to find her sword, but she could not. "A stupid way to die," she shouted at her gods. Odainat's face flashed past her, but she had no time to dwell on it.

There was but one chance to live. Zenobia waited until the swordsman was almost within range. As he prepared to run her through, she sprinted out of the way and dove between his camel's front legs. Wrapping herself around the animal's back leg, she brought it down with a crash that sent the rider flying. Zenobia winced as she scrambled up. She would have one huge bruise from flying camel feet. The curved sword of the Sassanian lay at her feet. She wasted no time and grabbed it before the enemy could.

He eyed her warily as he slowly rose to his feet. He stood motionless, no longer grinning like an ape. He took a step toward Zenobia and with lightening speed pulled a dagger from his belt. It glinted and whistled as it flew through the air. Zenobia dropped to the ground and squirmed away. The Sassanian was off center when he fell on her, and Zenobia was able to jab him in an eye and roll away. His hands found her throat, and she saw pinpoints of light as her life's breath was choked out of her. Zenobia reached for his sword, felt the warm, hard handle beneath her fingers, and brought the blade down across the man's back.

Instead of a cry, the Sassanian grunted and melted to the earth like hot candle wax, his hands still grasping her neck. Zenobia thought freedom would never come, but slowly, his grip loosened. She pushed the heavy, bleeding carcass off her, sat up, and took great gasps of air.

When Zenobia looked around, she saw the fight was over. Most of the attackers were dead or captured by her army. Ezechiel, who shouted orders above the din, was far away. Zenobia had ended up on the edge of the fight. She thanked the gods for her life as she searched the desert for her sword. She left the Sassanian sword where it had been planted in the enemy's back.

Her sword had scratches that could be removed by polishing. It felt good to hold it again, and Zenobia chose to carry it rather than sheath it. She glanced back at her camel who lay dead and was sorry for the creature. The camel master would be unhappy, for a good war camel took a long time to train.

The wind whipped her hair about her face as she walked toward the camel master carrying her battered helmet beneath her left arm and holding her sword in her right hand. She squinted when sand blew up and twisted around her, but she couldn't see anyone else. For a minute she thought her gods had spirited her away. She was alone surrounded by a sand tunnel that blotted out the sky. Its roar deafened her to all other sounds. The grains of sand penetrated her armor and irritated her skin. How could it work its way through her silk-lined leather undergarments so quickly?

Zenobia sheathed her sword to protect it and put on her helmet more to stop the roaring than for any other reason. She would have continued to walk, but she couldn't see. Her father had told her stories of people who wandered the desert after a storm until they died because they couldn't find the very people they'd been standing next to. That was unacceptable. To die in battle would be an honor, but to have your bones bleached by the sun after a slow death . . .

The wind stopped as suddenly as it had started, and Zenobia looked around. Ezechiel rode toward her, his camel's peculiar gait a welcome sight.

"Come, a storm races toward us." Ezechiel reached down and hauled Zenobia upwards.

She scrambled into the elongated saddle. "Sorry. The sword got in my way."

"One more bruise won't matter." Ezechiel gave the camel a short blast with the crop, and it lurched forward.

Zenobia clung to Ezechiel burr-like as they raced across the desert. She couldn't see anything; the helmet collected sand at an alarming rate. The sand scratched her ears, her forehead, and parts of her face that she didn't have covered by Ezechiel's back.

They caught up with the supply wagons and were about to go past when Ezechiel pointed to the left. "It's coming! Get down, get down!"

Zenobia half fell off the camel and hit the ground. She stifled a groan as her sword sheath jabbed her in the ribs. She had no time to think about injury before Ezechiel and the wagon driver jerked her to her feet. They pushed the wagon on its side. There should have been a loud noise as jars of water, grain, and wine broke, but the roar of the wind and rasping sand as it scuttled across the desert drowned out the crash of the wagon. Wine didn't have time to flow into the sand, but whipped across the desert until it evaporated. Grain became indistinguishable from flying grit.

The horses were cut loose from the wagon to fend for themselves. Ezechiel brought the camel around to the overturned wagon and forced it to its knees.

"In here!" he yelled.

Zenobia crawled into the tiny cave made by the wagon. "Where's the driver?"

"He went with the horses, the fool." Ezechiel pulled her to him.

Zenobia stiffened. "What are you doing?"

He wrapped his cloak about the two of them. "Protecting my queen from the sand. The camel blocks most of it, but as the winds get stronger, the sand will feel like a million knife blades pricking our skin."

They leaned back into the shell of the wagon. The wind roared louder and talk was impossible. Zenobia rested against Ezechiel's broad chest and smelled a familiar odor of sweat and scented oil that reminded her of Odainat. Thoughts of him always came at odd times. It felt good to be nestled in a strong man's arms. She realized, with a start, how lonely she'd been the last three years.

Her heart pounded faster, and she tried to wish away thoughts of passion that stirred in her. Ezechiel shifted and their chain mail snagged. Zenobia stifled a giggle as they both tried to pull away. Her nerves screamed. Ezechiel's arms felt hard and powerful and the ache for love was intense within her.

Zenobia buried her head into Ezechiel's shoulder and prayed for strength. Her gods ignored her, and with a whimper, Zenobia pulled Ezechiel's face toward hers and kissed him. He kissed her in return, and blood rushed through her body at a dizzying pace, blocking the sounds of the sand storm.

"No!" Ezechiel pushed her away.

"Please. I need you."

"Do you forget the speech you gave me about loyalty to Miriam? To my god? I believed your wise words. I told Miriam of my temptation and pledged my love to her anew."

"She forgave you?"

"Worse. She understood and loved me. She has never mentioned my indiscretion since."

Zenobia turned away from Ezechiel. He was as easy to love as Odainat, but Miriam loved him. "We must not hurt Miriam. Forgive me."

"Forgive me, for I wanted to make love to you, too."

"I will never mention this moment to you or to anyone. It will be erased from my memory."

"A wise plan."

"The storm abates. I hear men shouting for us."

"Good. We can gather our men and supplies and take the injured home."

"Ezechiel, you're a good warrior, a loving husband, and a fine father. I find those traits admirable."

"Thank you, my queen."

The morning sun fought its way through silk curtains and shone on Vaballathus and Arraum as they bent over their studies. Rebekeh liked the way their hair looked as if it were laced with diamonds.

"Rebekeh, I don't want to do this again," Arraum said.

"You hurried through your Latin and made many errors."

"I did mine correctly," Vaballathus said.

"Do not brag. You're doing your algebra over because you fabricated the answers," Rebekeh said.

"Ha!" Arraum said.

"Arraum, do not wish bad things for your brother. It is unseemly for a prince." Rebekeh tapped her finger on Arraum's papyrus. "That is the wrong ending."

"How do you know?" Arraum asked.

"Unlike you, I listen to Longinus."

At the sound of footsteps, Rebekeh looked up. Her heart beat faster as Tarab marched through the door and across the room, her face like a storm cloud. Panther switched his black tail, scurried across the room, and hid under Arraum's sleeping couch.

"Isn't this a pretty painting?" Tarab jerked the papyrus from beneath Arraum's hands and dropped it to the floor. "Are you learning your lessons well so that you may conquer the world like your mother? How wonderful." Tarab frowned as she read youthful scratches on another papyrus. "This is not perfect." She threw the papyrus to the floor. "Maeonius always did his Latin perfectly. My son is . . . was perfect."

Rebekeh stared at the woman before her. Tarab was unveiled and her long gray hair hung limp and disheveled. A chunk of hair had been cut close to the scalp. A month's regrowth stood straight up. Although Rebekeh knew Tarab's clothing was new, it was wrinkled and soiled.

The woman waved a dirty hand. "Why should two young monsters have such a beautiful place? Maeonius' apartment is small."

"Would you like for me to see if there's a more suitable set of rooms for you?" Rebekeh asked. She'd do anything to get Tarab to leave.

"No!"

"Perhaps there are too many bad memories for you there."

Tarab grabbed Rebekeh's arm and squeezed. "All I have are memories while she has two healthy sons. The gods have wronged me. She has wronged me. My son's death is on her head, and I'll make certain that she pays."

Rebekeh jerked her arm away. "You are mad. It is because of you that Maeonius died. It is because of you that Palmyra had a civil war. It is because of you that Zenobia's sons and I had to flee and hide. You! You! You!" Rebekeh shouted.

Tarab's fist crashed into Rebekeh's face and sent her stumbling into Vaballathus' table. Papyrus, pens, and ink crashed to the floor. Rebekeh stared at the flower pattern of black ink against pink marble.

Tarab pointed a long, skinny finger at Vaballathus. "You think you're going to be king of this . . . this empire, but I'll see to it that you never rule. Somehow, someday I'll make it so."

"Get away from them! Get out!" Rebekeh pushed herself between Tarab and Vaballathus.

"I go, but I will return. You'll never know when or where. Someday, I will have my revenge." Tarab whirled around and vanished like an apparition.

Rebekeh let out the breath that she held. "We need guards. Guards night and day. I'll send for Ezechiel."

"Does she hate us?" Arraum asked.

"Of course she does," Vaballathus snorted. "Maybe Mother will allow us to kill her."

"Vaballathus! Do not speak in such a manner." Rebekeh wanted to agree with him, for she realized what a hypocrite she was. She could kill, again.

"It would solve many problems if we could kill her," Vaballathus said. "I suppose it isn't proper if not on the battlefield."

Rebekeh coughed to cover up the chuckle that escaped before she could stop it. "Enough of this talk. Pick up the scrolls and get back to your homework."

"Rebekeh, how are we supposed to think when we have vivid memories of Tarab?" Arraum asked.

"Don't play the weakling. Aren't you the one who saved our little Panther kitty from the dog?" Rebekeh pinched Arraum's cheek. "So get busy."

"Yes, Arraum. We are brave. Remember, you kicked that ugly man who tried to kiss Rebekeh that time in the kitchen." Vaballathus stacked scrolls, pens, and an ink pot neatly on his table.

"Take your pen cloth and wipe the ink from the floor, Vaballathus, and speak no more. Time flees, and your homework waits." Rebekeh could feel her cheeks flame, and she knew they were red. Would she never get over the shame of hiding in a brothel? Perhaps death would have been easier.

Rebekeh turned toward the doorway at the sound of footsteps, and hoped it wasn't Tarab again. She relaxed when she saw it was her queen.

"I understand Tarab has been bothering you. How often does she play the tormentor?"

"Once or twice a day. No more than that. Today only once."

"She will be whipped."

"No! That will make her worse. She is not herself."

"You are too kind. Very well. She won't be whipped, but she angers me so."

"Tarab's mind is gone. The punishment she doles out to herself is worse than what you could do to her."

Zenobia sighed. "You are wise beyond your years and kinder than I."

"Thank you."

"Come here, Rebekeh." Zenobia gathered the girl into her arms. "You are so brave and intelligent. If ever I had had a daughter, I would have wanted her to be like you. You are eating better? I feel softness where I used to feel bone."

"I could not die. Rabbi Uriah and Longinus plagued me until I had to stay alive just to spite them."

"Good. Ezechiel sent word to me. His best men will guard you. Tarab will no longer be allowed near you, Vaballathus, or Arraum."

"Guards will make me feel more secure. She frightens me, and yet I feel sorry for her."

"Do not mistake her intentions. If she could kill me, she would. You, as my friend, are her enemy, too."

"Friend. I like that. Thank you."

The sound of running steps halted at the door. Both women turned. "Mokimu," Zenobia said.

"Where have you taken Tarab? My wife left our apartment

screaming revenge. Where have you sent her?"

"Nowhere. She was not here when I arrived." Zenobia stared. "Why is your face purple?"

"It is nothing."

Rebekeh gasped when she saw the huge bruise on the side of Mokimu's face that went from hairline to jaw. "Mokimu! You must let the physician tend to you."

He waved his hand. "I have no time. I must find her. Tarab is mad. She hit me with a brass vase as I slept."

"Why?" Zenobia asked.

"I tried to keep her from coming here yesterday, so she put a sleeping potion in my wine. Today, I would not drink wine, but the potion must have been in my food. I fell asleep immediately."

"I need to put her under house guard and confine her to the apartment. If she wants to leave the apartment to go to market or anywhere else, she'll have to go with you and two guards. I can't allow her to injure or kill anyone." Zenobia shook her head. "I feel sorrow for her."

"I have trouble feeling sorrow for Tarab." Mokimu gently touched his swollen and purple face.

"She is not Tarab," Rebekeh said.

Mokimu nodded. "Well spoken."

"You must sleep apart from her, Mokimu, or you may be killed." Zenobia chewed on her lower lip. "I'll arrange separate sleeping quarters."

"Thank you. I must go and find her." Mokimu left as quickly as he had come.

"Sorrow follows him," Rebekeh said.

CHAPTER
XVI

270 A. D. Palmyra, Syria

"Are we really allowed to go to the camel sale?" Arraum hopped up and down so hard his toga nearly unwrapped itself. He grabbed the material in time to prevent a disaster, looked sheepish, and grinned.

Zenobia laughed. "My youngest son, you are comic. So when did you start wearing togas?"

"I want to be a philosopher when I grow up."

"Silly," Vaballathus said. "You don't even know what a philosopher does."

"I do too! Longinus is a philosopher."

"So what does he do?"

"He teaches us and thinks great thoughts about the world. And he travels and people feed him because he's intelligent." Arraum arranged the folds of his toga.

"You can be anything you wish, Arraum, as long as it does not take away from your duties as a prince," Zenobia said. "I suggest that for now, you give up the toga and put on clothing that you're used to. Camels are unpredictable, and you wouldn't want to embarrass yourself in front of Chief Ahura Mazda and the entire Tanukh tribe."

"I'll be right back." Arraum disappeared out the arched doorway.

Zenobia grinned at the sound of his feet slapping against the marble floors. "Your younger brother has much energy and enthusiasm."

"Yes, especially at night. He chatters and talks to me until I can no longer keep my eyes open."

"He talks much because he observes all. Remember that when you rule Palmyra. He will be of great service to you, Vaballathus."

"I will remember."

Queen Zenobia, her two sons, Ezechiel, and Krikor, the master of the camels, trudged past the dusty market place. Six of her palace guards were behind them at Ezechiel's insistence.

Zenobia was glad for the veil she wore over her hair and across her face. It kept the dust from her nose. Hundreds of camels bawled, spit, stomped, and nipped at each other and the men who tended them. Some of the animals rested, their legs folded under them seemingly uninterested in the turmoil around them, but Zenobia knew better. She loved the brutes, but she knew their disposition. The camel masters cajoled, yelled, and swatted their charges, but nothing could make them move once the lofty beasts decided they wanted to rest. A well trained war camel, though, was unlike the typical caravan camel.

"When may we get closer?" Vaballathus asked.

"It would be disrespectful to visit a camel before we paid our respects to Ahura Mazda," Zenobia said.

"Will our respects be long?" Arraum asked.

"It will seem so to you. I hope you remember how to behave." Zenobia called out to a tribesman who bowed as she rode past. He'd been part of Odainat's army until age slowed him down. She paused at a giant blue and red striped tent with gold tassels that hung from every corner. Pale rose colored silk, draped across the door in swags, was filled with rose petals to filter out the camel smell that wasn't that offensive to Zenobia. It brought back memories of her father who took her to camel sales and showed her how to choose a good animal.

Two guards bowed and opened the drapes. She nodded her thanks and swept past them with the two boys, quiet now, Ezechiel, and Krikor. He was most necessary to her today. Krikor was the son and grandson and great-grandson of an ancient Krikor who had been her grandfather's camel master. All knew camels better than they knew men. Or women, for that matter. All the Krikors had shrews for wives. It occurred to Zenobia that perhaps the wives all had the dispositions of camels.

"My lady." Ahura Mazda rose from plump silk cushions and bowed. "How wonderful you look. If I thought that you would be my wife, I would give you a hundred, nay a thousand camels."

"You have enough wives, Ahura, but you tempt me just the same. You are still lean and tough." Zenobia chuckled. "I am having some fine wine delivered to you soon. Also, I hope that you'll accept our gift of dates. They are sweet this year."

"Please, no presents are necessary. Your presence is the finest gift." Ahura took Zenobia's hand and escorted her to a mound of pastel silk cushions at the head of his table. He kissed her hand before she settled onto the cushions. Two slaves, one at each end of the table, used huge jewel encrusted ostrich feather fans to cool the guests.

"You would please me, General Ezechiel, if you and Krikor, isn't it, would join me at the table. My, and who have we here? Two large young men who cannot be your sons, Zenobia." Ahura's eyebrows raised and he clucked his tongue.

"But they are," Zenobia said. She looked at Vaballathus. He was nearly as tall as Ezechiel. When had he grown so?

"They are men now, so should sit at the table with us and talk with adults. Have you put away all your childish toys?" Ahura asked.

"I have," Arraum said. He plopped down between Krikor and Vaballathus.

"Really? I confess that I have not." Ahura snapped his fingers. From the dim corner of the huge tent came a servant with a small monkey dressed in a red tunic trimmed in silver. A silver chain and collar kept the monkey under control.

"Oh!" Arraum said.

Vaballathus stared.

"Her name is Panya."

"Panya? That's Egyptian for mouse." Arraum slapped his hand across his mouth. "I mean, I think it's a nice name."

"You are right. I think she's tiny like a mouse." Ahura snapped his fingers. The servant unleashed the monkey who scrambled across the Persian carpets and onto Ahura's lap. Panya searched though the folds of his tunic until she found a chunk of bread. Her bright eyes surveyed the party who sat around the table. She leaped across the table, scattering golden plates of fruit and cheese as she went, and settled herself on Arraum's head.

The startled boy blinked, then laughed when the monkey started parting his thick dark hair and pawing through it. "What is she doing?"

"Looking for lice," Vaballathus screeched.

"I don't have lice!"

Zenobia roared so hard she felt tears come to her eyes. "Of course you don't have lice, but Panya doesn't know that."

"Yes," Vaballathus said. "She thinks every monkey has lice."

"Be kind to your little brother," Zenobia said. She collapsed against the pillows and stared across the table at Ezechiel and Krikor. Both grinned.

"How long does she do this?" Arraum asked.

"She likes you," Ahura said. "She thinks you're her family. I consider that a good sign."

Panya shrieked, jumped to the ground, and somersaulted across the Persian carpets before climbing a tent pole and swinging from the rigging. She bared her teeth and shrieked again.

"Why does she do that?" Vaballathus asked.

"Hmmm," Ahura said. "I think she's angry that she didn't find any lice in your brother's hair."

Zenobia, along with the others, chuckled at the startled look on Arraum's face. "Perhaps you could march across the desert with the army. We seem to march with lice."

"No thank you, Mother." Arraum wrinkled his nose. "But I don't want her to be mad at me."

"Feed her a fig." Ahura held a basket toward Arraum.

As soon as Arraum took a fig from the basket and held it up, Panya scampered down the tent pole and, sitting on Arraum's shoulder, ate the fig. She spit out seeds at an alarming rate and plastered Arraum's tunic with them.

"So, beautiful Zenobia, you have come to see my camels?" Ahura smiled. "You know the best camels."

Zenobia unfastened her veil and took a piece of bread. She allowed a slave to pour honey over it. "I know you have the highest prices."

Ahura chuckled. "I have the best camels, therefore should charge the highest prices."

"I am also your best customer. I buy more camels than anyone else. I should get a better price."

"You always make me give you extra bridles, camel saddles, and even a few boys to tend to the camels. All that is extra and I pay."

"As you should since you charge such high prices." Zenobia accepted a golden goblet of wine. "The wine is strong."

"Not too strong for you," Ahura said. "I know your strengths. I remember that your father brought you along when you were younger than Vaballathus so that you could bargain for him when he was so drunk that he couldn't."

"You always made his wine strong and you watered yours." Zenobia grinned. "It is the manner of all bargains, and so I take no offense."

"No offense meant. I admired your father. He was a good man, as was Odainat." Ahura raised his goblet. "To Odainat. The gods had need of him, and so he went."

Everyone touched their goblets together, even Zenobia's sons. She was shocked to realize this was the first time they'd been included in any adult function. Bless Ahura for treating them so. It was his subtle wisdom that showed her she had to work harder to prepare the boys for their place in the world. Her eyes met Ahura's and he winked.

"Thank you," she said.

"I thank you."

"Me?"

"I thank you for allowing my Bedouin tribes to roam freely about your country. I thank you for allowing my young men to train and fight with your army. I thank you for fighting the Persians."

"That Persian dog, Ardashir, murdered your Parthian King. We fight the son today. That was in your father's time and yet the hatred for the murder of King Artabanus lives still. I can understand that, for I hate the Romans who were the instrument of Odainat's death."

"You seek revenge."

"I do."

"It is a noble thing that you do. The best revenge is to take that which the Romans covet."

"Countries they've conquered."

Ahura sighed. "It is for the strong to fight the strong. We cannot help much, but I pledge more men for your army."

"And camels."

"Ah, you are shrewd to bring up that which you need based on that which I need." Ahura nodded. "How many of my camels do you want?"

"I would like two hundred of your best. Krikor will choose."

"Krikor will want my favorite camel; that which I ride."

"Perhaps." Zenobia looked at Krikor. "And perhaps he won't like your favorite camel."

"I may not have two hundred camels to spare."

"I know that you have more camels in the mountains to the northwest."

"I?"

"I have been told that you have forty-seven on the highest slopes above your summer home and another thirty in the foothills."

"Do you know everything?"

"Of course." Zenobia tossed a fig to the monkey. Arraum wrinkled his nose.

"You will want to eat before looking at my camels." Ahura snapped his fingers, and immediately servants with food appeared from the shadows. Silently, platters of gold and silver were set on the low table.

"Ahura, you have always set a grand table. I don't know where all these delicacies come from, but I may want to buy your cook." Zenobia sniffed at the tantalizing odors that came from a large bowl.

"You will not get this cook like the others. I married his daughter. She would slice my throat open in my sleep if ever I sold her father." Ahura grinned. "Did you know that I gave your messenger one of my captives?"

"The young lad that I sent yesterday?" Zenobia stopped eating.

"He seemed in need of a wife. I gave him a comely girl. She was ill-suited to our way of life," Ahura said.

Zenobia looked at her host. "You felt sorry for her, but didn't want anyone to know it."

"Not at all."

"Ahura, we all know that you have a weakness for young slaves. Those you don't marry, you try to find good places for."

"It's nothing."

"I assume the girl is grateful?"

"I think so. She seemed relieved to get away from . . . from one of my jealous wives."

"No doubt. I will make certain that she has a good home. Perhaps she can work in my palace. I always have need of more servants."

Ahura held up his hand. "Say no more."

Zenobia heard a screech and glanced at the monkey. It jumped from Arraum's shoulder to Vaballathus' head, took off across the table, and leaped over Ezechiel before it dashed out the door.

"No!" Arraum shouted. "Come back!"

"It is all right," Ahura said. "He'll come back."

Arraum scrambled up and followed the monkey out the door.

"Arraum!" Zenobia called. She sprang up and followed her son. An unnamed fear gripped her heart, and she prayed to Allat, the goddess who protects women, as she pushed her way past the throng that milled outside the tent.

"Arraum! Be careful."

"He follows the monkey that way, my queen." Her palace guard pointed toward the camel corral.

"Come with me, both of you." Zenobia flew across the hard packed sand. Ahead she saw a flash of red as the monkey leaped through the woven ropes that held the camels in too tight of an area.

"Arraum! Look out for the camels! They are unpredictable." She watched in horror as Arraum crawled through the ropes after Panya. The monkey turned and screeched at Arraum. Zenobia's heart froze. Camels milled about, trying to move away from the screaming primate. As she ran, too slowly it seemed, she could see Arraum lunge for the monkey. He grabbed the hem of his tunic, but could not hold on and fell beneath the closest camel. Her heart stopped as she watched Arraum scramble up.

She reached the ropes just as Arraum shrugged and turned toward her. "Thank goodness, you're all right." She reached across the ropes and hugged her son. "Did I not tell you that camels were unpredictable? Do I need to tell you you were rude to Ahura Mazda?"

Arraum crawled through the ropes and stood before his mother. "I am sorry. May I apologize to Ahura Mazda now?"

Trying not to grin, Zenobia ruffled her youngest son's hair. "I would expect nothing less than a perfect apology."

At first the rumble did not penetrate her consciousness, but in conjunction with shouting men and screams, Zenobia finally realized something was wrong in the corral. She looked up in time to see the monkey leap from one camel's back to another. It would've been funny except that the camels had decided Panya was something to be feared. They had not been trained to have a monkey leap across wave after wave of camel's backs. They spit, whirled around, and kicked at the camel masters. Camel-colored dust rose and camouflaged the beasts. Even the animals that knelt on the ground had risen, rump first, to be ready for flight. The problem was they didn't know which way to run, for they had no leader.

"Arraum, let's get out of here." Zenobia motioned to her two palace guards to break a path through the crowd.

She and Arraum had not traveled more than a cubit when she heard the stampede behind her. Zenobia grabbed Arraum's hand and ran diagonally across the compound as fast as she could go. Glancing back over her shoulder, she saw the camels surge toward them.

"Allat! Allat! Protect us!" Zenobia looked for anything to give them cover. Now all the people were running from the stampede, and she had trouble hanging on to Arraum. She stopped and grabbed the boy with both arms, threw him across her shoulder, and ran for a shallow wadi that she knew was ahead.

She slid down the side of the fissure, pushed Arraum into the bottom, and lay across the top of him. It wasn't deep enough, but it was all the protection they had. Had she stood, her head would've been above the wadi.

She could smell the camels coming before she felt the dirt kick down on them as the camels leaped across the crevice. The last of the noise died down as the camels drove themselves south. It would take weeks to round them up, and she could hear the camel masters swearing in a multitude of languages.

"Can we get up now?" Arraum asked. "You're heavy."

Zenobia giggled, mostly from relief, and pushed herself up. "I'm glad we're both all right."

A camel wheezed, and Zenobia looked up just as the injured animal tumbled into the wadi. She tried to jerk Arraum out of the way, but it was too late. The camel landed on her son.

She screamed and pulled at Arraum's arm to get him from under the body of the camel that thrashed around. "Ezechiel! Ezechiel!"

The camel's movements caused Arraum to scream. Zenobia pulled her dagger from the sleeve of her chiton and swiftly slit the camel's throat. Hot blood squirted out from the camel's carotid artery and drenched her tunic. She tried to pull the camel off her son, but could not. It was draped across his chest, legs, and had one arm pinned.

"Arraum, speak to me."

"It hurts," Arraum whispered.

Zenobia dropped down next to him and began digging the sand away so she could drag him from under the camel.

"Ezechiel! Ezechiel! Help us!"

"I am here." Ezechiel slid down the side of the wadi and fell to his knees beside Zenobia. "We are lucky. Some were killed."

"Arraum, speak." Zenobia scraped through the hard packed dirt that was beneath loose sand. "He has fainted."

"Get down here and dig," Ezechiel shouted up to soldiers who looked down on them. "Bring ropes to move the camel."

Zenobia ignored soldiers who scrambled down the side of the wadi. Her fingers bled where she had broken her nails. Twice she licked her fingers and held them under Arraum's nostrils. Both times he still had life.

A hand on her shoulder did not stop her.

Ahura spoke. His voice shook. "Zenobia. It is my fault. I should never have let the monkey loose."

"Do not speak thus." She patted his hand. "If fault is to be assigned, let it be mine for not having taught my son better."

"His face is pale. Does he still? . . ."

"He does." Zenobia sat back on her heels and watched as soldiers pulled the ropes taut that had been wrapped around the lifeless camel.

"Allow me." Ahura dropped down next to Zenobia and slid his arm under Arraum's shoulders.

"When we lift the camel, pull," Ezechiel said. "Ready! One! Two! Pull!"

Ahura pulled Arraum almost free before the men dropped the camel back down. Zenobia groaned with frustration.

"His legs are trapped, Ezechiel. Once more," Zenobia shouted.

"One! Two! Pull!" Ezechiel shouted.

Zenobia slid under the camel and grabbed Arraum's legs while Ahura pulled. She slipped and tumbled into the small depression she'd made by digging as a rope broke. The dead weight of the camel shoved her face into the sand. One hand was pinned beside her and the other hand was near her nose.

She heard nothing as the air was crushed out of her lungs. "Not now! Not this way. Allat, help your daughter again in her hour of need. I have to live to protect my sons from the Romans. Allat, help your daughter."

The weight was oppressive. Her back hurt; her shoulders were smashed; she couldn't breathe. She dug a shallow hole with one finger by her nose, but how long could she lay trapped without air?

As suddenly as it had happened, Zenobia felt weight being lifted from her back and shoulders. Someone grabbed her ankles and she was dragged across the sand and dirt. A whoosh of air whipped past her as the unfortunate camel was let down again.

"My queen, are you all right?" Ezechiel squatted down and stared at her. He brushed dirt from her face.

"I live. How is Arraum?" Zenobia stifled a groan as she sat up. She would be worse tomorrow.

"I have sent for your physician, Iason," Ezechiel said.

Zenobia crawled to Arraum and held a wet finger under his nose. She thanked Allat that her son still breathed.

"Zenobia, I have a wonderful physician who comes from Asia Minor. May I send for him?" Ahura asked.

She looked at his stricken face and reached for his hand. "Of course."

"I will hurry. We should bring the boy to my tent. It's closer than your palace."

"All right. That's kind of you." It mattered not where Arraum was treated. She watched Ahura clamber from the wadi. He was agile as were all the Bedouins who traveled her country.

"I should have stopped him, Mother." Vaballathus scrambled down the wall of the wadi. "I am his protector, and I should have stopped him. I was seated next to him."

Zenobia held out her hand. "Come. It was as much my fault as yours. I should have called to him sooner."

"My queen, I have come as quickly as possible." Iason stared from the lip of the wadi. He stepped carefully down the steep slope. His staff made holes next to each footstep, and he held on to a soldier who carried his bag of medicines.

With no further words, Iason knelt next to the unconscious boy. Quickly his deft fingers checked Arraum's arms and legs, his chest, and rib cage. "No broken limbs or ribs. He is lucky that his chest was not crushed."

He clucked his tongue as he checked Arraum's head. Zenobia knew better than to ask questions. The old Jew worked quicker when his concentration wasn't broken. He clucked his tongue again, then nodded to Ezechiel.

"It is safe to move him."

Ezechiel ordered two soldiers with a litter to carry the boy to Ahura's tent. Zenobia, helped up by Vaballathus, followed closely behind, her own pain pushed to the back of her thoughts.

Ahura had a physician waiting. Two couches had been placed in the corner of the tent. "I knew that you would want to be near your son."

Zenobia squeezed his shoulder as she passed him. He would feel the guilt for a long time although she knew there was no reason for it.

"I will have Panya destroyed," Ahura said.

"Oh no, my friend. Do not destroy such a charming pet. It is not anyone's fault. Don't your children like the monkey? And knowing the fondness of children for pets, didn't you do my sons a favor by bringing her out to entertain them?"

"A mistake."

"No, Ahura. The sign of a compassionate man. Don't let your heart hang heavy with remorse. It was an act of kindness. Even though the end result is an accident, the intent was noble." Zenobia turned at the sound of Iason's voice.

Iason nodded to the young man. "What is your name?"

"I am called Vanko."

"What medicines do you have?"

Vanko knelt in front of a leather chest with flowering plants painted in squares across the lid. He pointed to one of the pictures. "I have Galium aparine. It should be used on the boy's head injuries."

"I concur. It should be boiled immediately."

"I have already started the process. May I examine the boy's head?" Vanko unlocked the chest of medicines. "I would like to see the nature of the wound."

"Certainly." Iason pulled aside Arraum's long hair. "As you can see, he has a deep laceration and a section of skull has caved inward."

"Most serious." Vanko pulled a pair of scissors from a pouch that hung by his side. He snipped hair away from Arraum's head while he held the boy down. Each time the scissors clicked, Arraum whimpered and squirmed.

"Stop!" Iason shouted. "You'll do damage."

"We must do surgery or he'll die."

"Surgery! No! We will pray to the gods for his life."

"If he lives, with this indentation in his skull, he will be unable to talk, or worse, he'll be simple-minded. We need to do surgery."

"What makes you think you, as youthful as you are, can do surgery?"

"I have training from the Egyptians and the Greeks."

"It is an unknown factor. He could die by your hand." Iason shook his head. "I cannot allow it."

"If pressure is not released and the wound closed, this child will die."

"He may not. I have seen cases where . . ."

"Did they regain their full capacity? Or were they struck dumb or worse, raged at the gods, and could not be understood or controlled? Did they murder those who cared for them?"

Iason looked at his patient. "He is a sweet child by disposition. I would not have him injured in any way, but I cannot let you do surgery."

"I can," Zenobia said.

Iason bowed. "My queen, it is a risk that shouldn't be taken."

"Arraum is my child who is full of fun, of light, of laughter. I cannot condemn him to a world where he is angry and hateful. I would rather that he be dead." Zenobia glanced at Ahura, Ezechiel, and than back at Iason.

"Vanko is the best surgeon I have ever seen," Ahura said. "I trust him with my life."

"All right, then I shall trust him with Arraum's."

She looked at her physician. "You are a master of medicine, Iason. You decide what medicine will help Arraum during surgery."

Iason frowned. "As you wish."

Zenobia brushed dirt from her stola. "I shall stay with you, Vanko, and hold my son's hand."

"It is difficult to watch," Vanko said.

"It would be more difficult for me not to watch."

Vanko nodded toward his chest of medicines. "Choose what you will, Iason. I must prepare the instruments."

"Prepare them? How?" Iason asked.

"The Egyptians believed that boiling water killed the demons that caused corruption. I have found that to be so."

Zenobia settled down next to Arraum as Vanko and Iason argued over medicines and procedures. Iason was good, but he had old ideas. The young were the ones who helped medicine advance. It was that way with war and art and everything. Youth forced the world to change. Did she like it? She didn't know. Sometimes the old ways were more comforting.

Arraum's hand was hot and his face flushed. She couldn't bear another death. She couldn't have her family snatched from her one by one. She was aware of Vaballathus who sat near by. She smiled at him, but he couldn't return the smile.

"He will live." Zenobia motioned for Vaballathus to join her. She grabbed his hand as he sat beside her. "You must believe that he'll live."

"I should've . . ."

"Don't say anything. It was not anyone's fault."

"I hate sitting here." Vaballathus jumped up and paced back and forth across the layers of Persians rugs. He stopped and leaned against the massive tent pole. "I can't stay here. May I be excused?"

"Yes. Return before dusk. Take two guards with you."

"Guards?"

"We will always have enemies."

Vaballathus collapsed on a cushion. "I don't like having guards."

"You'll go nowhere without guards." Zenobia was surprised. She never had trouble with Vaballathus. It had to be as difficult for him as it was for her. She could choose the method of saving Arraum, but Vaballathus had nothing to do.

"Son, would you do me a favor? I can't go to the Temple of Bel to pray for Arraum's life. Would you do that for me?"

"Me? I have never prayed at the Temple alone."

"You're old enough. Take two Palmyran guards. They'll help you as will the priest. Go. I need the prayers sent quickly."

Vaballathus jumped up and ran out the door. Zenobia walked to the cot. She picked up a lock of cut hair that had fallen to the carpeted floor. It felt so silky. "Do the surgery without me," she whispered. She kissed Arraum's hot cheek and nearly ran from the tent.

"My deepest apologies," Ahura said. He came toward her, ghost like through the dust that still floated in the air.

"By the gods! Will you look at this mess!" Zenobia's mouth gaped. A half dozen tents had been knocked down along with several wagons. Men still ran, cursing, as they pulled camels back inside a makeshift fence of ropes.

"A bad thing is a camel stampede. I am glad it happens so few times." Ahura coughed. "How is Arraum?"

Zenobia shrugged. "I asked that your physician do surgery. I would rather that Arraum die than be simple minded or unable to talk."

"You are a wise and brave mother."

"It is in the hands of the gods."

"Come, let's go to my other tent. We will eat, then you may rest." Ahura took her elbow and led her toward a second brightly striped tent.

A shout caused Ahura and Zenobia to turn. Rebekeh ran toward them holding up her tunic and leaping across tent ropes. "My queen! My queen! Tell me it isn't true!"

"What have you heard?" Zenobia asked.

"I have heard that Arraum has been injured and may die." She grabbed Zenobia's hand. "Tell me it isn't true."

"Alas, it is true." Zenobia was startled when Rebekeh burst into tears. She pulled the girl into her arms and hugged her. "He will be all right. He's having surgery to his head. He'll be all right."

"May I see him?" Rebekeh said between sobs.

"You may, but you must know that he looks terrible." Zenobia walked with her arm around Rebekeh's shoulders as she led her to the other tent.

"I want to see Arraum before I go to the synagogue to pray for him." Rebekeh shivered. "God couldn't take him from us after having saved him. He has Latin homework that he hasn't finished. I found it hidden under his sleeping couch." She sniffled.

"He will live to finish his Latin. Come. We can't stay too long. The physicians prepare him." Zenobia shuddered. She prayed that Arraum wouldn't feel pain.

CHAPTER
XVII

270 A. D. Palmyra, Syria

    *Z*enobia stared up at the statue of Allat, the goddess of women. "Like you, my goddess, I wear a helmet and hold a spear. I do it to protect my sons and Palmyra." Zenobia allowed tears to flow. Here she didn't have to appear brave and all knowing. Allat understood her grief, her fears, her needs.

    Zenobia glanced at the guards who stood outside the entrance. The early morning sun cast long shadows of the men into the temple. The shadows lay across the cool stones like black spirits and further darkened Zenobia's mood. She was alone with Allat for the fifth time in five days.

    Zenobia placed dates, nuts, and dried fish from Lake Tiberias at Allat's sandaled feet. "I've come to beg you to save my son. He's a good son. I am an empress, but that means little when one's child is near death."

    Zenobia knelt before Allat. "I have lost much with Odainat's assassination. I've lost Adara's son. Need I lose more? To what end?" Zenobia prostrated herself before the statue. "I am a mere woman asking Allat to intervene with the fates. Allat has power over a mother's grief. Allat can crush grief with her generosity."

    Zenobia fasted, prayed, and chanted Allat's praises from sunrise until darkness settled inside the temple, and she could no longer discern Allat's features. One last chant, one last prayer, and Zenobia rose and backed from the temple. She turned and walked down the dozen steps to the street. She had trekked across town to the temple to show Allat humility, and she would return to the palace the same way. She had humbled herself and had been sincere.

Her unconscious son had been moved to his rooms at the palace at Zenobia's insistence. She wanted him near her and in a familiar place. Vaballathus, ever relentless, read his Latin stories to Arraum daily. He insisted that his younger brother would frown when Vaballathus explained the verbs.

Vaballathus sang Hairan's camel song to Arraum. Once Vaballathus had run to Zenobia and shouted that Arraum had smiled! She had wanted to believe him and had sat next to his bed while Vaballathus had sung the song over and over until the words burned her heart. Arraum never smiled even though Vaballathus insisted that he would on the next verse.

Poor boys. One awake and numb from singing and one asleep with no consciousness to hear the singer.

Zenobia strode quickly through the palace, ignoring everyone who wished to speak to her, and rushed into Arraum's room. Sconces and lanterns burned the darkness away except in the corners.

Miriam looked up and shook her head. "He sleeps still."

Zenobia sat on a stool next to her son. Already stubble grew where his head had been shaved. A curved scar, still deep red and crusted over started above his ear and ended a few inches behind it. "Does he sleep soundly or moan?"

"He sleeps soundly." Miriam felt his forehead. "His fever is down."

"I thank you deeply for watching him while I prayed to Allat."

"I shall pray to God for him tomorrow at the temple."

"If all our gods listen, then maybe he'll live." Zenobia held her son's hand. "He is such a little boy."

A piercing scream wrenched Zenobia from a fitful sleep. She awakened instantly and found her hand on her sword. It was her lover now.

She leaped from her sleeping couch, sword clenched in a powerful fist, and raced into the cella. Three guards stared toward the east window.

"Stop her! Stop her!" Mokimu shouted.

"By the gods!" Zenobia froze, her sword useless. Tarab, gray hair wild and undone, stood on the sill of the window above the wadi. Her stola hung in tatters about her body. Zenobia wondered when Tarab had grown so thin. Her bones almost pierced her dry skin. Sunshine framed her making her look like a goddess from the underworld.

"Get away from me. I go to join Maeonius."

"Wife, come down. I can't live without you. Don't do this."

Tarab tugged at her dirty stola. "I have no reason to live."

"You have many reasons to live," Zenobia lowered her sword.

"Don't speak to me. I hate you."

"Tarab, she is your queen. Show respect," Mokimu said.

"Don't admonish her," Zenobia whispered.

"Don't speak to Mokimu." Tarab looked out the window. "I don't want the last thing I hear to be your voice."

"Get down, Tarab. How can your death help?" Zenobia took a step toward her.

"Stand back." Tarab removed her sandals, balancing precariously on first one leg, then the other. She tossed them to the floor where they hit with a smack. "I won't need these."

"Do you think that I care whether or not you kill yourself?" Zenobia asked. "I don't care, but you're being selfish. Who will care for Mokimu?"

"He doesn't need me."

"But I do need you." Mokimu's voice was threaded with tears. "I have loved you since you were a young girl. I have loved you even though I knew I was unworthy. I prayed to the gods for your love."

"How foolish," Tarab said.

"Your hate for me will die with you," Zenobia said.

Tarab glared at her. "Hate comes from beyond."

"You will no longer torment me." Zenobia shrugged. "An easy way out for me. Guards! You're dismissed. We have no need of you. Mokimu, stay if you like, but I go to thank the gods who've answered my prayers." Zenobia turned and walked slowly toward the door. She closed her eyes and prayed.

She heard a screech behind her and turned just in time to see Tarab hurtle toward her. She dropped her sword and caught the woman. They fell to the floor, and Zenobia wrapped her arms and legs around Tarab. "Stop squirming. You'll not get loose."

"Let me go."

"Not until you promise not to leap into the wadi. I would leave you for the vultures."

"Yes, you would." Tarab squirmed again.

"A bitter meal for them."

Tarab lay perfectly still. "All right. Let me up."

Relieved, Zenobia released her sister-in-law. "You're free."

Tarab scrambled to her feet. She stared down at Zenobia. "Not yet. I'm not free yet, but someday . . ." Tarab motioned to Mokimu to follow her. He stood still and stared at Tarab's sandals that lay carelessly at his feet. He picked them up and studied them as if he had never seen them before. He smiled at Zenobia, then grabbed Tarab's arm and propelled her toward the door.

"Release me, Mokimu. I demand that you stop shoving me."

Mokimu whacked her on the behind with a sandal. "Hush, Wife, before I slap your troublesome mouth instead of your rear."

Zenobia could not believe the forcefulness that Mokimu showed. At this moment he had strength and control. She hoped it would last. Zenobia snorted. Poor man, to love such a woman. She should have let Tarab jump. It would've been easier, but she couldn't because of Mokimu's stricken face. The gods would have been angry as well.

She refused the hand of a guard and sprang to her feet, eager to start the day as she always did by visiting her sons. Zenobia walked down the hall to Arraum's apartment. When she peered in, Rebekeh was asleep on the floor next to him, and Panther was curled up next to Arraum. Zenobia stared because she didn't believe what she saw.

Arraum's fingers were intertwined with Panther's fur. "Rebekeh," she whispered. "Look!"

Rebekeh bolted upright, blinked, and jumped to her feet scattering linens everywhere. "I'm sorry, my empress. Forgive me."

"Look at Arraum!"

"Aye! The dead returns to life."

Zenobia felt Arraum's forehead with her wrist. "No fever."

"Mother, I'm thirsty."

Zenobia closed her eyes and knelt next to the sleeping couch. "Praise be to Allat. She has heard my pleas."

"Thanks be to God," Rebekeh said.

"Let me help you." Zenobia slid her arm under Arraum's thin shoulders and raised him.

"I need water." Arraum coughed.

"I'll get it." Rebekeh dashed to the table and picked up a clay pitcher of cold water. Her hands shook as she poured a cup.

Zenobia took the cup from her and held it to her son's cracked lips. He drank slowly, and water dribbled down his chin.

"More."

"All right." Zenobia didn't try to keep tears from flowing down her cheeks. "Send for Iason and Ahura's young physician from Egypt."

"Vanko is across the hall. Iason has been called to the barracks." Rebekeh ran from the chamber.

"Are you hungry?" Zenobia rubbed Arraum's stubby hair. "Your hair grows in dark and rich like the soil at the edge of the Nile." She stared at the horseshoe-shaped scar. It had healed clean without festering. The scab was solid.

"I'm tired."

"No wonder. Arraum! You're speaking clearly."

"Am I supposed to be quiet?"

"No. You talk as much as you want. Do you remember what happened?"

"Something about camels."

Zenobia's heart thumped. Was he simple-minded after all?

"He may never remember the accident or he may remember part of it." Vanko knelt next to Arraum and laid his head on the boy's chest. "His heart is strong."

"Why won't he remember the accident?" Zenobia struggled to keep her voice steady. It would do Arraum no good to sense her fear.

"We don't know. Many people with head injuries are like this." Vanko glanced at Zenobia. "It doesn't mean that he will be simple."

"How soon will we know?"

Vanko shrugged. "A few days, a few weeks."

"Are there medicines to help?"

"No." Vanko lifted Arraum's fingers on his right hand. "Can you wrap them around my hand?"

"I'm telling my fingers to move, but they will not." Arraum frowned. "I tried again."

Zenobia bit her lower lip to hold back a gasp. She had seen her grandfather thus after he had had a fit. He could only use one hand and never did he walk again.

"Use your other fingers to grasp my hand."

"I can do that."

"What is wrong with his hand?"

"I can tell you what is wrong." Iason rushed across the room, bowed to Zenobia and dropped to his knees at the end of the bed. "I came as soon as I heard."

"What is wrong? Can Arraum be cured?" Zenobia wanted to shake the slow-witted physicians who wouldn't answer her questions quickly enough.

"His head should never have been touched." Iason glared at Vanko.

"If I hadn't pried the bone away from his brain, he would have died."

"The brain is not important. It is the heart that we needed to protect. There is the seat of a person's being."

"Cease your arguments!" Zenobia shouted.

Both men froze.

"Not in front of the child. We'll talk elsewhere, but not here. Wait in my cella."

The men scurried from the room. Rebekeh dabbed her eyes with the hem of her tunic. "They frighten me with their talk."

"They know little." Zenobia sat next to Arraum. "Can you bend your legs?"

Arraum lifted his left leg, bent it and let it down carefully. He did the same with his right.

"It hurts like I've been kicked by our donkeys."

Zenobia pulled back the linen covering. "Still bruised but healing. The scratches are almost gone. Lift your arm."

"That's easy."

"Squeeze my fingers."

"I can."

"Squeeze harder." Zenobia tried to keep her face expressionless, but fear pushed itself against her hopes.

"I am squeezing."

"No, you're not." Zenobia ran her thumb over Arraum's fingers that she held in her hand. They were cold. "Bend your arm." She smiled when Arraum obeyed.

"Am I going to die?" Arraum's voice quivered.

"You are far from dying. You've come back from the edge of

death." Zenobia smiled. "I predict a long and healthy life for you. Allat has chosen to protect you."

"Allat will protect me?"

"Always, for once protected, always protected."

"Mmmm." Arraum's eyes closed, and soon he breathed deeply.

"Will his fingers ever work?" Rebekeh asked.

"I don't know." Zenobia patted Rebekeh's cheek. "You may sleep in your own bed. You need to rest so that you can care for Arraum. As he gets better, he'll get more restless."

"I'd rather stay here."

"As you wish. I have two physicians waiting for me in the cella."

Iason sat by the window staring at the sky. Vanko lounged against a pillar and kneaded his fingers together. Iason leaped to his feet and bowed when Zenobia entered. Vanko knelt.

"Rise." She glared at them. "I don't understand why two physicians can't work together. You, Vanko, know surgery, but not herbs and healing potions. You, Iason, know the potions, but rarely do more than set a bone or stitch a soldier's wounds. If either of you had tended my son without the other, he would have died."

The words hung like heavy spring clouds in the room. It was so still that Zenobia could hear birds calling as they swooped and dove into the wadi. Far away she could hear voices of women as they walked to the market place. The buzz of insects told her that morning was half over. Still she did not speak. What could she do to punish these foolish men who'd saved her son? Their fighting would have to be punished.

Iason stared at the floor. Vanko still kneaded his long, slender fingers. They were on opposite sides of the room and would probably never speak to each other again. A pity, for both had talent.

Zenobia chuckled. Vanko looked relieved at that, but Iason's eyes revealed his trepidation. "I have the perfect punishment. Iason, in the mornings between cock's crow and mid-morning, you will be the teacher."

"Of whom, my empress?"

"Of Vanko."

Iason's grin vanished as quickly as it had come when Zenobia glowered at him. Vanko looked like a pained school boy.

"Vanko shall be teacher from midafternoon until dusk," Zenobia said. She enjoyed the look of alarm on Iason's face. He knew her too well.

"Whom shall I instruct?"

"Iason. He is to learn your surgery, and you are to learn his potions. There will be no fighting between you. There will be open minds and a strong desire to learn. If either of you fail to learn the other's craft, then you will be exiled."

"Exiled!" Vanko said. "I have come here with Ahura of the Tanukh Tribe. I must stay with him."

"Shhhhh!" Iason hissed. "Be still or your head will be exiled from your body."

"Do your job well and there will be no trouble. You are dismissed." She almost laughed at Iason's hurried bow and his quick departure. Vanko was slower, but he followed Iason from the cella, his face nearly the color of his white toga.

Zenobia looked around the cella, then chose to recline on the couch that had been Odainat's favorite. Little had changed in the nearly three years since Odainat had been assassinated. His death had not yet been fully avenged, but it would be. Odainat's memory haunted her every minute of every day, but it no longer tormented her. She still had moments when something unexpected made tears flood her eyes, and she had to hide her sorrow lest some fool think she was weak. It was the little things that reminded her of her husband. A stranger who looked similar to Odainat; the phantom smell of the spice he wore; his voice directing her in battle. These were times of happiness that he was near and times of sadness that he was not. Both near and not near. How was that possible? Ah, the gods were almighty and did mock mere mortals.

Distant street sounds far below the cella drifted upwards to break the silence. Zenobia yawned and stretched. It was a rare moment when she was alone, and she savored it. She closed her eyes and almost slept.

Footsteps danced through her half-dreams, and she awakened with her hand on her sword as she usually did. Two people marched toward her, but the guards at the door didn't stop them.

"General Ezechiel." Zenobia let go of the sword handle as she surveyed the dusty man beside him. He was from one of her Palmyran infantry units. "What news have you brought us?" The man had spied for Odainat against the Persians all the years they had fought together, and now he spied for her.

"Much information about Claudius and Aurelian, my queen." The man bowed.

"You look as if you've traveled long and hard."

"I fear I've worn out three horses."

"From whence came you?" Zenobia asked.

"The Balkans."

"You have come a great distance." She looked at Ezechiel. "Is this news of Aurelian again?"

"Yes." Ezechiel nodded toward the man. "He has good eyes and ears. Tell the queen what you've observed."

"I fought in Postumus' army until his death, then I fought with Aurelian's troops."

"Postumus is dead?" Zenobia shrugged. "I am not certain whether the news is fortunate or unfortunate for Palmyra."

"How so?" Ezechiel asked.

"He kept the new emperor busy. A divided country is easier to conquer." Zenobia smiled at Ezechiel's frown. "You think I'm too ambitious."

He glanced at the spy. "This is not the time to discuss your philosophy."

"Really?" She hated it when Ezechiel was right. She stared at the spy. He had been a trusted soldier for many years, but men could be bought. "You fought with Aurelian?"

"For many months."

"Why did you fight the Goths in the Balkans and not north of Rome?"

"Claudius and Aurelian together beat the Goths at Lake Garda in the north. It was a good victory for the emperor—one he would not have won without Aurelian and the Dalmatian troops."

"Dalmatian troops? How did he come by that elite unit? I thought Cecropius led them." Ezechiel said.

"Cecropius was trapped by Aurelian into being one of Emperor Gallienus' assassins. He was executed by Claudius," the spy said.

"Forgive me, but your name has fallen from my memory. Are you Quillian?"

Quillian grinned. "I am."

"King Odainat always spoke well of you," Zenobia said. "Continue."

"Claudius was granted the title of *Germanius Maximus* by the Senate. He sent Aurelian and Marcianus to the Balkans with the Dalmatian Cavalry. It was at this time that Postumus was killed by his own troops. He stopped us from pillaging Mainz. It is a wealthy village. It was our right to do so, for how else are we to reap the benefits of dangerous fighting?"

"Did you lead the revolt?" Ezechial asked.

"Not me. I did not want to be noticed. If only one Roman soldier had served with me under Odainat, then I would be put to death." Quillian glanced at Zenobia, then down at the floor. "There are those who think that Rome and Palmyra are enemies."

Zenobia laughed. "We are enemies. It is a matter of time before we can meet Claudius and Aurelian on the battlefield. I welcome that battle more than any other."

"What of Postumus?" Ezechial asked.

"General Laelianus openly revolted against Postumus. They fought outside Mainz, then when Laelianus was defeated and killed, the troops were told not to pillage Mainz. Postumus said that they were not the enemy. They were the enemy. They had supplied Laelianus with troops who killed some of us."

"So Postumus was killed by his own men?" Zenobia asked.

"He was trampled to death by the soldiers, then his body cut up and fed to the vultures that hovered over the bodies of dead soldiers. There was a three-day celebration. I sneaked out with a few other soldiers, and as we rode to join Aurelian, Claudius caught up with us. He was happy to have more cavalry."

"Why did Claudius not take over the troops in Gaul?" Zenobia chewed on her bottom lip. She needed to know how Claudius thought. He was a good general, but she did not know what his tactics would be as an emperor.

"He spoke to us about that. He said that a war against a pretender was his own concern; whereas, a war against the barbarians was the states', and that concerns of the state must take precedence." Quillian looked at Zenobia, then Ezechiel. "I don't understand the meaning of his speech, but remembered the words for Palmyra."

"You did well," Ezechiel said.

"I am interested in how Claudius and Aurelian fight together," Zenobia said. "Can you tell me about that?"

Quillian pursed his lips. "Claudius is a great general, but not as clever as Aurelian. Together they planned to crush the Goths between them. Claudius retreated too soon. By then I was near enough to Aurelian, having joined his cavalry, that I heard him swear at the emperor. The battle was won by Aurelian because he pursued the enemy as they fled, but most of them escaped."

Zenobia laughed. "Then we'll pray that Claudius lives a long and healthy life. Aurelian might aspire to be emperor. That should never come to pass. How many troops does Claudius have? And Aurelian?"

"Claudius has nearly five thousand; Aurelian a few hundred more."

"A formidable foe. I like that."

"Careful, my queen." Ezechiel traced an old scar that zig zagged its way across his hand. "Your gods may grant your wish."

Zenobia flashed him a look through narrowed eyes. "I pray they do."

"What more can you tell us?" Ezechiel looked at Quillian.

"Nothing. I have told it all to you."

"Did you see any Roman activity in Asia Minor?" Zenobia asked.

"Nothing other than the ordinary."

"That is all. Get a good meal in the kitchen, then report to the barracks. We need you here now." Zenobia smiled. "There will be gold for your troubles."

"You're more than gracious. I do this not only for you, but for our beloved Palmyra." Quillian bowed and backed from the cella.

"Emperor Claudius and Aurelian are busy in the Balkans. That explains why they could not interfere with us in Egypt. They sent an ineffective general." Zenobia marched to the window and looked out. "It is time to expand our borders."

"Please be careful."

She whirled around. "Be careful? Why? The Romans have angered me, and I will retaliate with my strongest weapon—that of my ability to fight. You sound almost like a traitor. Are you with me or against me?"

Ezechiel closed his eyes and lowered his head. He clenched his fist around the hilt of his sword and swore.

Zenobia stared at him. What if he would not help her lead her men? What if he deserted her? Could she have him killed as a defector? Could she do that to Miriam and their children? To her-self? There was no one better to lead beside her than Ezechiel now that Odainat no longer rode next to her. She couldn't conquer the Roman world alone. She desperately needed him.

"Do you insist on going after more Roman land?"

"I do."

"Why?"

"I have to. They killed Odainat. They killed Hairan. They killed my heart and turned it to stone." Zenobia refused to allow tears to form. "If you don't join me, then I will go alone to a certain death. You know I can't lead the army without you."

"I know."

"The Romans have two strong generals; we need to match them." Zenobia could see Ezechiel fighting with himself. What more could she say to him?

It seemed too long a time before Ezechiel opened his eyes and looked at her. "I will help you, but I don't agree with your tactics. We should leave the Romans alone."

"Not now. Not while they are weakened from fighting the Goths. Not while I breathe. Not while Odainat lays dead in the funerary temple. Not while the hatred for their treachery still resides in my heart."

"I will be by your side, Zenobia. Always." Ezechiel walked to Zenobia and put his arms around her. "My heart sings whenever you're near."

Zenobia pushed him away. "Stop! What of our promise to each other and to Miriam? Go. I have my sons to visit."

Was it her imagination or did Arraum's fingers seem to grasp her hand? She looked down, then realized it was his good hand that held hers. She reached over and pulled his damaged hand into hers and rubbed it. He complained of it being cold. Rebekeh had his hand wrapped in a woolen cloth, but he still protested.

Longenius had suggested warm olive oil. That helped, but as soon as they stopped rubbing the warm oil into his hand, he cried about the coldness.

"I am sorry I cry, Mother. I don't know why I do that."

"It is no shame to cry. You have a difficult injury. It will take time to heal." Zenobia hugged her son. "I prefer the crying to the little boy who lay like a stone."

"I try to be brave."

"You are brave."

"I cry when I'm alone."

Rebekeh gasped. "Arraum, I promise that I will not leave you again." She turned to Zenobia. "I left him to run to the kitchen for broth and bread. I wanted him to eat."

"It's all right. I'll have servants here at all times so you may do whatever you think is needed for Arraum."

Rebekeh's tears dropped onto her tunic. "I failed him."

"I order you not to think that way. You have saved him with your tender care and loving manner." Zenobia smiled to soften her words. She turned back to Arraum. "Is there anything you want?"

"I had the most peculiar dream while I slept. I dreamt that Hairan's camel song was sung over and over to me by a monkey."

Rebekeh and Zenobia burst into laughter.

"What's so funny?"

"I think your dream was real," Rebekeh said.

"Would you like to hear the camel song again?" Zenobia asked.

"Yes."

"I'll send for Vaballathus. He is your singing monkey." Zenobia wiped tears from her eyes. Some were tears of happiness, but some were tears of pain.

CHAPTER
XVIII

270 A. D. Balkan Mountains

    *A*urelian pulled his woolen cape tighter about his shoulders and stepped into the darkness. He let the tent flap down slowly, the stiff leather difficult to hold. A light snow had settled on tents, supply wagons, trees, and the sparse grass during the night.

Across the valley burned minuscule fires of the Gothic army. After each battle, they retreated a little further south. He knew they were almost out of supplies. This was the third night in a row that the fires had been almost nonexistent. The men were weak; he could tell from the way they fought. Weak men, few fires. No supplies. One good thrust, and they could be driven into Thrace.

"Marcellus!"

"I stand next to you as always."

"A trusted friend." Aurelian slapped Marcellus on the back.

"You are uncommonly joyful." Marcellus chuckled.

"We are close to victory. I can smell it. Get the cavalry and infantry ready. One last push to rid ourselves of the Goths. Send a message to Claudius. He allows me to decide when to attack. Tell him the time is at dawn in two hours with cavalry and infantry."

"I'll go myself to see Claudius. It is safer if I carry the news. One never knows who spies on whom." Marcellus faded into the darkness, his figure appearing and disappearing as he passed rows of campfires.

The Goths shuffled along in ragged rows that matched their tattered spirits. Most of them were devoid of armor. Their only protection from the elements was mud-brown clothing that hung on gaunt frames. Matted hair caked with blood had been hacked off or tied back with scraps of clothing. Calloused feet attested to the months of marching and missing fingers and toes confirmed brushes with death.

Most of the men fought with homemade clubs. Few swords glinted in the early morning sunlight. Aurelian wished they would give up. He knew they were tenacious, albeit stupid for clinging to an impossible hope.

Claudius was in position on the other side of the Goths. Aurelian gritted his teeth in memory of the last meeting he had had with Claudius. Why couldn't the man see that attacking the entire band of Goths was useless? He remembered the motto of his own people —"Fight to the death. Freedom is everything." He'd tried to explain that to Claudius. The emperor refused to see what Aurelian meant and argued that Rome had superior fighting power, superior weapons, and food enough to keep the men healthy. He had no idea that men sometimes won in spite of destitution because their hearts were solid valor.

He doubted that any of the Goths lacked discipline. Claudius bragged about the discipline of the Roman army when in fact four of the divisions had refused to follow their leaders into battle. The retreat, if one could call it that when no blow had felled an enemy, had been ordered. That thought alone negated his cheerfulness.

Aurelian's boy helped him suit up and get on his horse. He couldn't remember the boy's name, but he was the son of some senator. The young man was mentally deficient and timid. Aurelian had been angered when Claudius foisted the half-wit on him. He often thought he was a spy. The boy had moments of clarity and insight about fighting that startled Aurelian. No one escaped spies.

He had a half dozen of his own; one right under Claudius' nose. Aurelian grinned. Lucine had grown to regard luxury as a necessity after catering to Gallienus. She was all too happy to let Claudius use her. She spied and greedily took Aurelian's gold. She liked telling tales about Claudius for revenge. Aurelian admired her cleverness. She already had a villa planned. Claudius rushed around worrying about architecture instead of battles. He was a simpleton when it came to women.

Thank the gods Aurelian could not be controlled by any woman. None. Not even his wife who was merely the manager of his household while he was out claiming victories for Rome. She would do well as his empress, but that didn't please him.

Harpinna snorted. Aurelian recognized the sound. The gods had damned him with this animal that was about to unseat him. "Hey!" He yelled for the lunatic that had helped him on the horse. The boy was good with animals.

The boy came running straight for the horse, pulled up short as if he couldn't judge distance, and stared into the horse's eyes as he leaned forehead against forehead.

Aurelian let out a disgusted whistle, nodded to the idiot, and rode toward the front of the lines that Marcellus had assembled.

"We are nearly ready," Marcellus said.

"And Claudius?"

"He awaits your signal."

"By the gods, Marcellus! What movement is that from the Goths?"

"They're on the move! How did they break past our lines?"

"They cleverly saw our weakness. They broke through where the Roman troops refused to fight. Sound the trumpets! We ride!" Aurelian tore across the distance that separated him from the Goths. Harpinna jolted him so hard with every pounding hoof beat that he thought his bones would break one by one. He clenched his teeth and swore at the lieutenants who had not kept their men in hand.

He looked across at Claudius' army who moved quickly to stop the Goths from escaping. Together he and the emperor would stop the enemy's flow, but many had already escaped.

Aurelian glanced back at the Dalmatian troops. They moved as one like the well-trained men they were. He would never have a problem with these men because he'd make certain they remained true to his leadership. It would be even more important later.

Aurelian ran over the first Goth that he came to at the end of the escaping enemy lines. The emaciated, ragged man crumbled down without a sound as he and Harpinna dashed through the group of soldiers. Aurelian swung his sword countless times. It was no contest. Most of the Goths were not armed.

He pulled Harpinna to a halt during a lull and looked around. The stream of Goths racing off to the south confused him until he realized that Claudius had sent in the infantry without cavalry backup. The fool!

Aurelian turned at the sound of hoof beats and waited for Marcellus.

"What's happened?" Marcellus shouted.

"Claudius is stupid." Immediately Aurelian regretted having said too much. Even Marcellus should not be trusted. No one could be trusted.

"What do we do?" Marcellus stared at the Goths as they streamed in front of the Roman army. "Claudius' infantry can't catch them."

Aurelian wanted to let Claudius lose this battle. If Claudius, favorite warrior of the senate, lost a battle there would be some way to remove him as emperor. Death. Claudius' death would put Aurelian in a favorable light. The Goths were fierce, and what more noble way to die than on the battlefield protecting Rome? If the gods would do what was right for Rome, then Claudius would meet his death here. And what if he, Aurelian, was looked on by the senate as having failed in his duty to protect the emperor?

"Marcellus! We ride to save Claudius." Aurelian had to try to save the emperor. It was the only way to vindicate himself beyond all doubt. He kicked Harpinna. The horse bolted forward at a pace that suited Aurelian for once. He would try to save Claudius. It would be up to the gods to do what must be done. If Claudius died, then Aurelian would know the gods blessed him. He would be emperor one day soon.

Aurelian grinned. And when he was emperor, Zenobia would cease being. He would see to it personally.

Even the mountains were hot with air that refused to stir. He and Claudius had fought the Goths all winter and most of the summer. The fine Roman army hadn't felled the stubborn enemy, but the plague had.

Aurelian stared at the row upon row of ill Roman soldiers. Fighting the afflicted Goths had brought them down in greater numbers than swords or clubs. Men died by the score each day, yet Claudius still lived. He was robust, ignorant of the momentous error he had made by not sending in both the infantry and the cavalry against the

Goths last winter. Claudius had allowed many of the enemy to escape. The war dragged on. Aurelian sighed. The war may be lost on the sick bed rather than the battlefield.

"Aurelian, come quickly. Claudius has good news that he wants to share with you." Marcellus grinned. "Another honor for our emperor, I assume. The messenger was from the senate."

"That is good news." Aurelian turned toward the huge tent further up the mountain that towered above his own. The stupid senators had no idea how their favorite soldier had lost the battle and now almost the war. Another award. Will the gods never stop showing Claudius favor?

"Come in, Aurelian." Claudius bellowed as usual when excitement filled him. "Let's have some of our finest wine. It was delivered with this." Claudius held a marble box. "You look surprised."

"Another honor. I am not surprised, for you deserve many. The surprise comes in that it took the senate so long to recognize your prowess on the battlefield."

"They are not fighting men, therefore they don't understand what we soldiers must do every day." Claudius motioned for Aurelian to come closer. "I have enough awards."

"Not enough, but more than many." Aurelian said.

"It is nothing. I do what I can for Rome. It is my duty," Claudius said.

"Gothicus Maximus," Aurelian said. "Another worthy title for an emperor who leads Rome to greatness."

Claudius grinned. "Not only a title, but these." He held the marble box toward Aurelian.

The box felt warm to the touch where Claudius had clutched it. Aurelian lifted the hinged lid. Nestled against purple silk lining lay a dozen gold coins that gleamed in the lamp light. He picked up one and read the inscription. "This is a great honor."

"I prefer the gold shield the senate has given me." Claudius pointed to the corner of the tent where, propped against a table, was a gaudy shield decorated with laurel leaves and Romulus and Remus, twin founders of Rome.

"That is more to my liking than the coins. You have many honors."

"Do I deserve such an honor from the senate?" Claudius held out a gold goblet. "Some wine to celebrate?"

Aurelian dropped the coin in the marble box and set it on the table. He hesitated before taking the wine. Two goblets of wine already poured. He suspected treachery.

"The wine is Rome's best." Claudius took a sip. He stared at his guest over the rim of the cup.

Aurelian sipped. "As usual, it is fit for an emperor."

"And his most trusted general."

Aurelian took a long drink. Did his stomach burn from the strong wine or something else?

"Let's sit." Claudius arranged his toga as he dropped into the nearest brocaded chair.

Aurelian waited long enough to show respect, then sat in the other chair. Was he feverish? Were his legs weak?

Claudius reached for the wine bottle and poured Aurelian and himself more wine. "How much longer do you think we'll be here?"

"Too long. We should pull in more troops, concentrate on this area, conquer these people quickly, and move on." Aurelian stared at Claudius who looked a bit pale. "We must replace our ill troops immediately. The plague has many men down."

"It will be done. As you leave, send me a scribe." Claudius' hand shook as he lifted the goblet. The wine splattered on his white toga. "It seems I've had more to drink than I thought. I started before you came."

"Perhaps a good night's sleep will help you." Aurelian stood. "I'll send in the scribe."

As soon as he felt his shoulder being touched, Aurelian awakened. "What do you want?"

"The emperor is ill and wishes to see you," Marcellus whispered.

"Ill?"

"Very."

Aurelian threw back his own linen covering that was covered with perspiration. He had slept soundly again. Or was he getting ill, too?

"Is Claudius suffering from the plague?"

"Probably." Marcellus helped Aurelian dress.

Incense burned strongly in Claudius' tent. The emperor's eyes flickered open, then closed again. Rosy cheeks attested to his fever while a ring of pale white-green skin around his mouth told of the nausea.

Aurelian glanced at Lucine who stood impassively near the sick bed. "Do you know of herbs to help him?" He asked the question in her language, faltering over the verb tenses.

"Do you want him helped?" She replied in the tongue that brought back fleeting memories of his mother.

"Of course I want him helped. Why wouldn't I?"

"You have a vision for your future."

"Give him medicines. You may have as much help as you want in gathering herbs."

"I have already gathered what I need. I saw his sickness creep up on him slowly, quietly. Rather like your ambition that snakes around the throne."

Aurelian wanted to slap her, but he knew he could not. Silly Claudius was fond of the spy and gave her anything she wanted. If he only knew where her loyalties lay. "Give him medicine."

"I already have. It is dangerous and must be carefully given." Lucine wrung out a cloth and laid it on Claudius' head.

She irritated him. Perhaps she'd poison Claudius and then Aurelian could have her executed. If Claudius died, he would be emperor. The senate had passed over him in favor of Claudius, but two things were now in his favor. He was trusted and admired by Claudius, and he had proven himself on the battlefield.

"Claudius called for you before his slumber," Lucine said.

"We need to make provisions since he can't lead us."

"He admires you, Aurelian." Lucine snorted. "I have no idea why."

Aurelian raised his hand to slap her, but Claudius groaned.

"Water," the emperor said.

Lucine pushed Aurelian away and knelt by the sleeping couch. "Here. Drink."

"Aurelian?"

"He is here," Lucine said.

"You must rid us of the last of the Goths."

"I will."

"You are in charge." Claudius coughed. "I have had papers drawn up and sent to the senate."

"I will try to be worthy."

Claudius lapsed into a deep sleep, his breathing barely discernable. Aurelian shook his head. "Lucine, can he be saved?"

"No."

The August sun beat down on Aurelian and Marcellus. It was unseasonably hot for the mountains. Even horses hung their heads and froth dripped from their necks. The men watched the imprisoned Goths wait for their executions.

"It is unfortunate that the emperor could not have lived a few more weeks. He should have seen the end of the Goths." Marcellus swatted a mosquito.

"I fear there will never be an end to the Goths, but for now they are beaten."

"Your brilliant strategy should make the senate sit up and take notice. They will appoint you emperor for certain."

Aurelian smiled. Any minute a messenger should arrive from the senate announcing his rise to the throne. "It was a chair that gave me the idea."

"How?"

"Threads. A single thread will not hold weight, but twisted together they hold a common soldier. So it is with the Goths. Together they were stronger than when separated. That's why I splintered them into smaller groups."

"Thrace and Lower Moesia have seen the last of those marauders." Marcellus laughed. "I think we can go home. I can't wait to go to the baths again. And drink. And find out if the brothels still exist."

"Rome." Aurelian nodded. "It will be good to go there."

"As an emperor."

"I have not prayed to the gods and asked to be emperor." Aurelian believed that the gods had a grand purpose for him, and to pray was redundant.

"You don't have to. The gods have always favored you." Marcellus stared across a meadow that had been turned to dust by the battle. "A messenger comes. See, he rides fast and carries the banner of the senate. He comes to give you good tidings."

Aurelian felt his heart turn over. At last.

The messenger reached him so slowly that Aurelian had time to list the proclamations he would make immediately. The senate had grown too powerful and stupid. He would take some of that power away. They knew nothing. His strength gave him followers—powerful men in the army. Many followers.

Dust swirled around the horse's legs as the messenger pulled up in front of Aurelian and Marcellus. He saluted.

Aurelian reached out and took his future in his hands. He hesitated a moment to thank the gods, then popped the seal on the scroll.

The words made no sense to him. Claudius' brother, Quintillus, was in Italy with his Balkan army. On hearing of Claudius' death, the troops had proclaimed Quintillus his successor.

Aurelian bit his lower lip to keep from swearing at the gods. He could not believe the senate agreed with the Balkan army and proclaimed Quintillus emperor. His eyes narrowed as he looked at his army. His Dalmatian troops were far superior to the Balkan troops. Perhaps it was a test by the gods of his will. Maybe they wished to know how badly he wanted to be emperor. He would show them.

"Away with you," he said to the messenger.

Marcellus stared at the retreating man. "What is wrong?"

"The senate." The messenger seemed to depart faster than he'd come.

Marcellus held out his hand. "May I see it?"

"Are you with me or not?" Aurelian held the scroll to his chest.

"With you? For what escapade this time?" Marcellus' face had changed from one of joy to despair in reflection of his general.

"Are you with me? No questions asked and none answered."

Marcellus stared at the tiny figure of the messenger. At last he nodded. "I am with you."

Aurelian grimaced as he handed the scroll to his lieutenant.

Marcellus let out a long whistle. "The senators are cowardly. They were afraid that if they chose you, Quintillus would attack them. He is closer than you, but not as powerful. What do we do?"

"We attack Quintillus. We fight to the death for the Roman Empire." Aurelian's hand tightened around his sword. "To the death."

"To the death." Marcellus grasped Aurelian's free hand. "I will follow you to the ends of the empire."

"I will send him a proclamation of my intent, then we march." Aurelian grinned. "We shall go home after all."

"Home. The very sound of it brings tears to my eyes," Marcellus said.

Quintillus' Balkan army hovered behind their leader. Aurelian glanced back at his battle-hardened troops. This would be almost too easy. The senators had misjudged him. May the blood be on their hands, not his.

Aurelian shifted in the saddle and nudged Harpinna forward at a faster pace. He was anxious to claim what was his. His men, led by Marcellus, had proclaimed him the true Roman emperor. It had been a hasty ceremony under the sun with a cool breeze blowing to remind everyone that a mountain winter was but a few weeks away. He wanted to go home where it was warm and sunny. His old bones needed the warmth.

"Quintillus' army is not happy to see us," Marcellus said.

"I doubt that Quintillus is happy to see us. He can fight the Goths, but not a Roman army. I hope he surrenders."

"If he does, what then?"

"I'll have him executed for treason. I have a document that states Claudius wanted me to succeed him."

"A forgery?"

"A well-done forgery." Aurelian adjusted his sword. "We attack in a matter of minutes. I am glad you chose to ride with me."

"I could never ride against you," Marcellus said.

"Look ahead! What do you see?"

"Odd. I see a single man in uniform riding toward us. The Balkan troops have pulled up short. Something is afoot. Shall I go meet him?"

"No. We wait. Halt our men."

Aurelian recognized the soldier as he drew nearer as one of the lieutenants from Claudius' first army. He couldn't remember the man's name, but it didn't matter. He may or may not be trusted.

"I bring good news to Emperor Aurelian," the man shouted.

Aurelian almost fell from his saddle. "What news?"

"The usurper to the throne, Quintillus, has departed this earth by his own hand. He admitted to a group of us that he was wrong to try to take the throne. His atonement for his stupidity is death."

"A trick of his, perhaps?" Marcellus asked.

"I have ordered Quintillus' body to be brought forth." He pointed behind him. "It is there."

Aurelian watched four men bearing a litter across the battle-field. They were in no hurry, but then Quintillus was heavy and the day hot. "Marcellus, ride back and prepare to lead our men if battle is needed. If I am killed by trickery, then avenge me."

"As you wish."

Aurelian waited until the men were more than half-way to him before he rode out to meet them. He couldn't believe that Quintillus lay dead. Blood had already dried on the toga that he wore. Quintillus had fallen forward on his own sword no doubt, or had been pushed on it. No matter, for Aurelian would not have his death investigated.

"I am the true Roman Emperor," Aurelian said. "At last."

CHAPTER
XIX

271 A. D. Palmyra, Syria and Milan, Italy

"This is interesting." Zenobia tossed the scroll aside and leaned forward on her forearms. The table felt cool in the early morning.

She glanced toward the window where Ezechiel stood. His broad shoulders carried half of her problems. Sometimes she wished for peace. Most of the time she wished for life—Odainat's life. Maybe she should've died, too. That had been Rome's plan.

"You look . . . pensive." Ezechiel had turned from the window.

The sun was just starting to rise, and it encompassed Ezechiel like a bright shroud. Zenobia shivered at that thought. "Odainat. I should've been murdered with him."

"Your gods spared you for your sons and for Palmyra."

"I'm tired. I'm tired of fighting. I'm tired of Rome. I'm tired of dust and heat and marching."

"Where is the exuberant woman who playfully restored the old monuments for Egypt? The people love you for that."

"Gone." Zenobia tapped the scroll. "Aurelian has control of the mints in Milan and Rome along with Caesius and Siscia. He not only had coins minted in his likeness, but he's deified Claudius. Why?"

"He was Claudius' best general and confidant," Ezechiel said.

"But he was not chosen by Claudius to succeed him. Quintillus was."

"Claudius was vain—he wanted his blood to rule albeit through his brother."

"His blood through Quintillus flowed right into the ground." Zenobia picked up a scroll. "Aurelian is an able politician as well as a general. He has the senate under control."

"Through fear. It took only one look at Aurelian's army marching toward Rome to switch allegiance from Quintillus to Aurelian."

"He would've had them all murdered." Zenobia let the scroll roll up with a snap. "Where is Aurelian now?"

"Fighting the Vandals around Budapest. They've crossed the Danube and have been raiding villages under Roman protection."

"Good. It'll keep him busy and away from us."

"Someday he'll come," Ezechiel said.

Zenobia stared past him at the white hot sun. "He has to come. Our destinies are intertwined."

Aurelian looked back at the Danube as he waited for Marcellus. When things were ready, they would strike. He turned at the sound of hoof beats and waited until Marcellus rode close. He lifted one eyebrow; he didn't have to speak.

"All the grain and livestock have been secured inside fortified cities as you ordered." Marcellus slapped a fly on his horse's neck.

"Good."

"Why didn't we attack immediately?"

"They'll give in more quickly without food." Aurelian looked eastward. "I have other battles to fight."

"Palmyra?"

"Zenobia. She flaunts her power. For the sake of Rome, we can not allow it."

"She is a woman and easy to beat."

Aurelian laughed. "She has Egypt under her control. Rome starves because we have no grain. She has cut off our supply. Do not underestimate the enemy. Do you know how a woman thinks?"

"No."

"I thought not." Aurelian smiled. "Zenobia starves us, but not for long. She will rue the day she took Egypt. Prepare to battle the Vandals in two days." Aurelian turned Harpinna toward his tent. He wanted good food, good wine, and a good woman—especially a good woman.

"Marcellus!" Aurelian bellowed. "Tell this ungrateful Vandal that every time he refuses to hand over two thousand of his cavalry, I will kill two hundred of them." Aurelian saw the chieftain blanch. So he did understand the language. Good.

"Take the first two hundred men and separate them out." Aurelian looked at the sky. "In one hour we will start the executions. Sharpen your blades. It is to be quick and clean. They are not to suffer for their leader's stubbornness."

He glanced at the chieftain who stared at his cavalry. The men were dirty, but not disheveled. They stared straight ahead and waited for their fate. It would be a shame to have to kill such well-trained soldiers, but he would if he had to. Aurelian admired the cavalry. They were dedicated to winning, well trained, and could ride better than many of his own cavalry. Their horses were shorter, stockier, and had a thicker coat. The animals were as sure footed on a bloody field of battle as they were in the mountain snow and ice.

Mixed in with the native horses from the Steppes of Russia were those of Arabian blood probably stolen from the Roman cavalry over the years of fighting.

The chieftain swore in his own language, then glared at Aurelian. "You were one of us."

"Never." Aurelian refused to speak in the chieftain's tongue even though he could.

"You were born near here and raised here."

"I never belonged. I saw the wisdom of joining the Romans at a young age." Aurelian swept back his arm to encompass his army. "What do you see? You see well-fed, well-trained men with the best equipment, the best leaders the world has ever seen."

The chieftain scowled and nodded toward his captured army. "What do you see? You see men who are loyal, who fight to the death for freedom from Rome, men who are brave beyond all expectations."

"Men who will die because of your stubbornness."

"My men are needed at home."

"Your men are not needed at home. They wouldn't be here fighting if they were." Aurelian looked at the sky. "See how the sun creeps across the sky. It foretells the death of the first two hundred men."

"The sun races across the sky to foretell of Emperor Aurelian's cruel ways." The chieftain sighed. "I can't let that happen. You will have your two thousand cavalry."

"Good. It would have been a terrible waste."

"I need to speak to my men. They need to understand why they have to go with you."

Aurelian stared at the crafty older man's blue eyes. A trick? He thought not. There was resignation, not deception in his demeanor. "And what shall the cruel emperor do to you?"

"I care not."

"Perhaps you should be allowed to go back north to tell your people of Rome's power. You should convince others to join our army."

"Death is preferable."

"Too easy. No, I will allow you to ride away on that stocky little beast of yours. That is the cruelest plan." Aurelian laughed. "Your countenance gives away your hatred. Go, talk to your men."

"Roman emperors have very short lives." The chieftain turned his horse away from Aurelian and rode toward his men.

Aurelian shuddered. What he said was true. There was deception and war everywhere. Some days he just wanted peace. Permanent peace.

A shout from Marcellus brought him from his musing. He watched his second in command ride toward him at an enormous speed.

"I have this." Marcellus pulled a scroll from his pouch and thrust it into Aurelian's hands. "I intercepted the messenger."

Aurelian frowned. Not much excited Marcellus. He read quickly. "Absurd. The Jurhungi marches toward Milan. We leave immediately."

"Now?"

"We must. It's a ten day march. How far behind are we?"

"Two or three days."

"Double time. We'll march double time. I'll lead the new cavalry plus our own; you stay with the supplies and the infantry. We'll wait for you at sundown. If you can, try to stay with us."

"As you wish." Marcellus saluted and rode away.

They were too late. Aurelian sat quietly on Harpinna and stared at the burned and ruined city that lay in front of him. People were streaming back through the broken gates in dirty, bloodied clothing. An old woman carried a baby. Both stared as if they did not see. Bodies of citizens lay scattered inside and outside the walls. The north gate had been shattered, and Aurelian stared down a cobblestone street darkened with blood.

Dogs howled. Aurelian shivered. The dogs always howled after a raid. Hundreds of them would lay across the bodies of their masters or children and howl. Later, hunger would drive them out of the city and they would run in packs. *Will it never end? Will Rome never rid herself of these damnable raiders?*

Aurelian sent a message to Marcellus to bypass Milan and cut across country. Marcellus needed to catch up with Aurelian's cavalry that marched toward the southeast. It shouldn't take long for Marcellus to pull both armies together.

The next morning before breaking camp, Aurelian heard the rhythmic marching of the Roman army. He glanced up from a map just as Marcellus rode up.

"Greetings, Aurelian. We rose before sunrise to get here." Marcellus looked at the sky. "It'll be a hot day today. The men are close to exhaustion. Do we march?"

"We have to, but we'll not march double time."

Marcellus stared at the ground. "We need a day of rest."

"And what do I tell the people we've promised to protect when they're beaten and robbed? What do I tell the women who'll be raped? Should I tell them the great Roman army was tired? They needed a nap?" Aurelian swore. He knew the men were tired. He knew they could hardly move, but he had a duty. Emperors who didn't perform their duties didn't last long. "The enemy is headed south toward Rome."

It was almost dusk. Piacenza was behind them. Aurelian guessed it had been spared by the raiders because the Roman army was so close. The citizens had cheered Aurelian and the army as they rode by.

Ahead lay a great wooded area where it would be impossible to camp. Aurelian didn't want to stop this side of the woods, either. They'd made some progress and were just beyond Piacenza. It would take an hour to get through the woods; then they would stop.

Aurelian could smell cool air that drifted toward him from dank earth beneath huge old trees that towered above them like columns in a temple. He peered into the semi-darkness. The lack of sunlight kept grass from growing. The only ground covering was from dried pine needles and leaves.

He and Marcellus were first into the woods and followed a trail only wide enough for two horses. The sanctity of the forest kept them silent. The only sound Aurelian heard was the soft plodding of horses and men as the army traveled farther into the deep woodlands. He liked the peace. The only other time he enjoyed quiet was when he and his wife, Severina, went to the temples. He could hear his own blood rush through his head it was so still. His eyes half closed and for the first time in months, Aurelian felt serene.

He saw the enemy pop out by the hundreds from behind the huge trees, but did not comprehend what happened until several seconds had passed. Aurelian shouted for Marcellus to sound the alarm, but it was too late. He drew his sword and swung at the first Jurhungi who ran toward him. Marcellus' horse banged into Harpinna, and Aurelian had to abort his swing to keep from slashing his friend.

Aurelian cursed, pulled his horse around, and swung again. He felled the enemy before the man could sever Harpinna's legs. Six more times he had to halt his swing to keep from killing one of his own men.

"It's no good, Aurelian! Our men die by the hundreds!!" Marcellus shouted above the din of clanging swords and moans.

"The Roman army never retreats! Never!" Aurelian surged forward and dispatched two more of the Jurhungi to their gods.

"Look around you! There won't be an army left to retreat! Don't let your pride overshadow your common sense. Save those you can." Marcellus grabbed Harpinna's reins and jerked the emperor around. "Look!"

It was all Aurelian could do to keep from gasping. Scattered across the ground two and three deep were the remnants of the greatest fighting army in the history of the world. Leaves and pine needles stuck to the wounds of the dead and dying like a macabre camouflage.

He pulled Harpinna around and shouted for the retreat. He rode quickly back the way they had come, racing through the trees and shouting for the men to flee. Twice Harpinna jumped over a pile of bodies tangled together—mostly Roman—and twice Aurelian almost vomited at the carnage. His army was shattered. He was shattered.

An hour after Marcellus and the men raced from the woods, they dared to stop and assess their losses.

"How many?" Aurelian asked.

"It is easier to count the living and walking wounded than to count the dead," Marcellus said.

"How many lived, then?"

"Fewer than three hundred."

"Post guards while we camp. Leave me. I need to think." Aurelian walked up a grassy knoll and stared back at the direction from which they'd come. The enemy had given up pursuing them a few minutes after they retreated. They were more interested in looting bodies, taking the fine Roman swords, armor, and horses.

Aurelian closed his eyes. He should pray, but he couldn't. Mithras had deserted him today. Why? What lesson was he to learn? Humility? He learned that too harshly. Strategy? He thought he knew most of it. Was he to choose his enemies carefully? What lesson did the gods want him to learn?

He stared toward the east. He would never lose another battle. He would be prepared for Zenobia no matter how she fought. His army would be bigger, stronger, and better trained even if it took months.

Right now he had another problem. Tomorrow what was left of his army had to continue to Rome. The Jurhungi wanted her riches. They had the advantage of numbers and distance. It would be difficult to catch them, but not impossible. Aurelian had already sent the recruiters out amongst the people. They should get a lot of young men from Piacenza whose faces wore looks of adoration for the army. He would have the numbers, but these recruits would be untrained. It would be best to scatter them among the trained troops.

"Marcellus!" Aurelian waved at him. "We leave at sunrise tomorrow to catch the enemy. I smell victory!"

"I believe you," Marcellus shouted in return. "The Roman army will never be bested."

"I need to talk to the men. Gather them together for me. Now."

Aurelian strode down the hill and into his tent. He poured thick wine into a gold goblet that he remembered had been Claudius' favorite. He didn't have a favorite goblet. He liked any made of gold. He sat at a table and picked up a pen. The bronze pen was serviceable, but ugly. He'd have to have nicer ones made. He hadn't had time to consider its ugliness before.

Aurelian laid down the pen. He didn't need to write notes. He knew exactly what he wanted to say to the soldiers. He had to make them want to march again even though they were near exhaustion and horrified at their loss. It was a good thing the Jurhungi marched toward Rome.

"The men wait." Marcellus held back the tent flap.

Aurelian nodded, brushed past Marcellus, and walked back up the grassy knoll he'd left a short time ago. He turned toward the men and waited for the murmuring to stop.

"I rarely address you men, for you are professionals and need little instruction. Today, I find that I must share my personal grief with you for the disaster that occurred this morning. It was my fault that I led you into danger. Many of you watched as friends and brothers died next to you. Some of you carry wounds from this morning that will leave a scar to remind you of your emperor's error. It is an error that will haunt me the rest of my life.

"If you want to help me regain honor for Rome, now is the time to take up our swords." Aurelian watched the men carefully. It didn't take much for an army to rebel and kill the leader who was perceived as a liability.

Most of the men waited quietly for him to continue. Aurelian looked into the eyes of one crusty old soldier. He could tell nothing about what the man thought.

"The Jurhungi march toward Rome where our wives, daughters, and infant sons live. The Jurhungi want the riches that Rome fought so hard to get. The Jurhungi want to burn our homes, rape our wives and daughters and kill our sons. Are we going to allow that? Are we going to allow the enemy to sack the greatest city on earth? Or do we march? Do we fight?"

The men were silent. Aurelian's ragged intake of breath startled him. Why did he dare risk talking to the men? Any moment they would be swarming all over him.

He dared not look toward Marcellus. He stared at the crowd before him. Slowly the old man in front raised his arms and shouted.

"We march, we fight, we kill!" The old man's chant was repeated in a wave that traveled from the front of the crowd to the back.

"We march, we fight, we kill!" was shouted over and over until Aurelian held up his arms.

The crowd stilled. Aurelian smiled at them. "Tomorrow I promise you victory. Tomorrow we save Rome."

This time he didn't stop the shouting.

"I see a great cloud of dust, Aurelian. Our cities haven't been sacked, so they know we're chasing them."

"Yes. We have caught them. They will die for what was done to us in the forest. Revenge." Aurelian grinned. "Prepare for triumph."

"Strike now?"

"No wait until they're closer to the Metaurus River. It is deep and treacherous. We'll use that to our advantage. It shouldn't take long for them to get to the river."

"A good plan."

"Always use nature against the enemy." Aurelian's bitter chuckle caused Marcellus' eyebrows to raise. "I re-learned that forgotten lesson from them."

A scant hour later and Aurelian felt satisfied that the timing was perfect. He gave the order to attack, and the Roman army swooped down on the Jurhungi. Aurelian rode in front of the cavalry with his sword drawn.

The enemy whirled around to fight, but were pushed toward the river as the Romans advanced. Aurelian heard the first splashes as men in the back of the Jurhungi army fell into the river. He slashed with his sword, shouted orders, and let his anger give him strength. It didn't take long for the stench of blood to fill the air. The enemy died by the tens because they were pushed together at the river's edge.

Aurelian quickly grew tired of fighting. He searched up and down the lines for the Goths' leader. He would kill him to shorten the battle. The Goths couldn't fight without a leader because they weren't as highly trained as the Romans.

It wasn't difficult to find King Cannabas. His cadaverous frame and stringy, gray hair attested to the hardships the Goths had encountered. The old man, crafty and devious, attacked them in the woods. King Cannabas may have won that battle, but Aurelian would laugh last.

Aurelian rode toward the king whose sword had killed many Romans. A shout burst from his lips and startled the king. He took just a second to ready himself for Aurelian's attack.

Aurelian pulled his mount beside King Cannabas and deflected the first blow from the old man's sword. The two leaders parried while their horses danced in circles unnerved by the violence of the sword fight.

King Cannabas' horse slipped, and the old king nearly dropped his sword. Aurelian took the initiative and, with three quick thrusts, knocked the sword from the king's hand. Cannabas backed his horse up until he was at the edge of the river.

"Like in the forest, eh? The trees kept us from victory; here the river is your enemy." Aurelian laughed as he killed Cannabas with a quick slice to the throat.

The leaderless Jurhungi jumped or fell into the river, sometimes leaving their weapons and armor behind. Most of them dropped fully armored into the water and sank.

The river turned bright pink from blood as Roman archers struck the enemy again and again. Men had no time to scream before being sucked under by a strong current. Aurelian knew that few would survive the tumbling water even if they managed to stay afloat long enough to be out of range of the arrows.

"Victory tastes as sweet as honey," Marcellus said.

"Sweeter when coupled with revenge. Shall we continue to Rome? I'd like to have a banquet to celebrate this victory."

"The senate will honor you for saving the city."

"Making the fight worthwhile." Aurelian stared at the water. Bodies floated like debris and drifted downstream. "Let's go home."

CHAPTER
XX

272 A. D. Palmyra, Syria and *Alexandria, Egypt*

"*I* must speak to you not as subject to queen, but woman to woman." Miriam twisted her fingers together.

"You are my truest and best friend. I don't think of you as my subject." Zenobia had never seen calm Miriam so agitated, not even when Maeonius had been roaming the streets. Two bright spots decorated Miriam's cheeks, and sweat clung to her brow. Her breath came in short, ragged bursts.

"No matter what you say, you are my queen. If I displease you by living, then you can have me executed."

"Executed!" Zenobia's raspy intake of breath echoed across the cella. No wonder Miriam had asked that the servants be dismissed.

Zenobia rose from her chair. "What have you done? Whatever it is, I can take care of it."

"It isn't what I have done, but what you have done."

"Me?" Zenobia's mind raced across the past. She could think of no insults to Miriam. Instead she remembered that Miriam had been treated as a sister. She and her daughters lived in luxury in the palace. The girls were being educated. They had everything in spite of Miriam's protests that she was spoiling the girls. Had she given them something that was against their religion? She thought not.

"Me?" she repeated.

"You and Ezechiel."

"Ezechiel?" Zenobia watched tears stream down Miriam's face. Whatever had she done to her best friend?

"You're so beautiful. I can't blame you."

"Blame me for what?" Zenobia's concern made her irritable. She hated puzzles. "Miriam, tell me immediately what I've done to you."

"Ezechiel. You're his weakness. He loves you."

"Ezechiel?" Zenobia fought to hide the truth. "He is my closest advisor, nothing more. We work well together and always have."

"He loves you. I can tell when he looks at you."

"Miriam, you're being absurd. He has always loved you. Why, sometimes I grow tired of his saying that you'd love to see this or have that when we travel. He thinks of you often. You and your daughters are the reason he has lived so long. He survives to come home to you."

"I know he loves you. He calls your name in his sleep."

"Ridiculous. He dreams of battles. When he calls my name, it's to chastise me for a mistake I've made or to warn me of danger. I do the same for him." Zenobia's breath came in shallow bursts. How could she make Miriam believe the lie that she must tell her? How could she deny that Ezechiel looked at her with soulful eyes and sighed when they were alone?

"I want you to grant Ezechiel and me a divorce so that he is free to marry you." Miriam's tears flowed anew.

"Don't be a silly donkey. He would sooner die than divorce you." Zenobia paced back and forth. "What could I do to convince you that he and I have no love for each other? Miriam, I still love Odainat and will until I die. He was the only man I ever wanted or will want. I will never marry again. I will never let another man make love to me. I would die by my own hand first."

"You don't want Ezechiel?"

"Of course not. I love Odainat even though he is dead. I wait for the day when our gods unite us."

"You don't love Ezechiel?"

"I admire him as a general."

"You can do something for me." Miriam whimpered.

"Name it."

"Send Ezechiel away so he won't look at you with love in his eyes. I can't stand to see him watch you. Send him away so I don't hear his honeyed words when he speaks of you." Miriam dropped to her knees. "I beg you."

"Miriam! Rise. Don't do this. Think about what you're saying."

Zenobia pulled her to her feet, then wrapped her arms around her. Miriam sobbed into her shoulder.

Zenobia waited until the crying subsided. At last Miriam pulled away.

"I'm sorry. Jealousy has made me stupid."

Zenobia kissed Miriam's cheek. "I agree with that. Miriam, I can't send Ezechiel away. He is needed here."

"I know."

"I'll talk to him."

"You can't!"

Miriam's horrified look told Zenobia she had said the wrong thing. She never understood her own kind. "All right."

"Send him away. You have other generals. Please. I feel like killing myself."

"Oh, Miriam. Don't think such thoughts."

"I tried to drink poison, but it was too bitter. It only made me ill."

Zenobia scrutinized Miriam. Her clothing hung off her, and her complexion was splotchy. How much weight had she lost? Miriam was sick with jealousy. Zenobia wanted to soothe her, but didn't know how.

"I'll think about your request. Maybe . . ."

"Thank you," Miriam whispered. She quickly left the cella.

Zenobia, stunned by Miriam's problem, dropped into a chair. Where could she send Ezechiel? And should she?

She didn't know how long a servant had been hovering in the doorway with a messenger behind him. She waved the servant and his shadow in.

"This messenger is from Egypt. Timagenes has sent him."

Zenobia sat straight and held out her hand for the papyrus scroll. She unfurled it slowly. Bad news could wait. She knew it was bad from the dirt encased messenger. His eyes were red rimmed, his hand trembled from exhaustion, and he could barely stand.

"Find a place for him to sleep. Take him food and water." Zenobia stared at the scroll. Finally she read, and as she did so her heart raced. She needed to talk with Ezechiel. She glanced up and saw Rebekeh in the doorway.

"I didn't mean to disturb you."

"You didn't. Run and find Ezechiel. Tell him quietly that he needs to come immediately."

"I just saw him in the kitchen pestering the cook." Rebekeh scurried from the doorway.

It seemed that Ezechiel materialized before her instantly.

"You were deep in thought," Ezechiel said.

"We have a long missive from Timagenes. He says that Rome is in the midst of a civil war. Aurelian's fine Dalmatian troops proclaimed Governor Septianius emperor. His reign lasted but a short time—he was dragged down and murdered by those who elevated him."

"That is good news. Aurelian will be too busy to bother us."

"There's more. The mint workers rioted because food is so scarce. There's no Egyptian grain for bread." Zenobia sighed.

"That is good news as well."

"I'm not certain. The beaten dog bites." Zenobia tapped the scroll. "Here it says mobs joined the workers and the citizens fought them on Caelian Hill. Before Aurelian restored order, many were killed."

"So why does that worry you?"

"I worry about Egypt. We can't bring down Rome if they fight us for Egypt."

"Does Timagenes ask for help?"

"Yes. He says that Aurelian even had several senators executed because they sided with the mint workers. Aurelian closed the mint to reform the monetary system. He has rationed food, and he's building new walls around the city to protect the people from the northern invaders."

"So our job becomes more difficult," Ezechiel said.

"Ha! Aurelian was even awarded the title of Germanicus Maximus as Claudius had been."

"Which do we do first—shore up Egypt or march on Rome?"

"We should do both, but I don't have enough men or supplies."

"Choose one."

"Egypt."

"Why?"

Zenobia smiled. "To keep the starving dog hungry."

"Who do we send to Egypt?"

"Who? Someone I trust. You, Ezechiel."

"Me!"

Zenobia started at the force of his response. "Who else would I send?"

"I don't know, but it won't be me." Ezechiel walked to the window, leaned against the frame, and crossed his arms.

"It won't be you?" Zenobia held back a gasp as anger surged through every part of her body. She stepped toward Ezechiel. "Attention!"

Ezechiel's puzzled expression changed to one of controlled indignation as he bolted upright into a military stance. His arm shot out at a perfect forty-five degree angle in a salute. He stared straight ahead.

"I am your queen. I have given you an order that if not followed is considered treasonous." Zenobia swallowed the last word involuntarily, but she could see by Ezechiel's eyes that he heard it.

"It is your choice," she continued. "You go to Egypt or you will be executed." Zenobia held her voice steady, but she wished she could retract the words.

"If I go to Egypt, I may never see Miriam again. If I don't go to Egypt, I'll never see Miriam in this lifetime." Ezechiel chuckled. "You have effectively trapped me."

Zenobia blinked. "I reacted as your queen rather than your friend. I could never execute you."

"Why not?"

"You and Miriam are my closest friends and advisors. I have been foolish." Zenobia wanted to ask for his forgiveness, but she couldn't form the words.

"I will go to Egypt."

"I'm not sure that you should go. It would be sensible for me to lead the army back into Egypt."

"You want to send me to Egypt. What do you plan to do?" Ezechiel asked.

"I'll recruit and train more troops. I'll make periodic trips to our frontiers." Zenobia stared deeply into Ezechiel's eyes. "I'll wait for Aurelian to come to me."

"He can't come soon. He still fights the Goths who are on this side of the Danube."

"Sooner or later. It doesn't matter. He and I will meet." Zenobia held out the scroll. "You may want to study this."

"Thank you." Ezechiel bowed and turned to go.

"Wait, there is one other matter." Zenobia took a deep breath. "Miriam is miserable. She fears that you love me."

"She is right."

"Don't speak words to force a truth where there is none." Zenobia frowned. "Miriam loves you beyond reason. She worries about the way you look at me."

"Is it possible to love two women at once?"

"No. You love the one who bore your children, washed your clothes, cleansed your wounds, and helped you after you had too much to drink. Go to her. Tell her you're going to Egypt. Love her."

"I beg you to care for her and my daughters while I'm in Egypt."

"You know I will. The boys love your daughters."

Ezechiel shook his head. "They love to tease them."

"Your family is safe in the palace with me. Now go and soothe Miriam."

"She will not want me to leave," Ezechiel said.

"You may be surprised. She is the wife of a soldier. Now go!" Zenobia pointed to the door. She watched Ezechiel leave. He did not glance back as he usually did. She would miss him, but it was for the best. She still loved Odainat, and she could never hurt Miriam, but Ezechiel was a temptation. He lived and drew breath and was infatuated with her. That flattered her, and if she admitted it, her heart beat faster when Ezechiel was near. It would be disastrous for all of them if she gave in.

"May I intrude on your thoughts?" Longinus asked.

"Yes." Zenobia smiled at the philosopher. "Are the lessons done for today?"

"My part is. Rebekeh is their task master now. She has no mercy."

Zenobia laughed. "She learns quickly. I'm proud of her."

"I keep her busy so she thinks of the future and not the past."

"Ah, Longinus, you are wise. I wish I were. Please come and sit near me so we can talk." Zenobia pointed to a chair across from her.

Longinus skirted around the low table that sat between the chairs. "The fruit looks wonderful."

"Part of the joys of controlling Asia Minor. It comes in fresh every day. You must try the wine as well." Zenobia motioned for Longinus to sit as she poured wine for the both of them.

"The conquest of Asia Minor pleases you," Longinus said.

"The taxes please me. It's a wealthy nation."

"It pleases you that you took it from Rome."

"True. I did it for Odainat."

"Revenge can turn bitter."

"I'll worry about that later."

Longinus sighed. "I hope all goes well for you—for us."

"Aurelian needs what I've taken. He'll come for me. He needs Asia Minor's taxes and Egypt's grain."

"Most of all he has to reduce your power. He can't let Palmyra best Rome." Longinus took a handful of grapes.

"That is his primary goal." Zenobia shrugged her shoulders. "We were friends of Rome until Emperor Gallienus had Maeonius assassinate my husband. The Romans chose this war."

"You chose to retaliate. I don't think Rome expected that."

"No. I was supposed to die, too." Zenobia sipped her wine. "Let's not talk of war. A game of Senet? You have won the last two games, so I challenge you."

"It is my pleasure." Longinus pushed aside the bowls of fruit while Zenobia took the Senet board and markers from the drawer in the table. She carefully set up the game board with black and white flowered markers.

"You move first, Longinus."

"Every time I move first, I lose."

"I know."

The rooftop was cool. Zenobia and Miriam stood side by side and stared at the city below. The sun dropped imperceptibly lower and lower. Shadows grew below sun kissed buildings and made them two toned. A balmy desert breeze gently lifted strands of hair that framed Zenobia's face.

"The days and nights grow cooler," Miriam said.

"Autumn comes quickly."

"Ezechiel has been gone too long," Miriam said.

"How do you fare?" Zenobia looked at her friend.

"I wish I had your strength. I wish I'd never begged you to send him away."

"I didn't send him because you begged. I sent him because Egypt needed him. Your words did not dictate my policy." Zenobia said the words softly so as not to offend Miriam.

"How do you live without the King?"

"I don't know if I am. The time has both flown and been as slow as honey since Odainat's murder."

"How so?"

"He died four years ago, yet it seems like yesterday. However, sometimes it seems that he is a distant memory, almost a remnant of my imagination." Zenobia stared at the Temple of Bel in the distance. "It saddens me to think that on some days I cannot see his face in my mind. I see his black beard tinged with silver, but I can't recall his eyes."

"I'm relieved to hear you say that. I thought something was wrong with me when I couldn't recall Ezechiel. I can hear his voice, however. Every night before I sleep, I listen to his words."

"He'll come home when Egypt is secure. He trains the Egyptians the same as I train our recruits from the countries we now control. Our army is growing." Zenobia leaned over the stone wall. "Look, your daughters chase after my sons with sticks."

"Oh, no! I'll stop them."

"Don't. My sons deserve it I'm sure. Rebekeh says that the boys play tricks on them all the time."

"They're growing up so fast."

"Too fast. Next year both will start military training."

"Does that frighten you?"

"Yes, but it must be." Zenobia watched the children disappear on the far side of the courtyard. The sun was gone. "Come, let's gather our offspring and have dinner together."

"I've looked everywhere, but I can't find the children." Rebekeh's voice trembled. "I've asked the guards to get lanterns and look for them."

"Where did you look?" Miriam asked

"The garden, the apartments, the kitchen. No one has seen them." Rebekeh's eyes were bright with tears.

Zenobia's heart pounded. She forced herself to calm down and think. It was less than half the hour when she and Miriam had last seen the four. A lot could happen or nothing. If one had been hurt, the others would have come.

"Rebekeh, did you call for them?" Zenobia asked.

"Over and over."

"I would guess they are playing a trick on you."

"Really?" Rebekeh's face turned from fear to anger. "I've never beaten them, but this time I may do so. That is a cruel trick."

"The guards will find them and bring them to us," Miriam said. "My daughters will be put to bed without dinner. They'll be confined to the apartment for seven days. That will drive them to think."

"Or drive you away." Zenobia chuckled even though something nagged at her. The children should've jumped out and scared Rebekeh. This wasn't like them. "I'll go and check with the palace guards to see how many are looking."

Zenobia walked casually from the cella, but nearly ran down the long hall as she went to find the head palace guard. She crossed the atrium almost as a run.

"Zenobia!"

She whirled around at the sound of her name. Mokimu ran toward her.

"I'm glad to have found you. It's Tarab . . ."

"I don't have time now. The children are missing."

"I know. Tarab has them."

"Has she? . . ."

"Not really. Come, they're in our apartment." Mokimu turned and led the way.

The children were seated at a table piled high with sweets. Giggles and laughter floated across the cella as Zenobia blinked. Tarab served honey cakes to the four children.

"These are Maeonius' favorite. He'll be here any moment to eat with us." Tarab smiled at Vaballathus. "You look so much like him when he was young."

Vaballathus stopped giggling. "I don't want to look like Maeonius."

Tarab glanced at each of the children. "All of you look like Maeonius just as brothers and sisters should."

"We're not his brothers and sisters," Arraum said.

"Of course you are." Tarab placed another honey cake on Arraum's plate.

"I don't like these." He pushed the plate away with his good hand.

"You do like honey cakes." Tarab pushed the plate back.

"How do you know? You're not my mother."

"Foolish child. You shouldn't tease me." Tarab placed a second honey cake on the plate. "Eat. These are the best."

"I'm not hungry," Arraum said.

Zenobia strode into the room. "There you are. All four of you are up too late. Say thank you to Tarab and go to your beds at once."

"No!" Tarab whirled around and glared at Zenobia. "You can't order my children around even if you are queen. Only my brother, the king, can do that."

"You can't talk to Queen Zenobia like that!" Shayna screamed. Her dark eyes flashed and Zenobia could see Ezechiel in his daughter. "It's all right. Do as she says and eat."

Shayna looked puzzled, but she dutifully bit into a cake. She nudged her younger sister and Kelila, tears forming, picked up a cake.

"I don't understand. . . ." Vaballathus said.

"It's all right. Do as Tarab asks." Zenobia put her hand on Tarab's arm. "You are very good to . . . to your children."

Tarab jerked her arm away. "Thanks only to Odainat do we have a roof over our heads. If you had your way my children and I would be food for the desert animals."

"I have not turned you out." Zenobia spoke softly. This was worse than any battle she'd been in. The children could be in danger, but she wasn't sure. There were no rules here, nothing that could have been studied to prepare her. "I believe you and the children belong in the palace where it's safe."

"Odainat forces you to keep us. I shudder to think what would happen to us if he were to die."

Zenobia's mouth dropped open. She looked at Mokimu.

He shrugged his shoulders. "She's been in the past for two days now. At first I thought it was reminiscing, but not now."

"Tarab, does Odainat still rule as king?"

"You know he does. Don't try to trick me."

Zenobia nodded. "Then you know as king that his commands must be followed."

"Of course I know that."

"King Odainat has ordered the children to his apartment. He wants to see them." Zenobia watched Tarab's face. It held no expression.

Tarab clapped her hands together. "Oh wonderful! My brother wants to see his nieces and nephews. I'll send Maeonius, too, as soon as he gets here."

"Maeonius is already with the king," Zenobia said. She nearly choked on the murderer's name.

"Children, do run and see the king. Do it now lest he become angry with you for being slow to obey him." Tarab smiled.

Zenobia nodded at Vaballathus. "You're the oldest so you must lead the others to the cella. Go quickly."

Vaballathus and Arraum moved quickly to the door. The girls were not far behind. None of them looked back, but disappeared down the hallway.

Zenobia backed toward the door. "I must go and tend to some business."

"Oh, yes. Some little war, I suppose." Tarab shrugged. "Go."

Mokimu walked Zenobia down the hallway. "I don't know what to do."

"We'll have guards posted around the clock. I didn't think she needed them any more, but I was wrong. She'll be followed discreetly. Perhaps a female companion might help. Does she like anyone in particular?"

"Miriam."

"Oh. Well, I'll talk with her about spending time with Tarab."

"I'm sorry about this."

"No harm done. Thank goodness. No harm done." Zenobia smiled at her brother-in-law. "You're such a good man, Mokimu. Tarab is very lucky."

Zenobia hurried toward her cella where sounds of excited, chattering children drifted toward her. She stopped in the doorway and looked at the two girls and two boys who'd surrounded Rebekeh and Miriam. They had no idea the danger they'd been in. Youth and innocence had advantages.

She motioned for Miriam to join her in the hall. As the two women walked away from Zenobia's apartment, they were both silent.

"Miriam," Zenobia whispered. "As good as Rebekeh is with the children, she can't be everywhere at once. Not only do we have danger from without, but now we have danger from within."

"I'm relieved that you see Tarab for what she is," Miriam said.

"She is a troubled woman."

"She is a dangerous woman."

"She'll not come near our children again." Zenobia stopped and took Miriam's hands in her own. "I am worried about Aurelian capturing my sons, so I want you to do two things for me. Promise that you'll be a companion to Tarab and will be my sons' guardian should anything happen to me."

"Nothing will happen to you."

"Promise me." Zenobia took her hand.

"You know I'll protect your sons as I do my own children." Miriam's eyes filled with tears.

"I knew you'd help me. I have the documents ready for you to sign."

"Documents? You are so formal."

"These times demand it."

Ezechiel stared at Timagenes. "You're sure."

"No doubt. Our informants believe he'll sail into Alexandria within ten days."

"There is no time to fortify the troops there. So who does Aurelian send? Or is he coming himself?"

"He sends a general who has the same last name as the other—Probus," Timagenes said.

"A second Probus? Perhaps he'll be murdered by his own soldiers, too."

"Better that it happen after we win the battle just as with the last Probus."

Ezechiel unfurled a papyrus map. "We'll march to here and camp beneath the great pyramids. We'll lose Alexandria, but we can hold Cairo."

"And go on the defensive later to get Alexandria back," Timagenes said.

Ezechiel ran a finger down the rough edges of the map and back up again. "We have to. We can't let Rome have a port for grain shipment."

"Zenobia would never forgive you if you let Cleopatra's palace fall into Roman hands." Timagenes laughed.

"Three hundred years is long enough. Send a message to the commander in Alexandria. Have him set up a signaling system from the light house to a series of riders. We need to know when Probus lands."

"A good idea."

"Can our troops hold him?"

Timagenes shook his head. "There are too many."

"We'll hold Cairo."

"May our gods be with us," Timagenes said.

Ezechiel sighed. "With summer near, I'd hoped to return home."

"You miss your family. A year is a long time."

"I miss my wife. I dream of her every night." Ezechiel smiled. "Love blossoms in this desert. I never knew what she meant to me until now."

"They are ready to attack," Timagenes said. "My troops will attack from the left flank."

"I'm not sure whether you should go up the middle with me or not. We need to break their lines. . . ."

"No," Timagenes said. "We'll have to fight front and back that way."

Ezechiel frowned. What would Zenobia do? He didn't know. Sometimes she fought like Odainat; sometimes she had her own tricks. Timagenes was seasoned and a veteran of desert warfare, but Ezechiel knew that he was too.

The Roman army spread itself across the desert sand like a gold and red fire bird. Early morning sun glinted off armor and swords. The reflection stretched wide and long like endless candles.

"We have no reinforcements coming," Ezechiel said. He handed a missive to Timagenes.

"It says Zenobia can't help because she's waiting for Aurelian." Timagenes frowned. "That isn't her usual position."

"No, something is wrong." Ezechiel adjusted his sword and nodded toward Probus' army. "As soon as we beat them, I'll take part of my men and go help Zenobia."

"After we take back Alexandria."

"It's on the way home." Ezechiel repeated the word home under his breath. It sounded good. He couldn't wait to see Miriam's laughing eyes. Shayna and Kelila would have grown, and he was sorry he had missed it.

Timagenes pointed toward the Roman army. "There are many."

"We've both fought large Roman armies before. Victory follows us," Ezechiel said.

"I'm ready, Ezechiel. Go with your god."

"And you go with yours." Ezechiel raised his sword arm. "Now!" He signaled both his men and Timagenes'. Timagenes and his men broke to the left as Ezechiel and his army surged forward.

Ezechiel swallowed as he rode toward the Roman army's front line of defense. He leaned forward, kicked his horse, and led his men into the line.

He was shocked when the Roman line held. He pulled his cavalry back and sent in the infantry. The lines still held, and Ezechiel was beaten back. He ordered the infantry and the cavalry to retreat.

"Again!" he shouted. He and his men rode forward a third time and a fourth. The Palmyran infantry tired rapidly, and there was no progress.

Timagenes and his men charged the Romans, but they, too, had to retreat. Dust flew around the men from both sides masking the glint of swords, but not the smell of blood or the sounds of men dying.

Ezechiel swore, then called on God for help. He led a charge a fifth time and finally hacked through the Roman lines. Blood splattered his chain mail, dried instantly and flaked off. His sword never stopped—arching and clanging, splitting and thrusting into flesh and bone.

Twice he had to stop because there were no men around him left to kill. He urged his horse over the carnage and found more of the enemy to send to their gods.

Then he saw him. Probus rode a white stallion and cut a grisly path through Ezechiel's men. Ezechiel forced his horse across bodies slippery with blood and gore until he was behind Probus.

"Probus!" Ezechiel shouted. "I've come for you!"

"And I for you." Probus turned his horse and charged. "For Emperor Aurelian!"

Ezechiel, shocked at Probus' quickness, had little time to position himself. As Probus came into range, Ezechiel lifted his sword and struck a glancing blow off Probus' helmet. Probus in turn swung at the Palmyran's midsection. Ezechiel twisted aside just enough so that the sword barely nicked his chain mail, but in doing so he made his horse stumble.

Ezechiel held on and loosened the reins. For one moment rider and mount seemed frozen in position, but gravity took over and both went down. Instinctively Ezechiel rolled away from his horse while holding his sword above his head. He leaped to his feet just as Probus rode past him. Probus' sword caught him in the upper arm. Ezechiel gasped, not from the pain, but from the incongruity of a useless sword arm. His muscles refused to work and his sword dropped to the bloodied sand.

He snatched up the sword with his left hand and waited as Probus turned toward him and ran his mount full speed. Ezechiel waited until the last possible moment to leap aside. He swung his sword. The scream of Probus' horse confirmed that he'd sliced through tendons and muscle. The horse fell and dumped Probus in a heap at Ezechiel's feet.

Ezechiel raised his sword with his one good arm and brought it down to finish Probus. Probus rolled away, and Ezechiel's sword vibrated as it buried itself in the sand. Probus leaped to his feet and swung before Ezechiel could pull his sword free.

Ezechiel felt hot blood run down his neck and across his chest. He tried to call out for Miriam, but only a gurgle passed his lips. His last thoughts were of her as he fell at Probus' feet.

CHAPTER
XXI

272 A. D. Palmyra, Syria and *Chalcedon, Asia Minor*

*M*iriam's tears finally stopped. She shuddered and nestled closer to Zenobia. Zenobia wrapped her arms around Miriam as they sat together on the queen's sleeping couch. Miriam had cried almost continuously for a week. She wouldn't eat and would hardly drink.

"Where are my daughters?"

Zenobia was so startled at hearing Miriam's voice that she didn't comprehend the question. "They're with Longinus and Rebekeh."

"Has anyone told them of their father's death?" Miriam's voice was so dry it cracked.

"I've told them. It was as difficult as when I told my sons about their father and brother."

"I should never have asked that you send him away."

"I would have sent him to Egypt anyway. It wasn't you who caused his death, but the Romans," Zenobia said. "Always remember who killed your husband and mine." She heard the bitterness in her voice.

"I wish he'd never been a soldier," Miriam said.

"Your god ordained it. Ezechiel is . . . was a great warrior and a great man." Zenobia's tears had dried the moment she resolved to kill Aurelian.

Her focus was split between breaking Rome and murdering the emperor who'd caused so much grief. Palmyra had kept the Persians from destroying Rome's desert frontier, and Rome's thanks was treachery. Zenobia vowed to repay Rome in kind.

"I'm so alone. I've never been without Ezechiel. We played together as children."

"You told me he tormented you."

Miriam smiled. "He did. I loved to hate him for it."

"You're not alone. You have Shayna and Kelila. You have me,
Rebekeh, and a score of other people." Zenobia brushed sweat damp-
ened hair away from Miriam's forehead. "Come, let the servants bathe
you with cool water. I'll tell them to get your tub ready."

"I'll do it for you, but it won't make the hurt go away. I don't
want to live without him."

"I didn't want to live without Odainat, but I did. I live to avenge
his death."

"I never understood your pain until now. I never understood
how someone so tough could collapse like you did."

"I wish you had never had to understand," Zenobia said.

"I can't fight the Romans the way you do."

"Yes, you can. You can help me manage the palace, the children,
the servants. I will have to work at training soldiers many more hours
a day." Zenobia looked out the western window. "Aurelian comes."

Rebekeh ran through the streets of Palmyra toward the barracks.
Perspiration flew off her face as she dodged pedestrians, carts, donkeys, and the vendors who sat cross-legged on blankets in the shade
of massive stone buildings. Ordinarily she would've followed the main
street with its columns and shade, but that was the long way to the
barracks. She had little time.

Dogs barked at her, but still she ran. Her clothing stuck to her
and finally she grabbed her skirts and hiked them up. People stared
at her, but stepped aside. She had to hold her skirt with one hand
and clamp her free hand over the pain in her side.

She ran past the guard at the gate to the base. He yelled at her,
but knew her name and didn't stop her. Rebekeh had to stop running just before she got to Zenobia's hut. She took great breaths of
the desert air and tried to calm herself. She reached the queen's of-
fice at last and leaned against the door.

Zenobia looked up from a scroll, dismissed the messenger, and
motioned for Rebekeh to sit.

Rebekeh dropped into a chair. She took the glass of wine that

Zenobia offered her, but couldn't drink it.

"Are the boys all right?" Zenobia asked.

Rebekeh nodded, then gasped, "It's Miriam."

"Miriam?"

"She has barricaded herself in her apartment. She refuses to come out."

"Does anyone know why she did this?" Zenobia rolled up the scroll and tucked it under her arm.

"She says she doesn't want to live without Ezechiel." Rebekeh blinked back tears.

"We'll ride back to the palace. Come." Zenobia rushed out ahead of Rebekeh and instructed a chariot driver to get them to the palace as quickly as possible.

The door was indeed barricaded. Zenobia pushed and Rebekeh helped, but to no avail. "It's probably that heavy chest. I wonder how she moved it?" Zenobia said.

"We have to get in. She may have already . . ." Rebekeh said.

"Go to the children, Rebekeh. Keep the girls away from here." Zenobia frowned. She could climb out the window from her cella and edge across the ledge to this window. It would be instant death if she fell, for the wadi was twenty feet below her. The fall would give her a minute of terror, then the rocks would give her a few seconds of agony. She shivered. She had to do it.

The ledge was wide enough for Zenobia to move sideways. She had removed her sword and armor and soldiers were stationed in her cella and below her at the far edge of the wadi. She had said a prayer to Allat and to Bel. She didn't have time to pray to any of the other gods. She worried that Miriam would take her own life. Why hadn't she seen it coming? Was she so oblivious to others that she failed to understand them?

Zenobia wanted to hurry, but it was all she could do to move one foot sideways, then the other. It seemed the forty cubit distance had doubled since she climbed out on the ledge. Another step, then another. She looked down and froze. The soldiers stared up at her from a great distance. The wadi looked evil with shadows that masked the bottom.

She listened, but no sound came from Miriam's apartment. A slide step. Zenobia held her breath and counted each step she took. She refused to look down again.

At last she gripped the edge of the window opening. She curled her fingers tightly around the corner and slid sideways across the opening. Silk curtains billowed out and wrapped themselves around her. Zenobia didn't want to be thrown into the wadi by curtains, so she fell backwards into the room. She leaped up and glanced around. The door that the guards had tried to break open was indeed blocked with a heavy chest.

Zenobia skirted the room and stopped at the doorway to Miriam's sleeping chamber. Miriam lay stretched out on the sleeping couch, her hand clutching a blue bottle that Zenobia recognized. Used in small amounts, it was a pain killer. If Miriam had drunk too much. . . .

She ran to Miriam and raised her. Miriam's eyes fluttered and she smiled.

"Miriam, how much did you drink?" Zenobia removed the bottle from her hand. It was empty.

"Enough. I will see Ezechiel soon."

"Where did you get this?"

"I stole it from Iason's medicine room. He is old and never heard me."

"You can't die and leave your daughters."

"I leave them to you. There's a note." She tried to point, but her hand dropped to her side.

Zenobia grabbed Miriam, turned her over so that her head hung toward the floor. She quickly ran her finger down Miriam's throat until, coughing and sputtering, her friend vomited. Pools of brown liquid decorated the marble. Zenobia placed Miriam in a sitting position on the couch and wiped her face with the bed coverings.

"I fight for your life just as I fight the Romans—with everything I have. I can no longer allow you to be alone. From now on, you will have three chamber servants to watch over you at all times. They'll report to me and will be paid well so that as long as you live, they'll have a good income."

"I want to be with Ezechiel. Don't you understand? I need to be with him." Miriam's tears flowed down her cheeks.

"I understand very well how you feel. Even after nearly five years I still yearn for Odainat. I dream of him. I smell the spices he used in his bath, and just when I think he is near, I awaken from a dream. That is the cruelest time of all. I understand your pain so well, Miriam."

"I know."

"You have to live for your daughters. What if you had died? What would they think? Would they think that you abandoned them? Left them to fend for themselves? Children need us. My sons are the reason I'm alive today. They need me and Shayna and Kelila need you."

"They would've been fine with you."

"I'm not their mother. They are your responsibility. Ezechiel would tell you that."

"Would he?"

"You know he would." Zenobia rubbed her fingers lightly across the back of Miriam's hand.

"I want to be with him."

"Miriam, no."

"I'm no good here."

"Every time Ezechiel went into battle, he expected you to care for his daughters. This is no different."

"I've never imagined life without him."

"The reality is that Ezechiel is gone, but you're not. If you had died, would you want him to commit suicide and leave the girls orphans?"

"Oh, no!"

"Then you must live for them. Ezechiel would want you to, wouldn't he?"

Miriam nodded. "Yes, he would."

"No more selfish attempts?"

"Selfish!"

"Think about it." Zenobia frowned. "Yes, selfish, so no more."

Miriam closed her eyes. "No."

"Promise your god you will live."

"I do." Miriam stifled a sob. "I want to bathe and put on fresh clothing. I need to see my daughters."

"Good. They need you to tell them everything will be all right. They need to pray with you."

"Your army grows daily, Aurelian," Marcellus looked across the shimmering gold, red, and silver of the Roman fighting machine. "Men cover the earth like a never ending fire."

"It's the largest army ever assembled in this century." Aurelian stepped outside the tent to join his second in command.

"Every able-bodied man wants to fight with you for the glory of Rome." Marcellus grinned. "How did you do it?"

"By winning."

"You pulled troops back from the frontier."

"To shorten the line of defense. We can leave fewer divisions behind to defend the Balkan area."

"You have a plan, but have discussed it with no one—not even me."

"True."

"I've wondered why all winter long you had men recruited and trained. I've wondered why you pulled together the Dalmatian cavalry, the Mauritanian horse troops, and regiments from all over Roman territory."

"You can't guess?" Aurelian grinned. "I've always said Rome needed only one emperor. We still have two."

"Two? There is only you." Marcellus frowned.

"Zenobia."

Marcellus whirled around and stared at the emperor. "By the gods! You're going to march across the desert and attack Palmyra!"

"We start tomorrow. I want to be there by early summer."

Water sparkled between the two continents as Aurelian and Marcellus halted their horses.

"Byzantium opened her gates to us. Such a beautiful city, don't you think?"

Marcellus shrugged. "It's too noisy and dusty. Rome is much grander."

Aurelian nodded. "On the opposite shore lies Chalcedon. And beyond Chalcedon is Ankara, Antioch, and Tyana. Those cities are the gateway to Zenobia."

"She controls Chalcedon."

"Does she?"

"For now."

"But not for long." Aurelian nudged Harpinna forward. The beast plodded slowly to the bridge, then stopped.

"It's a bridge." Aurelian kicked the horse. "It's only a bridge.

You've crossed them before." Aurelian kicked the horse again. Harpinna refused to move.

"Although tradition dictates that you go first, perhaps she'll follow my horse." Marcellus tried to hold back his laughter.

"Tradition doesn't matter when we hold up the Roman invasion and thus thwart history. Lead on."

Marcellus rode past the stone-like Harpinna and stopped a few feet in front of her. She moved until she was abreast of his horse.

"Aurelian, why do you keep such an animal? You could have any mount."

"I wish I knew. It's bizarre, but I'm attached to her. She's comfortable."

Harpinna lurched forward and nearly unseated Aurelian. "I like the challenge!" he shouted over his shoulder.

Marcellus signaled the rest of the cavalry and thousands of men started the trek from Europe to Asia.

Messengers continuously raced up and down the column of soldiers so leaders could be kept informed. Dust swirled around horses and men alike and formed a pale brown haze that was kept stirred up the entire day from dawn to dusk until the army was on the opposite shore where it surrounded the walled city of Chalcedon.

Aurelian dropped down on his bed glad to be rid of armor and sandals. He was too excited to sleep. Zenobia would not surrender no matter how many men marched toward Palmyra. She was a worthy foe, but no matter how tenacious she was, she could be beaten by sheer numbers.

Aurelian had hoped she would come to him so he wouldn't have to subject his men to desert warfare, but since her second in command—he couldn't remember the man's name—had been killed in Egypt by the Roman troops, Zenobia had stayed in Palmyra.

She wasn't idle. His spies told him she trained her men long and hard. She even had a regiment of Bedouins. It would be a difficult war, but Palmyra would fall even if he had to execute the entire city.

His immediate problems were Chalcedon and Tyana. Chalcedon was the key to getting Palmyra. Were they loyal to him or to Zenobia who controlled that city?

He sighed. How could he sleep with so much going on?

Aurelian finally dropped off to a fitful sleep webbed with spidery dreams of war. He awakened before reveille chilled by his own perspiration. He got out of bed and kicked the servant boy who slept under the map table. The fool scrambled up, blinked stupidly, and bowed.

"Hot water!" Aurelian bellowed.

He nicked himself on the jaw with the razor, swore, and dropped the blade into the metal wash basin. He grabbed a piece of scrap linen and stuck it to the cut. Aurelian expected a visit from the people of Chalcedon. The question was whether there would be a peaceful contingent of officials or an army ready for battle. He had no feeling for how much control Zenobia had over the most northern part of the land she'd taken from Rome.

Aurelian's eyes narrowed. He'd never allowed himself to utter or even think that Zenobia had taken land from Rome. Egypt was an invasion, but Rome had that country back. She hadn't taken it; merely occupied it. It was the same here. He would not take back the land— he didn't have to. Zenobia only occupied it. He'd march through Asia Minor and the villages and cities would greet him and his army as saviors. If they didn't, they would cease to exist.

He would wait for the officials of Chalcedon until the sun was overhead. If they hadn't come from behind their walled city by then to show loyalty to Rome, he'd invade their city. It would be wiped out.

Aurelian sat down and pulled out a rolled map. He wanted to check the route to Palmyra. Exactly how far was it? How hot was the desert? How many soldiers did Zenobia have in her army?

He leaned back, put his hands behind his head, and grinned. It would be most interesting to battle a woman. Most interesting.

Marcellus peered through the opening in the tent. "There seems to be a delegation who rides this way."

"Chalcedon officials?" Aurelian asked.

"Yes."

"When they arrive, make them wait outside."

Marcellus laughed. "You're up to your old tricks. Waiting makes them nervous."

"And shows subservience."

"Good. They come"

"Ask them to dismount, then make them stand. Check with me when you see the leader begin to perspire." Aurelian grinned. "It should take little more than a quarter of an hour."

Aurelian studied his maps. How long would it take to get to Palmyra? By now spies would have rushed to Zenobia and informed her of his progress. How long would it take? It depended on how many cities would throw open the gates to welcome him and how many would slam the gates in his face. All would be conquered. He would be in Palmyra in a month or two, but no later.

He heard Marcellus tell the delegation from Chalcedon that the emperor was quite busy, but perhaps he might be ready in a few minutes. Aurelian smiled. He could tell from his friend's voice that Marcellus enjoyed himself immensely in this role. He would have to allow him to play it more often.

Aurelian, curious and somewhat bored, bellowed at Marcellus. "Let them come in. I have a few minutes."

The delegation was made up of an old man whose long white hair floated past his shoulders. He was not perspiring. Why should he? He had already lived past his time. He would be easiest to talk with, for he had nothing to lose—not pride, not life, not anything.

The other two men were middle aged. One hawk faced man looked at Aurelian with small, dark eyes. His hands gave him away. His fingers intertwined with his toga as he twisted the material around his fingers much like a woman would under stress. The other man perspired so much it dripped off his face onto his clothing. Aurelian could smell the animal fear that wafted toward him from this man who hung back a step from the other two. Aurelian chose to stare at him while he found out what the delegation had on their minds.

"Are you ready for war?" Aurelian asked.

The oldest man spoke. His voice was resonant and the words spoken distinctly. An orator or a philosopher. Aurelian frowned. He'd prefer a soldier. A soldier would understand the implications of the Roman machine camped outside the city. He watched the old man carefully. The man's face was impassive.

"We are ready for war, if necessary," the old man said. "I am Catus. I was born in Rome and am a Roman citizen."

"As a Roman then you realize that Zenobia is not at all Roman in her beliefs, her religion, or her dress. In fact, she is an enemy to Rome and alien to all that is Rome. What say you to that?"

"It is true that she is not Roman. She is more Greek and Egyptian. Foremost, however, she is Palmyran. She derives her strength from Palmyra," Catus said.

"So you think that without Palmyra, she has no strength?"

Catus bowed his head. "Is that what you think?"

"Don't play the philosopher with me. I asked what you think. You're the great thinker, so tell me your thoughts. Zenobia is an enemy to Rome," Aurelian repeated.

Catus studied him. "It is so but hasn't always been."

"She has never loved Rome as much as she loved Palmyra," Aurelian said.

"Whoever decided that Odainat should be killed did not know the wrath of a warrior queen like Zenobia. Therein lies the cause of Rome's problems. They were brought on by Rome herself." Catus never wavered as he returned Aurelian's glare.

"You speak treasonous words," Aurelian said.

"I speak the truth. Truth is not treason."

Aurelian shook his head. "My army can reduce Chalcedon to rubble in a day."

"Yes, you can."

"Are you prepared for that?"

"No. We have sent word to Zenobia that you are here, but she can't get troops here in time. Those troops that were here have been called back to somewhere in the desert."

"There are none of Zenobia's troops in Chalcedon?"

"None."

Aurelian pondered this piece of information. She would set up a series of defenses, but where? She wouldn't wait until he got to Palmyra to fight. Or would she? Did she depend on the likes of these men to hold the cities she'd taken from Rome? That was her weakness. She took people at face value. She thought that they believed in her when in fact they would sway from one side to the other as blades of grass in the wind.

"Is Chalcedon going to bar the gates to me?" Aurelian asked.

"We have already opened the gates," Catus said. "Chalcedon welcomes the Roman emperor and his army. We are ready to be freed of the Palmyran oppression."

"Good." Aurelian stared at each man in turn. "Remember which ruler liberated you and which one put you in chains."

"Don't you think spring is a wonderful time of year?" Aurelian patted Harpinna's neck. She had behaved beautifully today, and he wondered why. He also wondered why he put up with her.

Marcellus glanced sideways at his emperor. "You are particularly jovial today."

"See what lays ahead of us?" Aurelian swept his arms out to encompass the view.

"Ankara. We've ridden a long way from Chalcedon. Do you think they'll really open their gates to us?"

"We have been told that there are no Palmyran troops there. Why is that?"

"Perhaps Zenobia has no men to spare. We are at least fourteen days from Palmyra." Marcellus looked to the southeast. "She may have pulled back her frontier as you did."

"You see the city of Ankara, Marcellus, whereas I see victory for Rome. Ankara will open her gates to us as Chalcedon did. They want to be liberated from the Palmyran tyrant. All the towns before us will swing open their gates, and we will spare them. After all, ordinary citizens were no match for Zenobia's army."

"We had garrisons there and in Chalcedon."

"Did we? Men trained by Zenobia and Odainat in Rome's name for Rome. Don't you think they trained them for Palmyra and not Rome?"

"Of course." Marcellus' face was pale and sweat lined his upper lip. "A true Roman army would not have lost Asia Minor."

"I'm glad you realize that. While I'm emperor, only Rome will train her army. Loyalty should not be suspect then." Aurelian stopped Harpinna. "We are almost there and look—the gates are open."

"Good. We'll have a hot meal and a soft bed tonight," Marcellus said.

"Let's go." Aurelian kicked Harpinna lightly. She responded like a well-trained animal, and he chuckled.

The thick wooden gates towered above Aurelian as he and Marcellus rode in. Aurelian smelled sap and fresh wood where weak planks had been replaced. Two hinges had recently been forged and stood out because of their newness.

Aurelian looked back at his army from the inside of the walled city. Shadows draped themselves across each soldier as they rode past the barriers thrown open in welcome. Or perhaps in fear, Aurelian didn't know. He wondered if the good citizens feared Zenobia or him the most. He pondered the question. She was a menace to Rome and dangerous. She was a brilliant soldier and leader of men. It would not be an easy battle to beat her, but he would never admit that—not even to Marcellus.

The clatter of the cavalry as the horses clip-clopped along the stone streets was the only sound Aurelian heard. He prayed to Mithras that this was not an ambush.

"Marcellus," he whispered.

"I see no one. Is it a trap by Zenobia?"

"Keep riding. We can't stop now." Aurelian glanced to the left and right. There were no people hanging from windows or in doorways of shops. The shop doors were open, but there was silence. Aurelian felt a shiver travel down his spine.

He breathed a sigh of relief when they reached the center of town. Two rows of dignitaries stretched across the top of the steps that led to a temple. On either side of them were priests in somber dark robes. People had gathered around the temple and eyed the cavalry with a combination of curiosity and trepidation.

Two priests beat gongs. The sonorous ringing vibrated Aurelian's breast bone, and he hoped it wasn't a signal to Palmyran troops. He'd only brought a light cavalry in with him. The infantry was a mile or two behind.

Marcellus whispered, "What temple is that?"

"I don't know. It must be one of their gods."

"Or Zenobia's."

"Do you see weapons?" Aurelian looked carefully at the men in the crowd.

"No."

A gentleman stepped forward and held out his hands palms up. "We welcome the mighty Roman Emperor Aurelian who has come to free us from the tyrannical Palmyran enemy."

Aurelian nodded.

"We have gifts for our hero. We have silk from the orient and spices from the Far East. We have perfumes and gems for your ladies. Your army will need provisions. We'll give you camels and food. If you would be kind and take our young men into your army, Ankara would be proud." The man bowed. "If you would be so kind, I have promised my son I would give you his horse. It's a fine war horse trained to perfection."

"Really?"

The man signaled, and the crowd parted. A young man led a horse forward whose coat was as black and shiny as obsidian.

Aurelian sucked in his breath. "He is powerfully built. His name?"

"Raven for his color."

Aurelian touched Raven's velvet nose. The horse snorted softly and nuzzled Aurelian's palm.

"He is gentle until battle, then he becomes formidable."

"I need a good mount." Aurelian ran his hand down Raven's flank. "He's a good horse. I accept your gift."

"Thank you, Emperor."

"What is your name?" Aurelian asked.

"I am called Belakab. I governed Ankara for Rome under Gallienus and Claudius. I hope to govern under you."

"I see no problem with that. I'm certain you're knowledgeable about our government and about the taxes we need to help protect your town."

Belakab nodded. "We think of ourselves as Roman, not Greek or Egyptian or Palmyran."

"You are a wise man, Belakab," Aurelian said. "Now show us where we may rest and eat. I am most interested in your gifts, but the young men whom you've promised for our army are even more interesting."

"They are the finest in Ankara."

"I will judge that for myself." Aurelian waved his hand. "Lead on. I am hot, tired, hungry, and dusty. You will remedy that, won't you?"

"Of course."

"We've marched ten days, Marcellus, only to be greeted like the enemy. Tyana has barred her gates. Look at the top of the walls. Archers." Aurelian could feel his jaws tighten as he clenched his teeth to keep from bellowing at the gods for this injustice.

"Palmyran archers. The best in the world are the Palmyran archers. There is no hope of taking that city from Zenobia."

"For shame, Marcellus. There is always hope for the Roman army."

Aurelian studied the town below. Towering walls made of native stone gleamed like winter wheat and enclosed the town. Four gates, one facing each direction, were dark and impregnable. The gates swung out rather than in, so that his army would have to batter them down while Palmyran archers assaulted them with burning arrows. The townspeople would pour boiling oil and water on his men. He would have his men throw up ladders to scale the walls, but they, too, would be in danger from boiling oil and flaming arrows.

"Zenobia is a thorn in my paw, nothing more," Aurelian said.

"You've been listening to Christian fables again," Marcellus said.

"Not really. It's just a childhood story that my mother . . ." Aurelian stopped speaking. "Now where did that come from?"

Marcellus shrugged. "Who knows when our childhood memories creep forth?"

Aurelian frowned at the town below him. Anger billowed inside him, and for the first time he knew he hated Zenobia enough to kill every man, woman, and child who stood between her and him.

"We'll conquer Tyana. It's another gateway to Zenobia." Aurelian turned his horse around, faced his troops, and waited for them to settle into silence.

"My fellow Roman citizens and soldiers. We have marched a long way across Asia Minor to recapture what was wrongfully taken from us. Before us is a small obstacle. Tyana has closed her gates to us and is protected by Palmyran archers. The battle will be treacherous, but you are the finest army in the world. There is treasure to be had in Tyana, for it is a wealthy town. I swear by the god, Mithras, that nothing in that town will be left alive—not even a dog!"

He was unprepared for his inflammatory speech to ignite his troops so quickly, but they were tired and angry, too. The shouts of revenge echoed over the heads of the thousands of men, and Aurelian grinned. This was the army that would defeat Zenobia.

Aurelian held up his hands and waited for silence. "We start with a siege of seven days. That should weaken their resolve before we batter down the gates." He nodded to his lieutenants and rode back to his tent. Marcellus would see to it that siege orders were carried out. Let Zenobia rot in Palmyra. He would take back his land until he reached her. No woman would do this to him.

"We are in the eighth day of the siege," Aurelian shouted. He glowered at each general in turn including Marcellus. "What is wrong with you? Why have you not conquered the city?"

No one spoke. Most of the men stared at the Persian rug as they stood inside Aurelian's tent.

Aurelian pounded the arms of his chair. "I have asked a question. Don't you dare refuse to answer me."

Marcellus spoke quietly. "Palmyran archers. They never seem to run out of arrows. The women are as adept at boiling water as they are throwing it on our men."

"Women! You let women prevent you from scaling the walls!" Aurelian snorted. "This is not a woman's war!"

"No, sir," Marcellus said.

"Get out. All of you get out."

Aurelian watched his generals leave as quickly as possible. It was difficult for twenty men to get through the tent flap at the same time. It was almost funny. Only Marcellus seemed at ease, but Aurelian knew it was an act. He could always tell when Marcellus was nervous because his left hand had a tremor. A very slight tremor that was unnoticed by most people.

He wished he hadn't blurted out that it wasn't a woman's war. It just brought out the fact that Zenobia had caused him as much trouble, nay even more so, than the barbarians. She had taken more land. It was a woman's war, and it shamed him that he had to fight it. He had to win. There would be much shame in losing to a woman and no honor in winning. Aurelian sighed. History would write of his deeds, but the record of his having fought a woman galled him.

Marcellus peered in through the tent flap. "Good news, I think."

Aurelian waved him in as much for company as for good news. "Pray tell."

"There is a man called Heraclammon who is a Tyana citizen."

"How did he manage to get out of the city?"

Marcellus shrugged. "He has important information for you, so he says."

"I have nothing better to do than to be entertained by a Tyana citizen. Bring him in."

The man bowed over and over as he was brought into the tent by two guards. Marcellus pushed him closer to the emperor.

"Speak," Aurelian said.

"I have valuable information," Heraclammon said.

"That means you want money."

"No, no. I want freedom. Nothing more." He bowed again.

"Are you not poor with starving children?" Aurelian asked.

"Since the Palmyrans have taken our city, I have become very poor. It is especially difficult now with the siege. My babies cry, and that makes my wife cry."

"So you don't want money to help your own children? That is foolish." Aurelian enjoyed watching the man squirm. "You tell me your information, and I'll reward you based on its value."

"You are too generous, Emperor Aurelian."

"Not at all. Quickly. Your information. I have little time."

"There is a way for you to enter the city without going through the gates or continuing the siege."

Aurelian looked at Marcellus. Marcellus shrugged. "Why haven't my good soldiers found this place?"

"They have been busy fending off Palmyran arrows."

"So where is this place?"

"There is a weakness in the northeastern corner of the wall. A well has eroded the ground there. On careful inspection, your men could see the difference in color. The mortar that holds the stones in place is soft. A battering ram would destroy the wall easily." Heraclammon peered at Aurelian from under bushy eyebrows.

"What is your occupation?"

"I am a stone cutter."

"So you know about mortar?"

"I do."

"Did you help build the walls?"

"No, but my grandfather's grandfather did."

Aurelian nodded. "You will be rewarded when we enter the city. Now return so that suspicions aren't raised."

"Thank you, Emperor." Heraclammon bowed and backed from the tent.

"Do you believe him?" Marcellus asked.

"Unfortunately, yes. There are always those who worship gold instead of their gods and betray their friends and family for it."

"Shall I send in the battering ram?"

"To the northeastern corner." Aurelian looked down at a map spread before him. "Now we can conquer Palmyra."

The northeastern wall had collapsed with just one well-placed thrust by the battering ram. As the Romans poured in through the wall, the Palmyran army, smaller in number than had been assumed, fled the city. Aurelian would seek them out and with them would be Zenobia. She would not allow her army to flee without coming to lead them. She had no second in command now according to Aurelian's spies, but used the general she thought could do what she needed at that moment. It was to his advantage that this impertinent woman had no trustworthy general.

Aurelian waited for the great gates to open. If the citizens were reluctant, he could understand. They had angered him and they should suffer for it. He wasn't angry though, and could hardly blame them. Which would he rather have—antagonistic and resentful citizens or happy and grateful ones? He had enough problems with Zenobia without having embittered people behind him who could turn against him as easily as they did Palmyra.

A plan formed and he turned toward his army. They quieted. It would be difficult, maybe deadly, if he couldn't get them to agree to his plan. Deadly for him personally.

"Roman soldiers are the best trained in the world. We have marched across many countries and two continents to be here today. This is a turning point in our quest to free our Roman friends from the clutches of Zenobia." Aurelian heard a murmur of confusion from the troops. He waited for silence.

"We can be considered conquerors or friends. We have that choice. I believe that Mithras has laid that choice before us as a test." Aurelian heard Marcellus' intake of breath.

"What are you trying to tell the men?" Marcellus asked.

"Listen." Aurelian patted Raven's neck to calm himself.

"I ask that you treat the good people of Tyana as our friends." He went on before the grumbling could get louder. "I ask that you spare them from looting, destruction, and the taking of women against their will. I ask that you behave in a compassionate manner to a people who had no choice but to obey the tyrant, Zenobia."

Marcellus groaned. "You promised that they could have the treasures of Tyana. It is a rich city, and they have earned the right to partake of her gold."

"I have reasons."

"Remember Postumus? His troops hanged him for denying them the very thing you're doing here. He wouldn't let them sack Mainz."

"How could I forget that? I know I'm in a dangerous situation."

"Look at the men. They grumble and whisper amongst themselves."

Aurelian nodded. "If I die now, Zenobia wins."

"If you die now, you won't care."

Aurelian raised his hands. "Good soldiers, I know that you deserve riches. But if you remember, I did indeed decree that no dog should be allowed to live. Well, then, kill all the dogs!"

Stunned silence was broken by ripples of laughter that soon erupted into a roar. The gates swung open, and Aurelian held Raven in place as hordes of foot soldiers swarmed past him into town amid shouts of "find the curs" and "it's a dog's life or no life."

Aurelian took a deep breath. The gods were with him still. "Send for Heraclammon. I want to give him the reward that he deserves."

"I thought you didn't like him."

Aurelian chuckled. "I don't like a lot of people."

Heraclammon walked as quickly as he could while bowing every third step. Finally, he stood before Aurelian's chair in a great hall of the largest house in Tyana. It belonged to the governor who had been overwhelmed with gratitude that he and his city had been spared.

Aurelian looked down at the bobbing man before him. "Heraclammon, you have done a great service for Rome."

"Yes, Emperor."

"You deserve a reward."

"You're most generous, Emperor."

"But on the other hand, you betrayed Tyana and her people. Weren't these your friends and family?"

"Yes. No. Some were, but Rome . . . Rome comes first in my heart. For the good of all and the good of Tyana I chose Rome."

"You betrayed Tyana."

"No! I helped Rome overcome Palmyra. Palmyra. I betrayed Palmyra." Heraclammon wiped sweat from his face with the end of his toga. "I didn't betray Palmyra because I was never her subject. I am always Roman. First a Roman. Last a Roman."

"You are a traitor to your own people. Do you know what I think of traitors?"

Heraclammon's eyes widened. He stuttered, then finally shook his head.

"I'll show you. Your reward for your traitorous activity against your own people is to be hanged." Aurelian signaled the guards. "Hang him in the town square. Tell all the people that Heraclammon betrayed them and let them have his body."

"Nooooo! Noooo! Where is my reward? My gold?"

"You assumed your reward was gold. It is not." Aurelian watched Heraclammon as he was dragged screaming from the room.

"You surprised even me," Marcellus said.

Aurelian turned to Marcellus. "I hate traitors."

CHAPTER
XXII

272 A. D. Palmyra, Syria

      Zenobia leaned against the low wall of the sleeping roof and watched the sun rise. She'd slept here the last three nights; it made her feel closer to the city. She liked to awaken to the sounds of her Palmyra coming to life.

      Deep purple shadows in the wadi turned blue, then gray as shafts of sunlight chased them away. The Palmyran buildings changed from charcoal gray to gold to blinding white. Her city. Her people. Both were under her protection not because of duty, but because of love. Without Palmyra, she would have no heart, no soul.

      She felt a presence behind her. Without turning, she asked, "Miriam?"

      "I came as soon as Rebekeh gave me your message."

      "Thank you."

      "You look troubled. Things aren't going well are they?" Miriam slipped her arm through Zenobia's and leaned against her.

      "No. Aurelian has been able to march halfway here with no resistance from Chalcedon, Ankara, or even Tyana. Our garrison at Tyana was betrayed, and they had to take flight. The army is on the Orontes River. I leave in a few minutes with the last regiment. We'll join the rest of the army."

      "How has Marinus done?"

      "He's young, but a clever soldier and a good leader." Zenobia turned to Miriam. "He will never be as fine as Ezechiel. Your husband had a gift."

"Your army is too large for you to handle alone. You needed a second in command." Miriam's eyes misted.

"I must go. I leave you in charge of the children and the palace. Rebekeh will help. If things go badly. . . ."

Miriam placed her fingers on Zenobia's lips. "Don't think it, don't say it, and it won't be."

Zenobia nodded. "Pray for us all."

Zenobia watched the small cloud of dust as it came closer. She glanced back at the armored cavalry, the horse archers, the foot archers, and the infantry who followed her. Her heart filled with pride. In a matter of days, her destiny would be set forever. The fate of these soldiers intertwined with hers, and she prayed for all of them no matter which gods they preferred.

The dust cloud came closer, and Marinus came into view. Zenobia urged Thabit into a trot and rode to meet her newest general.

"How many troops does Aurelian command?"

Marinus pulled off his helmet and wiped his forehead with a cloth, then shoved it back under his belt. His blue eyes squinted against the sun. His straight, dark hair was wet from perspiration and stuck to his head like it was painted on. "How many men do we have all together?"

"With the men that I brought—seventy thousand."

"He has no archers or armored cavalry, but he has more infantry than all of our army combined." He rubbed an old scar that ran down his unweathered cheek. "I have failed you, my queen."

"No, you haven't. You were betrayed by someone in Tyana." Zenobia shrugged. "We will fight and win. Think that no matter what."

Zenobia looked to the northwest. "Betrayal and trickery. That's the Roman way. We'll just have to think like they do."

"The Roman army will be here early tomorrow morning."

"We'll be ready for Aurelian. I'll lead the foot archers in first. I'll march them double time. Your job is to keep the horse archers from running over us and from outdistancing the infantry. Have the lieutenants march the infantry double time. We cannot let the army split. To do so is to invite defeat. We must hold Antioch or Palmyra is lost."

"If we can't hold Antioch, what do we do?"

"We will hold Antioch. We will stop Aurelian." Zenobia kicked Thabit and rode off to her tent.

Mountain shadows in shades of blue, purple, and dusty gray lay across the valley. Dusk cloaked her and the air cooled as soon as she left the sunlight. It smelled clean and cold like the Orontes River. She pulled Thabit to the right and rode along the river bank where the water bounced across ragged sand-colored rocks. Tomorrow's water would be colored with blood and the rocks would be hidden.

Zenobia looked to the east where the sky was still bright and the air warm. Brown and gray boulders jutted from the eastern mountain range made that much sharper by light and shadow. She imagined the sounds of birds—fluttering of wings, crooning chirps, rustling of leaves—as they settled down for the night. Their world would be changed tomorrow, too.

Zenobia dismounted, patted Thabit absently on the rump, and strolled into her tent. She sat down at the map table and shoved aside leather tubes until she found the ones she needed. She pulled out the map of the Orontes River Valley and studied it.

"Ah, Aurelian. You'll not come in from the west because the sun would be in your eyes. You'll arrive from the east through the widest and gentlest pass. We'll be ready for you."

Zenobia studied the maps and Aurelian's battle tactics with the Goths until darkness, velvety and black, engulfed everything but the table where she worked. She stretched and looked around. When had the soldier lighted the lamp? She sniffed the familiar scent of burning oil.

When had her dinner been brought to her? She touched the food; it was cold. It didn't matter. She couldn't eat. She stood and blew out the flame from the lamp. The pungent smell of smoke followed her to her cot.

Zenobia lay down in her armor and, although she didn't expect to, plummeted into a dead sleep.

Her eyes opened at the sound of the tent flap being pushed aside. The gray light that streamed in signaled dawn. She had slept without covers, and now she was chilled. It wouldn't be long until she was warm, then hot, then her body temperature would cease to be important as she concentrated on the battle.

"Good morning, Marinus." Zenobia almost leaped from her cot.

"What can you tell me about Aurelian?"

"He comes from the east with the sun behind him."

"As expected. Let's eat a hearty meal and pray to the gods." Zenobia smiled at Marinus. "You pray to one god?"

"Yes, I'm Christian."

"All right. You pray to your one god, and I will pray to all mine. Our gods will smile on us today."

"I pray that He does." Marinus saluted her.

Zenobia's heart constricted as she stared at Aurelian's Roman legions. They truly matched hers in number.

"Oh Allat. Protect your daughter." Again, her heart flip-flopped. She had studied Aurelian. She knew him as well as she knew herself. He would not retreat. He would not give up until either he was dead or she was. Never had a battle meant more to her personally or politically.

She heard the soft rustling of Palmyra's foot archers behind her as they put arrows to bows. Metal helmets and chain mail over padded leather protected them from most sword thrusts. Behind her foot archers were the horse archers and cavalry that Marinus had to hold back. The infantry stretched behind Zenobia almost out of sight. Aurelian's Roman soldiers would blanch at the sight of her powerful Palmyran army with its fine reputation for power.

Aurelian had been but a tiny figure when she had first seen him as he led his army down the mountain pass to the valley. How long would it take the grass to grow back after today? She scoffed at her peculiar thought and gave full attention to the enemy.

Now Aurelian loomed nearer. She imagined she could see cold anger plastered on his countenance. It would be replaced with resolve. Well, she was angry and resolute, too. How dare he kill Odainat. How dare he take the love of her life from her. How dare he have Ezechiel attacked and killed in Egypt. How dare he try to change the course of history.

She waited until the Roman army moved closer. They weren't in range of the arrows yet. The stirring behind her settled into an eerie silence as the archers waited for her command. She liked the silence; it signaled that her men were ready.

Aurelian closed the gap between them in a steady, maddeningly slow pace. Zenobia expected that technique. She had used it many times to unnerve the enemy. She waited. How did he expect to beat her without archers? Or were they hidden in the mountains? She glanced into the sun and shaded her eyes with her free hand. She saw nothing but boulders and scrubby gray-green growth. Her spies said he had no archers.

Aurelian stepped over the imaginary line, and Zenobia brought her sword down in a signal to charge. She waited until the archers were in front of her, then raced beside them.

"Kill Aurelian in the name of Odainat," she yelled as Thabit thundered toward the emperor.

Her adversary pulled up short and waited, but just before she got close enough to swing, he pulled away. She could hear his shouts of encouragement to his men, but all she could see was the sun glinting off his helmet as he rode up and down the front lines.

More arrows flew through the skies like dying birds and fell on the Roman infantry. Men screamed and grabbed the missiles that protruded from their bodies as they dropped to the brown earth already devoid of grass. Above the din of falling men, a bizarre cacophony of cracking shafts attested to the success of the Palmyran archers. Aurelian pulled his troops back in retreat.

"An old trick, my fine enemy. It won't work. You can't suck us into the middle of your army," Zenobia said. "It is one of my best weapons to fool the enemy. I'm glad you like it. But it won't work."

Zenobia heard a storm of riders behind her. "No! No!" she yelled. Palmyran horse archers pounded up and passed Zenobia on both sides with men riding as though they were one with the horse. They rode furiously through the foot archers until they were well past them.

Zenobia turned to find Marinus shouting for the horse archers to slow their pace. They paid him no attention, and she knew that unless she stopped their headlong race, it wouldn't be to victory, but to oblivion.

She kicked Thabit as hard as she dared; he bolted forward and raced to the front lines. "Slow down! Slow down!" she shouted, but not one of her men did. "You are being tricked by Aurelian! Slow down!"

She pulled back, stopped Thabit, and hoped the remaining horse archers would stop, too. They rode past her at a fierce pace. She reached out and grabbed the halter of a gray Arabian, but all it did was jerk the animal around and unseat the rider. He tumbled to the ground. He had just enough time to give her an incredulous stare before his own army trampled him into the ground. Zenobia moaned but refused to turn from the splattering blood that signaled his death. She hoped she would be punished for causing his death. How many more mistakes would she make today?

The Roman infantry swarmed around Zenobia's horse archers, pulled them to the ground, and slashed them to bits. The smell of blood and guts wasn't new to Zenobia, but this time it was more pungent, more disastrous, and more horrifying to her than any other battle she remembered. It was too late for her beloved horse archers and the foot archers. She had to save Palmyra and the only way was to save the infantry.

Thabit's scream caught her by surprise. He pranced in circles alternately rearing and pawing the air. He thudded down so hard Zenobia clung to his neck to remain in the saddle.

"Thabit! Not you, too!" Zenobia saw massive amounts of blood spurt from a gaping wound on his neck. She instinctively slapped a hand across the blood-pumping hole to stop the flow. Thabit's life gushed through her fingers.

The horse lurched forward, then fell to his knees. Zenobia untangled herself from the stirrups and reins and rolled away from her dying friend. She crawled back to him and held his head in her lap not caring if an arrow struck her.

Thabit, glassy-eyed and twitching, let out a shuddering breath and died. Zenobia's tears flowed freely and dropped onto her horse's lifeless eyes.

Arrows dropped around her so thick and fast that she no longer tried to avoid them. The closest ones struck Thabit.

A nudge to Zenobia's back brought her out of her stupor. She grasped her dagger as she rolled over to face the enemy. It took her a moment for her thoughts to sort themselves.

A gray riderless Arabian stared at Zenobia. "Help me to mount," she shouted at the nearest soldier. Zenobia whirled around and galloped toward a startled Marinus. She had no time to explain to him what had happened. He was too unseasoned; that was another mistake she'd made. Big mistakes led to big failures. She needed time to rethink.

"We retreat to Palmyra! Now!" she shouted to her general.

"Retreat? A hundred miles? A hundred mile retreat?"

"It's been done before. Aurelian retreated farther than that, then came back to beat the Vandals. We retreat to Palmyra. March the men double time."

"Double time? Across the desert?"

Zenobia stiffened. She didn't have time to explain that she over-trained her soldiers every day for these emergencies. She hadn't thought she'd ever have to resort to a massive long-distance retreat, but she was glad she listened to Odainat's advice from so long ago. "Be prepared for anything," he had said.

"We march double time across the desert. The Romans can't keep up. Now order it done!" Zenobia raced to the back of the lines and started the southeastern trek toward Palmyra. She didn't want to think about losing to Aurelian. She couldn't let that happen. How could she stop him? She knew the land around Palmyra better than he, but did she have enough men to fight in the open? No. Could she get any troops from Jordan? No. She had to depend on herself and her men.

"How?" The new horse pricked his ears at her voice. He apparently waited for a command. "Oh, you are a fine stallion. We are at the end of our clever ideas. Now we'll just have to fight with the weapons at hand. What are those? A walled city, but there are too many miles of wall to protect. We have resourceful women, but we don't have any that I've trained. None were interested. We have the Ain Efqa for water and plenty of food."

Zenobia looked back and saw that the infantry had turned and marched double time behind her. "My army looks as good in retreat as it does in advancement." She patted the Arabian on the neck. "That's an unfortunate observation, but true." Zenobia scratched a fleck of blood off the animal's neck. "I'm sorry." Zenobia sighed. "I'm sorry for everything, so I'll name you Sorrow."

"The walls. We need to be behind the walls." Zenobia pulled so hard on the reins that Sorrow reared up, then dropped down with a thud. She patted his neck as she turned around to seek out Marinus. She waved to him, and watched as he rode forward. He was too slow, so she galloped toward him.

"Yes?" he asked.

"Send a messenger to Miriam. Tell her to get the best builders in Palmyra to tear down the government buildings and the palace to build a wall that cuts the city in half. Use any buildings but the temples. "

"The government buildings? The palace? Cut the city in half?"

"Can't you see? We can defend half a city and win." Zenobia laughed aloud. "Tell Miriam to have a defense built on the western mountain pass where Aurelian has to come. We'll use it as a signal tower and a fort. Send the messenger now! Make certain you send the fastest rider and that he passes me on the way to Palmyra."

Sorrow didn't want to slow his flat-out run, but Zenobia pulled him to a slow trot. She heard the ear shattering bellow of a camel behind her and pulled Sorrow over. He snorted as the messenger, clinging to his camel, bolted past them. All was not lost yet.

"Odainat, how I wish you were here to guide me." Zenobia rode in silence. She didn't even acknowledge Marinus' presence or the palace guards who rode beside her. She knew they wouldn't have caught up with her if she hadn't slowed down.

"Miriam! Miriam!" Zenobia shouted as she raced through the remains of the palace.

"I'm in what is left of your chambers," Miriam said. She looked up from packing. "I'm taking a few of your things."

"You have done a wonderful job in getting the wall built. It's nearly done."

Miriam dropped a pile of folded silk into a leather box. "How close is Aurelian?"

"Two days."

"Rebekeh is with our children. She has them in the Diocletian Baths."

"Your choice, my friend?" Zenobia asked.

"It's back from the new wall that was built, but close to Ain Efqa. The street in front of it is broad and well-paved. You can ride your new horse anywhere from there. Part of the Baths is set up as a your headquarters. It's large enough to house the servants and us. I've ordered grain and food to be taken there."

"Miriam, you are brilliant."

"I am the wife of a soldier. Was the wife of a soldier. I learned much from Ezechiel and from you." Miriam's jaw clenched, and she turned away from Zenobia to busy herself with packing.

"I am forever grateful to you." Zenobia said.

"I am grateful to you. My children aren't orphans because you . . . you wouldn't let them be." Miriam pointed to the door. "Go to the Baths. You have work to do and so do I."

Zenobia grabbed Miriam and hugged her tightly.

"Oh, stop! You've grown strong enough to strangle an elephant!" Miriam chuckled and hugged Zenobia in return.

"I just plan to strangle one disgusting Roman emperor."

Zenobia stood on the wall by the north gate and watched the cloud of desert dust roll closer. It obscured Aurelian's helmeted and plumed troops, but did not hide them. Of course, he wasn't trying to hide. She grinned. This battle was hers to win. She wanted it desperately.

"He has twice as many soldiers as we do," Marinus said.

"We have the advantage of supplies and water. He has the desert."

"He can get water and supplies from the rest of the world. We have only Palmyra."

"Only Palmyra? We have the most beautiful city in the world." Zenobia gestured behind her. "The new south wall has been put up in haste and is ugly. We built ugly from beautiful, but Palmyra doesn't mind. She knows I'll take the scars away and make her lovely again."

Marinus frowned. "I hope so."

"Hope has nothing to do with anything. Fighting does." Zenobia checked the wall to the left and right. Her soldiers stood nearly shoulder to shoulder, but the absence of her expert archers distressed her. She had battle plans, but they seemed emaciated compared to the scrolls of drawings she usually had. These plans were simple by necessity.

Zenobia wiped her face with a warm cloth that Miriam had brought. Night time slowed the battle, but her men used that time to bury the dead without services or ceremony.

Aurelian's army surrounded the half-city and continued to pound it with battering rams, siege machines, and spears every minute of daylight and long after dusk. Zenobia had made it a habit to check his tent first thing in the morning and the last thing at night. She stared at his tent while she prayed to her gods for her men and sent curses to Aurelian and his army. She finished her evening prayers and curses, then dutifully followed Miriam to the bath house. She had learned that Miriam was more determined than she had thought. It was easier to obey her than to argue with her.

The ritual was the same. While she bathed, Miriam would order dinner brought to the section set aside for them. Rebekeh, Miriam, the four children, and Longinus gathered around simple food. It was sparse, but Zenobia had little appetite. Meal times were tense even though she tried to tease the children. Zenobia couldn't even play Senet with her philosopher friend, for neither of them could concentrate.

After dinner, she fell into bed, exhausted. Sleep was filled with unremembered nightmares that jerked her awake. Her bed linens were soaked with sweat. She knew she had a gaunt look about her face. She lost weight no matter how much she ate. Miriam was as stubborn about feeding her as she was about making her sleep.

Sleep had come. It seemed too soon for Miriam to be shaking her shoulder, and she pushed Miriam's hand away.

"My queen, Marinus is here with news." Miriam held an oil lamp. The light flickered against the walls and made grotesque shadows.

Zenobia groaned. "All right."

Marinus paced the small atrium that was the entrance to the baths. He blurted out, "My queen, Aurelian has more troops on the way. They will be here tomorrow."

"How many?"

"Our spies tell us twenty or thirty thousand. We don't have enough men. There is more I must tell you."

Zenobia nodded. "All right."

"The fort on the western mountain has fallen to Aurelian. Their spears fly over our walls like ravens."

Zenobia held her hands in front of her face. "Don't talk. Let me think." She stood as still as a statue in the funerary temple. Aurelian must have had these troops hidden. Roman trickery. She had to admire him for it.

"Marinus, you check the east gate. I need to know where the Roman troops are. Exactly. Draw a detailed picture. Go!" Zenobia shook her head as she watched him run from her rooms. "He isn't Ezechiel."

"He tries," Miriam said.

"He's too young and inexperienced, but he can be trusted."

"That is worth more than experience. Remember Abdas?"

Zenobia nodded, barely hearing the last words as she leaned her head against a column. She screwed her eyes shut and wiped out all the sounds that invaded her thoughts. It came to her suddenly. "Miriam, we have no choice. I need a camel. Send Rebekeh to the camel master."

"Rebekeh? She can't go. A young single girl shouldn't be on the streets in the middle of the night."

"By the gods, Miriam! This is war. Get a perspective on which rules can be broken!" Zenobia hated the sound of her voice. It had risen an octave, and she had yelled at her best friend. "I'm sorry."

To her surprise, Miriam giggled. "I am sorry. It's just maternal instinct. Or maybe I can hear my mother's voice admonishing me for sneaking over to see Ezechiel when I was but thirteen."

"Ezechiel. I miss him as much as Odainat, but in a different way." Zenobia patted her on the shoulder. "You run to the camel master. I need the fastest camel. I'm going to King Shapur for help."

"Your enemy? You're riding to Persia? My god, you'll be killed."

"I'll probably be killed one way or another. What choice do I have? Shapur has hated the Romans far longer than I have." Zenobia shrugged. "I will do anything to save Palmyra."

Miriam hugged her friend. As she turned, she gasped. "Who hides in the shadows? Show yourself whether friend or enemy!"

Zenobia drew her knife and stepped in front of Miriam. "Come out now or I'll come to get you."

Tarab, smelling of unwashed days and sweaty nights, stepped from behind a column. Her hair hung in dirty tangles that blended in with her clothes. "Kill me if you want. I don't care."

Zenobia put away her dagger. "Go back to your room. How did you get away from the guards?"

"I drugged them." Tarab's throaty laugh hacked through the stillness. "I'm going to watch you die. I'm going to help you die. You think you'll get help from the Persians? No, they'll never help you. I'll see to it."

"Don't be absurd. You have no power." Miriam rushed forward and pushed Tarab out of the atrium. "I'll get the camel master after I send Tarab back to her room with guards who aren't drugged."

Tarab jerked away from Miriam and disappeared into the shadows, her footsteps soft against the marble floor. "You'll die," she called back.

"Let her go. We don't have time to find her. I'll tell Mokimu to look for her in the morning," Zenobia said.

"Who are you really?" Aurelian didn't raise his voice. He knew the tone would make most men quake, but not the straggly gray-haired woman who stood in front of him each skinny arm held by his personal body guards. Marcellus stood by Aurelian's side.

"Tarab, sister to King Odainat and to that despicable Zenobia." She spat out the last word.

"You don't like the woman who claims to be a queen?" Aurelian asked.

"She is not my queen."

Aurelian grinned. "She is no one's queen although she pretends to be. How did you come here?"

"I rode a camel."

Aurelian laughed. "You rode a camel?" He looked at Marcellus who nodded.

"We saw the dust cloud from afar, so I sent the cavalry to check it out," Marcellus said.

"Maybe we can bargain with Zenobia for your life."

"Ha! She wouldn't pay a dead rat for me," Tarab said.

Aurelian's eyebrow's rose. "Really?"

"I don't care if I ever see her or Palmyra again." Tarab jerked her arms free of the guards. "I have information you need."

"What do you want?" Aurelian asked.

"Zenobia's death," Tarab said. Her eyes never left Aurelian's. "I know her plans. They involve the Persians."

"The Persians? Tell me what you know."

Tarab shook her head. "Promise that you'll protect me."

"Done. Tell me her plans."

"Zenobia rides alone to ask King Shapur to join in the fight against you."

Aurelian struggled to hide his surprise. "Why should I believe you?"

"You only have to send some of your men to the Euphrates to

learn that I speak true. She rides alone."

"Marcellus, take care of this," Aurelian said.

Marcellus saluted. "What of her?"

"Turn her loose—in the desert."

"What!" Tarab lunged toward the emperor.

Immediately two guards grabbed her. Tarab screeched and, leaning forward, bit the arm of a guard on her left.

Aurelian's eyes narrowed. "Wait! She can be of use to me. Keep her under guard."

"Marinus, I'll ride alone. It's less conspicuous." Zenobia looked down at her general from a perch atop a camel. "Have the gates opened. I don't have much time to get to the Euphrates River and cross it."

"Now isn't the time to be stubborn."

Zenobia's mouth dropped open. "Stubborn! Don't talk to me that way. Now open the gates!"

Marinus saluted her and signaled the guards. "God speed."

"Thank you." Zenobia rode through the gates. She picked her way slowly between campfires that the Romans had set up every hundred cubits or so. They were so arrogant that they thought the Palmyran citizens would be too afraid to leave the city. Their defenses on this side were thin and weak.

Zenobia glanced from one side to the other. Shadows of marching Roman guards crossed in front of the campfires and their voices drifted on the wind. She could smell the odor of seared bear meat and grease and the stench from latrines.

As soon as the campfires were behind her and she no longer heard voices, Zenobia leaned down and urged the camel into a flat out run. Wind tore at her head covering, and tears streamed down her face. She licked the salty streaks away. She hadn't cried for Palmyra, and she didn't intend to. She was glad no one saw these wind caused tears or they'd think she was weak.

She hadn't worn armor so there would be less weight. The only weapons she had were her bow and arrows, a dagger, and a sword.

It would take her two or three hours to get to the Euphrates River and another few hours to reach King Shapur. She grinned at the irony of asking an old enemy for help against a new enemy. She needed to be at the river before daylight.

Zenobia shifted in the saddle, held out her legs and flexed them. Her back hurt a little from leaning over for so long. She'd watched the moon move across the sky and expected to see the river any time. The ferry man would be given a purse full of gold coins for his task tonight.

She peered ahead and thought she saw the river sparkling in moonlight. She kicked the camel hard and it lurched forward.

"Holding back? For shame. You are a good camel, and we've done well." Zenobia watched the silver strip. As she got closer, it became more defined. The ferry boat was on this side, and that was to her advantage.

She slid off the camel and pulled him the last few feet to the ferry house. "Wake up! Wake up! You have a passenger." She stood at the door, the camel's reins in her hand.

The old ferry man stepped outside his house. His face didn't have the surprise on it that Zenobia expected, but had one of resignation. When he held up his lantern, she saw bruises on his cheeks and blood on his forehead.

"Did you fall? Are you hurt?" she asked.

Two Roman soldiers stepped out of the ferry house behind him. Zenobia drew her dagger and leaped forward. She stabbed the first soldier in the abdomen between the plates of armor, then turned and disarmed the second soldier before slicing his throat. She whirled around and drew her sword.

More than twenty men rushed at her. She slashed the air in front to keep them back. The hapless young soldier who stupidly stepped toward her lost his head. Zenobia took advantage of the momentary surprise of the Romans to dispatch three more men to their god, Mithra.

"Come and get me," she shouted. "Come and feel cold steel as it cuts into your warm blood!"

Zenobia identified the commander and moved toward him. She jumped aside as one man came at her from the left, then whirled around and cut him across both thighs. Before he had toppled to the ground, she turned and ran to the ferry man's hut. She put her back to the wall, pulled out her dagger, and waited. The camel bellowed in the distance. Her bow and arrows were hung over the camel saddle, but in such tight quarters they wouldn't be useful.

The Romans came at her in formation. She almost laughed at their need for precision. They danced toward her with swords, but pulled back. If they thought they could lure her away from the hut, they were mistaken.

She heaved her dagger toward a soldier in the front and felled him. He fell forward on the dagger that had pierced his armor and heart. The fall forced the blade out his back. Zenobia had the absurd thought that she wanted to retrieve that dagger. Odainat had given it to her.

Zenobia knew that these soldiers did not use spears or arrows. That was a mistake on their part, but bode well for her. She held her sword ready and prayed to Allat. Let them come. She saw movement to her right and left. They circled her like wolves circled lambs. It was over. She couldn't kill the rest of them, but she would send as many to their deaths as she could.

She raised her sword and waited. No one came near her. In fact, they stepped back. Zenobia looked up at the strange whistling sound above her head just as the fishing net fell on her head and clung to her body. She was trussed like a sheep. Her sword was useless, her dagger gone, and she had no one to get her out of the tangled net. She walked sideways along the wall, tripped once on the net, and righted herself.

"So the famous Queen Zenobia is in a bind," Marcellus said. "Seize her!"

"Marcellus, isn't it? Aurelian's second in command? Come and get me. I don't care if you kill me." Zenobia's voice sounded harsh and brittle.

"We have orders to bring you in alive."

"Alive! Has Aurelian lost his mind? Or does he grow soft in the head?" Zenobia spat out his name in disgust.

Four Roman soldiers came toward her. She glared at them. "Do you have the courage to remove the net?"

They didn't answer her, but gingerly lifted the webbing until she was nearly free. How stupid of them. She brought her sword up and speared the closest soldier. The second one jumped back, but not before Zenobia sliced off his ears in two swift movements. He fell screaming to the ground with blood squirting through fingers that held both sides of his head. She skewered him to the ground.

Zenobia laughed, pulled her sword out, and backed up to the

hut. "I am a slippery fish, am I not?"

Marcellus nodded. "So we have been told."

"There aren't many of you between me and King Shapur are there?"

"Fewer than I had started with." Marcellus turned and motioned his men at the back of the formation. "Bring her here."

Zenobia frowned. She didn't like the look of triumph on Marcellus' face. Bring who here? What tricks did he have? Romans! They were always full of tricks.

"I'm sorry, Zenobia. I tried to run." Miriam's face was as white as the moon.

"It's all right. The children?"

"Hidden."

"Rebekeh?"

"She is with them."

Zenobia smiled at Miriam. "You did fine."

"You were betrayed, Zenobia."

Zenobia looked around. "Obviously."

"If you come with us peacefully, then Miriam lives," Marcellus said.

"No!" Miriam shouted. "I don't mind dying. I'll be with . . ."

"Hush, Miriam! Say no more." Zenobia hoped Miriam would realize that she would endanger herself and the girls if she uttered her famous husband's name.

Miriam gasped. "I don't care if I die."

"You can save your friend by coming with us peacefully," Marcellus said.

"Let me die for Palmyra. Please. Let me do that for Palmyra and for you," Miriam said.

Zenobia shook her head. "No, there has been too much death." She handed her sword hilt first to Marcellus. "Take good care of that weapon. It was a gift from a great warrior."

Marcellus gently took the sword. "A gift from Odainat?"

"Yes."

"It is beautiful. Even though we're enemies, I'll care for it."

"Thank you."

CHAPTER
XXIII

272 A. D. Emesa, Syria and *Rome, Italy*

    *A*urelian bowed as Zenobia entered the tent. She hated him for it. Baskets of figs, grapes, and dates graced one end of the long table. Slabs of lamb and goat, fresh from the spit, lay on gold platters. Dark loaves of bread, lined in rows, were still warm from the brick ovens. Bottles of wine stood at attention beside bowls piled high with delicacies.

"I see you've found our food to your liking," Zenobia said.

"Yes, I do." Wine sloshed from a gold cup as Aurelian motioned for her to be seated. It splattered across the white linen cloth and left a trail of blood-like splotches.

Was this how her life would end? At the hands of the Romans? Ah, well. Longinus had said that her fate had been cast by the gods. Zenobia didn't want to believe the gods had been capricious—taking her to the heights and then hurling her to these depths. She preferred to believe she'd made her own destiny.

"Please join me."

Aurelian's voice interrupted her musings. Zenobia glanced about the tent.

"I've sent the guards away. This evening is for two mighty rulers."

"I lost the war. There is only one mighty ruler." Zenobia choked out the sentence. Truth was dry and difficult to swallow.

"I cannot negate your power, your army, and the fact that you took half of Rome's lands." Aurelian nodded toward a silk cushion, purple and gold tasseled. Fit for a queen. "Please," he said.

"Thank you." Zenobia settled herself on the cushion, her white stola whispering. She felt naked without her armor and sword.

"You must be hungry." Aurelian seated himself.

"No."

"Some fruit?"

"No."

"Wine?"

"No. I don't care to eat or drink before my execution."

"Execution?" Aurelian put down his wine goblet and leaned across the table. "I can't execute you."

"Why not?"

"Several reasons."

Zenobia snorted. "You have nothing to fear from my gods."

"I fear your people. They would rise up as one and attack Rome." Aurelian leaned back.

"There is no leader for them."

"Always a leader emerges. Your son, Vaballathus, would be a powerful force against Rome. I understand he has the best qualities of his father and his mother."

"You captured both sons along with me."

Aurelian laughed. "Didn't you know they escaped?"

Zenobia gasped. "Gone?"

"Stolen from under our noses by a winsome young woman and an old man."

Zenobia was startled to hear Aurelian's deep-throated chuckle. She held back a grin.

"So you see, your sons have been saved and you, too."

"An odd turn of events."

"Not for long. They will be found."

Aurelian's voice was brittle and swept over Zenobia like the winter air from high in the mountains.

"Do not murder my sons." Zenobia hated the sound of her voice. She had never begged in her life.

Aurelian poured a goblet of wine and thrust the gold cup into her hand. "You are pale. Drink."

Zenobia let the thick wine slide down her throat in one swallow. She held the goblet toward Aurelian. He poured. The Roman army was everywhere. Her sons, Rebekeh, and Longinus would not get far. It was over. The brief moment of hope for her sons was gone.

336

Life as she knew it was gone.

She put down the goblet and looked at Aurelian. "Do not harm my sons."

"We will make a trade."

Zenobia nodded. She had to do whatever it took to save the boys.

"I want the men who convinced you to attack Rome."

"Don't be stupid. No man convinced me to fight, save you. Look to your history. Emperor Gallienus couldn't keep the lands that had been amassed by others, and Claudius who, although a good soldier, couldn't keep the barbarians out of Roman territory. Almost a quarter of a century of ineptitude made Rome weak.

"Did Odainat tell you to conquer Roman lands?"

"Odainat died before that."

"On his death bed?"

"You had him assassinated. He told me nothing."

"Who then?"

"Rome was weak, and I was angry. Rome mewled and crawled and spit up like an infant who needed a mother. No man but Odainat would have had the courage to do what I did." Zenobia pounded the table with her goblet. "I decided! I decided!"

"I can't let people believe that. I'll have to find a man to execute for talking you into attacking Rome." Aurelian smirked. "You are a great warrior, but a woman. What man wants to be bested by a woman?"

"Don't flatter yourself. I almost brought Rome to her knees. No matter which man you choose to execute in lieu of me, everyone knows who I am. My destiny and yours intertwine through the years like a rose and a weed."

"I will have to find men to execute nevertheless."

"I don't see that as a strong solution. It'll make you look stupid." Zenobia held her goblet toward the emperor. "I need more."

Aurelian laughed. "You order me around like a servant. I like that. Bold to the end."

"Not that wine. It isn't as good as the other." She gestured toward a second bottle.

Again Aurelian laughed. "You may be haughty now, but there are ways to bring you down."

"Like Emperor Trajan, your conquest will not last. The desert has a way of swallowing our enemies."

He poured wine from the bottle nearest him. "This is Rome's best wine." He placed the wine in front of her. "You have no bargaining power. I can destroy Palmyra."

"Destroy Palmyra?" Zenobia thought quickly. She couldn't let him destroy her people. It didn't matter that she would no longer be ruler of Palmyra, but it did matter that all her friends, her family, her citizens be spared. They couldn't afford to lose their businesses, their homes, their lives.

"Palmyra is too far away. It would be a bother."

Zenobia had to convince Aurelian that to keep Palmyra was for his benefit. What did the Romans want besides power? Money! Of course. She drank, then looked at Aurelian over the rim of the goblet. "If you destroy Palmyra, you cut off your purse."

"You think Rome wants her?"

"I think Rome needs her. We have merchants, trade routes from the far east, spices. Our best source of taxes is silk. We have more silk than any other country in the world outside of the Far East. We have more silk than Rome. Think how your women would love you for bringing them silk."

Aurelian shook his head. "You are trying to use your feminine tricks on me."

"I'm not trying. I am using them. It works, doesn't it?" Zenobia smiled. Oh, how she hated this man who had taken everything she loved.

"You think I've forgotten about your sons. They'll be found."

"Let them live."

"So they can try to fight me in a few years?"

"They won't. I'm the one who needed to fight you. Execute me, but not them."

"If I execute you, then I'll do the same to them." Aurelian put down the wine bottle, leaned back, and made a tent from his fingers. He tapped his lips. "I think it would be too easy for you if I kill you. You would suffer more leaving lovely Palmyra and being forced to live in Rome."

"I'd rather die."

"My point is made." Aurelian slapped the table. "My mind is made up. If you live, your sons live. It is such a fitting punishment for a woman who thought she could rule my world."

"I did rule your world. I ruled it for three years. I took that which Rome thought couldn't be taken. I beat you."

"You're the captured one."

"Am I? I'll never fear the assassin, but you will."

"I have no such fear." Aurelian glanced away.

Zenobia leaned forward. "Then you should, for let me promise you this. By all my gods that I hold holy, I will find a way to have you murdered. If I live, you die."

"You can't goad me into fearing you. You can't force me to execute you although I'd like to see you suffer. Suffering would change that prideful nature of yours."

"You think I'm proud? No, I'm angry. I fight best when angry. You've been warned." Zenobia put down her goblet.

"I'll warn you. I'm going to take you and your sons and that wife of your General Ezechiel, his daughters, and whomever else you hold dear to Rome. You'll all be my prisoners. You'll be marched through the streets of Rome in a parade to show my citizens how powerful I am. I think it would be most appropriate for the richest woman in the world to wear all her gold jewelry and her crown. I think the most fierce woman warrior in the world should also march in her armor."

"That would serve no purpose."

"You can't walk while weighted down with gold."

"I can."

"We'll see."

Zenobia paced back and forth in the atrium of a patrician home in Emesa. Aurelian had been afraid to return her to Palmyra. He had said that water from Ain Efqa gave her strength. Ain Efqa had nothing to do with it. Her people gave her strength.

Miriam let out a cry and sat up. She looked around, shook her head, then settled back on the couch. Zenobia watched her toss and turn. Miriam feared for Kelila and Shayna as much as Zenobia did for Vaballathus and Arraum. Both of them prayed to their respective gods for Rebekeh and Longinus' safety. Roman troops examined every Palmyran building and looked behind every rock in the western mountains. Three weeks had passed and no one had told where the children were hidden. It was if they had all been made of fog that dissipated when the sun shone.

Zenobia worried that some zealous Roman soldier would find the children and do them harm. When she had voiced her opinion to Aurelian, he'd just laughed. He'd promised her that they were worth more to him alive than dead. She and Miriam wanted to believe him, but still they worried.

Aurelian had questioned her at length about Marinus and Longinus, but she had shrugged her shoulders and told him that Marinus was nearly worthless because of his youth and inexperience and Longinus' intelligence made him stupid. Why, he couldn't even beat her at Senet. She feared for those men.

A soldier called out to Zenobia. She turned. "What do you want?"

"Aurelian demands an audience with you."

"What if I refuse? Will you and several of your compatriots drag me bound and gagged to your emperor?"

"No. He asked that you decide whether you're curious enough about your sons to pay him a visit."

Zenobia felt her legs turn to water. Her heart beat faster than it did in battle. "Have they been captured?"

The soldier shrugged. "I don't know."

"All right. I'll come." She stepped in front of the messenger and strode toward the villa that Aurelian used as his headquarters.

"Thank you for coming," Aurelian said as she stepped up to the table. He had maps scattered across the top.

"Don't be inane. You promised me news of my sons."

"They are the strings that tug at the heart of a mother. I pull the strings and control the woman."

"If my heart were made of stone, I'd be happier."

"Spoken like a true warrior queen."

"Enough. What of my sons and Miriam's daughters? Of Rebekeh and that fool who calls himself a philosopher?"

"The late Dionysus Cassius Longinus?"

"Late? What have you done to him?"

"Did I forget to invite you to his execution?"

Zenobia felt dizzy. She groped for a chair and sat down hard. "Execution?" she whispered.

"I should have told you so that you could've watched. I did us both a favor. He confessed that he convinced you to invade Egypt, Asia Minor, and other Roman territories. He said he argued long and hard, but you finally gave in."

"You know that's a lie! I decided to invade! I decided to seek revenge for Odainat's death! I did it! I did it!"

"Not according to Longinus." Aurelian studied his nails. "No, I can't believe that a woman would think of these manly things on her own, so I had no choice but to execute the traitor to Rome."

"How did you? . . ."

"Find him? Easy. He was foraging for food for your sons when captured. We found the boys, the young Jewess, and your general's daughters."

"How are they?"

"Frightened, but I find that amusing. They're in the villa where you and that woman friend of yours live. They're upstairs." Aurelian laughed. "They've been under your nose for two days now."

"You're incredibly irritating. So all the children are fine. Do you treat them well?"

"Like kings and queens."

Zenobia frowned at him, then took a deep breath. "How did you execute Longinus?"

"We returned him to Palmyra and hanged him by the Oval Piazza. Tarab told me it was your favorite part of the city. I thought it appropriate."

"Tarab? My sister-in-law?"

"Tarab and I have had several conversations."

"You didn't torture her? She is harmless."

"You like Tarab?"

"No, but she can't help herself. Let her alone."

"I don't bother her. She bothers me."

"I can see to it that she's kept confined."

"That won't be necessary. She's lost in the desert by now."

"Send someone to find her before she dies. Please." Zenobia blinked to keep tears from revealing how close to a break down she was. She didn't like Tarab, but she was Odainat's sister and a princess. She deserved something.

"Do you know who betrayed you the night you tried to flee to Persia to seek aid from Shapur?"

"I assume that one of your guards saw me ride through your lines."

"No. Tarab came to me with the information. You see, without her help, we might not have captured you or stopped this silly little war. I believe Shapur would've sent troops to help wipe us out."

Zenobia shook her head to clear the thoughts that tumbled through her brain. "Tarab?"

"Yes, pitiful demented Tarab brought down one of the mightiest warriors in history. Incongruous, isn't it that a weak mother of a murderous son was able to finish the job for him."

"I hope she dies in the desert."

Aurelian laughed and Zenobia hated him all the more for it. She knew that laugh would haunt her for years.

The sunrise, hidden by Rome's buildings, shone directly in Zenobia's eyes, but she didn't blink. She was a warrior. Especially today.

Zenobia flexed her shoulders to test the weight of the gold necklaces, the Palmyran royal torc, and the jewels. The amount of large stones that nested in the pounded gold surprised her. She had no idea her royal treasury was so vast.

Perspiration trickled down her spine beneath her armor, but she was used to it. This would be more embarrassing than difficult. She had kept herself in fighting condition on the ship and in the grounds of her new villa. She would never allow herself to grow soft. She would be ready.

The trip across the sea depressed her at first, but Miriam had reminded her that to give in to those feelings meant that Aurelian truly had won. Zenobia had been relieved when Aurelian did not punish Miriam and her daughters, but allowed them to accompany her along with Rebekeh.

Rebekeh's devastation at the death of Longinus had been replaced with resolve to right a wrong. She, too, had been counseled by Miriam. Odd how Miriam's soft ways got them food, water, and a decent place to sleep on the ship. She'd even made friends with Aurelian's concubine, Lucine, who chose to spend time in their quarters more than in the Emperor's.

Zenobia turned to view other members of the Emperor's parade of people and things he'd conquered. Ebony-skinned men and women, naked and chained together, stood defiantly in front of a line of caged beasts. A spotted leopard paced around the perimeter of its cage and snarled at the sticks poked between the bars. Stick-wielding boys jumped back and squealed, then approached the cage again.

An elephant trumpeted; a white donkey brayed, and monkeys rattled the bars on their cages and screeched as they bounded from one side to the other. Camels, laden with bolts of silk and spices from Zenobia's personal stores, rested in a double row behind the cages.

Vaballathus and Arraum stood next to their mother unencumbered by anything but their thoughts. Zenobia had instructed them daily on what to expect and how to behave as they were marched through Rome.

Aurelian would make a grand show of the triumphant hero. She would do everything in her power to negate that.

The crowd grew still, and Zenobia glanced to her left as people stood on tiptoe and stared.

"Look at that, Mother," Vaballathus said. "What are those animals that pull the Emperor's chariot?"

Zenobia stared at six delicate horned deer in deep blue leather harnesses with gold tassels. "Reindeer," she said. "I've seen drawings of them. They come from far away lands that are cold. I wonder if they like Rome's hot weather?"

"Will they die?" Arraum asked.

"I hope not. We've seen enough death of men and animals." Zenobia said a silent prayer for Thabit who haunted her memories almost as much as Odainat did.

Aurelian stared at Zenobia as he drove to the front of the parade. He stopped near her.

"Zenobia! How do you fare this fine day?" He looked up at the sun. "I think it will be another wonderful summer day. The sun burns bright and hot."

Zenobia shrugged. "It is cooler than the desert."

Aurelian studied her. "You don't think the Roman sun will wilt the desert flower?" He laughed at his own joke.

"No."

"I think you'll drop to your knees."

"I won't."

"I'll give you all the jewels you wear if you survive my victory parade."

"These jewels are mine and not yours to give."

Aurelian laughed. "To the victor belong the spoils."

"What spoils did you win, Aurelian? You beat a mere woman. What victory is there in that?"

"I enjoy taunting you, Zenobia. You, though born a woman, are still a warrior. At first I gave no thought to the problems of fighting you without Odainat, but my mind was changed when I learned of your strategies. You are better than most of my generals. Too bad we are no longer allies."

"That is no fault of mine, but yours. Rome chose to pay Maeonius to murder my husband. That was a mistake. Your second mistake was to keep me alive. With each breath I take, I plan your assassination."

"I don't fear you, Zenobia."

"Good. It'll make my plan easier."

Aurelian chuckled. "If you make it to the end of the parade, the jewels are yours to keep." He slapped the reins and drove away, the metal rims grinding against the stones that made up the pavement. Dust swirled up and, curtain-like, hid him from view.

Zenobia glanced at her sons. "His extravagance and barbed generosity will be the end of him. Jewels are better than Rome's minted coins in the market place."

"What will you buy?" Arraum asked.

"Peace," Zenobia said. "The parade has started. Walk tall and don't listen to the jibes that the Roman populace will hurl at you. You are Palmyran."

She smiled to herself. Let Aurelian have this day. Her day is in the future.

Miriam gasped at the pile of jewels that lay on the table in Zenobia's apartment. "Why is Aurelian being so generous with you?"

"I don't know, but don't trust him," Zenobia said.

"I know," Lucine said. "He plans to marry you to a senator."

"What! Why?" Zenobia stared at the woman. She didn't quite trust her although it seemed she hated Aurelian nearly as much as Zenobia did. "Why would he make me marry a Roman senator?"

"There would be a certain pride for a senator to have you as a wife."

"There would be a certain pain for any Roman who approaches me with such a ridiculous idea."

"Lucine," Miriam said, "what would happen if Zenobia refuses such an order?"

"It depends on Aurelian's mood, but I think he fears Zenobia and would not force her."

"He'd better fear me. I plan to . . ." Zenobia stopped. Lucine had claimed that she hated Aurelian, but she had been with him for several years.

Lucine grasped Zenobia's hand and looked into her eyes. "If ever you need someone to help rid this world of that pig, then let me help. I'm able to go where most people can't."

Zenobia withdrew her hand. "Don't listen to the ravings of a bitter woman. Forget what I've said."

Lucine nodded. "I must go." She glanced down at the pile of jewels. "No one thought you could march through the hot midday sun and survive, but you did. You looked as fresh at the end of the parade as you did at the beginning." She whirled around and left.

Miriam waited until Lucine left the villa before she spoke. "I like her, but I'm afraid to trust her."

"She may help us." Zenobia frowned. "I don't know whether to trust her or not, but she's a good spy for us."

"That she is."

Zenobia grabbed a handful of jewels and held them up. "This is Aurelian's downfall. I promise you."

EPILOGUE

275 A. D. Rome

Zenobia smiled at the tall, slim woman who came toward her. "Rebekeh, you look beautiful as always. How was the gossip at the market today?"

Rebekeh leaned down and kissed Zenobia's cheek. "I have come with more than gossip. Lucine sends news of Aurelian."

"You've come to tell me of his assassination."

Rebekeh's mouth opened and she gasped. "How did you know?"

"She knows a great deal," Miriam said from the doorway. She came in followed by Kelila and Shayna. "Girls, take this silk to the seamstress down the street. She knows what needs to be done."

"We want to hear what Rebekeh says," Kelila wailed.

"No. The less you hear, the safer you'll be. Now go." Miriam shooed them out of the atrium. "Your sons are safely hidden until this entire thing is over."

"I've waited three years for Aurelian's death," Zenobia said.

"Do I have to wait three years to find out what happened?" Rebekeh asked.

Zenobia laughed. "Tell me what is rumored, and I'll tell you the real story."

"You planned his death, didn't you?"

"He planned his own death when he had Odainat assassinated. I merely supplied the gold." Zenobia motioned to two chairs opposite her own. "Do sit. It will be a most pleasant tale."

Miriam giggled. "Zenobia never quit fighting. We didn't want you to know for your own safety."

"You never spoke of Aurelian since he put us here."

"I chose not to remember that disagreeable portion of my life." Zenobia stared across the cool water of the pool. "Aurelian knew that to spare my life was worse than death. He kept me from Odainat's side. I could take being paraded through Rome, as he had promised, with all my gold and jewels draped around my neck. I never faltered that day."

"You could've killed yourself and been with Odainat."

"The kind emperor said that if I died by my own hand, you, Miriam, my sons and Miriam's daughters would die."

"Oh," Rebekeh said.

"Aurelian took more than Odainat and Hairan from me. He took Palmyra."

"He gave you a villa befitting a queen." Rebekeh's arm swept back to take in the vast atrium.

"He did that to appear magnanimous."

"It has been better than a prison," Miriam said. "So I applaud his generosity."

"I was to marry one of his supporters, thus the villa." Zenobia snorted. "I had other ideas, however. By the time I was done with the lowly senator, he feared for his life. I vowed no man would ever be my husband save Odainat."

"Now our enemy is dead," Miriam said. "Tell Rebekeh the story."

"There isn't much to tell. I have money and still have power."

"A lot of power. Many people hated Aurelian, but he surrounded himself with trusted guards," Miriam said.

"His most trusted general, Marcellus, met an untimely death on the battle field last year, so Aurelian had to rely on Mucapor. That man loved gold more than Aurelian."

"Your gold?" Rebekeh asked.

"My gold."

"So tell us the gossip," Miriam said.

"He was stabbed to death by Mucapor and four of his men. They waited until the bodyguards left the emperor to chase two young men who had thrown stones at Aurelian. . . ." Rebekeh gasped. "Vaballathus and Arraum!"

"Hush!" Miriam clamped her hand across Rebekeh's mouth. She waited until Rebekeh nodded before she took her hand away.

"Weren't you afraid for them?" Rebekeh whispered.

"Yes, but they needed to help me." Zenobia pursed her lips. "No one pays attention to young men. They were able to drift in and out of the army barracks, take verbal messages to Mucapor right under Aurelian's nose, and bring me information from Lucine."

"Do you hear that?" Miriam asked. She looked down the hall-way that led to the sleeping chambers.

"What?" Rebekeh asked.

"Footsteps. Quiet footsteps," Miriam said.

Zenobia pulled a dagger from its customary hiding place. It was the one Odainat had given her many years before. Marcellus had retrieved the dagger and kept it until he could give it to her. He had done the same with her armor and sword although those had never been worn again.

"Mother!" Vaballathus whispered. "We are home. It's the safest place for us. Lucine showed us a short way through an orchard."

Arraum strode across the room and kissed Zenobia on the top of her head. "We guessed that no one would suspect us, and even if they did, you'd kill them."

Miriam and Rebekeh laughed.

"They are right, Zenobia," Miriam said.

"Yes, they are." Zenobia held back tears. "You've made my life worth living again. Aurelian is no more."

Printed in the United States
34722LVS00004B/24

9 780965 972130